Dongola
Berber
RED SEA
Khartum
Kasala
Keren
Massaua
SUDAN
KORDOFAN
El Obeid
Sennar
ABYSSINIA
Gondar
AFAR
Ambara
Takale
Fashoda
Shoa
Harar
Nuer
Sobat
Denka
Aden
Makalla
Mokha
Hodeida
Zeila
Berbera
Daror
Ras Hafun
Sokot
C. Guardaf
Nogal
Melmil
Dollo
Bad
Bonga
KAFA
Lado
Gondokoro
Bari
Dufli
Albert L.
Mruli
UGANDA
Rubaga
Victoria Nyanza
Kavirond
Samburu
Kenia
Tana
Ukamba
Kilimanjaro
Masai & Wakuavi
Shabele
Logh
Bardera
Jub
Warsheikh
Mukdishu
Merka
Brava
R. Jub
Kisimayu
Pata
Malinde
Rabai, Kisulutini & Ribe
Freretown
Mombasa
Pemba I.
Equator
INDIAN
OCEAN
UNYAMWESI
Ujiji
Unyanyembe
Gonda
Mondo
Saadani
Pangani
Mamboia
Mpwapwa
Zanzibar Mbweni & Kungani
Bagamoyo
Dar es Salam
Kilwa
Lindi
Uranga
Mangwangwara
Kazembe
Bemba
Bandawe
Rovuma
C. Delgado
Masasi
Newala
Comoro
Ibo
Mayotta
C. Amber
Nosi Be
Meto
Luri
Lomwe
Mozambik
Majanga
Maravi
Zumbo
Tete
Sena
Manika
Blantyre
Mandala
Angoshe R.
Shirwa L.
Mopea
Kilimani
Zambezi
Antananarivo
Tamatave
Antongil B.
Ste Marie
MADAGASCAR

DAUGHTER
of a
DAUGHTER
of a
QUEEN

DAUGHTER
of a
DAUGHTER
of a
QUEEN

SARAH BIRD

ST. MARTIN'S PRESS ⚏ NEW YORK

DAUGHTER OF A DAUGHTER OF A QUEEN. Copyright © 2018 by Sarah Bird. All rights reserved. Printed in the United States of America. For information, address St. Martin's Press, 175 Fifth Avenue, New York, N.Y. 10010.

www.stmartins.com

Designed by Steven Seighman

Library of Congress Cataloging-in-Publication Data

Names: Bird, Sarah, author.
Title: Daughter of a daughter of a queen / Sarah Bird.
Description: First edition. | New York: St. Martin's Press, 2018.
Identifiers: LCCN 2018010894 | ISBN 9781250193162 (hardcover) |
    ISBN 9781250193186 (ebook)
Subjects: LCSH: Williams, Cathay, 1844–approximately 1893—Fiction. | United States—
    History—Civil War, 1861–1865—Participation, Female—Fiction. | United States.
    Army—African American troops—Fiction. | Cross-dressers—United States—Fiction. |
    Women soldiers—United States—History—19th century—Fiction. | Women slaves—
    United States—Fiction. | GSAFD: Biographical fiction. | Historical fiction. | War stories
Classification: LCC PS3552.I74 D38 2018 | DDC 813/.54—dc23
LC record available at https://lccn.loc.gov/2018010894

Our books may be purchased in bulk for promotional, educational, or business use. Please contact your local bookseller or the Macmillan Corporate and Premium Sales Department at 1-800-221-7945, extension 5442, or by email at MacmillanSpecialMarkets@macmillan.com.

First Edition: September 2018

10 9 8 7 6 5 4 3 2 1

Dedicated to those who seize what an unjust world refuses to give

Acknowledgments

The list of those I have to thank is long and starts with the remarkable June-teenth cowboys and cowgirls who first introduced me to the tale of Private Cathy Williams in the late seventies.

I am forever indebted to Pam Black for lighting the fire with her words, "My students need books about heroes who look like them," and to Emily Haas for fanning it.

I must acknowledge Mary Williams, Fort Davis NHS, as an early advocate and protector of Private Williams's legacy.

I would like to especially draw attention to the work of Barbara Richardson, who in her books, *Black Directory of New Mexico* and *Noteworthy Black Women of New Mexico*, as well as in her conversations with Pam Black presented an illuminating portrait of Private Williams found nowhere else.

I also offer heartfelt thanks to the men and women of the Buffalo Soldiers Heritage and Outreach Program; the Buffalo Soldier Society of New Mexico; and to Paul Matthews, founder of the Buffalo Soldier Museum of New Mexico for their vivid reenactments and help with the details of army life and dress. The Fort Davis National Historic Site and the Fort Clark Springs Museum were also both invaluable resources that allowed me to imagine myself into Cathy Williams's world.

I give thanks to the Dobie-Paisano Fellowship at the University of Texas for a wild and open space where Williams could come to life.

I am grateful to the Meryl Streep Screenwriters Lab for its support and to the dear and wise friends I made there: Lyralen Kaye, Kim Turner, Vanessa Carmichael, Billie Mason, Janet Stilson, Tracy Charlton, Jan Kimbrough,

Anna Hozian, Kellen Hertz, Gretchen Somerfeld, and Peres Owino who provided an invaluable African perspective.

I offer appreciation to all who guided me along this path by reading early drafts, providing critical insights, offering counsel, and sharing bottles of wine and cups of tea: John Pipkin, Carol Dawson, Anne Rodgers, Kelly Harrell, Tiffany Yates Martin, Clare Moore and Sarah Phelps, Satori Shakoor, John Jones, S. C. Gwynne, Ben and Sharie Fountain, Steven Harrigan, Elizabeth Crook, James Magnuson, Brenda Bell, Saundra Kirk and all the Chickas of Victoria Cottage, Christine Swanson, Scottie Gissell, Chris Tomlinson, and Michael Hurd.

Special thanks are due to Ann Weisgarber for telling me how the novel begins.

Among all my readers and advisors the most important are my sisters, Martha and Kay Bird. I won the Sister Lottery with two darlings who will not only read endless drafts but constantly lift me out of the pit of despair with encouragement, enthusiasm, and cheese.

For more unearned generosity and kindness than I deserve or could ever repay, I thank the luminous Kristin Hannah and Christina Baker Kline.

I am profoundly grateful for the extraordinarily happy new home I have found at St. Martin's. I have been bowled over by the enthusiasm and expertise of everyone there from visionary publisher Jennifer Enderlin, to Lesley Worrell, the creator of the perfect cover, to my boundlessly energetic friend, former aerobics instructor, and now marketing guru, Gillian Redfearn. I am thrilled to be working with so many gifted and passionate bookpeople, Brant Janeway, Erica Martirano, Jordan Hanley, Dori Weintraub, Sally Richardson, and George Witte.

Finally, most crucially, I give thanks for a woman whom I feel Cathy Williams guided me to, the sublime Monique Patterson, editorial director extraordinaire, and her rock-star colleagues, Alexander Sehulster and Mara Delgado-Sanchez.

Needless to say, none of this would have happened without the empress of agents, my brat sister, Kristine Dahl.

And, of course and always, my essentials remain George, Gabriel, True, and the inspiration of Lt. Colista McCabe Bird, R.N.

A tribute in fiction inspired by the singular decision made by Cathy/Cathay Williams, the first woman to enlist in the peacetime U.S. Army, and the only to ever serve (1866–1868) with the fabled Buffalo Soldiers.

Girls want marvelous adventures just as much as boys do.

—L. Frank Baum, author of *The Wizard of Oz*

"I reckon that I is a hundred and three or a hundred and four years old. I was a woman grown at the end of the war.

"I ain't had no daddy 'cause queens don't marry, and my mammy, Junny, was a queen in Africa. They kidnaps her and steals her away from her throne and fetches her here to Wake County in slavery."

—Ann Parker, age 103 (?) when interviewed in the Wake County Home, Raleigh, North Carolina, by Mary A. Hicks

The option of a white man's republic ended at Appomattox.

—Daniel Fried, America's most senior diplomat, retirement speech, 2017

BOOK ONE

Back South

Chapter 1

———

ere's the first thing you need to know about Miss Cathy Williams: I am the daughter of a daughter of a queen and my mama never let me forget it. That's right. Royal blood runs purple through my veins. And I am talking real Africa blood. Not that tea-water queens over in England have to make do with. My royal blood comes from my grandmother, my *Iyaiya,* as we called her in Fon, our secret Africa language. And don't go picturing one of them sweet old grannies like you got nowadays with linty lemon drops tucked into her apron pocket for the grandkids. No, she had possum teeth, filed to points so, if need be, she could rip an enemy's throat out, for my grandmother was one of the Leopard King's six thousand warrior-wives, what the French called *les Amazones.*

The second thing you better get straight about Miss Cathy Williams is that, even though I had the misfortune to be born in Missouri nearly fifty years ago, somewhere in the vicinity of 1840 to 1844, depending on how Old Miss told the tale that day, I am not a Southerner. Only two things in this world the South is good for. Hookworm and misery. I've lived here in Trinidad, Colorado, for over twenty years and it'd take chloroform and a gun to ever get me back to the South. What I'm trying to say is I am a Western woman and that is what that dandified reporter from the *St. Louis Daily Times* never understood about me. Just because I was from the South, that pinch-nosed weasel expected me to be a grinning old auntie, calling him "suh," shuffling her feet, and talking about dem ole days back home. When I didn't turn out to be some green country gal fresh off the plantation never knew the touch of shoe leather and was, instead, a person who could talk just as proper as him when she was of a mind to, here's what that skunk dump wrote in the January 2, 1876, edition of the *St. Louis Daily Times*. He wrote that I received him "with an assumed formality that had a touch of the ridiculous."

"Assumed"? Because I knew when to say "ain't" and when not to?

How do you answer back to a newspaper? With just a few words, that bowler-hatted jasper made me out to be a fraud and every word out of my mouth a lie. No wonder folks don't believe me when I tell them I was a Buffalo Soldier. Having both my feet amputated last year has not strengthened my case either. The way I'm being whittled down, I reckon I might have another year, two at the most, to set the record straight before they fit me out for a pine box. So, with Miss Olivia Hathcock, teacher at the Trinidad, Colorado, Free School for the Children of Colored Miners, taking down my words that is what I intend to do.

No point in starting off with whatever date Old Miss wrote in her book to record the births of the slaves born onto their miserable tobacco farm off on the far west side of Missouri in a region so Confederate it was called Little Dixie. No, my real life, the one I was meant to have, did not start until an August night in 1864, three years into the war, when I watched the only world I'd ever known burn to the ground and met the man who was to be my deliverance and my damnation, the Yankee general Philip Henry Sheridan.

The first time I laid eyes on Philip Sheridan, the man might of been Satan himself. He was mounted up high on a black horse must of been sixteen hands tall set smack in the middle of fires roaring so loud that Sheridan had to yell orders down to his blue-jacketed demons in a voice that thundered like Judgment Day. The Yank soldiers swarmed through the farm, torches held aloft, kerchiefs tied over their noses against the smoke. Tears washed white streaks down their soot-blackened faces. They were burning Old Mister's tobacco crop and the smell, like ten thousand men smoking stogies, could of harelipped a bull ox.

My little sister Clemmie, a wisp of a girl subject to many a nervous complaint, trembled in terror against me, for the white preacher had warned us that Yankees were minions of Lucifer. "They'll slice you open," he promised whenever the occasion had presented itself. And many times when it had not. "And let their dogs drag your guts out so you can die watching your entrails being devoured."

Sheridan might of been Satan himself, still I could not take my eyes off of the man. When I separated him from his mount, though, I found I was looking at a squatty little fellow with black hair so short it looked painted on, a long body, strong, broad chest, short legs, not enough neck to hang him with, and arms so long that if his ankles itched he could scratch them without stooping. He had a head like a bulldog, big and round, with a hard set to the jaws that signaled once he sunk his teeth into a thing, either him or that thing'd be dead before he turned it loose. It was a head molded by the Creator to do one thing on this earth. And that one thing was fight.

There wasn't but one Yankee fit such a description, the dreaded General Philip "Little Phil" Henry Sheridan. Even the Feds called him "Smash 'em Up" as that's what the young general was given to yelling as he rode, laughing and cursing up a blue streak, into battle.

Old Mister and his Secesh friends despised all Yankees, but they hated Sheridan worse than any other Federal. They called Sheridan's habit of burning everything in his path "despicable and unspeakable savagery and against every rule of civilized behavior." Unlike, say, shackling up humans and working, flogging, or starving them to death. All in all, I was inclined to like the man.

"Burn it all, lads!" Sheridan bellowed over the sound of the flames crackling and roaring. "Burn the Rebels' food and burn what they'd sell to buy food! Burn every grain of Rebel wheat and every kernel of Rebel corn! Burn it to the ground! I want the crows flying overhead to have to carry their own rations!"

Before that moment, I had never heard this exact brand of Yankee being spoke, and though it hit my ear like a handful of pebbles hurled against a window, I had to admit that the General, as I came to think of him then and forever after, could preach him some damnation.

Out beyond the dirt yard where the soldiers had gathered us up at bayonet point, flames flowed over the fields like a river of blazing orange spreading into an everlasting lake of fire. It roared so loud it took me a minute to make out the caterwauling of Old Miss.

"You are the devil, Phil Sheridan!" Old Miss wailed, gathering her three wormy offspring to her side. "The very devil himself, for only a demon of the lowest order would burn out a poor woman with a husband lying fresh dead in her parlor and leave her and these poor innocent children with nothing to eat!"

"Don't be calling me a devil, woman," Sheridan said, his queer accent turning "devil" into "divvel."

"The Union Army has burned your crops, madam, we have not slaughtered your sons. And we shall not be laying a hand upon your daughter."

He pointed a righteous finger toward the pasty-faced Little Miss, trembling in her pinafore worn now to a gray rag beside the two Young Sirs, both bowlegged with rickets.

"You traitorous Secessionists brought this miserable war on yourselves. Insisted upon it. Sought to sunder our country in two with it. War is brutal, my good woman. I do not make it any more so than I must."

The three gray curls that hung down either side of Old Miss's long face hopped around like fleas as she'd had no tonic to calm her nerves for the three long years the Rebellion had been grinding on. "We'll starve!" Old Miss cried, so pitiful you'd of never guessed at the blackness of her heart.

Never of imagined her looking bored and peevish when my grandmother, my Iyaiya, was led away, naked but for a rag twixt her legs, in a coffle of other wore-out slaves, all chained together like fish on a trotline. Old Mister had sold her for ten dollars to a turpentine camp down in Alabama, where they'd squeeze the last bit of work and life out of the captured queen in a dank pine forest. Bored and peevish was also how Old Miss had looked when my mama's other babies were sold away from her. It was how she looked when Old Mister took my beautiful baby sister, Clemmie, up to the house to use like a man uses a wife.

"You have left us nothing," Old Miss shrieked. "Nothing!"

Looking at Old Miss then, with all three of her children alive and clinging to her, their fine house standing proud, I thought, *Nothing? Why, that stupid woman hasn't touched even the least little hem of "nothing."* But she was starting to, and for that I was glad.

"How will we feed ourselves?" Old Miss whined.

Sheridan roared down at her, "Rebel, don't be adding lying to the crime of high treason against the United States of America. Feed yourselves with the silver you've buried."

That shut her up right quick. We all knew that Old Miss had buried her precious silver even before the war started.

"Or would you prefer that I hogtie your youngest son?" Sheridan asked. "And hold him over a fire until the fat and the truth is rendered out of him?"

We had all heard about how bushwhackers had done just that over to Glen Eden plantation where they had strung Mister Pennebaker up over a low fire until they cooked the truth out of him, and he directed them to the fork above Perkins Creek where he'd buried his valuables in a barrel.

"Might that not encourage you to reveal where you've hidden the spoils which, by all rights, belong now to the Union Army?" Sheridan prodded.

Old Miss's jaw worked as she bit at the inside of her mouth. Her eyes twitched about in the rabbity way she had, but she didn't answer.

"Speak no more of the hardships you've endured," Sheridan said. "Not with more than half a million souls, yours and ours, lying in their graves because, for the most selfish of reasons, you willful, prideful, ignorant, arrogant, traitorous Rebels would destroy the finest country our Almighty Lord ever set upon His benighted earth."

I could see from the start that Phil Sheridan was a serious man.

With Old Miss shut up good and proper then, Sheridan demanded of one of his officers, "Have all the contrabands been accounted for?"

For the first time, the soldiers shone the torchlight upon our faces.

Mama, who was standing to my right, and Clemmie, to my left, huddled up closer against me. Fear was making my sweet little sister vibrate like a hive humming with bees. Old Mister's nasty doings had taken all the starch out of her. And that is why I had been forced to slip a brown recluse spider into his pocket to bite the hand that had interfered with my baby sister. His blood had gone bad and, with all the fit men carried off and no one else left to run the place, he'd had to make Mama overseer. After the bitten hand turned black, Old Miss took her nasty husband into town to have it cut off. But he died anyway. I thought that was the happiest day of my life. This one, however, was showing fair to beat it out.

I wanted to tell Clemmie not to be afraid. That no one's guts'd be getting dragged out by dogs. My little sister had never been able to fully understand that white folks generally preferred the more economically satisfactory practice of working us to death over outright killing.

Me? I was more excited than scared for, no matter how bad the Federals were, I saw no way they could be worse than what we had here.

"Madam," Sheridan boomed down at Old Miss, "are these all your Negroes?"

"All that your cowardly marauders and scavengers have left us," Old Miss sniffed, as though it wasn't the Rebs and general riffraff bushwhackers who'd carried off, first the strong men, then the weak, and, finally, the boys.

A Yankee with silver oak leaves on his shoulder straps stepped up and asked, "Sir, should I confiscate the contrabands?" The officer had the toady-ing manner of the worst kind of overseer sucking up to the master. I figured him to be either the General's overseer or he was angling for the job.

The General had what you might call a salty vocabulary and he roared, "Colonel Terrill, need I remind you that we are on a _____ foraging mis-sion? And it's been a damn _____ miserable one so far? We've barely liber-ated provisions enough to keep our own _____ bellies full and you're proposing we add a pack of _____ Negroes to the quartermaster's load? No, Colonel, I'll send a detachment later to take them to a freedman's camp. I've no intention of feeding every _____ pickaninny between here and Washington, D.C."

"Begging the general's pardon, sir," the colonel went on. "I hate to men-tion it, sir, but your staff's head cook did requisition a helper, sir."

"Solomon needs a helper?"

"Yessir. Cook's helper, General. For the officers' mess, sir."

"What happened to . . . ? You know." The General circled his hand in the air, urging the name to come forth. "Fat wench. Front teeth knocked out. You know."

"Betsy?" the colonel supplied. "Betsy died of the bloody flux."

The General shook his head and sighed with annoyed regret. "It's what I have always maintained, the Almighty did not fashion woman for the life of a warrior. All right, Terrill, requisition a cook's helper. But I will have no more _____ females serving my staff, do you hear me?"

"Yessir, sir, General, sir. Couldn't agree more, sir. No females, sir."

"Don't want to _____ see them. Won't _____ have them dying around me. The rigors of battle require a man's strong constitution. What is needed is a darkie buck. Stout, husky one with the constitution of a _____ mule."

From atop his fine steed, Sheridan appraised us, his finger twitching back and forth as he passed over first one slumped specimen quivering before him then the next: Auntie Cherry, who was too blind and crippled up to do anything except stick a finger in a baby's mouth when she cried from hun-ger. Hettie, who, though still strong and able, was eliminated since she was not only female, but also convinced that she was still back in Georgie eat-ing crowder peas, the result of Old Mister laying into her with a singletree yoke several years back. Old Amos, though technically a man, still didn't make the cut as his fingers were knotted up like a corkscrew willow to where he couldn't hold a chopping knife right. Even Maynard, a near-grown man-boy, who believed he should have been made overseer instead of Mama, did not capture the General's fancy.

Then Sheridan's eye fastened on me for, as had become our habit since Old Mister's blood went bad from the spider bite and Mama was made overseer, I was wearing britches and in no wise gave off the look of a female. I felt Mama stiffen at seeing me being included in all this mule talk and her fury jumped into me like a spark off a fuse.

Being treated like beasts at auction didn't bother the rest of them. They were all slouched over and beat-down-looking, trying not to attract attention. They didn't know whether these white Yankee men wanted to free us so they could roast us on spits like the preacher and our masters told us they planned on doing, or if liberation really was at hand. It hardly mattered, though, for we all knew that, one way or the other, long as whites were running the show, it'd be bad for us. So I couldn't fault them for keeping their heads down and waiting for this latest misfortune to blow over.

But in the months Mama had been running the show, me and her had lost the habit of being sized up like broodmares and we both bristled. Iyaiya had drilled it into Mama never to show weakness before your enemy and Mama had passed that rule on to me. Since any and every white man, no matter what color uniform he wore, was Mama's enemy, she drew herself up tall and proud and locked eyes with this general.

In the gaze that passed between them it was clear that Sheridan saw who was before him because puzzlement clouded his expression as two things he had never put together before collided in his head: warrior and woman. He shook his head and moved on to the last candidate, me.

"That one!" He pointed at me. "The tall one there! Splendid specimen."

I brightened. It was hard to hate someone who called you "splendid."

"He'll do," he pronounced. Then General Philip Sheridan spoke directly to me for the first time. "You there," he said. "You won't die on me, will you, boy?"

Whether I was about to be liberated or roasted up, I was hard set on the one thing I'd always cared most about: making Mama proud of me. As I gathered myself up, I thought about Daddy telling me how he'd made his way amongst a certain sort of white gentleman who enjoyed a bit of sass. I judged the General to be of that sort and shot back, "No, sir, I be singing at your funeral, sir. You can count on that."

Everyone except my mother sucked in his breath and stepped away from

me. Even Clemmie put some air between us. Sheridan's dark eyes ceased reflecting the least little bit of light and narrowed down to draw a bead on
me. If he could of shot bullets from those black eyes, I'd of come down in a
pile right then and there. Yankee or Rebel, a white man was a white man,
and I had taken a fatal step over the line. Slaves were lashed to death for
imagined slights. Who knew what my bald-face sass would get me?

Old Miss's face pruned up with the fear that the Yanks would take out
my impudence on her and she went to babbling and wagging her finger at
me. "That one. That one is incorrigible. Ever since the bucks were taken and
her mother was made overseer after Mr. Johnson fell ill, she has run wild.
Lord knows we tried to beat the devil out of her, but he would not come."

"The devil, you say," Sheridan repeated and I knew I was done for. With
strong hands to do the job, Old Miss could now order the hide to be whipped
off me.

Instead, Sheridan just studied me as he scrunched his face around so
that the tips of his black mustache twitched to one side of his mouth then
the other. At last, he let out a bark of a laugh and told the colonel beside
him, "They told me at West Point that *I* had the devil in me, didn't they,
Terrill?"

Terrill mumbled some mealy-mouthed answer I couldn't hear, but the
way Sheridan's question had caused the prissy colonel to tighten his lips told
me that the West Point comment had been a pointed jab.

"Devil's just another name for spirit. Lad's got _____ spirit!" Then Sheridan mused, "His is a comical race of japes and buffoonery. Wouldn't hurt
to season Solomon with a wee bit of levity, now would it, Terrill?"

"Indeed not, sir!" the colonel agreed before the question was all the way
out of Sheridan's mouth. "Although, if I might add, sir. Your head cook did
specifically request, if not a female, at least a house servant who knows a bit
about cooking."

Well, that was it for me. Any skink slithering past knew more about
cooking than me. But instead of asking what I knew, the General bellowed,
"This is the United States Army, Colonel Terrill! Not _____ Delmonico's!
Solomon will get the best of a bad _____ lot and make _____ do as we
all make _____ do." He wiggled around in the saddle, settling his rump
in good and solid, as if the colonel's comment had unseated him. Then he
proclaimed my destiny. "It is decided then. You"—he pointed at me—"shall
come with us and be my cook's helper."

Mama wailed, "No, massuh, please, not my child! My child is my heart, massuh. I gon die without my heart."

I had not heard the word "massuh" slip from between my mother's prideful lips since all the men had been carried off and Old Mister had made her overseer. She'd say "sir" and "mister," "ma'am" and "miss," but never "massuh" and would of switched me if I had ever uttered it. And she never spoke in such a pitiful, mush-mouthed way.

Her begging, though, had no effect on Sheridan who answered, "Then send him with your blessings, Mammy. Your blessings and prayers to our Lord Jesus and his Holy Mother that the Union Army shall smite the Rebels and you shall be the last mother whose son is ever taken from her."

Mama's protests that I wasn't no mother's son were lost in Sheridan booming out the order, "Colonel! Liberate the boy! He is now, officially, Union contraband!"

Terrill leaped forward, grabbed me roughly, and promised, "I shall personally ensure that he is delivered to headquarters, sir." Then he shoved me in the direction of a bunch of soldiers, yet still I would not turn loose of Mama.

I was immediately swallowed up by a sea of blue coats. Hands popped out every sleeve and they all took to shoving me along, every soldier jockeying to see who could show off how tough he was by pushing me the hardest. They tried to yank me out of Mama's arms, but she clung so tight my bones popped. And I was clinging right back for though it was my dream to answer the call of my blood and be a warrior as Iyaiya had been, I never figured Mama and Clemmie wouldn't be fighting alongside me.

The white soldier boys hoisted me up into the air. The instant they ripped Mama's hands from mine, my mother shed the first tears I had ever seen fall from her eyes. Seeing that Mama loved me in the regular, American way made love gush so hot and hard through me that I, too, might of cried had I not been within the General's sight.

I reached out for Mama, but the soldiers pulled us apart and floated me over to Old Mister's buckboard. The wagon bed was crammed full with three miserable baskets of sweet potatoes, a couple of hogsheads of parched corn, our last scrawny pullet, and a few other sundry items left after three years of foragers stripping us like a plague of locusts from Revelations.

When they let down the back gate, a bushel of sweet corn tumped over, and the ears went rolling everywhere. The soldiers mashed me in next to a hogshead of cured tobacco held back from last year for Old Miss's personal use, and tried to slam the gate closed, but it banged hard against my knees. I had to tuck my long legs up until I was squatting like a bullfrog, knees beside my ears, before they could get the gate latched. Soldiers gathered up the runaway corn, threw it in, and seemed to be aiming specifically for me, since every ear knocked me in the head.

The buckboard bounced around when the driver, a tall white soldier with shoulders hunched up like a vulture, climbed onto the foretop and took the reins. He went to harring up the mules and the wagon creaked and started rolling away down the trail. As I was parted from them, Mama and Clemmie broke away from the soldiers. They had about reached me when a big iron X dropped down and stopped them in their tracks. Two soldiers marching behind the wagon had crossed the bayonets on their rifles and wouldn't allow my sister and my mother to come any closer.

Mama yelled to me in Fon, a language that she had never before spoken when whites were around as she would have been flogged for doing so. "Remember who you are," she said. "You are *N'Nonmiton*. You are the daughter of a daughter of a queen who was one of the six thousand virgin warrior-wives of King Ghezo, the greatest of the twelve kings of Dahomey!" The words rang with the strange music of the tongue we shared.

The sweat that glazed Mama's dark skin shone in the firelight. She tugged down the neck of her bodice to expose the five neat rows of scars that glistened there like black pearls between her collarbone and her heart. Holding my gaze, she touched the scar beads.

In answer, I touched my own set of identical scars and cried out to her in the language of my cradle, *"Ma'ami! Ma'ami!"*

Clemmie bleated out my name, "Cathy! Cathy! Cathy!"

As they fell farther and farther behind, Mama reached her arms out to me. I tried to yank mine loose, but they were mashed in tight next to my knees. All I could set free was my voice, and I yelled, "I'll come back, Ma'ami, I promise! I'll come back for you and Clemmie!"

I finally managed to work my arms loose and hold them out, leaning so far over the gate that I touched the bayonets. When I hit iron, the soldier turned his weapon and poked at me like he was transporting a bear. He kept on poking until I squatted back down.

We rolled on and the dark night closed in around the wagon. I stared so hard that my eyeballs ached trying to hang on to the sight of my mother. But Mama shrunk away until the rock that had always anchored my world was whittled down to a frail silhouette swaying in front of the flames.

And Clemmie? I couldn't see Clemmie anywhere. My sweet, sad little sister had vanished altogether.

Chapter 2

⁓

Though that buckboard wobbled and those iron wheels hit every rock and gulley along the trail, I hauled myself up and stood so I could watch until the fire wasn't but a lonely ember far off in the dark. When even that was swallowed up by the night, the strength left my legs. I sunk back down onto the hard boards of the wagon, not caring that I was wedged in tight as a bullet in a chamber.

Much as it hurt to leave Mama, it was the pain of knowing I had abandoned Clemmie that stabbed the dagger in my heart. Though I had killed Old Mister, still worse might await her if Old Miss put her on the auction block. The most dangerous thing one of our girls could be was pale and pretty, and Clemmie, who favored our handsome daddy, where I took after our strapping mama, was both. Anger heated my tears as I thought about a hand touching her. One that I could not set a brown recluse spider upon.

With no one to hear me except a single lonely chicken, and the creaking of the wagon covering any sound I made, I carried on snorting out big, wet sobs that didn't stop until I noticed flickers of torchlight off in the woods. The flickers traveled alongside us. Someone was out there in the woods tracking us. Tracking me.

Rebels had only two ways for any slave they caught with Yanks to go: back into slavery or up a tree at the end of a rope. Or worse if they had the time. Burning alive and skinning were two favored pastimes. In the whole, long war, Seceshes never took one black prisoner of war. It was slavery or death if they caught you.

The ones tracking me now, though, had to be pattyrollers. Bad as regular Rebs and bushwackers were, pattyrollers were the ticks on their bellies, for those night-riding fiends believed Jesus had appointed them personally to torture and terrify all blacks and to pay special attention to contrabands. Pattyrollers wouldn't take the Yanks on straight. Didn't dare fire on anyone with a gun who could fire back. Instead they'd creep around in the dark like they were doing now and shoot all the freed slaves they could pick off. Then disappear back into the shadows before the Yanks could come after them.

I felt them now. Out there. Watching. Waiting to get a clear shot as soon as the moonlight hit me right. Next, I heard them making the gargly sorts of moans night riders made to terrify us into a case of the screaming fantods. I ducked down far as I could, but the moans approached even closer. They had a horrible rusty sound to them like they were coming either from a man in a grave or a man meant to put me in one.

I was about to meet my maker, sent by an enemy I couldn't see. My heart thumped hard on that fearful prospect and I prayed that Mama and Iyaiya were right and that Jesus had got it wrong. That it was okay for a captive, a warrior, to kill her enemies the way I had laid Old Mister out. My preference would be to hunt elephants with Iyaiya for all eternity rather than sizzle in the everlasting fires of the white preacher's hell. Finally, I realized that the moans were coming from close by. Very close. In fact, they were coming from inside the wagon itself.

"Who's there?" I felt around for a weapon. My fingers closed around the handle of one of the curved knives we used to chop tobacco, the ones that had left my hands filigreed with white scars. I held my breath, but the only sound was the creaking of the wagon and the clatter of the stolen freight, until from practically right beside me came a low groan, "Waaa-tuh."

In the deep shadows cast by the woods we were driving through, I could barely make out what I realized with a start was the form of a man laying atop some sacks of grain not an arm's length from me. His head lay toward the gate and a white bandage covered his eyes and a good part of his high forehead. The rest of him was lost in darkness.

He cried out for water again. Weaker this time. I could barely hear him as his calls were quickly lost in the rattle and jouncing of the wagon. I felt around. My hand fell on the round lumps of sweet taters in a tow sack. The pullet in a cage squawked when I felt of her. I pricked my finger on the tip of a tobacco knife. But I found no water.

The man stopped groaning, but his labored breath went on, itself a cry for help. I scrambled closer, feeling as I went. Finally my hand fell on the cool, moist curves of a keg. I unstoppered and smelled of it. Cider. I dipped the long tail of my shirt into the keg until the cloth was sopping. Then, more by feel than sight in the darkness, I found the man's mouth and squeezed the cider in. He gulped it down. Though it gave me the creeping fantods to touch a white man, I wet and squeezed the shirttail a dozen more times before he heaved a great sigh of relief and whispered something I couldn't make out.

I was close enough that the hard metal smell of blood along with sweat and gunpowder filled my nostrils. When the wagon pulled out from under the black shadows cast by the trees canopying the road, silver light fell on the man and I could make out his uniform. Union blue. At least he was a Yankee. There'd of been no more cider for a Reb.

The dim light of a clouded moon caught on the brass buttons running down the front of the soldier's jacket. They shone with the care that the soldier had lavished on polishing them. On each button was a fierce eagle, a shield over its breast. In one claw the eagle gripped an olive branch. In the other he held a bundle of arrows. Those buttons, gleaming in the moonlight, were the most beautiful things I had ever seen.

The soldier croaked out something I couldn't hear and I leaned in closer. He whispered in my ear, "Thank you."

Two Yankees in one day, two white men, one a general, now this regular soldier, had spoken to me.

I lifted my head to answer him at the same moment that the moon sailed out from beneath the clouds and shone down bright, revealing a sight that caused me to wonder if I had taken leave of my senses. For there, beneath the white of the bandage, I saw that the Yank's face was near as dark as my own. I could not conjure how these two colors, the blue of his suit and the black of his face, could possibly go together.

"Are you still there?" The soldier's whisper was hoarse and dry as sand. I watched his fine full lips form the question, the moon silver-plating the tip of his tongue when it peeped out on the word "there." I had never stared hard at a man's face before. Never had the least desire to do so. What I could see of this face, though, stopped me dead and left no choice but to study it. I tried to answer and was surprised to find that my own words had dried up in my throat.

"Hello?" His voice was husky, scratched raw by thirst and battle and pain.

"I'm here," I whispered, barely recognizing my own voice for it had gone soft and gentle.

"You . . . you're . . ." I had to lean so close to his mouth to hear him that his breath warmed my ear when he said, ". . . a woman."

"I am."

"You're a . . . a . . . black woman." I had never before heard anyone put those two words together the way he did. Like they were poetry. Like they were a prize and he had just won it.

"I am."

"My prayer has been answered," he gasped.

The effort caused a horrible rasping and rattling cough to overcome him.

I fetched up several more soppings of cider until he was breathing easy again, then I asked, "What prayer is that?"

"Not to die alone."

He spoke the way Daddy had. Educated and with none of the slurry drawl that made Southerners sound lazy or slow or both. And not hurried-up and mean the way Yankees talked, either.

"I didn't dare to ask for a black woman to comfort my last moments on this earth. But the Lord knew what was in my heart and He sent you to me."

His words and the feel of them forming against my ear caused my belly to quiver and my cheeks to warm like I'd been caught at something shame-ful. I answered as Daddy would of, clear and powerful and polished, for I needed to sound smart when I told him, "You are not going to die." It was both an order and what I suddenly wished for with all my heart.

He answered, "Yes I am," like it was a fact beyond disputing. In little halting bursts, with many stops to rest and allow me to trickle cider into his mouth, the soldier related, "I was near gone already when Sheridan's scav-enging party came upon me. I'd been left for dead after a little skirmish my unit got caught up in just north of here."

"Your unit? So this blue suit? It's yours?"

Again, in the halting way of a dying man, he managed to say, "I put the blood in it. Put the sweat in it. Figure that makes it mine as much as enlist-ing did."

"You're a soldier? A signed-up Yankee soldier?"

He told me how there were lots of black soldiers, tens of thousands. All fighting and dying to end slavery. Speaking wore him out, though, and with a long sigh, he slumped even more heavily into the sacks of grain. His head listed to the side as though the spirit had left him.

After several long, motionless minutes, I placed my hand beneath his nose. A long time passed before I felt the warm puff of a weak breath. I started to take my hand away, but the soldier leaned into my palm, and nestled his cheek up against it like a dog wanting to be patted. So I stroked his cheek, and comfort I never knew I had to give flowed out of me. The relief of a human touch allowed him to lower his guard so much that a few whimpers of pain mixed with the fear of the death coming up on him slipped from his lips.

The feel of his cheek skin was finer than when I was allowed into the big house and would run my hand against the silk-smooth wood of the maple banister. Other than Clemmie's, I had never stroked another person's cheek. Certainly no boy's. Mama had warned me from early on that to catch the eye of a boy, black or white, was to make a misery of your life. What befell Clemmie proved her warnings true.

Maybe because my nature had never come, I didn't have the slightest interest in boys the way most girls did. Far as I was concerned, they were just girls in britches. Though, by and large, a sight stupider, dirtier, meaner, smellier, and a whole lot louder. Now, though, a queer giddiness lit me up like hundreds of fireflies were zipping around inside my belly. For a second, I almost understood how girls went calf-kneed and forgot their raising when they were sweet on a boy.

The soldier slept and I was fixing to pull my hand away, but the instant I did, he groaned deep in his throat. The groan sounded like the noises that came from the other side of the cabin we shared with Maynard and his mama when one of the men visited Maynard's mother, a woman who was as man-fevered as they came.

The soldier leaned his cheek further into my palm and I left my hand just where it was, nuzzled against his warm skin. He slept and we traveled many a rough mile in this manner, my hand holding off troubled dreams and fears of the grave. I slept then woke without knowing when I'd dozed off and never certain I was truly awake as we rolled through forests shrouded with Spanish moss and swirling with foggy mists.

The days passed. I gnawed on sweet potatoes and fed the pullet parched corn, and other victuals the Yanks had stolen. The wagon only stopped when the driver—who had his rations on the foretop with him and never once looked back or spoke a word to me, and would of been happy if me and the soldier'd both gone cold—had to do his business.

Soon as he set the handbrake, I would jump off, hurry to relieve myself, and gulp down some water before I soaked my shirt, kerchief, and any other bit of rag I could lay my hands on. I'd bring the sopping cloths back and squeeze out a good drink for both the soldier and the pullet in the cage who'd become a friend with her fretful clucking.

It was during one such foray that I listened in on the white soldiers talking soldier talk and got the lay of the land as to where we were headed and why. Our destination was a place called Harper's Ferry where Sheridan was gathering up the Army of the Shenandoah along with the Sixth Corps of the Army of the Potomac, four infantry and two cavalry divisions. All told the soldiers reckoned he'd have him a force of fifty thousand men. This figure was beyond my power to conjure. They were fixing to have one whale of a showdown with the Rebs, who were massing their own men to the south under a general by the name of Jubal Early.

I couldn't say how many days passed, other than to note that I had made a considerable dent in the sweet taters, when I started awake from a dead sleep one night with a heavy feeling pressing in on me. Terrified, I checked on the soldier. He was taking his murmurless rest, and though he didn't wake, he did swallow a mouthful of cider before sagging back into a deep sleep.

The more time that passed with us bundled up so close, the greedier my palm grew. Soon, it took to sliding down to mold around the strong place where his jaw curved. Then to stroking his neck where the blood pulsed and the apple Eve gave Adam that got stuck in all men's throats ever after rippled when he swallowed. I brushed my fingertips across the wide flare of his nose, the bristly rasp of a mustache, the softness of his full lips.

That last, touching his beautiful lips, caused a spirit to take possession of my soul and that spirit desired the touch of those lips against mine. Though I attempted to rebuke such a willful spirit, a weariness greater than any I'd ever known came stealing over me. It made my head so heavy it drooped on my neck like a giant sunflower, forcing me to lean in closer. Then closer. I inhaled the scent of his skin, his breath. I leaned further.

Just as my lips touched his, the soldier woke. His croak of a voice after such a long silence startled me by asking, "May I . . ."

I jerked my head away and, from a respectable distance, answered, proper as I could with my heart thumping like a scared rabbit. "Yes? May you what?"

"May I . . ." His hand, trembling and weak, rose. "May I touch your face?"

I pulled back even further. All the sweet touches and words would stop the instant his fingers found the truth written on my dark face for even a blind man to see: I was a plain girl.

"Well, now," I stammered. "I don't know about all that."

"I am dying," my soldier stated flatly. "Let the feel of the face of a kind woman accompany me to the grave."

He reached his hand toward me, palm up, begging. Though I still worried about what he would see with his fingers, I could not deny a dying man his last wish. I guided his hand to my face. The tips of his strong fingers brushed across my cheeks, nose, forehead. They stroked my eyelashes gently, then traced the outlines of my lips. The breath bunched up inside my lungs as he saw me the way Auntie Cherry saw after her eyes went cloudy and gray.

He considered what his fingers felt and said, "You are a handsome woman. Gallant and stouthearted."

That queer giddiness came over me even stronger then for I felt the soldier had seen me better than anyone outside Mama and Clemmie ever had. Aside from the handsome part, he didn't just see who I was but who I dreamed about being. It was like when Daddy first laid eyes on Mama and knew right off that she was quality.

He laid the flat of his hand against my neck and then ran his fingers across my collarbone. "What are these?" he asked, his fingertips resting on the top row of scars like a piano player with his hands on the keys. "Who did this to you?" The way he asked, harsh, like he would of taken out after whoever had cut into my flesh, like he would of protected me, made me want to rest my head on his chest and never lift it from that spot again.

"No one put them on me," I answered, my voice so soft, I had to whisper directly into his ear. "My mama marked me the way her mama marked her. And all the girls were marked when . . ." I couldn't say "when their nature came." Instead, I just mumbled, "When it was time."

My scars were lies for my nature had never come. When I was seventeen and still had never bled, Mama said it was because I was not a female who would ever be claimed by a man. That I was meant for better than to be a brood sow for some short-weight plowboy. Might have been that or might have been the fact that us field hands had naught but a handful of ground corn and what we could steal and scavenge to eat and because I worked too hard for a womanly nesting to take hold in my nethers.

Clemmie, though, she worked in the house and ate regular and never lifted anything heavier than a feather duster, and her womanhood arrived when she was fourteen. So that's when Mama decided to mark us both.

I told the soldier how I had kneeled in front of Mama and she used a blackberry thorn to pluck up bits of my young hide, which she then lopped off with a straight-edge razor Clemmie had borrowed from Old Mister for just that purpose. After Mama dotted me thusly thirty times, she rubbed a handful of ashes and some pinches of her snuff into the cuts to stop the bleeding and make the dots puff up pretty.

"Did it hurt?" my soldier asked.

"Getting ashes and snuff rubbed into cuts leaking thirty trails of blood down your chest?" My answer pointed to the foolishness of the question. "But I was Mama's Africa child and if I ever let the water fall from my eye those tears would of washed away the strength and magic and power Mama had cut into me. Then I'd be like everyone else: a slave not a captive.

"But Clemmie, Lord." I chuckled at the memory. "Where I'd made myself into a stone on the bottom of a clear river the way Mama had taught me, Clemmie boo-hooed buckets. That's because she was Mama's America child and never knew Iyaiya the way I had."

I wished I knew the American words for the chant Mama repeated through all the cutting, so that I could tell that to my soldier, too. But it only came back to me in Fon: *I cut strength into you. I cut belonging into you. Me to you. You to me. We to our people, to our ancestors, and to our children to come. I cut a warning into you that no unwelcome hand shall ever touch you and go unpunished.*

That last is why I'd been obliged to kill Old Mister, for he had put his unwelcome hands on my little sister and had to be punished. I didn't tell that part.

The soldier stroked the tips of his fingers across the beaded rows soft as a bird brushing me with its wing and my breath stopped. "You know who you are," he whispered, as though that was some kind of miracle. "You haven't forgotten. They haven't taken Africa from you. How is that possible?"

"Iyaiya's stories," I answered. "She told them to me every night until Old Mister sold her off. Then Mama told them. They were our lullabies. Now I tell them to myself in the moments before sleep catches me."

"Tell me," he asked. "Tell me about Africa, about the home I never knew. Tell me your lullabies."

Chapter 3

ow I wished I could of told those stories in our secret queen language that we spoke when there were no whites about. Iyaiya and Mama and me could paint curlicues, do backward flips, and run across rainbows in that limber tongue.

Though I missed the musical way the words loppity-lopped like a creek tumbling over smooth stones when the tales were told in Fon, I stumbled along, hobbled by having to speak American and said, "My grandmother, my Iyaiya, wasn't but a knobby-kneed girl when a scout arrived in her village. He had been sent by King Ghezo who was the greatest of the twelve kings of Dahomey and the one that freed his kingdom from the rule of his brother Andandozan. Old Andandozan, who was crazy as a peach orchard boar, was partial to feeding his prisoners of war, alive and hollering to hallelujah, to the pet hyenas he kept special just for that purpose.

"But it's King Ghezo we're talking about now and it was one of his scouts who came to my grandmother's village and put all the young virgins to a test. After picking out the six fastest girls, he made them charge through a wall of acacia thorns."

"Acacia?" he asked.

"I don't mean the kind we have here. I'm talking Africa acacia where they sprout needles three, four inches long that can slice you up clean as a straight-edge razor."

The soldier sighed, settling in like a child being told a bedtime story, and I picked up my tale. "Only one girl went at that barbed barricade not once, not twice, but three times, and that was my grandma. So the scouts took her to the capital of Dahomey, Ouidah, to see if she had the grit to be N'Nonmiton."

"N'Nonmiton," he repeated, enjoying the feel of the word.

"When my Iyaiyah first came upon the city of Ouidah, she was struck dumb by its magnificence. A mud wall, near thirty feet high and two and a half mile long, wrapped around the whole city. On top of the gates set a dozen enemy heads shriveled black in the sun, each one with its own bib of dried blood. Off in a special area were a hundred acres of royal residences, tombs, and memorial shrines all shaded by thick palm trees. King Ghezo and his six thousand virgin queens lived in a palace at the very heart of the capital. But what really impressed Grandma was that King Ghezo had him a low, wooden throne setting on the skulls of four enemy kings that his warrior-wives had laid on the cooling board for him in battle. Iyaiya wanted nothing more than to live with the king in Ouidah and be one of his wives."

The soldier gave a throat rumble of interest, encouraging me to go on.

"For the next few months, hundreds of the strongest, fleetest girls from all over the kingdom of Dahomey were brought to Ouidah to be trained and tested. They ran barefoot over burning sand, shot flintlock muskets with flowers scrolled into the silver trigger plates, wrestled each other, and stormed more of those acacia-thorn barriers. The same time they were getting deadened to body pain, trainers were working on deadening their mind pain."

The soldier nodded like he approved of this toughening and I went on. "This they did by having the new recruits climb up a sixteen-foot platform. At the top the girls found three dozen prisoners of war, gagged and trussed up like shoats going to market. In the large central gathering place below, a mob howled for the blood of their enemies. Each new girl had to heave a prisoner off the platform so the howling mob could air them out with the sticks they had sharpened for exactly that purpose and then tear the ventilated carcasses into little souvenir chunks.

"Any girl who hesitated or whimpered or let the water run from her eye was sold to the Portugee for a miserable sum, because who wanted a girl in the first place? And a coward to boot? My Iyaiya hurled captives off the platform easy as chunking rocks into the river. And sang while she was doing it."

The soldier's forehead furrowed and I realized that I'd gone too far and shut up. He was too American for Iyaiya's story.

A moment passed before he asked, "Well? Was she chosen?"

"Of course."

He murmured in an interested way and I went on.

"After my Iyaiya was taken on as one of the king's wife-warriors, she was given all the tobacco she could smoke and all the palm wine and millet beer she could drink. And when she set foot outside her royal quarters, one servant stood waiting to shade her head from the sun with a parasol and another ran ahead ringing a bell to warn the men to lower their eyes and not to look upon one of the king's virgin wives.

"But what I remember best," I said, "was her describing how she wore a blue tunic and carried a saber that gleamed like the sun. And how, when she stood, shoulder to shoulder, with the bravest, strongest girls in all the kingdom, the line they formed was as straight as a bar of iron. And dignitaries from around the world came to marvel and call them *les Amazones*."

Just like Iyaiya, my voice swelled with pride. But it all drained away when I reached the sad ending of her tale of glory.

"My Iyaiya used to say that the only regret she had about being an Amazon was that she hadn't ripped the veins out of the neck of the Yoruba warrior who captured her while she was out hunting a rogue elephant with a dozen other warrior-wives. The Yorubas did to her exactly what Iyaiya's people would have done to any enemy they captured: they sold her off to the Portugee."

I hated that part of the story. It was like dreaming of running and waking up to find the manacles still around your ankles. So I quickly added, "Iyaiya never thought of herself as a slave, though. She was a captive. And that's what she raised Mama knowing and what Mama raised me knowing: we were captives. Prisoners of war. Never slaves. Captives."

"Captive," he whispered, seeming to like the sound of the word. Then a long, low breath whistled out of him and he said, "I wish I wasn't going to die. You are fit to be the wife who would bear me the children not broken as we are."

Wife? Children?

I could not speak.

"Dying has made me bold," he gasped out. "Made me greedy for what I will never have." He took hold of my hand, and for the first time in my life, I understood what shy meant. Though I wanted more than anything to show off, to be someone for him, I couldn't of spoken if Jesus had been taking orders for salvation.

In the silence, the pain came back on him hard and I saw that he was one of those, like Daddy, who had such a big, busy brain that it actually hurt for it to lie fallow. That the ideas and stories in his head meant more to him than the world outside it.

I saw I had to come up with another story to occupy his mind and was grasping for one good enough when he asked, "Your parents? How did they raise you so strong?"

Chapter 4

——

Oh, he loosed the floodgates on that one. I blew straight past shy as I pondered on how best to tell the wonderful tale of my daddy and my mama. Though my mother was a monstrous large woman, even taller than me and brick-built from the ground up, I didn't want to reveal the manliness that we shared. Instead, I started off, "If you were American, you'd say my grandmother raised Mama hard and that Mama raised me hard. But that was the Africa way and I was Mama's Africa child."

The soldier sighed with satisfaction, signifying that that was the answer he wanted to hear. The one that fit with all the other answers he had stored up in his busy brain. After gathering up his strength, the soldier said something that had the shiver of prophecy about it. "That Africa raising will save you. It will make you strong enough for freedom. While others, the weak, will fall by the wayside."

"Well," I whispered. "I don't know about all that."

I was putting on, answering his truth with a lie, for he was right. Mama raised me knowing God-sure that we were better than the others. So I went on and admitted as much, saying, "Knowing we weren't slaves, that we were better than the tore-down souls around us, did not make us popular, but Mama never gave a shovelful of fleas about being liked."

He snorted the hint of a laugh then sucked in a quick breath that signified pain had stabbed him, and I rushed to chase that hurt away by telling him of the great pride of my life: my daddy.

"Now Daddy," I said. "Daddy was the opposite of Mama in every way you can conjure up. He was a free man born in the free state of Ohio and

educated at the Society of Free People of Colour for Promoting the Instruction and School Education of Children of African Descent. There he
learned to read and write, speak like a city preacher, and earn his keep as a
tailor of fine gentlemen's clothing."

I continued. Daddy was my brag story and it bubbled up out of me
like a spring. As I knew it would, that earned the happy murmurs and the
soldier's breathing settled back down.

"Daddy made his living traveling about. He hired out to gentlemen
wanted quality. Wanted a fine collar lined with horsehair canvas and lapels
done with hand pad stitches so they'd lay down smooth. These were all
things that Mr. Chastain Pennebaker over to Glen Eden plantation, a two-
hundred-slave for-real plantation, craved. Mr. Pennebaker was a vain man
always looking for ways to show he was a real planter and not just some
no-ham-and-all-hominy, dog-dirt-poor dozen-slave farmer like Old Mister who never had any more idea how to turn black muscle and brown dirt
into a decent tobacco crop than a kitten'd know how to gin a bale of cotton.
And that's why Mr. Pennebaker sent all the way up to Ohio for Daddy."

The soldier gave a contented nod.

I went on, holding out the shiniest parts of me to him, those being the
parts about Daddy. "Daddy could not only tailor to Mr. Pennebaker's finicky standards, but he spoke American better than anyone else, black or
white, in the tricounty area. Mr. Pennebaker liked his work so much, he
issued him a pass to come and go as he pleased."

I didn't bother adding that Daddy crowed about how he was as slithery
good as the serpent in the Garden of Eden at flattering white people and that
he had buttered up vain Mr. Pennebaker until the planter took him on as a
pet. Not only did Daddy get that pass, he also got away with all manner of
offenses would of gotten any other black man flogged or lynched. But
Mr. Pennebaker wouldn't stand for any rough handling of his "little
monkey."

"It was that very pass," I continued, "that allowed Daddy to attend a sociable over to Chalmers McWattie's place. And that is where he met Mama.
Daddy was the only man ever laid eyes on my mother smart enough to see
right off that she was quality, sewed up with stitches so fine and strong they'd
never show, never sag, and they'd never, ever give out. Daddy invited her
to dance a Walk-Around-Joe with him and that was all it took."

That appeared to bring a calming picture to the soldier's mind and the pain stitching what I could see of his face unraveled a bit. So I left a few particulars out. Especially the one that had come to me courtesy of a big old lumbering clay-eater out of Cape Girardeau County, name of Handy. Handy had been at that sociable and ever after liked to do his own little reenactment of Mama and Daddy meeting. Though never in Mama's presence for Handy used a small, spotted dog to stand in for Daddy. Bending over at the waist and holding the dog by its dainty paws, Handy would play Mama and lead that little dog about on its hind legs.

All this is by way of saying that Daddy was a man as compact as Mama was mountainous. Though Daddy might have been somewhat undersized in the torso and limbs, with stubby fingers on hands that stopped closer to his waist than to his crotch, my father had the head of a lion to accommodate his extra-large brain.

I skipped over the dog-dancing part and moved on to what I figured the soldier would enjoy more. "Like Mama," I said, "Daddy carried a high opinion of himself and didn't think it was worth being loved by a woman unless she put equal high stock on her own value. And there weren't many like that among the other slaves as being someone's property tends to have a deflating effect on the psyche," I added, quoting Daddy.

"Amen," the soldier croaked, too excited to let pain stop his words.

"Yes, Daddy saw right off that Mama was made of oak and iron-bound," I said, not adding that, though there was close on two foot of difference in height between them, he knew they were made for each other.

Daddy might, indeed, have been a midget as the bullyboys and clabberheads claimed, but to me, he was a giant and, though he would vanish from our lives whenever work or the whites carried him away, he always came back to us.

"Daddy was genius smart," I stated, seeing no reason to slice that fact any thinner. "He taught me about the Articles of the Constitution. About the eleven planets spinning around the sun, Mercury, Venus, Earth, Mars, Jupiter, Saturn, Uranus, Ceres, Pallas, Vesta, and Juno. He read and reread to me the copies of *The Colored American Deliverer* published in New York City that he smuggled with him down South."

"But you yourself don't read?" The soldier's hand went limp in mine. His disappointment surprised me. As if the most dangerous thing next to a gun a slave could be found with wasn't a book.

He caught himself and said, "No, no, of course not. I just thought . . ."

What? That I measured up to you?

"Ciphering," I said quick. "Daddy and I concentrated on ciphering since ten fingers and ten toes were a lot safer to own than books. Instant Daddy learned me my numbers, I could add, do takeaways, times, goes intos, all in my head. Numbers came to me natural as blinking."

The soldier gave no answer except to make a low, growly sound for he had again, mercifully, taken leave of his senses. With my free hand, I wet a rag, flapped it about in the night breeze to cool it some, and daubed his throat where the blood flowed hottest.

All this talk about Daddy forced the memories I kept buried to rise from their graves and, once again, I was five and it was Christmas. We had our one full day of the year off and were waiting on Daddy to come visit. When he hadn't shown by the time the sun went down, Mama went crazy for worry that the pattyrollers might of got him. Even before the Rebellion, those calamitous vigilantes were hoodooing around the woods checking passes. If they caught a person of color without one, the acts of wickedness they committed were beyond imagining.

I was ordering my own imagination not to creep one inch further when the soldier's hand trembled in mine then went cold as death as he struggled to suck in air. A terrible rattle came from the back of his throat that meant the end was coming on fast unless I got him help. The sound unstrung me and my own breath came hard. Panic rising, I searched frantically about the wagon for something, anything, that might save him. I felt like I'd found a gold nugget in a river, but that a swift current was snatching it away and sending it, glinting with every hope I'd ever have, tumbling from my grasp.

And then my soldier went silent.

Chapter 5

I raised up to yell for the driver to stop. Before I could open my mouth, though, I saw that we were coming up on an aid station of some sort.

"Hang on," I begged my soldier, hoping that some part of him could hear. "I can get you help now. You'll be fine. Just fine."

There, on the outskirts of camp, was a row of tents large enough to stand up in. Cedar boughs to keep out insects and clean the bad air decorated each one. The flaps in the front and sides were open. Wounded men were laid out on cots with the blanket pulled away from stubs of missing arms and legs that had been stitched up with wide tracks of black catgut like embroidery around a hem.

"Hospital tents," I told him. "For soldiers. Real soldiers like you. We made it. Driver's headed there right now. You'll be resting on a cot before you know it."

But when we reached the tall hospital tents, instead of stopping, the driver veered away like he hadn't seen them at all and made for a desolate area back beyond camp. Though it was dangerous to speak out to a white man, I didn't have a choice. I yelled out, "Sir! 'Scuse me, sir. Sir?"

For the first time, the driver looked over his shoulder at me. Most of his face was covered by an assortment of whiskers—mustaches, sideburns, and whatnot. Out of that foliage peered a pair of hard blue eyes shot with blood by short nights and long days of trail dust.

"Sir," I said, turning all humble and meek, the way most men of any color preferred to be addressed, "aren't the hospital tents back yonder?"

The driver curled his lip up to reveal a limited selection of stumpy brown teeth, let fly a thin stream of chaw juice and said, "Not for you Ethiopians they ain't." He tipped his head toward my soldier and added, " 'Specially not dead ones."

Without thinking, I scrambled to the foretop, jerked the reins from the driver's hands, yanked hard to turn the wagon around, and was rewarded with a string of curses regarding my race and a righteous clout in the nose from a fist hardened by years of mule persuasion. Catching me off balance, the blow pitched me back into the bed and I only righted myself when the driver whoaed the mules and we stopped at a desolate place on the far edge of camp. A raggedy pack of contrabands, escaped slaves, and other hard-luck cases sprung forward.

"Got 'nother one for you, boys," the driver informed the contrabands, cocking his head back toward the soldier. "Haul him to the boneyard. Throw that there other one in with him for all I care. I'da dumped him out myself except Sheridan wants him delivered to headquarters."

The instant one of the men grabbed hold of my soldier, I screamed, "No!" with all the force of my voice, which was a mighty one when I chose it to be. With no more thought than I'd give to drawing a breath, I threw my body across the soldier and announced, "This man is alive! He needs doctoring! Water! Food! Medicine! He'll be fine!"

The men cut glances back and forth until a snowy-topped gent with a few scraggly white hairs poking out of his chin like bean sprouts inquired gently, "You touched in the head, son?"

It was then that I saw that my soldier's struggle for breath had ended. The half of his well-made face not covered by blood-blacked bandages was serene and at peace now that he'd stopped fighting the pain. He had been taken home. I lay across his chest, not letting the men take him, and said Iyaiya's prayers asking that his ancestors would be waiting for him. I told him I was pleased to have made his acquaintance and then I kissed him good-bye.

That kiss unleashed a torrent of abuse and rough handling from the men, who cursed me as a sodomite as they drug the soldier from his bed of grain sacks. A dark stain of blood marked the spot where his head had been. My soldier hung between the men, limp as a gutted animal. His head, thrown back, neck to the sky, bounced with every step as they made their way to a great pit in the distance. At that pit, men with bandanas over their mouths and noses were shoveling lye powder on those who had already been laid to rest. I turned away, unable to bear any more.

"You got a name for that last one?" a thin private holding a tattered notebook and the stub of a pencil yelled up at the driver.

"Last what?"

"The soldier the graves men just took away?"

"Oh, the nigger," the driver grunted. "Yeah, they gave me his paper when they loaded him up." He pulled a document folded in eighths from his pocket and handed it down to the private. The private, a nearsighted boy with narrow shoulders, practically put his nose on the document as he copied my soldier's name from the limp document to the list he held.

Looking up, he asked, "Where are his personal belongings?"

"Say what?" the driver asked.

"His effects? He was a soldier. I have to collect his personal effects."

The driver's face soured.

"What all he had on him," the graves private explained. "Money. Bible. Penknife. Shaving glass. Last letter home. Such like. It's regulations. Have to collect them. Store them in this here personal effects box." The private held up a pretty pine box a bit bigger than a cigar box, and added, "We have to store a soldier's effects for when his kin comes to claim his personal belongings."

The driver shooed him away, saying, "You want to go paw through a dead nigger's pockets, go on ahead," then went to yelling at the mules, "Back! Back!" to get the wagon turned around.

As the driver backed up the mules, I called out to the private, "Sir! Sir!"

The boy glanced up at me.

"What was his name?" I asked.

The private stuck his nose back down on the list and, as we rolled on into camp, he hollered after us, "Swayne! His name was Private Wager Swayne!"

Chapter 6

A good deal of time passed, though I can't say how long, for after my soldier died I stopped keeping track not only of time but most other concerns as well. Like living or dying. Losing my soldier made me fear that I would never see Mama or Clemmie again in this life. And, if what Old Miss used to tell me was true—that I was bound to burn forever in the next life for the willful ways she hadn't been able to beat out of me in this one—I wouldn't be spending eternity with them, either.

I had just about accepted that I'd end my days thumping about in the back of a wagon when I awoke one morning and saw that we had fetched up in a new world. Just ahead, a vast city of dingy white tents rose from the misty dawn, sagging swaybacked in the scant light.

A bugle was tootling as we approached the edge of all those tents strung along in rows look to have been laid out with a plumb line. White men commenced to spilling from the tents. Stretching, scratching their bellies and posteriors, pulling trousers over their drawers, shouldering on suspenders, hotfooting it to the woods to pee, hawking, spitting, and blowing out their noses on the ground.

It surprised me that Yanks woke up making the same disgusting noises and doing the same disgusting things as every other man I had ever known. Some of them bent over buckets and splashed water on their faces and the backs of their necks. A few waited in line for a turn in front of a shaving glass tacked up on a tree.

Farther on, we passed soldiers already turned out in uniform. Those blue suits must of had extra starch in them from the way the men snapped up tall and straight when they put them on and went to either saluting or being saluted at. Saluting. I liked this handsome way of greeting and showing respect. The sight was a fine one and made me ache for wishing I could of seen the dead soldier standing up straight and proud in his shiny-button uniform.

In the center of camp was a row of tents high enough to stand up in. Outside the middle one, several officers were gathered around a couple of upturned barrels, heads down, studying hard on a map spread out there. The wagon halted. The driver hopped off, marched right up to the cluster of bosses, saluted and announced, "Reporting as ordered, General."

The man in the center lifted his head and, sure enough, there was the General himself, burning hot holes into the driver for interrupting him.

"Sir," the driver stuttered. "The, uh, contraband you wanted delivered? I got him here." He shoved his thumb back at me.

Still puzzled and annoyed, Sheridan turned those devil-dark black eyes on me. I drew myself up and, without thinking, my hand snapped to my forehead hard as a cleaver hacking into a hambone, and I saluted the General.

Sheridan's heavy, black eyebrows jumped like he couldn't make out the sense of what I was doing. I might of been a dog with my paw tapping my forehead as far as he was concerned. His hard jaw set even harder. It was clear that the General had no more recollection of me than any of the other thousands of threadbare contrabands tramping the countryside.

Sheridan was about to turn his back and condemn me to join the ranks of those lost souls, unrooted from the past and given no future to aim for, when his overseer, Colonel Terrill, stepped forward. "Sir, this is the fine buck you liberated. You wanted him delivered here to serve as your cook's helper and I took personal responsibility for that charge."

The General gave Terrill a peeved look that went beyond what any soldier would of gotten for expecting to be thanked for following an order. It seemed that Sheridan genuinely detested Terrill and I wondered again why he kept the man around.

"Then take him to my _____ cook. Jay-sus, Terrill, what would I be wanting with that _____ while we're discussing strategy?" Though technically fighting to free us, the General had a world of high-caliber insults to hurl upon members of my race.

"Begging your pardon, General, sir," Terrill stammered. "It's just that

you did make a point of . . ." The colonel trailed off for his boss was paying him no more mind than a grub worm underfoot and had gone back to
poking hard at the map, making swooping gestures with his hand, pointing at one officer then the next, all while questioning the legitimacy of each
man's birth and the virtue of his mother.

"Are you deaf?" Terrill barked at the driver, his sniveling ways gone
now. "Get that . . ."

The wagon jerked away, and in the hail of insults and curses that Terrill
hurled after me, I could hear the hint of a Southern accent.

We circled back to a cluster of patchy tents and lean-tos set off behind
the nice, fancy tents. In the open yard in front of them, iron tripods held up
cauldrons the size of hogshead kegs over fires of logs so stout they put out
heat had me sweating before we even came to a halt.

Ahead of us was a line of more wagons filled with foraged food being
unloaded by the contrabands and runaways who swarmed about. Other freed
slaves busied themselves poking the fires, adding more wood, pouring buckets of water into the heating pots. A couple of men sat cranking the handles
on big grinders. One for coffee. One for corn. Every time the drawer of a
coffee grinder was full, the fellow cranking'd spring up and run to dump it
in one of the pots.

With each dump, the man at the center of it all would crack the fellow
on the back of his head with the cast-iron ladle in his hand and holler, "Keep
a-crankin', son! General likes his coffee strong enough to fight back! Rest
of all y'all," he yelled at the ones lolling about, "what is your affliction? Were
you all born tired and raised lazy? No work, no food. I ain't y'alls' master. I
didn't put no cash down on a single one of you. You starve, makes me no
nevermind."

He noticed our wagon, pointed the ladle at it, and ordered a couple of
men, "Eli! Jonathan! Get them provisions unloaded."

Before I knew it, the strong country boys, both of them already a little
stooped from having spent their early years hunched over chopping and hoe-
ing, shoved me aside like I was a barrel of wormy apples. I ended up standing
alone in the middle of a whirlwind of to-and-froing, all spinning around the
boss cook wielding that ladle like a mule skinner cracking the whip on his
sullen beasts.

He was a sight. And not one for sore eyes. The man had one of those long,
narrow faces made for frowning and scowling. Which he did plenty of.

Freckles spattered his high cheeks like specks of molasses. Skinny as a scarecrow, he had a strange menagerie of garments flapping about him. He wore a top hat looked to have been sat on a time or two, a pair of bottle-green britches near covered in gaudy patches, and a drummer boy's short, shiny-buttoned jacket that had a scorched-looking hole below the shoulder where the previous owner had been shot.

But oddest of all, he had a long, stretched-out rat, might of been a baby weasel, running free across his shoulders, goosing its head out like a snake about to strike, then darting back behind the cook's neck to poke his head around on the other side. Most disgusting of all, though, when that varmint decided it didn't like what it saw, it ducked into the cook's shirt and skittered around until it found a comfy spot then nestled there, pouching the shirt out like a roll of squirming belly fat.

As the men unloaded the food stolen off of Old Mister's farm, the boss cook inspected every keg and barrel. When he peered into a lumpy tow sack, he proclaimed, "Hallelujah! Sweet taters! Can make the General his pie now. Eli, dump them out over there." He pointed to a low bench next to where I was standing off to the side, away from the commotion. The bench had a fine Green River knife with a stag-horn handle stuck into it.

Eli, acting like he was a house servant and me a no-count field hand, about ran me over as he went to dump out a small mountain of sweet potatoes beside the bench. A couple of the taters took hard bumps and cracked open, showing bright orange meat against the mucky black dirt.

When one of the men hauled in that last scrawny pullet of Old Mister's, the boss cook glared at the empty wagon and demanded, "That all the meat they brung?"

" 'Pears so, Mr. Solomon."

Solomon.

"Well, dog it to hell. Quartermaster ain't sent two beans out in over a week. Commissary's empty. Not enough here for a stew for two white ladies much less the officers' mess. Jonathan, go on and forage me up some meat."

"Naw, suh, cain't do that. Ever farm herebouts been stripped clean."

"Well then, go on shoot some varmints for this stew."

"I already done got every jackass rabbit in three counties," Jonathan answered.

Solomon hoisted up the rifle and issued a general order to all the assorted shirkers and hangers-on, "Half a sweet tater for anyone brings me a squirrel or a jack. Hell, coon or possum'll do."

Jonathan snatched the old musket up and the others crowded around as he bore his prize away. It was a rare thing for a black man to be in possession of a weapon and they intended to make the most of it. The boss cook yelled after them, "And don't come back empty-handed. You know the General. You black he think you can make cobbler outta clay."

"And hash out of horse shit, isn't that right, Solomon?"

At the unmistakable sound of General Sheridan's voice booming out behind him, Solomon jerked to attention like a rifle been shot off next to his ear. The General stepped into view and Solomon and I both saluted.

"General, sir, didn't know you was . . ." Solomon's pitiful wheedling trailed off. Sheridan didn't bother to return our salutes the way he did with the blue suits. Just waved them off like we were children playing at being soldiers, tipped his chin at me and asked Solomon, "So, what do you think of the helper I emancipated for you?"

I drew myself up in my raggedy britches, hair uncovered and going ever which way, and for the first time, Solomon took me in. He was none too pleased with what he saw.

"Him?" the cook asked, his face as sour as if he'd bitten into a green persimmon. "Beggin' your pardon, Gen'l, suh," he continued, turning down his boss voice and general intelligence level until he sounded like an old plantation uncle. "But I do believes I specifically requested a girl, suh. A house girl. Least a house *boy*. I'm 'bout wore out with these ignorant field hands, don't know 'nough to cook an ashcake. Don't stay long enough to learn. Had a whole bunch run off just yestiddy. Not even worth catchin' they names."

Boss cook was mealymouthing and the General was not one for mealymouthers. "By thunder, Solomon, I'll not have another _____ pox-ridden female cooking for me and my officers. You'll _____ make do with this fine, husky buck."

For some reason, hearing the General call me a "husky buck," even a fine one, made the feel of the soldier's palm stroking my cheek, telling me I was a handsome woman, come back and my heart knocked sideways with hurt. I wanted to yell at them that a blind, dying man had enough sense to know that I was female. It felt so much like these two were stealing away the one pretty thing that had ever been mine that I rared back and spit out, "I *am* female."

Solomon stared at me like I was a two-headed calf and asked, "You? A girl?"

If the General was surprised, he didn't show it. "Enough of this. Solomon, you asked for a female and I have fetched you a female," he said, just like he'd transformed me on the spot. "And there's an end to it." To me he added, "Solomon is the finest _____ cook in this man's army. So mind what he tells you. Especially about sweet potato pie."

At that Solomon grinned like a simpering fool and the General lashed out, "Get to it, the both of you! I'm hungry enough to eat the hind leg off the Lamb of God!"

Solomon chuckled and called after Sheridan's retreating back, "Don got that on the menu, suh. But we sho' nuff gon get you that sweet tater pie. Gen'l likes his sweet tater pie. Yassuh. He sho' do."

As soon as Sheridan was gone, the cook's grin dropped, replaced by that green-persimmon look of disgust. He stuck his face so close to mine the critter in his shirt bumped its snaky head on my belly and I saw that the man was old. Had to be within sniffing distance of forty.

"You a girl," he demanded. "Why you wearing britches?"

Any other female would of been bulled down by his rough-and-haughty manner, but Mama had taught me all about rough and haughty. And all about scrawny men like Solomon. How they puff themselves worse than a mean dog ruffling its fur to look bigger and scarier than they are. She always told me that the worst thing to do, mean dog or mean man, was to back down. I had to stand up to him from the get. Ruffle myself up even bigger than he was. Let him know I wasn't to be trifled with or I'd have a snout up my ass the rest of my livelong days.

So I got right up on him, stood tall enough that I could see the bald spot size of a half-dollar top his head, and I answered back smartly, speaking the way Daddy would of, "I wear what I please, I do what I please. Back home my mama, she ran the place. She's the daughter of an Africa queen. And that makes me the daughter of a daughter of a queen."

That cut him right down. It surprised me how quick he folded, and respectful now, he said, "Daughter of a daughter of a queen. That right?"

"Right as rain in August. Solomon." I made his name sound like I was saying "Fool." And I sure didn't add any "mister." Slave days were behind me. Smash 'em Up Sheridan himself had said I was emancipated. I was done forever with "mister."

"So that how it is," Solomon said, not asking, just nodding his head in agreement.

I'd never seen a man break down so easy. Even Mama generally had to throw a few punches. But I figured the boss cook had just felt the power of my Africa blood. With considerable satisfaction at having established myself, I folded my arms and agreed, "Yeah, that how it is."

Without another word, Solomon shoved me so hard I near knocked over the bench he slammed me down on. "You a queen. Here's your throne. Now get to skinnin' them taters 'fore I forget General sent you. If he didn't have his eye on you, I'd chop you up into little queen pieces and make me a queen stew! Fit for a king. Which right now means me, *Mister* Solomon Yarnell out of Van Buren County, Tennessee."

My hand was on the Green River knife and I was on my feet before another thought went through my head. I jabbed that steel blade in Solomon's direction to show I meant business and I wouldn't have him or anybody else knocking me on my ass.

But Solomon just smiled, held both hands out high with his palms up, and said, "Come on ahead then," daring me to move on him. He stood there cool as a frog's belly, which cut my heat enough that I saw the obvious: I was surrounded. As far as the eye could see there was nothing but soldiers and tents with soldiers in them. I was bobbing on an ocean of armed men. And Solomon was one of theirs. And I was not. I sunk back down on the bench.

"Like I thought," he said. "All vine and no taters." Then he leaned in and laid down the law like Moses giving the Israelites the Ten Commandments. "You listen to me, your majesty. 'Less you the daughter of the daughter of Ulysses S. Grant hisself, you shit in shoes just like the rest us. Ain't no more do what you please. Them do-what-you-please days is over. You in the army now, Queenie."

He went on for a good bit more, elaborating on how ignorant, worthless, and ugly I was. Finally, checking to make sure that none of the others were paying any attention, he whispered, "You smart, you keep that Queenie nonsense to yourself. Hear? Fact is, you gon live a lot longer you don't let on you female at all. Girl on her own? No man to protect her?" He shook his head. "Shee-*yit*. This pack of shiftless, passin'-through dogs? They'll use you like a rented mule then leave you behind so Rebs can lynch what's left of you for a traitor. And that ain't plantation scare talk." He placed his varmint on the bench, slipped a lasso of twine around her neck, tied it to the bench, ordered me to watch the snaky thing, and left.

I was trapped good and, oh, how I hated being trapped. Hated how the dying soldier had opened a tender place in me only to have it stomped on. Hated that I had failed Clemmie. Hated that I had left my mama with tears in her eyes. Mostly I hated how weak it all made me feel. How ashamed Mama would be if she could see me brought so low. All those hates boiled away the tears choking up at the back of my throat and turned them to hot steam that drove my hand as I stabbed the knife back into the bench.

The cook's varmint came skittering up then to investigate and I saw that it had black button eyes, a pink nose, and a black mask over its eyes like a raccoon. While I was studying it, the thing struck quick as lightning, put its pink nose on my hand, and would of climbed right up my arm, but I jerked my hand away and buried it deep in my armpit.

I had landed in a low spot and tried to comfort myself by imagining I was back with my soldier. Suddenly though the men with bandanas tied over their mouths like stagecoach robbers intruded upon my sweet memories and they were blown away in a cloud of lye powder whirling up from a burial pit.

It hurt to think of that terrible white powder falling across the soldier's soft lips the way the moonlight had during those long nights in the wagon. So I made my mind go blank and sat there like a stone that nothing and no one could hurt. Like a tombstone with the name Wager Swayne chiseled into it.

Chapter 7

I t was high noon when Solomon and his boys returned with a string of jacks all skinned and dressed out. I jumped up off that bench and hurried to meet him.

While Solomon was explaining to his boys how he wanted the jacks chopped and seasoned, I broke in and informed him, "I can pot a mess more varmints than y'all did. And I won't ruin the meat with gut shots, either," I added, nodding at one critter been blown into tatters.

"You don't say," Jonathan said in a sneery way.

"You don't believe me, give me that old musket you got, and I'll show you. I'm a dead shot."

I made to grab for the gun, but Solomon jerked the long arm away, saying, "Shot dead, more like it. Slave with a gun? Any white ever seen that, you'd of been swinging 'fore nightfall."

He got that right. Horses and reading and rifles, they were all forbidden. You got caught riding or reading, there'd be a whipping. Maybe worse. But a rifle? Lord. That'd guarantee you a long drop from a short rope.

"Yeah," Solomon's boy Eli put in. "How'd a slave ever get a gun?"

"Took it off a dead Rebel," I answered, and my head filled with the sound of buzzing like a hive been bust open. That was the sound that had led Mama and me to that dead Reb one day when we were out clearing timber for a new field. The bees had turned out to be a cloud of green-eyed flies feasting on the pulpy remains of what we figured to be a Secesh deserter. His right leg was swole up to where it had ripped open the leg of his trousers. "Copperhead," Mama said, naming the viper that had bit him.

"He had a rifle beside him," I explained. "A beautiful German yagger."

I knew the name, for Mr. Pennebaker had one and never tired of gassing on to Old Mister about his fine German yagger rifle with its stock special-made of fine burled wood and a patch box, muzzle, and trigger guard of polished brass.

"And what?" Solomon demanded. "Your sweet old master put up some targets? Took you out and learned you how to shoot?"

"No, my grandma did."

"Your grannie?" How they hooted at that.

"Well, not her so much as the stories she'd told us about being—"

Solomon cut me off, saying, "Seems you're mighty good with stories."

I sulled up then like a possum playing dead at him calling me a liar to my face and didn't go on to explain that I'd watched Mr. Pennebaker load and shoot his yagger a hundred times. Or that Clemmie stole pinches of black powder and minié balls from Old Mister for loads. Or how, with my strong, steady hands and eagle eyes, I was a natural. How I got to where, using the flip-up rear sight, I could peel a squirrel off a high branch fifty yards away. I wished most fervent that I had my yagger at that very moment, for I would of shut them all up with a few dazzling shots. But my beloved long arm was in the woods back home where I'd hidden it inside a hollow ash tree. Someday, I swore, I would reclaim it.

Without another word, Solomon grabbed me by the collar of my shirt, dragged me back to the bench, saw the mess I'd made of the few taters I'd tried to skin and the big pile I hadn't touched.

"Get your filthy hands off—" I started, but the poke of the Green River knife digging into my throat shut me up quick. Pausing only to stuff a couple of potatoes into his pockets, Solomon drug me off.

The camp was a town of canvas and mud that went on for miles in all directions. After tromping past endless rows of the regular soldiers' low tents, we approached an open field. Here new recruits were attempting to march to the beat pounded out on a drum by a redhead boy looked to be all of ten years old. They succeeded only in tangling themselves up like a nest of snakes.

I couldn't make out the strange army commands the jug-eared drill sergeant was barking out. The aspersions he cast upon them, though, came through loud and clear. He called them hayseeds, Paddies, dagos, Limeys, Krauts, Wops, and greasers. Mostly, though, he shouted out, "Hay foot!

Straw foot! Hay foot!" This made no sense until we drew abreast of the marchers and saw that the plowboy soldiers had tied a wisp of straw to their right foot and hay to the left so as to tell one from the other.

Farther on, veteran soldiers who had some polish on them were lined up in three rows. They could of been windup toys the way they all moved together when the man in charge yelled out orders. At the commands "Handle cartridge," "Tear cartridge," "Charge cartridge," the men in the first row pulled out a cartridge, ripped it open with their teeth, and poured the black powder and bullet down the barrel of their upturned musket. I imagined the balls they fired cutting through a line of Rebels and could of watched all day. But Solomon, his face set graveyard grim, dragged me on.

In the middle of camp we came across a fellow, mother naked, stuck in a barrel. His arms poked out the two holes that had been hacked into the sides and his head popped up through another hole at the top. His face was sun-scalded red as a boiled tomato where it wasn't flaking away entirely. The ground around the bottom of the barrel was wet from him doing his business right there. I reckoned he must of slit someone's throat in their sleep to rate such a punishment and wished I could read what the sign hanging from a knife stabbed into the barrel said.

"Food thief," Solomon informed me like he knew my mind. "See now how serious General takes feeding his army?"

Like all of the questions he asked, Solomon didn't expect an answer to this one and he hauled me away, blowing on about how Sheridan had come up through the Quartermaster Corps. How, like all great generals from Hannibal to Napoleon, he knew that an army marched on its belly. "No food, no fight. Got that, Queenie?" Not being fond of answers, he carried on, words stomping out of him as fast as his feet, telling me how he believed that Sherman, "that'd be General William Tecumseh Sherman," got the idea of something called "total war" from Sheridan.

"Total war, know what that means?" he asked.

Of course, the man didn't give a slick shit what I knew and went right on. "Doesn't mean just fightin' on the battlefield. Means Sherman is shuttin' down the Confederate's pantry. Means cleanin' out every Rebel farm, plantation, and vegetable patch between here and Atlanta. No food. No fight. It was our General's idea first, though, and he's gon win the war with it," Solomon carried on. "Just as soon as we get this army assembled and start marching down the Shenandoah Valley. Food, baby sister. Food is the key.

And you know who holds the keys to *that* kingdom?" He pointed to himself. A cook, a pot-scrubber, and a stew-stirrer. He believed he was the big dog. Crazy coot.

At the edge of camp, just before the woods started crowding in, the marching and shooting fields stopped. In their place were a couple dozen ramshackle lean-tos and curtains of dirty quilts hung over lines running between trees to make a bit of private space.

Closest to camp, laundresses were hard at work. An acrid stink spewed out from where one woman was dumping a bucket of rancid fat and potash for making soap into her pot. At another cauldron, a bony girl with chicken-wing shoulder blades stirred a black pot of dirty clothes set over a low fire. A couple of her brothers poked bits of kindling into the fire.

The mother of the skinny children, dressed in a long skirt, long apron dotted with scorched spots from where cinders had landed, kerchiefs around her neck and over her hair, put her back into scrubbing some man's dirty drawers on a washboard set in a galvanized steel tub of gray water. The big sister, tall and gangly, the way I always was, distributed the clothes she wrung out across any shrub or tree branch hanging low enough for her to reach.

A baby sat in the dirt, naked and ignored, nose boogered up, wailing so big drool poured out of his mouth. The whole family watched us pass with eyes hollow and haunted as any slave's. Maybe more since they didn't even have the dream that freedom was going to be one tiny bit better than slave time.

After we passed the laundresses, we reached another set of crude shelters where Solomon yanked me to a halt. The tattered tents and lean-tos appeared deserted. Or they did until Solomon called out, "Hello, ladies!"

Then, like gophers popping out of their holes, heads started to poke out from tent flaps and around the edge of blankets hanging off lines. Women, sleepy white women, appeared. They took one look at us and immediately vanished. One gal, however, opened her mouth to reveal an empty hole with but two gray teeth left, and bawled out, "Darkies down the end!"

At the last couple of shelters, five girls with some color to them scampered out. Bedraggled as they were, they'd done what they could to spruce up a mite. A light-skinned girl had rubbed berry juice on her lips and cheeks and tucked a flower behind her ear. They were all tugging on their bodices to show more of what their mamas had given them. They were slinking this way and that with a hand on a hip cocked to the side and big smiles on their faces that never made it to their tired eyes.

"Hey, Solomon, whatchoo brang me?" the light-skinned girl called out.

"Brought you a new recruit," he answered, yanking me forward. I tried to jerk free, but stopped when the Green River poked at my throat again. "That what you want?" he hissed in my ear, grabbing so tight on my shirt that he cut off my wind and I couldn't of answered if I'd wanted to.

"You see them?" he asked, like I had any other choice.

I clawed at the collar that was strangling me, but Solomon just choked up on it harder.

"Any man here can have 'em for a piece of hardtack. You don't have no hardtack, you can have 'em you punch 'em hard enough. You wanna be a hardtack girl? That what you want, Queenie? 'Cause I'd be real happy to make that happen. Pure dee delighted, truth be told."

I was near passed out when he turned loose of my collar. I gulped in enough air to spit back at him, "I'll run away."

"Where you run to?"

"Home."

"What you eat? They burnt you out."

"I can hunt. I was the best shot on the place."

"You can't hunt no varmints been burnt up. You gon go back, take the food outta your mama's mouth? Huh? That what you do?"

The mention of Mama snatched my breath away and took the fight out of me worse than the choking had.

"Don't matter. She's long gone anyhow. Sheridan already sent out units to gather up every contraband they found and carry them God knows where. Total war. No slaves, no food. No food, no fight. Your mama and everyone you ever knew is gone. You got nowhere and no one to go back to."

I felt like I'd stepped into a sinkhole. Dropped straight down into a dark place with no bottom, no escape, and no Mama or Clemmie. Though I didn't let it fall, water stood in my eyes at the thought.

"Dry your tears, Queenie. Only one thing world cares less about than a black man's tears, that a black woman's. You be dead soon anyway. You not half as tough as you think you are."

Solomon plucked a sweet potato out of each pocket and held them up. The whores swarmed over him like he was waving around a Liberty dollar. One big ole heifer pulled Solomon's head down and mashed his face in her titties. Another with a washboard for a chest, seeing she couldn't compete in the titty department, backed her bony behind up to Solomon's crotch and pumped away until his willie poked out and tented up the front of his trousers.

The light-skinned one, though, didn't need to do anything nasty. She just crooked her finger at Solomon and he followed her to a quilt thrown over a line between two trees. The lack of a real tent didn't matter. If a girl is pretty enough, nothing mattered, the men will come for you. Come and do what they want. I already knew that.

Not ten seconds later that quilt came alive with the shapes of elbows, hips, and butts bumping it out here and there. A barrel, half the staves pulled out for firewood, stood next to the quilt curtain. The girl's head appeared and she rested it atop the barrel, her hands folded under her ear. She was naked from the waist up and Solomon had a hand holding on to her shoulder, pulling back while he pumped into her. He scooted her back and forth on the top of that barrel. And though she let loose with a few big moans as if having splinters ground into her chest was a pleasuring experience, her eyes were way off somewhere far and gone. She took a sight more notice of a ladderback flicker pecking its way up the side of a tulip tree than she did of Solomon. Then, like she had just remembered that she had a man's hambone all up in her, she let out one of her fake good-time groans.

Her gaze fell on me and, still getting rocked back and forth across that barrel, she watched me with no more or less interest than she had paid the flicker. When the shoving stopped, she lay quiet, only reaching back to pull her skirt down before she raised up. Then she just stood there, bodice off, ninnies out for the world to see, flower behind her ear drooping now down her neck, and she stared at me like I was the one had just let herself get plowed way a bull plows a heifer. Then, like she knew me, knew who I was, she winked. At *me*.

That wink, as though she'd read my future and saw *me* with *my* head atop a barrel, gave me a feeling so near to drowning that I couldn't draw a breath until I ran away from her, away from the hardtack girls, away from the launder women with babies they couldn't feed blubbering at their feet.

Tough? Solomon didn't know the first little thing about tough. He didn't know Africa tough. But I'd show the fool.

Chapter 8

~

As I had nowhere else to go, I went on back to what passed for Solomon's kitchen. With the boss gone, Jonathan and Eli and them were cutting up, shoving each other around, showing their big teeth in big laughs, having a high old time. They paid me no more mind than if I'd been a June bug skittering underfoot. They treated me like I was a field hand and they were house servants too high-nosed to even cut a glance my way. Which was fine by me. The less truck I had with them, the better.

I didn't want them or any of the other shiftless drifters knowing a thing about me. Least of all that I was a girl. Someone they could take and rake across the top of a barrel. I plopped down on the bench and, cursing under my breath, set to peeling Solomon's damn potatoes.

It was past dark by the time Solomon came back from his visit with the whores. I had a pile of skinned taters on the bench next to me and a pair of hands that appeared as if I'd stuck them directly into a thrashing machine. I don't know how it was that I could gut and skin a deer with a penknife, whittle a cob into a passable pipe, and chop an acre of tobacco without a scratch, but getting the peel off a tater flat bumfuzzled me.

Solomon stood above me and stared hard at the fat peels piled at my feet. When he shook his head in disgust he fanned the smell of lilac water and fornication my way. "Left more meat on the peel than you took off." Then he ordered, "Scrape them peels until you got enough for pies."

"It's too dark to see."

"There's your first cooking lesson then: get it done while sun's up."

I scraped by firelight until the embers burned down. Then I scraped by nothing until the moon rose. When I finished, I laid my head down on the bench, my hand under my head, cupping the spot the soldier had stroked. It seemed like less than a minute passed before the infernal bugles were squawking.

Chapter 9

For the next few weeks, camp life went on around me like it was happening in a dream. Every time a bugle blew, men would line up in some new spot. They lined up to march. To practice shooting. To hold tin plates out for a ladle of something from a steaming pot. Even lined up for a turn in the privies if they didn't quick step off to the woods. There was a rhythm to camp life that soothed me. It put me in mind of all the training that Iyaiya had told me she'd done with her sister warriors. How it had had a purpose: to take many and make them into one.

I wished I was marching along smartly in a blue suit and practicing killing Rebs. Doing something important. But day after day, all I did was fetch water, gather firewood, scrub pots, and peel an everlasting pile of taters. And not one bit of it was ever to Solomon's liking. Man just loved to find some speck I missed cleaning off a dirty pot and yell, "You want them Rebels to win this war?"

Then he'd make out like I'd answered, "Oh, yessir, my dearest dream is to be a slave again and die chopping tobacco for a man who made free with my little sister and sold off my grandmother and one little brother and two other baby sisters."

Then, like I'd actually said all that, he'd snap back, "Is that why you're trying to give the General the flux? Get you some wood ash, sand, and scrub this pot out right. Better you wear out your arm scrubbing than the General wear out his bowels purging. And pull a comb through that nappy mess top your head. You are an embarrassment to this unit."

"Thought I wasn't supposed to let on I'm female."

"Not asking you to be female. Figure that's way above your bend. Just try for human."

"What? You think you perfect as a painting hanging in the parlor?"

"Always got an answer, don't you? Even though you don't even know what the question really is, you always got an answer."

"Me? You're the one with all the answers."

Solomon snorted. "You know what your problem is?"

"Doubt I need to. Pretty sure you're fixing to tell me."

"Damn right, I am. Your problem is you're used to not mattering."

It wouldn't of taken a schoolteacher to read the sour look I shot him.

"Oh, I ain't saying you don't matter. You matter plenty. *To yourself.* Not talking about that. I'm talking about mattering to the world. You think you the wrong color to matter. Think you don't . . ." He never finished. Just shook his head like I wasn't worth his time and concluded, "Just think you don't."

One morning in early September, Solomon rousted me out before the bugler even got warmed up. He was lit up like a man been hitting the apple-jack barrel and he had no time for my complaints. "Sherman did it," he announced, beaming from ear to ear.

"Did what?" I croaked, my mouth moving though my brain was still asleep. A shiver went through me. I rubbed my hands along my upper arms to chase away the chill that had settled in during the night.

"Took Atlanta. General's gon want to celebrate tonight. I'ma see if the commissary has any them desecrated vegetables. Make up a burgoo for the man invented total war."

After setting me to husking and hacking kernels off a hundred ear of corn, Solomon left, and I was too busy to worry overmuch about what desecrated vegetables were. Army had its own name for most things. I fetched up buckets of water and set them to boiling in the big cook pot. I skinned, dressed out, and cut up the squirrels Solomon's boys brought in and tossed them in with the kernels.

Solomon returned with a small sack that contained a rectangular lump size of a brick and about that heavy that looked like a big chunk of sweet feed flecked with green and orange. He pitched the lump into the pot along with heavy dousings from his precious box of spices: salt, pepper— both black and cayenne—curry powder, and fistfuls of the crumbled-up leaves he gathered on his own. He stirred it all with his long-handled ladle, dipped up a bit, tasted, shut one eye, pondered, took another taste, shut the other eye, and announced, "Needs onion."

"Commissary's out."

"Mother Nature's commissary's never out." He held up a tow sack. "Go on, gather me up some wild."

I jumped to my feet, eager to be set loose, to get out in the woods on my own. Letting Solomon see my shiny excitement was a mistake.

"Second thought," he said, snatching the sack away. "I'll go myself. No telling what you'll bring back. Here, mind the burgoo." He shoved the ladle into my hand and left.

We'd been getting on tolerably well and it wrathed me up to have Solomon do me that way, holding out a couple hours of freedom then snatching them back. He knew how much I hated being trapped doing woman's work. He didn't know that it always made me think about the woman's work Clemmie was forced to do. By Old Miss during the day. By Old Mister at night.

After an hour of boiling, the green and orange brick loosened up into strips of what might once have been carrots, green beans, parsnips, peas, and celery. I even caught sight of a few shriveled-up purple knots that might once have had a passing acquaintance with beets. The burgoo rolled beneath the ladle as it started boiling. The dried carrots uncurled. Steam rose from the pot. Sweat beaded up and ran down my face. The steady boil turned to furious bubbling and, of a sudden, those desecrated vegetables plumped out and sucked up so much water that the stew started to go dry. Solomon would hide me if I ruined the General's and his officers' celebration supper, so I stirred hard to keep the bottom from burning, but that only made it worse. Soon I was scraping at the bottom and every scrape brought up charred flakes of scorched food.

I tried to lift the pot and move it off the flame, but I could barely heft the massive cast-iron thing when it was empty. Full as it was, all I managed to do was burn the bejesus out of my hand. With the scorching smell getting stronger, I had no choice but to dump in another bucket of water to cool it all down. I was stirring the extra water in when Solomon finally returned. He sniffed two times, grabbed the ladle out of my hand, stirred, saw the soupy mess with big, black scorched flakes floating around in it, and proceeded to curse me and my ancestors back to Adam and Eve.

"Damn you, girl! You trying to ruin my food or is it possible a body can cook as bad as you without trying?"

"What the hell's I supposed to do? It was burning."

"You blind? You supposed to do like you seen me doing a dozen times a day." With the toe of his shoe, he pushed a log burning beneath the pot off to the side. "You couldn't figure to do something that simple? You really that stupid?"

Stupid.

With that one word, quick as cocking the hammer back on a flintlock, my fist was balled up, pulled back, and ready to fly before I got hold of myself, and froze.

"What? You gon chug me one? That it, Queenie? That your plan?"

My arm quivered from the effort of not burying my fist in his face. But that was what he wanted. What he'd been goading me to do since he first laid eyes on me, the helper he didn't want. The second I touched him, Solomon'd cut me loose. Tell everyone I was female and let them tear me apart like a pack of wolves. I was tough. Too tough to let him bait me that way. Much as it pained me, I lowered my fist.

Instant I did, though, a nasty smile cracked across Solomon's face. He was gloating. Gloating just the way Old Mister used to gloat. Pleased with himself. Pleased that he always got whatever he wanted. Pleased that he got Clemmie.

I slugged Solomon.

Chapter 10

My fist had barely finished connecting with Solomon's jaw before I was packed up inside the barrel FOOD THIEF had recently vacated. The stench that rose from that container was so rank I feared that FOOD THIEF had died and decayed while confined there. The barrel weighed in the neighborhood of fifty pounds. I could stand up, but the barrel dug hard into the tops of my shoulders when I did. The worst pain, though, was the humiliation.

A unit marched past, and every head swiveled in my direction. Shame heated my cheeks.

Solomon wrote two words on a piece of paper and stabbed the sign into one of the staves like he wished he was punching it between my ribs.

"What's my crime?" I asked.

"BAD COOK."

"That's no crime."

"To the General it is. To me it is. Whether you steal it or burn it, you're taking his food."

"Solomon, wait. You can't—"

"Can't what? Leave you here to piss and shit down your leg until the sun turns your tongue into a stone in your mouth? You got off light, Queenie. Only reason you're even still alive is 'cause the General took an interest in you."

"Solomon, I tried."

He thumped his hand down on the top of the barrel so hard I staggered and tumped over. No turtle on its back could of been more helpless than

I was with the stumps of my lower arms flailing about for the ground they couldn't reach and my feet kicking uselessly on account of my knees being trapped in too tight to bend much.

Solomon glowered at me, his arms folded across his chest, and watched like I was a beetle on its back, waving its tiny arms in the air. Finally, he righted me. Again he pounded so hard on the barrel that my teeth clacked together. "You maybe might of tried with your hands," he thundered. "But you for God sure never tried with your heart. 'Cause you think you're too good, don't you? Too good to help make a decent meal for men ready to lay they lives down so your pitiful self can be free."

It wasn't the first time I'd heard him go on like that, but at that moment I couldn't put up with one more annoyance, so I came back, "The Yank soldiers? They ain't fighting for me. You, neither. We're nothing to them. They're fighting 'cause they'd get shot or hung if they didn't."

Solomon shook his head like I was too sorry to waste words on and said, "I hope you rot in there. What you deserve."

I didn't give him the satisfaction of calling after him, begging to be let loose. There wasn't anything that cook could dish out that I couldn't take.

First few days were tolerable. Sun hadn't sucked all the water from me yet and I had figured out a way to take the weight off my legs by bracing up against my knees and posterior. If it wasn't for having to pee down my leg, I'd of enjoyed the time off from fetching water and scrubbing pots.

Two nights of not sleeping and days with no water, though, and I was all kinds of miserable. My legs had seized up and I came near to strangling myself the few times I dozed off and went slack. Every bone in my body ached and my mouth was dry as dust. Worst, though, was when the soldiers came by to laugh and make smart remarks. A couple of them relieved themselves on the side of the barrel.

One joker cracked an egg on my head. I appreciated what dripped into my mouth, but the green-headed flies that came for what dried in my hair drove me half-crazy. The lowest moment, though, was when General Sheridan rode past on his black gelding. I knew he recognized me because his face curdled with disgust. Shame made me wish I would hurry up and die on the spot.

Knowing I would either die in the barrel or come out as a laundress or a hardtack girl opened my eyes to my own mule-headedness. Suddenly, I realized that I had taken to thinking like a man. Which is to say, I had stopped allowing the possibility that I might ever be wrong.

With my eyes open, I finally saw what had been in front of me the whole time. I saw that behind the scraggly whiskers most of the "men" in camp were boys no older than me in age but a heap younger in knowing. And, like boys, what they did most of when they weren't marching or cleaning was play.

As soon as the bugler blew what I'd learned was retreat in the evening, all the soldier boys fell to cutting up. They ran foot races, wrestled, and made towers of themselves, stacking one on top of the other in a pyramid with the smallest drummer boy scrambling up a staircase of soldiers to perch at the top for a few trembling seconds until they all collapsed. They played cards, checkers, dominoes, chuck-a-luck, and a Yankee game called baseball, running full-out if they managed to whack a wad of horsehair tied into a ball.

What they were most partial to, however, was fighting. They fought foraged cocks when they could get them. They conducted heated battles between ants and the lice they picked out of bedding, the seams of uniforms, and off their own bodies. But mostly, what they fought was each other.

When they'd broken enough bones doing that or just generally wore each other out, they talked about the sweethearts and wives they'd left behind. One loudmouth whose eyes crossed put it out in his strange Yankee talk that his girl was "none of your one-horse gals." I took that to be good, as was his brag that she was a "regular stub and a twister." He liked to read her letters out loud. And, though they mostly concerned how the hens were or were not laying, she always ended with the sweet words "My pen is bad, my ink is pale; my love for you shall never fail." I reckoned stubs and twisters weren't too particular about their sweethearts and would take even a cross-eyed loudmouth into their hearts.

When campfires grew bright in the gloom of an evening, the soldiers would hunker down and one of them'd commence tooting on a fife or sawing away at a fiddle. Then, sounding like a choir of track hounds with toothache, they'd sing sad songs about the dear mothers and sweet homes they'd most likely never see again. The singing eventually made the younglings among them put their heads down between their knees, and then their shoulders would rise up and down, and shake from crying. They were that homesick. And scared of dying.

The third night I was barreled up, I'd been shivering and listening to soldiers snore for a few hours when a little fellow in a short drummer boy's jacket tippy-toed out of the darkness. He was one of the boys I'd seen crying over his dear mother and sweet home. He had no more whiskers yet than God gave a guppy and I feared he had come to jab me with his saber or some other such mischief.

Instead, he held his tin cup to my lips and tipped cool water down my parched gullet, then fed me tidbits of salt pork and hardtack he'd saved out from his own rations. He'd already gone to the trouble of softening the jawbreakers in coffee and picking the drowned weevils out.

As he refilled the cup from his canteen and watered me again, he whispered that, though most of the others didn't care any more about the coloreds than they did the lice that was eating them alive, him and his folks back in Maine were abolitionists. I had heard of such before when Old Mister would cuss the like so fierce he jeopardized his religion. I never reckoned, though, that such a cloven-hoofed menace would appear and hold a cup of water to my lips. Or that one would whisper in a sweet voice, high and piping as a meadowlark, that he'd joined up to fight so that I could be free and never again have to live like some slave he knew of name of Uncle Tom. Whose master, Simon Legree, made Old Mister seem like Baby Jesus in the manger.

I thanked him for the food and water and for coming to fight for me.

He patted me on the head for some time, enjoying the springy feel of my hair. This caused him to talk about how much he missed his good old dog Buttons. After sniffling back a few tears, he slipped off back into the night.

Next day, a strange quiet fell over the camp. The men didn't heap themselves up in big piles or wager on which fellow could drag a Dutch oven farthest with a rope between his teeth. Instead, they huddled up and jawed the way men on both sides of the Mason-Dixon Line are wont to do, with a lavish of pointing this way and that, chin stroking, and undertaker-serious nods. Then one'd break away from his confab and scamper off to caucus with another one. I'd catch a few words here and there. Most puzzling of all was how they kept asking each other if they'd "seen the elephant." The day ended without a touch of the usual merriment for a new grimness had fallen on the camp.

Before sunup, Solomon roused me out of a crouching half-sleep by slamming a dress, apron, and comb down on the head of the barrel and declaring, "Up to me, I'd let you rot. General's taken pity on you, though. Fairer sex and all that bull hooey. He even gave me the money to get you outfitted from his own pocket. So if you want to come outta there, you gon have to come out proper. You come out ready to help the General win this war. You come out in a dress, your hair fixed. You come out with your mind right. You come out like you are somebody, hear me?" He shrugged and added, "Or you stay in this barrel and starve. That'd be my druthers. Either way, we move out today."

Grumpy as he was, Solomon couldn't tamp down the excitement in his voice when he added, "Shenandoah Valley Campaign's about to commence. Gon drive them cursed Seceshes off of Mr. Lincoln's back porch and all the way back down South to hell where they belong." He started to stomp off like he had a Johnny Reb waiting to be herded back to hell at that very moment.

"Solomon. Solomon!" I yelled at his retreating back.

"What," he answered, prickly, not turning around.

"Thought you said a female'd get tore up."

"A female without a man or another whore with a pepper pot to watch her back will. But if you come out proper, you'll come out as the General's girl, and no one'll mess with you."

I had my useless arms out waving at the dress I couldn't reach. "Mind handing me that?"

He didn't move.

"Sir," I added.

He still didn't budge.

I sweetened my voice and said in a girly simper, "I would be much obliged for your help, sir."

Solomon handed me the dress.

Long before the sun rose, I'd been to the creek and was washed up and dressed. My life had been saved and I set my mind hard on making it into one the General would tip his hat to next time he saw me. A salute. That's what I really wanted. I wanted General Sheridan to look on me and see someone worthy of saluting.

When I had my hair plaited back smooth and neat like Clemmie had showed me, I presented myself to Solomon. He looked up from stoking the fires under the officers' coffee water, nodded, and said, "All right then, baby sister. I hope you're ready to see the elephant."

Chapter 11

⁓

The elephant was war and, over the next few weeks, I came to know the beast from tail to trunk. But that morning, when I went back to the officers' mess, those who saw me took me for an entirely different person than the reprobate they figured had perished in the barrel. Solomon had put it out that, though I was a girl, the General had me under his protection and they were to leave me be or answer direct to Little Phil. That was as good as quarantine with yellow fever for keeping the men away.

All that day we crammed Solomon's kitchen wagon with pots, ladles, Dutch ovens, various knives and long forks, coffeepots, grinders, and what stores of sugar, salt pork, parched corn, desecrated vegetables, and flour as remained. The soldiers packed their knapsacks with field rations of hardtack, salt pork, and coffee. Then they stuffed in their Bibles, their letters from home, and tintypes of their wives and sweethearts. With tent halves and bedrolls strapped on the packs, they were ready to march.

By the next morning, the tent town was torn back down to muddy ground polka-dotted with black holes where cook fires had been, the stink of latrines now replacing the clean smell of the woods. From dawn all through the night, companies of infantrymen marched out, cavalrymen rode, and each regiment's wagons followed carrying the field officers' baggage, rations, telegraph equipment, blacksmith necessaries, and kitchen supplies.

Swallow-tailed guidon banners snapped in the breeze, fresh-polished tack creaked, bridles jingled, horses nickered, and sergeants hollered out, "Left!

Right! Left! Right! Left!" for the hay and straw had been removed from the new boys' shoes and they marched like soldiers. Our columns must have stretched four miles or more. I fell into rhythm, marching with them alongside the cook wagon.

We made a fine parade and, though I was tickled to be part of it, it didn't take more than a mile before I missed my britches for I had lost the knack of accommodating a skirt. Where britches were barely more trouble than a second skin, Solomon's infernal dress was like wearing a long broom. I marched the miles, dusty and muddy alike, sweeping up the trail with that cursed garment.

I'd swapped a few taters for a broken-down old pair of brogans from the graves detail and I had them strapped on my feet with pieces of twine. There were so many holes in the soles, though, that it was little better than going barefoot. I kept falling behind the cook wagon every time I veered off into the woods to fetch strips of smooth bark off a paperback maple to stick in the shoes and cover the holes. After my last bark hunt, I had to run to catch up with Solomon. When I did, he peered down at me, panting alongside the wagon, and grunted out, "Up here," like each word was costing him a greenback.

I didn't wait for a second invitation, but hopped onto the buckboard's foretop next to him and we rode on in style, part of the Army of the Potomac's Cavalry Corps under the command of Major General Philip Sheridan himself. Up high, I saw that the Shenandoah Valley was as pretty a stretch of country as the Maker had ever fashioned, green as a billiards table where it wasn't covered with miles of field crops, mostly wheat that shimmied golden in the sunshine.

It was a right chill morn and there was enough of a nip to the air that I welcomed the feel of Matildy's warm body curling about my neck. Solomon shook his head at the sight of his pet draped over my shoulders and muttered, "Just like a woman. Go to the one hates her."

"I don't hate her," I protested. "Like everything else about the army, she's tolerable once you get used to her."

The cool weather and excitement of moving out worked a tonic on Solomon and he actually laughed as he snapped the reins on the mules. And though the contrary beasts didn't vary their speed a whit, Solomon sat up like a dandy on race day and crowed, "Damn Rebs won't be crawling up this valley any time soon, slipping in Mr. Lincoln's back door. Think they can steal the election from him." He snorted at the idea then blowed on about how bad it made Mr. Lincoln look that he couldn't even sweep the Rebs off his own back porch, which is what he called the Shenandoah Valley.

Seems all I had to do was put on a dress, plait up my hair, and call him "sir" and Solomon became my buddy gee. He jabbered on for the next few hours like we'd been old campaigners together forever. And, though I never would of told him, Solomon Yarnell showed himself to be the second-smartest man I'd ever known, right after Daddy. He turned that clanking, creaking wagon into a classroom and his subject was the Civil War.

"We don't get started cleaning them Seceshes outta the Shenandoah Valley before the election come November," Solomon explained, "Yanks might take a mind to elect that chickenshit traitor Union General George McClellan." Only person Solomon hated more than Old Jube, the fearsome Rebel General Jubal Early, who was leading the Rebs we were chasing, was Lincoln's opponent in the election six weeks away, the chickenshit traitor McClellan who'd once commanded the whole Union Army.

"Back in '62," Solomon went on, "Lincoln gave that chickenshit traitor one hundred and twenty thousand men. Blast if McClellan couldn't of squashed Lee right there and then. Drowned the whole damn Confederacy like the sack of rabid pups they are. War'd been over two years ago. But would that pusillanimous nancy boy attack? No, he would not! Kept telling Abe he had to have reinforcements. McClellan stalled. Wouldn't attack. Gave that sick pup of a Confederacy time to grow into the rabid dog it become. Now McClellan has the gall to run against Old Abe on a peace platform. Peace platform! Know what that means?"

I thought about Mama and Clemmie and answered, "Means slavery would be legal and even if you could escape there wouldn't be anywhere in the whole country to run to."

"All right, baby sister, you listening." Solomon nodded approvingly. "You learning. If the chickenshit traitor gets elected, it all goes back the way it was. Means we live in a country ruled by the wicked and all the fighting and all the dying and all the misery was for naught." His voice was mournful and lost when he repeated, "Everything goes back way it was. Only worse."

A cold, sick feeling came over me as I thought of what the Rebs would do if they ever got power over us again.

Thousands of feet pounding in time like a big heart beating became the music that chased off such gloomy thoughts. We were the Army of the Shenandoah and we were marching to battle to keep Old Abe in the White House, to keep the country together, and to rid it of the abomination of slavery. We'd win this war for Mr. Lincoln. All of us. Together.

When the sawed-off drummer boys and fife players went to tootling and *pah-rumping*, the soldiers and all us contrabands joined in singing, "Mine eyes have seen the glory of the coming of the Lord. He is trampling out the vintage where the grapes of wrath are stored." Our voices joined up together and rolled on mighty as a wave and caused tears to jump out of me from a place I never knew existed before.

I swallowed them back hard and fast, but Solomon caught sight of their gleam in the hard morning light and nodded. Just one slow dip of that crumpled top hat of his, but it was enough to show that the very same tears were stinging his eyes. That he knew what was in my heart because it was in his heart, too: we, all of us marching south, were in this together.

Chapter 12

⁓

For the next few weeks all I saw of the great beast of war was the tail. The hind end of all the battles fought up at the front lines. And those battles were so terrible and so plenty that in a war that had nothing but terrible battles, the road from Washington, D.C., to Richmond that cut through the Shenandoah Valley came to be called the Bloodiest Hundred Miles in America.

Just after dawn, the boys marched off to face the enemy, stepping high and acting brave even if they'd just aired their paunches, heaving up that morning's coffee and hardtack. The lucky eventually came back, stunned faces black with gunpowder, the smell of cordite and fear heavy on them.

The less lucky were carried back in tall, rickety ambulances to join the poor souls waiting for the sawbones to turn them into cripples or corpses since there wasn't but one treatment in those days: amputate.

The ones who came up flat out of luck didn't return at all. On the banks of Opequon Creek or Tom's Brook or up on Fisher Hill, those mothers' darlings were laid to take their eternal rest, never to rise again.

Every battlefield had a Dying Tree, the highest, prettiest tree around where friends of the mortally wounded dragged them so that the dying boys might take their leave of this world amidst a bit of beauty. I was haunted by the sight of those doomed faces, watching out of their hollow eyes as we left them behind. Too tired to struggle anymore, they had a kind of glow on them like they were already halfway into the next world and didn't bear us any grudge for abandoning them.

In spite of our terrible losses, we ripped through the Breadbasket of the

South, burning fields heavy with a harvest the starving Rebs needed to survive. We gathered up their livestock, scattered what horses and mules we didn't need, and freed the slaves to wander where they would. What the General had done to Old Mister, he was doing now to every farmer and plantation owner who had the misfortune to be in his path. Every day, the sun rose on a vision of the Shenandoah Valley's fresh green heaven ahead and the smoking, charred black inferno we left behind. We were shutting down the South's pantry. No food. No fight. It was a new way of doing war and it was an awful one.

The fear of returning to slavery, and believing that I could help Mr. Lincoln keep that from happening, made me into the best cook's helper Solomon ever had. I skinned peels off sweet potatoes so thin you could of read through them. Water was always fresh and plenty and at Solomon's side even before he hollered for it. Pots were scrubbed until any fine lady's dainties could of been sudsed out in them.

As soon as we started running into new units with their rearguard of contrabands, I spent every second when I wasn't scrubbing or fetching, asking if anyone had seen my sister or my mother. I explained that my sister was a quiet, sweet-faced girl, frail and fine-boned, and that my mother was a mighty woman, sturdy and tall as me, both of them marked with rows of scars pretty as strings of pearls resting above their hearts.

Lord, the answers I got.

I heard tales of every bump and pockmark ever to blight a female body. And I won't go into detail on the ones who peeled off shoes or hiked up shirts and lowered britches to display their own disgusting assortment of warts and bunions. And scars. Lord, the libraries of scars I was shown. I saw backs had been lashed until it looked like garter snakes were writhing across them. And ankles and wrists with thick bracelets of scars from iron manacles. Though those marks told the story of how much worse than me others had suffered, no one had seen Mama or Clemmie. Then one day, I met up with a fellow said he'd followed Grant from Shiloh to Vicksburg. I showed him the pearl scars on my collarbone and asked if he'd ever seen the like.

"'Deed, I have," he answered even before I could describe Mama and Clemmie. Figured I either had a confabulator on my hands or one of them'd go on and describe every skin peculiarity he'd ever come across. Which he did. Though he wasn't particularly old, the man didn't have a tooth in his head. Watching his baby mouth open and close, gummy balls of spit stretching between his lips, gave me the creeping willies to where I could hardly look his way.

So I wasn't paying much mind when he raised his hand up high and asked, "These gals you's hunting? The old one tall? Strong? Skin near coal black? No titties to speak of?"

I started to walk away for all in the world this jasper was doing was throwing off on me by guessing how my mother would look based on my appearance.

"The other one?" he called after me. "Little frail thing?"

I stopped.

"She 'bout yay high?" he asked.

I checked and could see Clemmie fitting right in beneath the palm he raised up to his shoulder. Not a height anyone would of guessed from looking at me.

"Pretty gal?" he asked.

Also not what a body'd reckon from looking at me. I nodded.

"Both of them all bumped up here." He drew his fingers across the space between his collarbone and the place where his chest swelled.

He had every speck of my attention now. "Yes," I said, barely breathing. "You know where they are?"

"'Deed I do." He nodded slow, pleased with himself that he had something I wanted.

"Where? Where are they?"

"You want to know where that pretty li'l gal and the big 'un are at?"

"That's what I'm asking you."

He paused and inspected his nails. "How much's it worth to you?" he asked.

I saw the way things were going and, not caring for his approach, I clamped my hand around his throat, put the Green River to his neck, leaned in and growled in his ear, "Enough to stick this knife in your throat and lick your blood off the blade when it comes out." Hard cases like him sometimes required a persuading detail or two.

He pursed his lips even farther into his mouth like he was pulling the strings of a reticule tight. He was pretty sure I wasn't going to put him under, but didn't care to place a bet on how bad I'd hurt him. "Last time I saw that pair," he said. "I was throwing dirt on their naked bodies for they had already had the clothes stole off them."

My hand dropped. "You're lying."

"Why'd I do that? I was lyin', I'd tell you I knowed where they are. Make you pay to find out. Naw, they dead."

That toothless hole went on opening and closing right in front of me, but the words came from far off as he went on, "I was on buryin' detail. They was scrubwomen. Heard they took sick with breakbone fever. Bad way to go. Might could be the worst. Way they seize up there at the end. Trying to scream but can't pry they jaws open."

I felt my hands rising up to stop the man's words from hitting my ears. I forced my hands down but couldn't stop my feet from carrying me away from the sight of that gummy mouth. Still his words followed me. "Though lockjaw, now, lockjaw'll take you down hard. Wouldn't want no . . ."

I ran and didn't stop until my legs gave out on me.

Chapter 13

The next week, we encamped at Cedar Creek and Sheridan swore that that was where we would hold the line. That he and every soul under his command would die before he'd allow the Rebs to cross Cedar Creek.

Third night there, I made the General his cup of tea way I knew he liked it. Dark as tar, with a touch of blackstrap molasses and two tablespoons of a new delicacy, Gail Borden's milk that came in cans they called "airtights."

I handed the cup to Solomon, but he passed it back. "You take it to him tonight."

"Me?" I asked, certain I hadn't heard right. Solomon had been nice, almost gentle with me, since the night a week back when I told him about Mama and Clemmie. He had even patted my back a little and given me Matildy, saying I needed the company, something warm to love on when sleep failed me. Next morning, after I'd cried until dawn, he let me sleep late then did most of my chores himself. And now here he was telling me to take the General his tea.

I was so nervous walking to Sheridan's tent my hands were shaking with the bumfidgets. The General always stayed awake, studying maps and writing dispatches and whatnot, long after the rest of the camp had doused their candles and slush lamps and turned in. So, as usual, his was the only tent glowing in the darkness. It reminded me of the pumpkin lanterns Little Miss and her brothers were partial to carving back before the war when there was food to waste.

As I approached, I heard the General chanting low in the "me boyo" accent that I'd come to learn was Paddy Yankee. Through a slit in the flaps, I saw that he was on his knees beside his cot praying to the Irish goddess he favored. He clutched a string of beads and said one prayer for each pearly bead he counted off. When he ticked off the last one he whirled the cross hanging from the beads around his head and shoulders.

He brought the cross to his lips to kiss and I caught a glimpse of the Irish Jesus nailed there. I had heard about Jesus and the Crucifixion and the Crown of Thorns from the white preacher Old Mister made us listen to, but the only cross I ever saw was two plain boards nailed together. This was my first look at the fellow himself bleeding and near naked and drooping from where he was nailed to the cross. It was gory enough to have come out of one of Grandma's stories and it raised my opinion of Jesus considerable.

I tiptoed to the flap of the General's tent and though I was barely breathing, Sheridan grabbed up his saber and whirled around, ready to skewer any intruder. He had a ferocious, slaughter-minded look on his face would of done that lunatic King Andandozan with his bone-crunching hyenas proud.

Recalling my father's instruction in correct speaking, I plucked myself up and piped out, "Begging your pardon, General, I am here to deliver your tea."

And just that quick, the warrior switched off and Sheridan said, "Ah, my tay," in his Paddy manner. "Come in. Come in."

I pushed through the canvas flaps. Inside, the air smelled of cigar smoke, kerosene, camphor, sweat, and gun oil. A rug, a genuine parlor rug, covered the dirt floor. He had himself a cot, a spindly table, and a chair cut out of a barrel half so that it had a back. On the table was a saucer with the butts of several stogies crushed out on it, a gold-nibbed pen, and a stack of laid paper. His hat and greatcoat hung from a nail pounded into the back support.

Sheridan's dark eyes were bright and quick as a hawk's. It seemed he recognized me. But that might just of been my pride hoping such a thing was so since I wanted the General to see what I'd made of myself since being a no-count pissing down her leg in a barrel.

"Put it there." He nodded to the table.

I placed the mug on the table next to the saucer of stogie butts and waited for my next order. But the General's attention had already turned to a map spread over another table and I backed quietly away, leaving him to reckon how best to smite Jubal Early so that Lincoln could get reelected and I could stay out of chains. I was content knowing that I'd made the cup of tea'd help him do that, and was almost through the canvas flaps when Sheridan, eyes still on the map, raised a finger, pointed it in my direction, and said, "You."

I stood unbreathing. He turned to face me, jiggling that finger my way as though he was trying to shake something off it. "You, you are the contraband I freed, aren't you? The one who intends to sing at my funeral."

He knows me. General Philip Henry Sheridan knows who I am.

I was as proud as Iyaiya must of been when the scout saw *her* for who she really was. I wished more than anything that my soldier could of seen me at that moment. A grin I couldn't control went east and west, and I popped back, "Yessir, I'm keeping in tune, sir."

Sheridan tipped his head to the side, and the lantern light fell full on his face. He was as fierce as any Africa warrior. Even the ones from old times like Iyaiya who sharpened their teeth into points to rip the throats out of the king's foes.

My heart lurched and my smile dropped, though, when I saw that I had riled him. The thing about the powerful is that sometimes they like a peppery comment from those beneath them so they can laugh along and show what sports they are. And sometimes they don't. And what with interrupting his Mary prayers and all, it appeared that this was a don't time.

"Sir, I . . . Sir . . . I . . ."

"You what? *Don't* want me dead?"

"Last thing on earth I want, sir. What I want is for you to stomp a hole in Jubal Early so wide the whole Union Army can ride through it and squash them Rebs like the vermin they are. That's what I want. And unless God's a possum that is what General Philip Henry Smash 'em Up Sheridan is going to do."

He gave me something in the vicinity of a smile and said, "Good night, contraband."

Without thinking, I saluted him, but the General's back was already turned.

Chapter 14

I was up before dawn next morning, setting a big slab of corned beef to boiling so as to leach some of the salt from the hunk of meat. We had us a world of provisions now pouring in from every bit of the Shenandoah Valley that our troops had captured. To say nothing of the supplies that came in after we took the Central Virginia Railroad. Jubal Early was starving and the General was eating corned beef.

I was chopping up the eighteen head of cabbage that came along with the beef when Solomon, stretching and scratching, appeared and told me, "You're gon help serve tonight."

"Did the General request me?" I asked. "By name?"

Solomon crunched into a pale triangle of cabbage heart, which he considered a delicacy, and snorted. "Name?" He flapped his lips like a horse, snorting at my foolishness. "Took the man three years of me cooking every bite of food he put in his mouth to learn my name. Here." He pulled the sliver that remained of his bar of soap from the inside pocket of his jacket and handed it to me. "Go on, get you a bath. You smelling a bit blinky."

"What? And you think you a lilac in spring?"

He ordered me to git and I slipped away on down to the source of all that water I'd been hauling up to camp, the famous Cedar Creek that marked the line General had beaten the Rebs back to. The line he swore Jubal Early and his demon hordes would never come north of while he drew breath.

I followed the creek until the noise of camp fell off, lost in the wind rustling through the tall, shaggy cedars it was named for. When that and the soft gabbling of turkeys off in the brush and a few melancholy hoots from an unseen owl were the only sounds that could be heard, I found myself walking through a quilt brighter than any stitched by the hand of woman. High up along the ridge tops, yellow chestnuts and red oaks looked to be on fire. Mid-slope, the maples were orange as a patch of pumpkins. The lowlands along the creek were roofed with clouds of yellow leaves puffing out from tall poplars. The carpet was sumac gone red as rubies with Virginia creeper hanging wine-purple in the dark shadows.

I felt like I was off in the woods with Mama again back during the winters and fallow times when we were sent out to clear the woods to make new fields for more tobacco. I started out fetching water and bundling pine knots. Time I was twelve, though, I was taller and stronger than any boy on the place. With my skirts looped up around my waist, I could swing a broadax sure and steady from can't see to can't see and was cutting half a cord a day like any man.

As soon as we got out of hearing of the others, Mama schooled me on what I needed to know when the three of us escaped. How to rub coal oil with snuff and cayenne pepper mixed in it on your feet to put the dogs off. Where to find mulberries, gooseberries, hickory nuts, and acorns. How to eat cattails, monkey flowers, and milk thistle. How to use sneeze weed to open up your head and cure deafness. Mostly, though, Mama showed me how to move through the woods so not a leaf rustled, twig cracked, nor bird left its nest. When I got to where I could sneak up on Mama herself, she gave me the most important lesson of all—how to follow the North Star to the free states.

Now, as I strode along beside Cedar Creek, I felt like Mama was with me, just ahead, out of sight, leading me to a safe place where no prying eyes would find us and she could tell me Iyaiya's stories.

A distant gurgling promised that a swimming hole deep enough that I could have a proper dunking was close. I followed the sound to where vines grew thick along the creek, parted them, and peeked through. What I'd taken for gurgling was the sound of two whites, up to their posteriors in the water, naked as newts, loving on each other.

The woman had the perfect hourglass of her back to me. It shone pale as polished ivory in the dark shade. She blocked my view of the fellow who was larruping at her neck, but I caught a glimpse of his uniform on the bank and was considerably relieved to see that it was blue. He was one of our boys and had plucked himself a lovely local flower. Most of him was hidden from my view. And then the soldier kneeled down in front of the gal, gripped the pillows of her hindquarters with his long fingers, and pulled her to what had to be his mouth.

I found this queer Yankee procedure puzzling in the extreme, however the country gal appeared quite content with it and grew more so every minute it continued. She threw back her head, revealing the pale arch of her neck. It was stretched tight as she gasped, sucking in and blowing out harder and harder until a rush of moans that trailed off like a mourning dove's call slid from between her parted lips. Then, wobbling in the fellow's grip, she fell silent and he rose to hold her.

Yank or Reb, no white would tolerate a colored spying on him sparking in such a peculiar manner, so I commenced backing on out of there. Just as I did, though, I caught a glimpse of the soldier head-on. Beneath his hair, barbered off neat as Sheridan's, was a face I took to be a young boy's as it was entirely free of whiskers, stout jaw, or apple of Adam. In addition, he also had him a pair of bouncy titties with nipples big as silver dollars. As I'd never set eyes on a boy, white or colored, built like a broody hen that way, I had to conclude that what I was looking at was, not one, but two women.

After a good deal more kissing and splashing and giggling, the couple waded arm in arm to the bank where both of them proceeded to put on uniforms. I blinked several times to make sure I was seeing what I thought I was seeing as they helped each other wrap bindings tight around their breasts, button their jackets up, and get their caps set on straight.

I slipped away like Mama had taught me all those years ago. Not a twig snapped as I made my way back down the creek. Barely pausing to wash under my arms and up my skirt and rub my teeth and tongue with a bit of ball moss, I flew back to Solomon with my amazing revelation.

All Solomon did, though, when I told him about the white ladies in the blue suits was to slurp up a taste of the stew and tell me, "Too salty. You didn't boil the beef long enough."

"Solomon, didn't you hear me?" I waved my arm toward all the soldiers and said, "There are women in some of those uniforms."

"You just now figuring that out?" he asked, tossing a handful of pepper into the kettle. "Chunk in some them Irish spuds. They'll do to soak up the salt you failed to get out."

"You knew? About the women?"

"'Course I knew. They's lots of them. Were more at the start when they all thought war was going to be like skipping off to a picnic. Seen 'em come in with their husbands, their sweethearts. Surprised it took you spying some lady lovers naked to take notice. Given's how you're near female yourself."

"So no one cares if a woman signs up?" I asked, ignoring his jibe about me being "near" female.

"Oh Lord, here we go again. You gon tell me 'bout your warrior-lady blood and what a dead shot you are and how you'd be better at soldierin' than Robert E. Lee and Gideon what led the Israelites combined, they only gave you the chance."

"If no one cares, then I got the chance, right?"

"Hold up there, Dead Eye. Didn't say that. Them two lady lovers? They already been reported to Sheridan. Heard it myself. A woman comes in with her husband, boyfriend, that's one thing. But two women?" Solomon made a face like he was smelling spoilt milk. "Uh-uh. That won't pick no cotton. It's all over once they get reported. Them two gal boys be gone by retreat."

"What about a woman come in on her own?"

Solomon snorted like the question was too stupid to answer and said, "Woman alone? She be *dead* by retreat. Used up in ways I will not specify. Now switch your fanny, Queenie, you burnin' daylight. Tonight's a big night. One of Sheridan's favorites's coming for supper. Brigadier General George Armstrong Custer. Boy General himself in from the Western front."

Chapter 15

⁓

Solomon," the General said that night, hoisting a cup of what the camp surgeon who'd contributed it called *"spiritus frumenti,"* but which looked, smelled, and had the merrying effect of whiskey. "Me own ma herself couldn't have done better with the corned beef." The more *spiritus* the General imbibed, the more Irish he became. Couple more tipples and I reckoned he'd be up doing a jig.

"Thank you, sir," Solomon answered, briefly dipping his head into the globe of candlelight that domed up around the men gathered at the table outside the tent.

"Hah," I whispered to Solomon. He caught my meaning: the General liked my corned beef. Mine. Not too much salt. Good as his ma's.

The General had George Armstrong Custer set right beside him and they kept their heads tipped together whispering and passing comments like a couple courting. As for Custer, the Boy General was a peacock of the first order. He had long yellow hair he shined up with grease that hung in long curls that bounced off his shoulders. And his uniform! Where all the other officers might as well been wearing tow sacks for how crumpled and baggy and speckled with cigar ash and hardtack crumbs they were, Boy General could of stepped out of a bandbox. He was that pretty and shiny new.

It was hard keeping my eyes from him, mostly on account of he gussied himself up with the exact intention of drawing every eye his way. Like the prettiest lady at the ball, he expected folks to make over him.

"Sheridan," Custer said, producing a bottle. Being careful to hide the label with his hand, he filled the General's cup. "Libbie sent this down with her regards."

Usually Sheridan was a gulper and a bolter, stuffing victuals down his flytrap like a man shoveling coal into a boiler. Except when he forgot the whole matter of eating entirely until he nearly fell out from hunger or thirst. But now, for the first time, I saw him taking dainty sips of what Custer had poured and glorying in each one.

"Jesus, Mary, and Joseph," the General exclaimed, "if this isn't Bushmills whiskey from County Antrim I'll be a Hottentot with a bone through me nose!"

The Boy General sat back and beamed.

"Well, I'll be jiggered," Sheridan said. "Your wife, the lovely Libbie, is as clever as she is beautiful."

As Custer refilled Sheridan's glass, the other officers cut glances back and forth that any slave could of read a mile off. They were blowed up like toads at the Boy General for shining up to the master. They were even madder at themselves for not thinking of it first and maddest of all at their wives, who weren't Lovely Libbies with an eye toward getting them that next promotion. But that wasn't the only trick the intruder had up his sleeve.

Custer clapped his hands, called out, "Sergeant!" and a noncom with a fiddle tucked under his arm stepped forward. "General," Custer said, "name your mother's favorite tune."

"Me boyo, no one outside of County Cavan, Ireland, would have ever heard of me ma's favorite tune."

"Try my man, here," Custer insisted. "Sergeant Paddy O'Hoolihan." The General hooted at the name, then sighted in on the fiddler like he was a doomed squirrel and barked out some growly words sounded like "See an Owl Run."

The sergeant, a stumpy fellow had that kind of thin Irish skin that went to wrinkling and spotting about the time its owner shucked off diapers, tucked the fiddle up under his chin and sawed out a few notes caused the General to rear back a hair. Then, in a voice mournful as a mother sheep bleating over a dead lamb, the fiddler sang,

> I wish I was on yonder hill.
> 'Tis there I'd sit and cry my fill.
> And every tear would turn a mill.

From the look on Sheridan's face, it could of been his own mother crooning. Custer smoothed his mustaches even smoother, looking, as usual, a mite too pleased with himself.

The only one of Sheridan's other officers I knew much about was his aide-de-camp, Colonel Aloysius Terrill, who I'd met on that fateful night when Sheridan plucked me off of Old Mister's farm. In the time I had been at camp, I'd learned that Terrill was a finicky, high-nosed fellow out of Covington, Virginia, who took a bath every week and was forever bustling about Sheridan. He clipped the General's cigars, wrote down official dispatches, checked that the inkpot was full and the quills sharp for Sheridan's personal letters, and generally fussed over him the way a wife would. In Terrill's case, however, the wife of a man who clearly could not stand her.

And, now, just like a wife whose husband was paying too much attention to a woman younger, prettier, and a heap more fun than she was, Terrill glared at the Boy General who was making Sheridan laugh with bits of whispered gossip and comments about this one and that. Sheridan and Custer were two bad boys egging each on. General loved being a scamp and Terrill was more a scold than a scamp.

When the air was blue with cigar smoke and the kind of cussing'd make a peg-leg pirate blush, Terrill snapped his fingers and twirled them around the empty glasses. Solomon and I filled them up even though the bottle was right there in front of that prissy colonel. When Terrill's glass was topped up, he abruptly raised it in a jerky fashion as the man was incapable of ever acting natural, and said, "A toast to the General for he has broken the Confederacy. Thanks to Sheridan, the Rebels' backs are against the wall and they shall crumble now that we've whipped them on the battlefield and starved them out at home. To the General!"

"To the General!" the men roared, and down the gullet went every drink except for two: the one sitting untouched in front of the General and the one in front of Custer. The two men just sat there trading low-lidded glances like someone had passed wind. Little by little, the clinking and guzzling stopped. When the officers saw that their commander had gone black in the eyes and wasn't drinking, the jolly drained off fast and silence fell heavy on the little party.

Even the fiddler noticed and stopped playing so that, though the General spoke quiet, we all heard when he asked, "Terrill, tell me, Colonel, have you ever been hungry?"

Solomon caught my eye, but I didn't need his warning. The General's anger was as easy to read as thunderheads gathering in the north. Terrill, though, Terrill didn't have the sense to look up when the sky went dark and he answered in his highborn Southern Yankee way, "Well, ah, rations have, ah, upon occasion, ah, been short." The poor fellow sounded more sheep than man with all his ah-ah bah-bahing.

"What I mean, Terrill," Sheridan pressed. "There on your father's *plantation . . .*" Sheridan never missed an opportunity to bullyrag his adjutant about coming from a rich Southern family. "Did ye ever have to go to bed night after night with your guts rumblin' from hunger?"

"I'm not sure I—"

"I mean, Terrill, did you ever have to listen to your wee brothers and sisters cryin' themselves to sleep?"

Terrill, finally feeling the horns sinking into his hindquarters, pulled himself up straight and stammered, "No, but I fail to see—"

"Failure to see, Terrill, precisely. I'd count failure to see as the greatest weakness of your kind. Colonel, what place did you graduate in your class at West Point?"

"General, we've already been over this. Several times."

"What place, Colonel?"

Reluctantly, he answered, "First."

"First, yes. Yes, now I recall. First, that's right. And you, Custer, where did you graduate?"

"Dead last, sir," the Boy General piped right up, like him near washing out was some kind of blue ribbon.

"And myself, Terrill. Tell our guests what you know of my history at the Point."

"I don't believe I recall the particulars, General."

"Thirty-fourth out of fifty-three. That was my rank. But there is something more notable about my time at our alma mater, is there not, Terrill?"

"I wouldn't know, sir."

"Oh, come now, Terrill. Don't be modest. We share a bit of family history, do we not?"

Terrill worked his jaws, his nostrils flinching from anger held in.

"Why, indeed we do," the General persisted. "Let me tell the lads the story. I was suspended, wasn't I, Terrill? Sent down my third year. I'd gotten into a bit of a scuffle, right? And who was my opponent, Terrill? Came from the finest of families. Big fellow. Had half a foot and fifty pounds on me. Who was that lad? Terrill, remind me. Who was he?"

Maybe it came with being a warrior, or being short as he was, but there was a meanness to the General. When he took out after someone, he was a rooster wouldn't stop until he pecked feathers down to blood. I'd seen him do it myself many a time. Pitch in after a man just for the fun of it. Terrill, he'd lost a lot of feathers in his time. Still Sheridan went on pecking. In the next few minutes I learned why the General kept him around to do just that.

Finally Terrill unseamed his lips and the words burst out. "My brother, sir. You beat my older brother, William, near senseless." Terrill wasn't tripping over any "ahs" now. "After you attacked him with a bayonet."

"In a fight he started by calling me . . ." Sheridan snapped his fingers like he couldn't recollect the particulars. "Help me out, Terrill. What was it your brother called me?"

"I don't think—"

"Oh, is that the way of it, then?" Sheridan said in a viperous low tone. "You don't see *and* you don't think. A blind idiot I've got for an aide, is it?" Of an instant, he slammed his fist down on the table and roared, "Colonel Terrill, I order you to tell the assembled what your brother called me!"

Terrill sat grim and white as death while the others looked everywhere except at him. Finally, he whispered, "A mick . . ."

"Eh?" Sheridan said, putting his hand behind his ear, playing at being deaf. "I'm not sure we all caught that."

Seeing no way out, Terrill said, "A mick nigger."

"Ah, yes, mick nigger, that was the charming term used by your charming brother, that I had no choice but to defend myself against. Then your family saw to it that I was tossed out for a year, didn't they, Colonel?"

Terrill bit his words back.

"Terrill, you are an ass if you presume to know how ferociously a hungry man will fight for his home, his family, his dignity. You and your sort might count a man out because he's hungry and ragged, but that would be a grave mistake. A very grave mistake, indeed."

Terrill's nostrils flared and he breathed heavy as a man'd run five miles. All at the table took to studying their spoons, the dirt under their fingers, anything that'd keep their eyes from falling his way.

The silence went on uncomfortable long before Sheridan hollered at the fiddler, "Paddy, pray tell me, laddie, will you not be giving us a tune with some fun to it? A jig perhaps to cheer me boyos up? Faces around here are as long as old Abe Lincoln's himself."

The fiddler struck up a jig and the men fell all over themselves clapping and playing at having fun. Even Sheridan went along, pretending to be having a high old time until, halfway through the tune, he smacked his hands on the table, stood, and announced, "Carry on with your festivities, gentlemen. I must leave in a few hours for Winchester to confer with the secretary of state. I trust you won't let Old Jube cross Cedar Creek and take back the Shenandoah Valley in my absence."

Everyone *har-harred* at that except Sheridan, who suddenly seemed uneasy and troubled in his mind, the evening's previous jackassing forgotten. He motioned for the camp commander, Major General Wright, to join him and they slipped outside. I exchanged a look with Solomon as we gathered up the dirty dishes. We both knew something was up and that the General needed looking after. Solomon tipped his head toward Sheridan. I put down my stack of plates and followed.

Outside, a big, low-hanging harvest moon gave the camp a ghostly silver glow. The air was crisp enough that mist wreathed Sheridan's head when he spoke. Even hanging back in the shadows as I was, Sheridan's order to Wright was clear. "General, I am leaving you in command of the Army of the Potomac's cavalry. Mind that pickets are posted every night."

"Yessir, General," Wright answered in a jolly way as though he and the General were still throwing back Mrs. Custer's whiskey. "But we'll have to stake it pretty far south, hard as we've pushed those damned Secesh back. Yes, I doubt Johnny Reb will be disturbing our peace much anymore now that you've dealt him a mortal wound."

I couldn't believe the man was saying such a stupid thing.

There was a sharp edge in the General's voice when he asked, "General, were you not listening to a _____ word I just said? A wounded _____ snake can _____ kill a man fast as a healthy one."

Sheridan pivoted on his heel and, without returning Wright's salute, stomped away. At that moment, the General must of been pretty sure he was surrounded by saps and nincompoops and he'd have to win the damn war all by himself. Everything in me wanted to tell him he wasn't alone. That all he needed do was say the word and Cathy Williams'd follow him through the gates of hell.

Chapter 16

"What in holy hallelujah?" Solomon, looking around his mess, demanded the next day after Sheridan and his cavalry corps rode off. All around us soldiers, sergeants, commanders, even the other contrabands in Sheridan's staff who usually at least tried to look busy, were lolling about, taking their ease. "Did Robert E. Lee surrender and nobody told me?"

The whole camp had turned into a county fair with troopers pitching horseshoes, playing music, smoking rabbit tobacco, and generally loafing about. Solomon glanced around at the shiftlessness and asked me, "They think the damn war's won already?"

Since he couldn't do it in words, Solomon chastised the lazy white boys by working his crew double hard, patrolling the mess area, scrubbing little bits of rust off the cast-iron pans with sand, and grinding up enough parched corn to feed Pharoah's army twice. The others grumbled at Solomon doing them that way now that Sheridan and his officers were gone and the Seceshes all but whipped. I even acted mad myself. But I wasn't.

I was well acquainted with Rebel snakes and I knew that the General was right: they had enough poison stored up in them to snuff your candle not just when they were wounded, but even after they fell down stone-cold dead. Fact is, the Rebels were trapped so tight in their harebrained dream of what the South was, even death wouldn't release them. So Sheridan was right to be worried about the near-whipped Rebs, and I worked that day like he was standing there watching me.

That night, as I slept, Wager Swayne came to me as he had many and many a time before. The dreams always ended with him being fit and alive. He'd sit up, take the bandage off his eyes, declare he felt grass-fed and groomed twice, hop off that wagon, and take my hand to help me down.

We'd run into the woods, which were misty, yet bright and sparkling with light, find a nest full of turkey eggs, or a hive of generous bees and have ourselves a treat. Then, while he was stretched out on a blanket of primrose, bee balm, black-eyed Susans, larkspur, and butterfly weed, I'd flap my arms and soar off into a sky bright blue as a prairie lily. After I took his breath away with the audacity of my swallowtail swooping, he would be overcome with admiration and holler up to me, "My pen is bad, my ink is pale; my love for you shall never fail."

In the dream I had that night, though, when I lifted the bandages from my soldier's face, graveyard things wriggled where his eyes had been. I jerked awake to escape the ugliness, then fell back asleep five more times and four more times horror waited under the bandages. Once I found Old Mister staring up at me with his vacant eyes, brain-fevered from dying of the spider I'd put to bite him. Then it was Old Miss squinting hate at me. Then there were rows of dog's teeth, spiders, and snakes where the soldier's eyes should of been. The fifth time, though, Daddy was hidden beneath the bandages. My father was alive and he told me he was on his way home to me and Mama and Clemmie and would never leave, and I sobbed until I woke myself up. After that, I slept no more.

The next night, scared that the graveyard things would come to disturb my rest again, I went to find peace where I always had in the past, off by myself in the woods. I wandered out a quarter mile or so to the perimeter of camp where Sheridan had his picket line posted with guards switching off every two hours all night to make sure no Rebs crept up on us.

I found the wooden picket stakes driven into the ground to mark right where the watch should have been, but there wasn't a soul about except for an owl hooting high up in an oak tree. Hoping it was just that one guard who'd abandoned his post, I hurried along to the next set of stakes. Nothing and no one. When I saw that every blessed post was deserted, I tore out for camp like a kerosened cat.

"Solomon," I gasped, out of breath when I got there. "There's not a single, solitary guard out there on the picket line. We don't have any lookout."

Though I expected him to leap to his feet and sound the alarm, Solo-

mon stayed right where he was, resting his behind on a stump, digging at
the bowl of the clay pipe he took in the evenings.

"Didn't you hear me?" I asked when all he did was poke around with a
twig until the embers flared, sending sparks into the dark night.

"I heard you fine. Also heard Terrill and Wright laughing about General maybe being a little spooked. Maybe needing the Rebs to seem worse
than they are to impress folks in Washington. Maybe needing to big himself up enough so's he'd get him another star."

"You hoaxing me?"

"Cathy, we beat them Rebs like a drum. We beat them, burned them,
next little bit we gon bury them. You been jumpy as a wild yearling since
General left. Rest easy now. Not a Reb within a hundred miles. Least not a
live one. 'Sides Sheridan's only twenty mile away in Winchester."

"Twenty mile? Might as well be twenty thousand, them Rebs sneak in
on us."

Solomon rolled his eyes and took a long, sucking draw off his pipe, signifying that he was wore out with my foolishness.

Though I planned to stay awake and on guard all night long, sleep overtook me. This time I dreamed my grandmother's dreams. In them, I wore a
necklace of boar's teeth and fired an ancient flintlock musket that had a garden of flowers scrolled on the silver trigger plate. I fired until the rifle grew
too hot for me to hold and still King Ghezo's enemies marched forward.
They held fiery spears above their heads and carried shields of flame out
front. They were coming to kill us. Or worse, they were coming to take us
as slaves and sell us to the Portugee.

As I watched my bullets bounce off the attackers' shields, I realized that
the attackers had survived Sheridan's Burning. They were demons from the
other world, and no human hand could kill them for they were already dead.
As they drew nearer, I found my legs had disremembered how to run. I could
not escape even as I saw that, there at the front, leading those dead soldiers,
was Old Mister, his black and rotting hand held high. He had come to seek
vengeance on me, his murderer.

Clemmie appeared at my side, clutching me and whimpering, "Stop him,
Cathy. Stop him. Don't let him touch me."

As she went on begging, "Save me. Save me. You have to save me," I
realized it wasn't Clemmie at all. It was Iyaiya and she was screaming back

to me from the coffle of slaves being marched away to be fed alive to a pack of cackling hyenas.

I wondered idly in my dream how I'd come to know what a hyena shriek sounded like. But the nonsense of it did nothing to stop the nightmare and the awful cries went on causing my heart to race until I woke up, gasping. But though my eyes were wide open, the hideous hyena shrieks did not stop and I knew them then for what they were: Rebel yells.

Chapter 17

The shrieking surrounded us, but it was dark and a thick fog clouded our camp so that I couldn't get a fix on where the demons were coming from.

A Yankee private, wearing nothing but the long muslin shirt he slept in, came out of his tent. His sleep-dazed bunkies trailed behind. He put his hands on his waist and yelled, "This someone's idea of a joke?"

In answer, a crimson flower blossomed across the front of his pale undershirt. "What in the name of—" he started to ask, irritated as if a strange bug had bit him. But he pitched down dead before he could finish.

A volley of lead thick as hail falling sideways cut down every man beside him.

The way they fell—dropping to their knees like they were praying, not fierce or fighting, dying without a word much less a fight—was so different from Iyaiya's glorious battle stories that I couldn't credit what I was seeing. It couldn't be an enemy attack, I thought. I must still be dreaming.

But the balls pinging off black cast-iron pots, tearing bark from trees, and kicking up dirt near my feet convinced me otherwise. Clumps of rags lifted from the ground nearby and turned into contrabands who'd been sleeping raw out in the open.

"Rebels!" I screamed. "Get down!"

They dropped back to the dirt and minié balls whizzed over our heads.

"Rebels!" we all hollered loud as we could, trying to rouse the white soldiers nearby.

Like dogs hearing their names called, though, it was the Rebs we roused and they swarmed out of the woods and came raging through the rows of tents. The sight of an army of half-starved, crazy-eyed men in ragged uniforms gray as the fog screaming their hyena screams froze my brain. I watched bullets ripping into tent canvas and heard men, asleep a moment before, shrieking in shock and agony, but I couldn't move.

Instead of sabers glistening in the sun and rows of advancing enemies, an ashen cloud swirled through the camp. Rebels and fog. It was impossible to tell one from the other. Instead of soldiers marching forward, powerful and brave, there were scrawny boys dying as they hitched up their trousers. I had no place to point the warrior courage I had believed was in my blood. Faced with real battle for the first time, I was scared down to my toes. Lily-livered, teeth-chattering, yellow-bellied, pants-pissing terrified.

Certain that Solomon, the veteran campaigner, had known enough right off to take cover, I snatched up his old hunting musket and dug in beneath the stout logs of the woodpile. Burrowed in like a badger in a hole, I prayed for the only thing that mattered to me at this the moment of my greatest test. And it wasn't courage or teeth sharpened to points. It was my life. Pure and simple. I prayed the Rebels wouldn't find me. I prayed they'd take every other soul in camp but not find me. Nothing and no one could of poked me from my hidey-hole. And it was there I had my first look at the whole of the elephant, every terrible part of that frightful beast.

In the row of tents nearest the mess, a young captain pulled a jacket on, then stared wide-eyed with fear at the Rebel fog screaming his way. A grizzled old sergeant with a bugler at his side shouted to his superior officer over the roar of shrieking Rebs, the crack of muskets firing, the screams of dying men, the terrifying *whump! whump!* of mortars landing, "Captain, give the order for the troops to form up!"

"Where's the colonel?" the captain whimpered like a lost boy. "What's the colonel say?"

"He ain't here! Give the goddamn order!!" the sergeant bellowed. But the boy captain stayed still as a rabbit staring at a fox, while a dark spot spread across the crotch of his pants.

The sergeant, seeing the captain had pissed hisself, cursed, and ordered the bugler to sound formation. The young bugler died fitting his horn to his lips. The captain, who'd yet to unfreeze, fell next.

"Fire at will," the sergeant commanded all the soldiers who could hear him. The Yankee boys, finally recalling that they were soldiers, shouldered their arms, and drawing beads on an enemy more fog than foe, blasted away at anything that moved.

"Reload!" their brave sergeant ordered. "Fire at—" A minié ball cut his last order short, yet his troops kept fighting.

Thunk! Thunk! Thunk!

A volley of shots hit the logs I hid behind and I hugged the ground so hard the smell of dirt and damp filled my nostrils. Through a chink between the logs, I saw gray ghosts creeping out of the fog. The Rebels were shooting anything that moved then stabbing a bayonet into the bodies.

My nightmare had come to life. The dead killed by the Burning were coming for us and the living couldn't stop them. They hadn't yet noticed the gang of ex-slaves, runaway and emancipated, huddled off at the edge of camp, hiding in sparse cover. But they would. They would come for them and do them worst of all.

I was hidden, but the others, they needed to break for the tall timber. Scatter. Fan out. Head north. And they needed to do it right quick. But they had done nothing but obey orders their entire lives and nobody'd ordered them to run. They were frozen up stiff while the Rebs kept creeping closer.

I thought of Iyaiya on the Other Side watching me and seeing how the royal purple blood she had given me was running yellow in my veins. Though the thought mortified me all to pieces, it wasn't enough to force me to move. No, that didn't happen until who should appear amidst the helpless band of ex-slaves but Solomon Yarnell, bright as a new penny in his green britches and shiny-patched vest. The man didn't even have sense enough to take off that damn top hat. He was out there shooing the others toward the woods like he was driving sheep. And they were too scared and balky to move.

"Y'all git!" he ordered. "Now! Rebs is comin'! Git into them woods off yonder! Move!" he yelled, but they stayed put. Who could blame them? We'd all come from places where woods might be full of Rebs waiting with chains and whips, track hounds, and nooses.

One second there was nothing but fog, the next a Reb with a slouch hat pulled down over his eyes materialized pointing a rifle at Solomon's back. "Well, now, what we got here?" he asked in the sneery way of the Southern yahoo. "Put your hands on your head, Uncle, and turn around."

Instead of obeying, Solomon showed more guts than any other man, white or black, in or out of uniform, I'd ever seen. Solomon crossed his arms in front of his chest and real slow, annoyed, almost bored, he faced the Reb, looked at him with an expression of disgust that said he had seen enough jackasses of this Reb's class and would rather die than deal with one more, and stated, "Uh-uh."

Solomon's defiance rendered the Reb apoplectic for the man had his heart set on a gratifying show of cowering and kowtowing. After a close-up cursing that left Solomon's face drenched in Secesh spit but caused no other reaction, the Reb jammed the barrel of his rifle into Solomon's mouth and yelled, "You traitor! We took you out of darkest Africa, got you civilized, gave you the word of our Redeemer Jesus Christ, and this is the thanks?" He lowered the barrel to Solomon's crotch and continued yelling, "I'll shoot it off, nigger, don' think I—"

The Reb lived long enough to see he'd been shot dead by me, a daughter of darkest Africa. I rammed in another charge as fast as any soldier been drilling for months could have done.

"I was fixin' to disarm the man," Solomon said casual-like, though he trembled as if he had the ague. The next instant a bullet blew Solomon's hat off. I whirled around and plugged the shooter while he was ripping open a paper cartridge with his teeth.

I said "I" did it, but it wasn't me at all who hastened those Rebs to their Maker for I wasn't in my body anymore. I had left the real me huddled up in terror back behind those big, stout logs. From somewhere off high and distant, I looked down and saw this other me help Solomon lead the contrabands to safety in the woods.

Not three seconds later, an artillery barrage thundered down onto the exact spot they had just vacated. We were all knocked sideways to the dirt as trees fell around us. Solomon took the fall on his hip so as not to land on Matildy, who was quivering and chittering beneath his jacket, and we dug in, hiding ourselves under the fallen branches.

The Rebs advanced. I reloaded. Three gray jackets strutted into the bombed-out place where our mess had been. I aimed and laid out the one in the lead. The other two scrambled for cover. I reloaded twice and shot. No fire was returned. The rest of the contrabands scattered. Like them, I was still terrified, but now I knew something they didn't. Something that Iyaiya and Mama knew and only Solomon near getting laid out had showed me: fear can be ordered about.

When Rebels surged in from all sides with more coming on, a Yankee boy hollered, "We're surrounded!"

Seeing their camp overrun, their commanders and friends lying dead at their feet, the soldiers lost hope and began stampeding in the one direction that meant safety, meant home. They fled north. They abandoned camp. They surrendered the General's line at Cedar Creek and they took to their heels.

The Rebs took out after the fleeing Yanks.

"Solomon," I said, crawling from my blind of fallen boughs. "We have to hold the line for the General."

"The line? Baby sister, in case it's escaped your attention, the line just packed up and run off."

"Grab a rifle, Solomon, we'll pick off what we can."

He yanked me back down. "What we'll do is, we'll wait until night falls then try our damnedest to slip on outta here without getting killed or captured by some Reb itching to venge himself on a slave not grateful enough for the chains he put on him."

"Chains that'll be put right back on us if we let those devils run us off. Sheridan loses Cedar Creek and Mr. Lincoln'll lose the election to that chickenshit traitor McClellan who wants to make peace with the slaveholders. Then we for sure be back in chains," I said, already leaving.

"Cathy!" Solomon called after me as I skinned out, fully expecting to give my life that day for my commander. Oh, I was still plenty afraid, but I'd demoted fear to just another condition you have to work around. Like being tired or hungry or hurting. I ran through the abandoned camp, grabbing up abandoned Yankee cartridge boxes where I could. The Rebels had swarmed on past and I didn't see one again until I came to the quartermaster's tents set along the Valley Pike road for supply deliveries.

There a great flock of starved Rebs had congregated. They had thrown down their weapons and were stuffing their flytraps with salt pork, hardtack, molasses, and every other edible they could get their hands on. I even saw a couple attempting to gnaw on a brick of desecrated vegetables, though they'd of had more luck gumming down an actual brick.

I dropped back into the woods that ringed the clearing and climbed the tallest tree I could find, figuring I'd pick off a few of those gluttonous Rebs before they plugged me. All I knew for certain sure was I'd rather die than either let the General down or ever again be that whimpering coward hiding in the woodpile. Cursing the burdensome skirt Solomon made me wear, I shinnied up the tree until I had a clean view of the hogs at the trough.

I was sighting in on the wide target of a broad-shouldered old boy punching his bowie knife into one of the General's airtights of condensed milk when the whole flock of them scattered like a covey of blue quail and I spotted what had caused them to run: roaring down the Valley Pike was General Philip Henry Sheridan.

He must of heard the artillery from Winchester twenty miles away because he was burning a breeze down the pike, making for camp like he had Lucifer himself on his tail. His horse's nostrils were open wide and showing red. The Morgan's black coat was frothed white and his hooves were striking fire. It was a sight to stir the soul.

The road was lined with the Yankee yellow bellies who'd turned tail and were fleeing. Sheridan boomed at them, "Come on back, boys! God damn the _____ Rebs! We'll make _____ coffee out of Cedar Creek tonight!" He held his saber out in front, pointed to camp, and bellowed, "Smash 'em up, boys! Smash 'em up!"

The General swept up those chickens and made them into eagles. They turned around to follow their commander and charged back into camp. Their ranks swelled until the field below my post in the tree was flooded with waves of blue jackets. They fell on the plundering Rebs whose hands were so slick with pork grease the little piggies could barely grab up their rifles.

For the next few hours, I remained at my post and potted as many Grays as I could. Toward twilight, I emptied my last cartridge carton and shinnied down the tree to hunt out more loads. I hung back in the woods until I saw a Reb shouldering his arm to shoot a Union private in the back, then I plugged him. I ran out and was claiming his rifle since I knew it was already loaded when I heard, "A wench! A darkie wench."

The Reb who was fool enough to yell out his amazement at my presence was as bad a shot as he was good at warning me he was there, and his shot went wild. I fired directly at him. Sadly, the barrel of the rifle I'd grabbed was out of true. I didn't know to correct for the pull to the left, so my shot went wild as well and we stood there, both of us alive. Since my rifle didn't have a bayonet, I swung it around and was fixing to club him with the heavy stock when someone behind me blew a hole in the middle of my attacker's chest, throwing him onto his back with his arms flung out wide on either side.

That same someone then grabbed the rifle from where I held it behind my back. I whirled around, ready to bust a head open, and bumped right into Sheridan's horse's whiskery muzzle. Sheridan's brave warhorse snorted hot breaths onto me from the red chutes of its nose and his master, who was holding the rifle he'd yanked from my hands, yelled down, "Who authorized you to take up arms! It is against the natural order for a woman to bear arms!"

The General was wild-eyed and panting as hard as his mount. I'd heard that battle took a true warrior that way. Heat they called it, the heat of battle, and I knew it myself now. "Yessir, General. Careful, though. Barrel's out of true."

The General blinked at me as though a gopher had popped up out of its hole and started quoting Scripture at him. In just that amount of time the battle craziness left him. He handed back the rifle. "By thunder, contraband, you held our ground, didn't you?"

"I tried, sir."

"You didn't cut and run, did you, contraband?"

I couldn't answer for that is what I had really wanted to do. Would have done, too, if that Reb hadn't tried to blow out Solomon's lamp.

"Good work, contraband." Sheridan was already wheeling the gelding around, searching among the dead for a Graycoat might still need killing when I called after him, "Sir. Sir!"

He looked back.

"Name's Cathy, sir. Not 'contraband.' Cathy Williams."

He snorted, shook his head. "Cathy Williams, it's a damn shame the Creator did not fashion you a man. If I had a hundred men brave as you, we'd have this _____ war won already."

I wasn't a man and I sure wasn't brave, but he was still right.

Chapter 18

⁓

"Mopping up" is what they called the minor skirmishes we dealt with over the winter as the starved-out Rebels made their last, futile stands. It was one of the coldest winters in memory, and we stripped timber off every house and barn and chicken coop in five counties to build shacks with wood floors to keep us from freezing. We even put up tall windbreaks for the horses and mules to shelter behind when the wicked winds came screaming down off the Allegheny Mountains.

Near the end of winter, we rolled out again, following Sheridan's advance deeper and deeper into the burned-out heart of Dixie. By early April, we were headed to a place Solomon said was called Apoplexy. It wasn't the strangest town name I'd heard by a long shot, but it certainly held its place among the oddest.

The morning when we set out was chilly and damp. Solomon and I had a system where one drove and one slept. It was late in the day when Matildy and me snuggled up amongst the sacks of feed we toted for the mules. I never once rested on those sacks without recalling Wager Swayne laid out the same way. As usual, I dropped off to sleep with every word that had passed between me and my soldier singing in my head, a lullaby to replace Mama's.

I was dead asleep when the bomb exploded. My eyes flew open and I beheld a night sky bursting with flames. Matildy dug her claws into me tight enough to hang on but not to really hurt. She cuddled up and made her whimpering noise that, over the past seven months, I'd come to know meant she was scared. I stroked her sleek little head and the whimpers turned to a low chittering. All up and down the line horses whinnied, mules brayed, and wagons clattered from being jostled by spooked animals.

"Lord, save us," I said aloud, terrified of the Rebs' mighty new weapon.

Solomon cackled and asked, "Don't tell me you so country you never seen fireworks before?"

For the first time since I'd known him, the face that Solomon tipped up to a sky exploding with colors and light was filled with happiness.

"Somebody celebrating good news," he announced. "My guess is word come down that ole Bobby E. Lee's finally gonna roll over and play dead."

He snapped the reins and we drove on to our destination, which I came to know was called "Appomattox."

Chapter 19

⁓

We set up camp on a rise above the village whose full name was Appomattox Court House on the eighth day of April in 1865. No one slept much that night as the grapevine was singing too loud. By sunrise even the contrabands digging sinks knew that General Grant had decreed that Lee would surrender, not in the courthouse as you might have expected, but in a redbrick farmhouse outside of town. On April 9, around noon, right after Solomon got the new crew of contrabands he had working for him lined out, we skinned out to join those gathering within sight of the farmhouse.

The crowd grew larger as the morning wore on. Though I had long ago accepted in my mind that I would never see Mama or Clemmie again on this earth, my heart would not be convinced, and as I always did, I searched for their faces amidst the strangers gathered on that hillside. My eye went to the female faces. A mother standing next to her man, red headkerchief faded to pink covering her hair, long, dirty apron, bare-butted child on her hip, two others clinging to her rag of a skirt. A flock of hardtack girls squinting into the sun, bodices pulled up proper. A clutch of hard-worn laundresses. Even a few ancient grannies with cob pipes stuck into toothless mouths.

"History gonna be made right down there, baby sister," Solomon kept announcing, pointing at the two-story, redbrick farmhouse with its wide white porch running the length of the first story and a balcony doing the same on the second. Our soldiers were posted on every step of the broad stairs leading up to the front door. Color guards lined up outside, their regimental banners flapping smartly in the breeze. Grooms stood at rigid attention, holding the reins of the horses belonging to generals who were already inside. Sheridan's black gelding that he now called Winchester in honor of the horse's epic ride was easy to pick out for he shone like wet tar in the sun.

Solomon and I exchanged approving nods, proud that our general had the finest mount. "What's Grant ride?" Solomon asked.

"Chestnut sorrel," a tall man with a face wide as a shovel said.

"General Grant knows his horseflesh. Cain't no one say otherwise."

I wanted to brag on my General's horse who saved the whole Union Army at Cedar Creek and was such a hero he had already been immortalized in a poem that was famous far and wide. That poem and the heroic ride that inspired it was so popular it had changed folks' mind up North about how Lincoln was conducting the war. Just as I was about to pipe up and tell how my General and his horse had gotten Mr. Lincoln reelected, a man near old as Methuselah ordered us to hush and added in a deep, rolling voice, "He's here."

We all fell silent then. We didn't need to see Robert E. Lee in his spotless dress uniform, golden sash dancing at his waist, black boots freshly polished, prancing up on an iron-gray horse with a long black mane and tail to know who we had before us.

The ex-slaves next to me shuffled around, their gazes bending down to find their feet. And, even though I was high up on that hill, standing above the commander of all the ones who had fought and died for the privilege of owning me and my people, and I was free now as the birds flying over our heads, my stomach pitched. It was all I could do not to cast my eyes down as well. That's how strong the feeling was that a master, any master, *the* master, had ridden in amongst us. For us Lee was every dashing Southern gentleman riding proud and tall on account of him believing he was a knight in shining armor in spite of the fact that he held a whip ready to lash anyone bold or foolish enough not to bow their head when he passed.

None of us exhaled until he dismounted, climbed the front stairs, and disappeared into the house. I imagined Robert E. Lee walking into the room where my General sat waiting. I imagined Sheridan letting his fearsome black-eyed gaze show Lee the terrible death that waited for him.

"You see Lee's knees shakin'?" the shovel-headed fellow asked. "That man scared."

"Should be," Solomon said. "He know what they do with rebels."

"Hang 'em," several men chimed in.

"Ones who lose," agreed Solomon. "Gonna do him like Washington did Benedict Arnold for he's ten times the traitor Arnold ever was."

Glee rose in me at the prospect of seeing the tips of those polished black boots pointing down when the leader of the Secesh Army hung from a tall cottonwood.

Solomon's motion was seconded. "Traitor tried to break up the Union and he will swing for it. Him and all the leaders of the Rebellion."

"Man's gon come down them steps in chains," came one prediction.

Chains. We all liked that idea.

"Might not come down at all," someone else suggested. "Might burn the traitor down on the spot."

"Shootin's too good for him," a man in a slouch hat disagreed. "Lynch him!"

"Like the Bible says," the old man intoned, " 'Lord God of Hosts, do not show mercy to any wicked traitors.' "

"And Robert E. Lee is one wicked traitor," Slouch Hat concluded. "He gon hang. All them gon hang."

"Hang traitors and shoot deserters," said a man with a battered campaign hat squashed down on his bushy head of hair. He wore a sack coat that bore dark rectangles on the shoulders where a captain's straps had once been sewn. The insignia might have been gone, but this fellow still wore that rank in his words as he told us how it was gonna be.

"They'll hang all the leaders of the rebellion who fought to destroy the United States of America, right down to the majors. Won't be a telegram pole or sturdy oak won't have a hung Reb dangling from it. And them flags they rallied behind? The Stars and Bars? Grant'll make the biggest bonfire you ever seen out of them." He nodded his head with such certainty, we all nodded along with him as he muttered, "Treason, uh-huh, no worse crime. Wouldn't be surprised if, after they burn all the flags, and hang all the leaders, they make it a crime to even say the word 'Confederacy.' "

We all amened that.

Half an hour later, a Union soldier with a wild, untended beard that had a stogie jammed into the middle of its whiskery mess, rode up at a full gallop on a chestnut sorrel.

"Unconditional Surrender Grant." The old man pronounced Grant's nickname like he was saying "Holy Lord Jesus Christ."

If General Grant, savior of the Union, hadn't had those three stars shining on the shoulders of the rumpled private's blouse he wore, you'd of thought the man incapable of commanding his way out of a privy. Next to the pristine Lee, Grant in his borrowed, mud-splattered uniform looked like a mule skinner at the end of a five-day spree.

But when U. S. Grant dismounted and charged forward, his wide, flat-brimmed hat leading like he intended to knock the redbrick farmhouse down with his head, and then clomped up the stairs loud enough that even us way up on the rise could hear, it was clear as day that this soldier didn't need a pressed uniform to command. He and Sheridan had a lot in common in that respect. Bulldogs, both of them.

As the hours passed the predictions about Lee's death, and all the rest of his top men from Jubal Early to Braxton Bragg, turned so gruesome that, in the end, we had half the Rebel army greased up with pig lard and locked in a bear cage.

Given how greedy we were for the sight of the Confederacy shamed and brought low, it was a sore disappointment when, early in the afternoon, Lee strutted out every bit as dapper as when he'd pranced in. An orderly buckled his horse's throatlatch and Lee reached up and drew the forelock out from under the brow band, then gently patted the gray's forehead before mounting up.

To our utter stupefaction, when the leader of our enemies, the man most responsible for upward of half a million souls being ripped from this earth, rode away, General Grant saluted him. Our jaws unlatched and we gaped, listening in disappointed astonishment to the peaceable clop of hooves as Robert E. Lee was borne away, whole and unharmed.

I thought of Iyaiya's stories. How, if a warrior got beat, she had to expect to be put in chains or have her head decorating the top of a gate. I was feeling cheated of the blood vengeance we'd fought for when Bible man boomed out, " 'He hath showed what is good. Showed y'all what the Lord require of thee. Got to do justly, and to love mercy, and to walk humbly with thy God.' Mercy, y'all," he repeated in case we'd missed his point. "Our General's doing what Lord Jesus want him to."

There were a few "amens," which didn't mean that if Lee hadn't been chunked down to us from the top of a tower, most of us wouldn't of taken a sharpened stick to that fine Southern gentleman.

Into the quiet moment of disappointment that followed someone whispered, "War's over." A few seconds later, volleys of celebration shots rang out until it sounded like a full-fledged assault was in progress. Instant the shooting started, though, Grant clomped down the stairs and marched into the sunny yard, head out, ready to butt through whatever brick wall he encountered.

Ulysses S. Grant held up his hand and the firing stopped. He unclamped his thin lips from the stogie he had wedged there and thundered in a voice harshened from a lot more than cigar smoke, "The war is over! The Rebels are our countrymen again, and the best sign of rejoicing after the victory will be to abstain from all demonstrations in the field."

For a long moment, the only sounds we heard after that was the nicker of the Union generals' mounts, the clanking of bridles as they slung their heads about, and wind rummaging through the high boughs.

Finally, the Bible man asked, "Any y'all recollect that today is Palm Sunday?"

Chapter 20

After that, chain of command broke down fast among everyone except the army regulars, who were few and far between as most of the soldiers were civilians, farmers and shopkeepers, who couldn't wait to leave. First to vamoose were the homesick boy drummers and buglers. Without them to sound out orders, the army's clock was broken and all us as had been slaves made the acquaintance of a powerful force we had never known before: free time, our own to do with as we chose.

For the next couple of days, we scratched about like hens for any scrap of information that might come our way concerning the surrender agreement. In specific, what it said about us.

"Way I heard it," a fellow with a pair of bushy muttonchops winging out either side of his head declared, "we all's to be divvied up. Straight down the middle. Half go North to freedom. Half go South back to bondage."

"You's all kinda liar," another disagreed. "Ain't gonna be like that at all. They's already built the boats gone carry us back to Africa."

That caused a mighty stir with all gathered putting in their opinions on life in Africa as if we were standing on the dock at that moment. While we were arguing about whether we'd be greeted as long-lost relatives or chunked in a big pot and boiled for dinner, a piercing voice cut into our chin wag and demanded, "Would any of you care to know what the document in question actually says?"

Though the question wasn't stated in a loud voice, the tone of it cut so clean through the hubbub that every single one of us fell so dead silent that I expected to turn and see a white man.

But the man, compact built and fine dressed, was as dark as me. He wore a mustache with waxed tips pointing directly east and west and a small afterthought of a beard on the chin. He had a kingly bearing about him that made you wonder, "Who is this fellow?"

A gold watch chain looped from one pocket of his waistcoat. From the other he plucked a pair of spectacles and, with more hemming and hawing than seemed entirely necessary, he curled the wire arms around his smallish ears. Next he produced a newspaper clipping that was limp as a rag from much handling. The crowd fell silent for many among us had never before seen a person of color who could read.

Mr. Spectacles waited until even the wind had stopped soughing in the high branches before he held the wilted article up with an outstretched arm and spoke in a piercing voice that drilled straight into your brain and etched the words directly there, "You have before you today a transcript of the Articles of Agreement Relating to the Surrender of the Army of Northern Virginia."

Someone chimed in with a chorus of "uh-huhs," "amens," and "thas rights." That someone might have been me for I was distracted by wondering if this small fellow, along with being able to read, might not also possess Daddy's ability to discern a woman of quality. For though he couldn't of held a candle to my soldier, and caused none of the firefly flutters he had, it was clear that, like myself, this fellow was a bend or two above the ordinary run.

The small ovals of glass in front of his eyes turned to silver as they caught the afternoon light while he read. Though he quickly lost most of us in a thicket of brigades, detachments, divisions, and corps, we listened as though hearing the word of God. He finished, dipped his head, peered over his glasses, saw our stupefied confusion, and summed it all up this way. "With God as their witness, those damn Rebs agree to lay down their weapons and never again take them up against the government of the United States."

Oh, that brought on a hallelujah chorus to beat all.

He continued, "Grant's going to give all the Johnny Rebs parole and let them return home. He won't send a one of them to prison."

Though we had seen it all our lives, we were still stunned by this fresh evidence of the murders, treason, and other unspeakable devilry a white man could get away with. No chorus filled the silence this time. There would be no justice. I knew that what Grant and Lincoln and who all else had drawn those terms up might of thought to be mercy was a calamitious mistake. Though beaten and burned out and laid low, the Confederacy was still a snake with poison enough to kill off half a country.

I told Solomon, "Sheridan would of sent them all to hell." Everyone within hearing distance told me to tell it. Tell the truth.

When our cries for revenge rose up, Bible man shouted us down, saying, "We ain't what we want to be. And we ain't what we gon be. But we surely ain't what we was."

A moment passed before someone called out the question that was at the top of all our minds. "What's it say about us?"

Mr. Spectacles answered in that voice made to carry to the top of the mountain we all wanted to climb. "The Rebels cannot claim you for you all are free men. Lincoln already emancipated you two years ago. He just had to whip the Rebs to make it stick."

We exploded with joy, cheering the well-dressed stranger as if he were the one who'd personally unshackled our bonds. When he was finished, the crowd bunched up like an adoring congregation, paying their respects to the preacher. Several even asked to touch the scrap of newspaper he held as though it was the very document that had ended their days of bondage.

That night, we all went to sleep praying for daylight, for the final surrender would take place the next day.

And I was there for every minute of it, hypnotized by seeing nearly thirty thousand Rebels lay down their colors and their arms. I grinned for twelve hours straight knowing how aggravating it was for the poor Southern boys who'd never had anything in life except being better than girls and coloreds to see me up there lording it over them at the moment they had to holler uncle. I hurt from wishing so hard that Clemmie and Mama were standing beside me.

When the last Johnny Reb shuffled off, most of the contrabands, finally convinced they were really free, drifted away. Some headed back to where they'd run off from or been plucked from to see who was still alive back home. Some cleared off in any direction but south. But a few stayed tight on the spectacled stranger for he had offered to help us with reading documents and making our way through the scary new world we'd been turned loose in.

I went to start after him myself, but Solomon stopped me with a hand on my arm, a sour look wrinkling his face.

"What?" I asked. "Man can read. Can help us with whatever papers come our way. Might keep us from getting bamboozled. He seems to know the way of things."

"Man seems a lot of things," he said, peeved. "Lot of miles between seeming and being."

"Aw, Solomon, you're just jealous 'cause folks are paying him all the mind." It was true, Solomon liked being top dog and wasn't shy about baring his teeth and bristling up when a challenger came too close.

"Because he can read?" Solomon demanded. "Because he can write? I'll tell you what, that man there, he'd steal the butter off a blind man's bread and put him on the wrong road home."

I laughed at Solomon's jealous words and he stomped off.

Meanwhile, the happy band gathered up around Mr. Spectacles was already heading off. I consulted Mama and Iyaiya on whether I should follow him or Solomon, then waited for their sign.

No sign appeared to nudge me in one direction or the other. And, in that moment, I felt as bewildered and scared about what was to come next as any of the others. The only two people in the world I cared about were dead. I had nowhere to go. And no one who cared if I got there.

Except for Solomon.

It hit me then that if I had a friend, he was it. With no other choice, I started off after him. The last thing I heard from the stranger was the Bible man asking him, "What's your name, son?"

Mr. Spectacles stopped, turned back so all behind could hear, and answered in his distinct voice, "Vikers. They call me Justice Vikers."

Chapter 21

That night, in spite of Grant forbidding it, no power on earth could of stopped the rejoicing. Not after four years of fighting and starving and dying. Especially since all the generals had ridden away to Washington to meet with Lincoln to figure out how to shrink the military from the near two million that had fought against the Rebellion down close to the sixteen thousand it was when the Secesh traitors started the whole mess.

Most everyone, both white and black, except for Solomon and me and a few ancient aunties, went down to the woods outside the village and commenced to throw the biggest shebang ever held. Solomon refused to join in the festivities, saying he'd seen a right sharp of snot-flying drunks in his time and had no need of making a special trip to see more. So we watched the hullabaloo from up top the rise.

Outside the courthouse, a proper band, not some piddly fife-and-fiddle job, played "When Johnny Comes Marching Home." Overhead fireworks exploded like a century of Fourth of Julys crammed into one night. Great dandelions blew golden fluff into the night and giant chrysanthemums opened their red petals. For a spell, I was content to sit and ooh and aah with the old folk.

Then a mighty burst threw crazy bolts of light across all the faces below, black and white, and I could see them down there having a high old time. Next, the black sky went noontime bright as a fountain of silver lit up the heavens and rained sparks down on the merrymakers. The band played "Aura Lea" and sang about the "maid with golden hair." In the sporadic flashes of fireworks light, I saw frozen glimpses of couples dancing. Most were just ordinary whores and their customers, but they were all raised up high in their joy to a place I longed to visit just once in my life.

"Solomon, let's go on down there."

My friend sat on a tree stump, one leg folded over the other, one arm tucked up in his armpit, the other holding his clay pipe to his mouth, all settled in the way he liked. He tugged on the pipe, puffed out a cloud of smoke, knocked the edge of the pipe on the heel of his boot, and said, "No, thank you, Queenie. This is where we were posted. Where we supposed to be."

"Solomon, there's no posting anymore. Everyone's run off or been mustered out. Don't you understand? War is over. We can do what we want. Go where we want. This is the start of a whole new life for us. We did it, Solomon. We won. We got a right to celebrate."

"Won? What you think we won?" he barked back.

"Freedom, Solomon. We won freedom."

He harrumphed and said, "You'll see what black folk won. War was the easy part, buttercup. Peace with white folks gon be a whole new war. War we be fighting alone. You think them Rebs we saw riding off back home gonna be a hair different from what they were before the war? Only difference now is they hungrier, poorer, and meaner 'cause they got a grudge. Think they were done wrong.

"Since they'd die before they ever admitted what fools and traitors they were, every one of them beat Rebs'll go to his grave sure as God that we, all us ungrateful slaves, were the reason for every bit of the misery they brought on themselves. Bad as they were before, they gon *punish* us now."

"All we got to do is stay away from them. We can go north."

"What? You think the Yanks'll be a whole lot better? You think they'll be waiting up North to give us their own good jobs? Nice houses to live in? Plates of fried ham and redeye gravy? Huh? That what you think?"

Though I told him that, of course, that wasn't what I thought, he still said, "You dreaming, buttercup. North. South. White man's a white man." He drew heavy on his pipe like he had just spoken the final word and the case was closed.

Well, it wasn't. "Dog you, Solomon," I said. "If it was raining silver dollars you be moanin' 'bout you forgot your umbrella." I stood up, brushed bits of grass from my skirt, and smoothed the hair back behind my ears.

"Where you think you're going?"

"Don't think, know. I am going down there and have me a dance or two with a free man."

Solomon jumped to his feet and blocked my way. "No, ma'am, state that crowd is in, wouldn't be safe for a young lady without an escort."

"Why, Solomon Yarnell, I do declare," I trilled out, the way those sap-headed Southern belles back in Missouri used to. "Ain't you the gentle-man." The instant I said it, though, I realized it was true. That's exactly what Solomon Yarnell was. He was a gentleman. And had been from the start.

He tapped out his pipe, stuck it in his pocket, and grumbled to Matildy, "You heard the lady, best put on your dancing shoes."

I ran to yoke up the team. If this was the first and maybe only time I was to be squired about by a fellow, I reckoned we'd do it in style. Also, I was imagining Justice Vikers watching me ride in and had to admit that I wouldn't have minded seeing that impressive gent again.

By the time we navigated the back road down to the village in the pitch-dark night, the party was roaring and most in attendance had celebrated themselves into a state of paralysis. Leastwise that's what we made out from the sound of the goings-on for we couldn't yet see them, as groves of thick woods surrounded the open field where the revelers were dissipating them-selves in the light of bright bonfires made of torn-down Secesh barns. We left Matildy tethered in the wagon we parked at the edge of the woods and commenced to make our way towards the spree.

Halfway through the woods, we spotted a pack of rough-looking jas-pers malingering about a sad little campfire, passing a jug around, joylessly working at getting drunker than boiled owls. The gang was dressed in scraps of Yankee uniforms and civilian clothes, though these lowlifes were probably wearing Secesh gray a few days back. They looked to be hard cases who'd been heading nowhere fast when the war bumped into them and, now that the shooting was over, they were continuing on in the same direction.

Though they were ossified good, it wasn't moon-howling, cutting-up drunk. It was mean, spoiling-for-a-fight drunk. It was the grudge-holding drunk of men drowning their sorrows. Men who reckoned they'd been done wrong. Just like Solomon predicted.

We were giving the jackals wide berth, keeping far back where they could neither see nor hear us, when the familiar gleam of a patch box, muz-zle, and trigger guard of polished brass caught my eye, for they were all at-tached to a yagger rifle. *My* yagger rifle.

Chapter 22

⁓

S olomon," I whispered, "that's my rifle. That's my yagger I left hidden back home in the trunk of a hollow tree. One of those crackers found it."

The long arm I had taken off the snake-bit Reb deserter lay unattended, even prettier than I remembered her. That was my rifle all right for I had not seen another like her amidst the vast assemblage of weapons I'd noted over the past months. A pang cinched me up tight and I was so overtaken with longing for Mama and the times we'd had with that selfsame rifle that no power on earth could of stopped me from reclaiming it.

The instant I moved toward it, though, Solomon clamped a grip on me could of halted a buffalo and whisper-hissed, "What on God's green earth you doing?"

"Getting my rifle."

"Getting kilt more like it."

"Can't kill what you never hear or see. Solomon, I can do this. I have to do this."

"You push it, Queenie," Solomon said in a despairing way. "Always push it. World's gonna push back. See if it don't."

But he set me loose and I advanced. No snake slithering across a plate of glass could of been quieter. When I came close enough, the sludgy, ignorant twang of the most miserable specimens of Southern manhood assailed my ears.

The fellow who had stolen my yagger was a bony specimen wearing greasy buckskins and a coonskin cap appeared the coon been eaten by a bear and vomited up directly onto the man's head. He was squabbling with a squat, beady-eyed individual, had a round face shining with grease, most likely from salt pork handed out by the conquering Yanks.

The fatty said something I didn't catch and Coonskin Cap barked out in a nasal whine, "Whud you jist call me, Loudermilk?"

Loudermilk raised his voice and answered in a mocking la-di-da way, "Why, Dupree, my good man, I am surprised you failed to catch my drift. 'Specially as I was speakin' in your native tongue. Allow me to repeat myself, Dupree."

With that, Loudermilk tilted his chunky butt to one side, lifted a meaty haunch, and let loose with a rump ripper fueled by four years of beans and bad water.

The rifle-thieving Dupree was on his feet and plunging into the withering brown cloud Loudermilk had released quick as could be. They were all spoiling for a fight and would of preferred to thump a few Yankee or ungrateful black gourds, but they took this one and every one of them pitched in. It must of seemed to most of those rednecks that they'd gone to war for less than a fart, so why not bust some knuckles over a real one?

Once the thrashing started and they were occupied grinding their knuckles into each other's eye sockets, booting one another's groins, yanking out handfuls of hair, and trying to bite an ear or two off, my yagger was easy pickings. I snatched it and vanished.

Oh, how I gloried in having that fine firearm cradled in my arms once again. I ran to Solomon, expecting him to be as happy as I was. But he had sulled up on account of my pushing it and going against him and he wasn't speaking to me.

His mood brightened, though, when we emerged into the open field and found folks having all kinds of times out there. Everyone was jubilating. Bluecoats from every Yankee state in the Union along with swarms of freedmen camp followers, vendors selling tonsil oil, turncoat Rebs, drifters, bunco men, and cutpurses.

Clumps of drummer boys, unused to the strong spirits being passed about so freely, lay dead to the world like so many rag dolls left outside. I searched for the young fellow who brought me water and hardtack when I was barreled up, but didn't find him and said a prayer that he had survived the Rebellion and was making his way home safe to his abolitionist ma and pa.

Fiddlers, drummers, and fifers who hadn't lit out for home or the nearest city with gaslights and loose women for them to waste their separation pay on played lively tunes. Grizzled veterans capered about the bonfires grabbing any soldier, officer or enlisted, who passed their way by the arm and swung him around like they were do-si-doing at a barn dance. Long lines snaked into the tents where the hardtack girls had set up. They were charging two dollar a head and still couldn't keep up with business. At those exorbitant rates, even a fair portion of the washerwomen had temporarily shifted from the cleaning to the dirtying business.

Most of the suds ladies, though, confined themselves to selling dances as soldiers were happy to pay two bits just to whirl around with a woman in their arms and laugh and stick a Rebel cap on her head. It was quite a hoedown, with soldiers from every unit in the Union army represented. I'd learned to pick them out by their speech and I heard Irish Yankee, Boston Yankee, New York Yankee, German Yankee, and Swede Yankee all wove into the soft brown velvet of my people's way of speaking. Which, to my ears, was how the Lord had intended his creatures to speak.

I was gawking about like the most country hayseed when a fellow with a wide mouth and teeth spaced far apart as a gator stepped up, pointed at my chest, and asked, "What you got there?"

That was when I noticed that while retrieving my yagger, my bodice had come unbuttoned, revealing a fair amount of my bosom. I quickly closed it back up and snapped, "Nothin' that you'll ever put your nasty hands on."

"Calm down, sister. I got no interest in that washboard of yours. What I meant was them scars."

That stopped me cold. "You mean these?" I asked, touching the scars. "Why you asking?"

He shrugged. "No reason. Just ain't never seen the like except on one other gal."

"What other gal?" I asked, slitting my eyes against this fool.

"Gal follows Grant's camp."

"What her name?" I demanded.

The man tapped his forehead. "Was right on the tip of my tongue."

I felt Solomon move in close to me, lean down and whisper, "Don't do this to yourself, Cathy. Don't go opening hurts been healed up."

"Solomon, that hurt will never heal." I turned back to the man and asked again, "What her name?"

The man snapped his fingers and said, "Clemmie! That's it, gal's name's Clemmie."

"You knew Clemmie? You knew my little sister?"

" 'Knew her'? I'm still knowing her!"

"No . . ." I was trying to sort out the right words from the tornado whipping through my mind when he said, "Y'all wait right here where I can find you. I be back directly," and disappeared into the crowd before I could stop him.

For one stupid second, I believed Gator Mouth would bring my little sister to me. Then I accepted that either I'd never see him again or, if I did, he'd be dragging along some warty girl just happened to have the same name as my sister. My dead sister. Though I knew I was a fool for letting even the tiniest green sprig of hope sprout up, I still felt low and let down even with all the uncorked happiness churning up around me.

The band struck up a comical version of "Dixie" made up on the spot for the occasion. Those still conscious raised an unholy ruckus howling out the new words, "In Dixie Land we'll take their land and make them die in Dixie! Took away, took away, took away Dixie Land!"

"Forget it, Cathy," Solomon said, and I took note of the fact that he'd called me by my name. Twice. I smiled at him, and set on putting pain aside for that night, I even joined in shout-singing, "Took away! Took away! Took away Dixie Land!" Determined not to let Gator Mouth spoil our fun, I grabbed Solomon's arm and jostled him in a kidding, maybe even a flirty type way, until he opened his mouth and added what turned out to be a right agreeable baritone. When he sang out ". . . and make them die in Dixie!" the third time, he was grinning big and both the business back in the woods and Gator Mouth had been forgotten.

A whiskey vendor came our way with a jug and a tin cup. Solomon handed over a few pennies from a pocket inside his vest and bought us each a blast. The man waited impatiently for me to slug down the stiffener so that Solomon could take his turn with the man's single cup. It was the first strong drink ever passed my lips and I liked it fine. It had a pacifying effect that calmed me the way hearing Scriptures does some folk.

Just to be ornery and aggravate the white vendor, Solomon was taking dainty sips out of the man's cup, pretending to savor the rotgut while the vendor told him to step it up since a passel of thirsty guzzlers were waiting.

I'd never worn a corset, though I was acquainted with that instrument of torture from helping Old Miss get harnessed up. Still, I felt like I'd been laced into one my whole life and that my first cup of joy juice had caused all the stays to bust loose, letting me breathe freer than I maybe ever had. Feeling all let out, I rested the yagger in a safe, dark spot, and asked Solomon straight-out, "You plan on inviting a young lady to dance?"

Instant I issued my invitation, Solomon slugged down his jolt, tossed the cup somewhere in the vicinity of the vendor, and raised his arms into dance position perfect as a gentleman at a cotillion. I stepped right into them and, for the first time since I was pulled away from Mama and Clemmie, I felt like I had a partner.

Solomon held our hands out so that they made a prow to cut through the ocean of people. I was feeling as though we were about to launch on what I'd begun to suspect would be a long journey, one that might last the rest of our lives, when a heavy hand clamped onto my shoulder, jerked me around, and I came face-to-face with Dupree.

Chapter 23

B eneath Dupree's coonskin cap was a pinched, weasely face even more starved out and pie-eyed up close than it had been from a distance.

"Whar's my rifle?" he demanded.

"I don't know what you're talking about."

"I knowed you took my yagger. We had us a lookout posted what seen you make off with my weapon. I was occupied or would of come after you directly. So give it over fore you find out what happens to a nigger wench steals off of Hiram T. Dupree."

Seeing the odds tilted heavy against us, I was about to show him the yagger when Solomon said, "Remove your hand from the lady."

Dupree swiveled his dim, bleary-eyed gaze to Solomon and asked, "Whud you say? Boy?"

"I said," Solomon repeated, "take your grimy paw off the lady." This time, he accompanied the order with action and jerked Dupree's hand off me. The instant Solomon's black hand touched Dupree's white one the air became charged the way it does before a thunderstorm.

Almost more amazed than outraged, Dupree stated, "Boy, you done put your hand on me."

Once the crime was named, his gang fell on us and we were locked in strangleholds and neck locks. And, though we hollered and struggled for help, none of our own people came to our aid. They just looked on and let that pack of hyenas drag us back into the woods where, I expected, they'd finish us off in ways too awful to name.

When they got us back to their campfire, I wriggled free and kicked a couple of them where it hurts a man most. Then I chugged Dupree a stout one in the mouth and the few teeth he had left in his head gave way and came gushing out in a spray of what looked like kernels of corn mixed with blood and slobber. Solomon proved himself to be all wool and no shoddy in the fighting department as well. He had a reach you wouldn't of expected on a man of his height and a solid upper cut that came all the way up from Alabama to flatten a couple of them egg-suckers.

Then Solomon and me backed toward each other so that we put a solid V of fists between ourselves and the trashy skunks. We were holding our own and edging back away to safety when one of the polecats slipped around behind and coldcocked me with what felt like a round jack sap to the back of the head, and I went down heavy as a dead beef.

When I came to, I was on the ground staring up at a rockslide of fists raining down upon me. Those crackers were refighting the Rebellion and there wouldn't be any surrender this time. I prepared myself to meet Iyaiya, Mama, and Clemmie. Then, just as the fellow with the bassoon butt was fixing to plant his boot in my face, a shot was fired and he dropped down dead on top of me. Another shot was fired, this one more of a boom than the first, which had had a crack to it, and it blew another fellow out of his clothes. I squirmed out from beneath the dead man in time to hear another shot fired and to see the skunk punching Solomon come down in a pile.

I figured a band of Yankee snipers had finally come to our aid and were hiding out in the woods picking Dupree's gang off one by one. The gang arrived at the same conclusion, for they left off murdering us and, not knowing where the snipers were, they all clumped together, whirling from side to side and darting glances about, looking for the attackers they reckoned had them surrounded.

Dupree, drooling red slobber, had lost, along with the majority of his teeth, every bit of his bullyboy spunk. The next shot fetched off his cap, revealing that the only hide he had atop his newborn-bald head had been coonskin. Whimpering like a wormy pup, he crouched down, held his hands out in the direction the shots were coming from, and pleaded, "Let us go! We didn't intend no harm! Please, Grant told y'all to leave us be. It's peace now. Y'all can't just shoot at us like—"

Of a sudden Dupree, having seen something emerging from the woods, stopped wheedling, and sounding like he was about to perish from the dry wilts, whispered, "Oh, Lord God Amighty," and fell silent.

For out of the shadows stepped all the freedmen and women I thought had abandoned us to our fate. Leading them was none other than Gator Mouth. Not a one of them spoke, nor did they need to. With three of Dupree's ranks dead and the rest near to it from fright, the mangy pack did not require any persuading to clear off. They backed away, bit by bit at first then in a wild, galloping stampede, tearing over one another in their hurry to escape.

"You see them crackers turn tail and run?" Gator Mouth asked again and again, each time to greater and greater amusement as our rescuers were doubled over laughing until they came close to airing their paunches from sheer gut-cramping mirth. Once I collected myself, though, I realized that not one of those folks had any iron on him.

"Who did the shooting?" I asked.

Before anyone could answer, the distant notes of the band whipping into a schottische, a lively Kraut tune that made for good dancing, caught their attention and the freedmen and women rushed off to join in.

When they'd left, I called out for our rescuers to make themselves known so we might thank and reward them for they had surely saved our lives. Expecting a couple of burly pistoleros to appear, I was taken aback when a plump girl bearing my yagger stepped into the firelight. No doubt her accomplices were remaining out of sight to cover her.

The girl wore sparkly earbobs of the sort no laundress or cook could earn in three lifetimes of boiling clothes or victuals. Her face, a delicious color this side of caramel, was rouged up and powdered as befits a fallen Daughter of Eve. She was a comely young woman with glossy hair that hung in springy curls and a figure, though gone to fat at a young age, was still fetching enough that it was easy to see how she could command a pair of sparkly earbobs.

"I am mighty obliged to you," I started off, not knowing how to go about the business of thanking this stranger and her partners in hiding for saving me and Solomon.

Solomon went to put his hand into his vest pocket, but the girl whipped a derringer from the well-padded holster of her cleavage, cocked it, and ordered in the growly voice of a gin-soaked bawd, "Hold it right there, Top Hat!"

"I ain't armed," Solomon protested. "I got money and figured on giving you and your buddies, wherever they're hid, a reward."

"You saved our lives," I said. "Tell us your name."

The hussy made no answer, for my question had caused her to start bawling like a baby. In that instant, the hands of time turned back and I didn't need her to cry out in our Africa language, "Am I that fat and ugly that you don't even recognize me?" to know that I was being held at gunpoint by my baby sister.

Chapter 24

A nd then my head took over and told me it couldn't be. "No," I said, backing away from this pretender. "My sister is dead. Talked to the man who buried her."

The girl stepped closer, took my hand, and stuck it down her bodice until I felt five rows of puffed-up scars, round as pearls. She put her hand on my scars and the presence of Mama and Iyaiya came on so strong I could smell the licorice root they both were given to chewing. There was no denying it: the bawd was my sister Clemmie. Once the truth of it came clear, I saw that the only thing truly different about her was that the woebegone look that had fallen upon Clemmie after Old Mister began having his way with her had vanished. Though gone to fat and to the bad, little sister had been returned to me as bright and shiny as she had ever been. I fell into Clemmie's arms.

I can't say how long we'd been clinging to each other and sobbing before Solomon said, "This must be the famous baby sister Clemmie." He said it like she was his family, too, put his arm around both of us and added, "We heard you was dead."

Clemmie and I wiped away tears and snot and she answered, "No, I'm alive."

"She never stopped looking for you," Solomon went on. "There wasn't a black face we come across, she didn't search it. About wore the neck of her dress out, tugging it down, showing those Africa scars, asking if anybody'd seen the like."

I never suspected that Solomon had ever much noticed what I did unless it was not chopping or cleaning or serving to his liking. But he had. He'd been paying attention the whole time.

"No," Solomon went on, "she never stopped looking. Not for you, nor . . ." He glanced my way and added, "Nor your mama."

The way Clemmie froze, only her eyes darting to find mine, I knew for the first time that Mama was gone and a crumbling that started in my knees overtook me, for until that moment, I had not truly believed that Mama was truly gone.

I wobbled and Clemmie stepped forward to grab me. "Could you give my sister and me a moment?" she asked Solomon.

I collapsed, sobbing, into Clemmie's arms; she welcomed me with a kick in the shins from her boot so hard that the pain snapped the tears right off my cheeks. Before I could hit back, she grabbed me by my shoulders and ordered, "Get a hold yourself, right now this instant."

"But Mama," I whimpered.

"No!" she shouted sharp and hard, way you would a dog messed on the carpet. "No! Ain't having that. Not one bit of it. You listen to me. Mama went North, you hear? Went North to be with our daddy—"

"But they said Daddy was—"

"Shut your mouth. Shut it. Don't let that word come out of your mouth or enter into your mind. Mama and Daddy are up there in Illinois now eating biscuits and honey. He's doing his tailoring and she's taking care of him. They have them a sweet little house with hollyhocks in the garden."

I was seeing my sister for the first time. Who she really was. She was ten times tougher than I would ever be and had seen grief I could not imagine. She was tough enough to decide she wouldn't allow the cruelties of a wicked world to break her down or destroy her memories.

"Now that is the picture of Mama and Daddy I want and I will not let you or anyone else take it from me."

I nodded, swallowing back my grief. So, though my little sister did hold me and let my tears run down her neck, we spoke no more of Mama. I told her my tears were for joy at finding her again and, by the time the crowd surged in around us, pushing and jostling toward something behind us, tears of joy were what they had become.

Suddenly, a marching chant rang out from the distance.

Say that in the Army, chicken's might fine
One jumped off the table, started marking time
Say that in the Army, coffee's mighty fine
Looks like muddy water, tastes like turpentine
Say that in the Army, biscuits mighty fine
One rolled up off the table, kilt a friend of mine

Sound off!
One! Two!
Sound off!
THREE! FOUR!

I glanced up and found that, for some reason, whoever was counting cadence was causing everyone to stare off with looks on their faces like Jesus was behind me raising Lazarus from the grave. When I finally threw enough elbow to twist around and get a look, what I saw was more miraculous than a dead man rising.

The crowd parted and a detachment of black soldiers—real soldiers, not the scruffy work gangs of contrabands I'd seen in their cast-off jackets and seat-blown trousers digging graves and chopping kindling—came marching up. And here's the miraculous part: these troopers were carrying rifles and they were wearing the blue suit. Crisp new uniforms, not ones ventilated with bullet holes and bayonet stabs. These soldiers had their shoulders pinned back, spines straight as fence posts, heads held high. They were ready to look anyone, black or white, straight in the eye with no fake smiles or shift-down glances. These were real, full men. Real, full human beings.

A brass band struck up the "Battle Cry of Freedom" and, with the stern profiles of our men marching past—Spencer carbines resting on the left shoulder, stiff right arms ticktocking back and forth with each step, keeping time—we sang along with the chorus.

The Union forever! Hurrah, boys, hurrah!
Down with the traitor, up with the star;
While we rally round the flag, boys, rally once again,
Shouting the battle cry of freedom!

Hurrah, boys, hurrah!

It was the first time the song had ever been about *our* boys and we couldn't shout *that* battle cry of freedom loud enough.

Even the band, playing atop a low stage, was made up of a dozen of our boys. Soldiers holding torches took places around the platform and the light gleamed up onto the brass curlicues of the horns the musicians held to their mouths. Their forage caps were on straight, not hanging off to one side or the other trying to look jaunty the way the contraband soldiers wore them. No, these caps sat right so that the golden horns embroidered on the round tops all faced us and we knew that they were in the United States Infantry. They were bona fide marching soldiers.

Another unit of soldiers paraded in and lined up, four abreast on either side, in front of the stage. This group wore caps that I knew for a calcified fact no other black men had ever worn atop their heads. They weren't infantry. These caps were embroidered in gold with the crossed swords that meant they were better. They were the best. Like Sheridan, they were cavalry. They were riding soldiers.

"Company halt! Parade rest!" their top sergeant called out. The ground beneath us thundered as all the men stomped a foot down and set their rifle butts down next to the toes of their boots.

"To the right!" the sergeant bellowed. Every soldier jerked his head toward his right shoulder and stared hard into the shadows where the jingle of a bridle and some loud snorts told us a man ahorseback waited.

"Salute!" Their hands snapped up so hard and so fast that I was sure some prissed-up white commander was waiting out there to make his big entrance. Maybe it was even that show-off Boy General Custer with his greased-up yellow ringlets. I heaved a sigh of disgust and bid farewell to the little fairy tale I'd just been telling myself where my people were the equal of whites, running the show, being saluted. That happy vision crumpled: the white boss was coming.

The ones up near the front of the crowd saw him first. It made me sick the way the men pawed the hats from their heads, children pointed, and women put a hand to their mouths or sent fingers fluttering at their necks.

If I hadn't been boxed in so tight I'd of left then and there. The last thing I ever intended on doing again in my life was stare up at some white man lording it over me atop a horse. With Solomon's arm still cocooning my shoulders and Clemmie snugged up next to me, though, I reckoned I could stomach the sight of this showboating jackass making his grand entrance.

But the commander who rode up to the edge of the stage wasn't white. In fact, he had skin near as dark as my own, fine full lips, a strong, wide nose, and a high, noble forehead. He dismounted, stepped onto the stage and gazed out at us. Though the soldier had never seen me before, he immediately picked me out of the crowd and stared right into my eyes.

I didn't know how it was possible, but he knew me. I was for God sure of it because, for the second time that night, a ghost had appeared. Like Clemmie, Wager Swayne had come back to me.

Chapter 25

S ister, what's taken you?" Clemmie hissed in my ear.

"Clemmie, I know him. I know that man. And he knows me. He recognizes me."

Clemmie snorted. "Yeah, that man recognizes you all right. Recognizes you and every other calf-eyed female out here mooning after him."

Clemmie was right. All the women had been struck dumb by the sight of the soldiers. And deaf, dumb, *and* blind by the sight of one of our men ahorseback, riding tall and proud commanding them all.

"Put a blue jacket on any old hog," Clemmie said, "and women lose they minds. Put a gun in his hands, mount him top a prize steed? Lordy God, I mean."

Still I couldn't stop staring.

"Girl, quit eye-eating the man," Clemmie ordered.

But I couldn't. Those were the lips I had taken my first and only kiss from. I knew they were. I felt it down to the tips of my toes. And, the way he looked at me? In spite of his eyes being bandaged when we met, I was sure as the sun rises in the east that he knew me. That he felt the connection I felt.

Clemmie whispered, "Solomon's getting jealous."

"What? Solomon?" I whispered. "Jealous? You mean me and Solomon? Naw, sister, ain't like that at all. He's just a friend."

But Solomon's arm tightening around my shoulder, pulling me back the tiniest bit away from my soldier, wasn't a friend's arm. Clemmie saw that and hissed into my ear, "Might not be like that for you, but I know a jealous man when I see one."

I cut my eyes as far as I could without turning my head and there it was, clear as day, Solomon glaring up at my soldier, tight-jawed and stiff-necked with jealousy. He snugged me in closer.

"What I tell you?" Clemmie asked in a low voice, proud of all she knew about reading the ways of men.

"But he's so . . ." Though the band was ripping through one of Sheridan's favorite songs, "Nelly Bly," and Solomon couldn't have heard me over the banjos plunking along with the horns, I still whispered the last word, ". . . old."

Clemmie looked him up and down. "Still got his own teeth. Hair. Maybe he ain't no hero on a white horse, but I tell you one thing."

"What's that?"

"That man is the reason you alive."

"Naw, sister. *I'm* the reason I'm alive. Me and General Sheridan. Clemmie, you seen it yourself. Sheridan picked me out special that night on the farm. I was the General's girl. No one dared lay a hand on me."

"Yeah? Fine, if that makes you happy, then you go on and believe that a white man, a general, was watching out for you. You also go on and believe a hero in a blue jacket's gon pluck you up, ride away with you on the back of his pure white horse."

Clemmie wasn't being ugly when she said that. Just speaking the truth that anyone with two eyes could see. I always regarded myself as a person who faced facts head-on. And the fact here was: girls as plain as me didn't catch the notice of a man fine as the one who'd dismounted and was now standing at attention with his men. Girls like me counted their blessings if a man as good as Solomon cared to put his arm about her shoulders.

The final, and most important, fact of all was this: no matter how I might dream it was not so, Wager Swayne had died. I had seen him carried away to be buried. Those were the facts and I saw that I better figure out how to accept them, and do it fast, or miss my chance.

With one whip of his baton, the band director snapped the song shut. The musicians left the stage and the sergeant took it. He strode out and studied us until even the slightest whisper and cough had died away into a breathless silence.

I leaned forward, straining to hear every word he spoke, so that I could match them with how my soldier spoke. No matter what sense and the facts told me, no matter that he'd never choose me now, no matter that I'd seen him carried off to the burying pit, I still believed and I still had to know.

He spoke. "The war has been won! We are free!"

For a second the silence held. It was like we had all just heard the news for the first time. Then everyone went to whooping and hollering, happier and lifted higher than we had been even when we saw Robert E. Lee surrender. I couldn't open my mouth, though. I was lost in comparing my memory of the soldier's voice with the one I was hearing. They matched. I believed again. That was Wager Swayne.

The crowd quieted down and he started back in. He said, "I am . . ." Then time stopped while I waited for him to say the name I knew was his: Wager Swayne.

". . . First Sergeant Levi Allbright . . ."

Levi Allbright.

". . . of Troop D, Ninth Cavalry, and I come to you tonight with a message."

As the sergeant spoke, I understood why I had believed that he knew me. He stared at every one of us, man, woman, and child, the way he had at me. Like he knew us. The real us. Not the pitiful bunch we were then. No, Sergeant Allbright saw who freedom would make us into.

"Men of color," he went on, his voice sounding less and less like my soldier's with every word. "We must use our freedom well." This voice now rang out strong and vibrant with life and clear as church bells on Sunday morning. Compared to it, Wager Swayne had sounded like what he was, a dying man. My dreams had gotten the better of me. Made me see, and for a moment hear, what wasn't there. Much as I wished it, this wasn't the kind and true man who had touched my face and breathed his last to the sound of my voice. The only place where that sweet soul still lived on was in my dreams and no amount of wishing otherwise would ever change it.

"We must heed the words of Brother Frederick Douglass well," First Sergeant Levi Allbright proclaimed. "'Once let the black man get upon his person the brass letters, U.S., let him get an eagle on his button, and a musket on his shoulder and bullets in his pocket, there is no power on earth which can deny that he has earned the right to citizenship!' My brothers in freedom, let us earn that right!"

Solomon took his arm from my shoulders and the three of us clapped until our palms smarted. Sergeant Allbright couldn't speak two words without the cheers breaking out again, but he was a commander and knew how to make himself heard. He told us that the army had set up six brand-new colored regiments that'd be sent out west of the Mississippi to fight the heathen savages.

Most important, we'd get paid thirteen dollars a month. After a lifetime of earning naught but parched corn and floggings, that was a sum to make your head spin. Then he added one last particular that made it all seem like he was laying out a path specially for me to follow. "Our commander is to be General Philip Sheridan, whom Lincoln has named Governor of the Fifth Military District."

I glanced at Solomon. He was nodding, and I reckoned he was as pleased as I was that we had the chance to serve with our old commander again.

"I grew up out West," Sergeant Allbright continued, "and I know that a new world awaits us there. A world of promise and plenty, where a man can be judged as a man. Uncle Sam stood up and fought a mighty war so we might be free. Now, I say to you all tonight, my brothers in freedom, stand up with your Uncle Sam and help him win the fight to make the West a land of peace and prosperity for all. A land where we can live our lives and raise our children to be free citizens of these United States!"

Oh, we cheered aplenty at that. Brothers and sisters alike.

"A recruitment depot will be established in town tomorrow. Inspections start at dawn. Those qualified will be transported to Jefferson Barracks in St. Louis to be trained for service in the United States Army. Who will join me?" he shouted, holding a hand high. All the men shot their hands up. "Who will join your brothers in the Ninth Cavalry?"

The brass band broke into a march that could barely be heard over the crowd roaring like the Gates of Heaven had just been swung open for them as Sergeant Levi Allbright and his men marched offstage. Even Solomon was swept up in the jubilation, waving his hat over his head and shouting hurrahs for the mighty Ninth as the soldiers marched away.

I had to holler in his ear for him to hear me. "You gonna join up?"

"Me? What they want an old man like me for?"

"It's like you always say," I reminded him, "you need an old dog for a hard road."

He tipped a little smile at hearing his own words come back to him and said, "Tell you what, though, I'd sign on as cook if it meant I'd be feeding our . . . our . . ." His voice wobbled and he stopped for a few seconds before he could finally finish up. "Our own boys wearing, really wearing, the blue suit."

There was too much feeling in both of us for talk, so I took his hand and squeezed it. Solomon's eyes snapped open wide and, after considering for a moment, he squeezed my hand back. An understanding passed between us then that somehow the two of us, maybe even our children if the Lord saw fit, were going to be part of the new world out West where black men wore the blue suit and rode horseback and defended their own.

A fiddle band took the stage and tore into a lively breakdown and clumps of dancing and whooping erupted here and there.

"Cathy," Clemmie said, her cheeks flaming with excitement. "My unit leaves tomorrow. I'm going with them. Come with me. Both y'all. We can be together again. Things be different for black folk out West."

"What you say, Queenie?" Solomon asked. "Baby sis is right. They'd hire us no question. You, me, Clemmie, and Matildy out West? Cooking would still be better than a day of picking cotton, right?"

"Go with them to cook?" I asked.

"What else you thinking about?"

"Enlisting, of course. In the cavalry."

"What?" Solomon said, like he hadn't heard me right.

Before he could say anything else, I rushed to ask, "Aren't you about sick of cooking? I know I am. Solomon, listen, you're not too old to enlist. Wear the blue suit. I could . . . I could—"

"Uh-uh," he said, trying to stop what he knew I was about to say.

I said it anyway. "Solomon, I could enlist with you."

His mouth dropped open, but before he could object, I rushed to remind him, "Lots of girls did it during the war. You know they did."

Solomon laughed, pretending I was joking, and told Clemmie, "Now I know for sure your sister is crazy as a betsy bug."

"Crazy?" Clemmie said. "That girl is wild! Wild as an acre of snakes. Always has been. You never seen the like. She be dead now our granma hadn't thrown a protection spell over her."

I ignored Clemmie and told Solomon, "Solomon, I'm serious. We go in together like them other couples you say you seen, we can do it. *I* can do it. Be hard. But we'd have each other's back. I'd be looking out for you way you've always done for me. Where else we gon make thirteen dollar a month? That's twenty-six between the two of us. We do our hitch, two, three year? We'd have enough saved up to buy us a place. Place out West where we can live the way we want to live. No one ever tell us what to do again."

Solomon said to Clemmie, "Tell this fool to stop talkin' like a crazy lady."

"Why not?" I asked. "They did it. Them other females. Why can't I?"

"Why not?" Solomon asked. "How about it was wartime for starters. Everyone spread all out in tents. Off by themselves. And those young soldier boys? The drummers? Most of them *looked* like girls. And since it was wartime, army let anyone in. You had teeth enough to rip open a powder cartridge, you were in. Peacetime be a whole other deal. No Rebels trying to destroy the country, they gone get picky. Have a hard look at what they're letting in. Top of all that, all them other females were white."

"What?" I interrupted, tired of his eternal gloominess. "You don't think I'm good enough to wear the blue suit? My color wrong?"

"Not your color we're talking about, you know that."

Solomon drew away. I was left alone and, after all the merriment, lonely. This mournful feeling caused me to see clear what I was doing: throwing away what I had right in front of me to go chase after a dream didn't even exist just like I'd mooned after a soldier who no longer existed. I needed to be the girl I believed I was. The one who faced facts. Right then and there, I made up my mind.

"Solomon," I said, "I'd rather die than stay here in the South. I want to go out West, but I can't do it alone. Wouldn't be safe on my own. I'd rather join up and serve. But, if I did, without a partner, other soldiers'd kill me or worse if they ever found out. No, can't risk either one alone. The three of us, though, you, me, Matildy, out West, we stand a chance of making us a decent life. Have some dignity. Some respect. Have . . ." I paused. "We'd have each other. How's that sound?"

Clemmie put in, "Sounds like you're proposing a damned tactical maneuver's what it sounds like. Solomon, what I think my sister is saying is, I think she's asking you to marry her."

Solomon nodded slowly. "That so? Thought she might be."

"Well?" I said, already getting huffy at him not jumping at my proposal.

"Well," Solomon started off, then stopped, took my hand, looked into my eyes, and said, "I suppose that'd be all right."

Maybe the words don't sound romantic writ on the page, but we were pledging our lives to each other and that beat romantic all to smash in my book. Solomon and I would leave the misery of the South and go out West. We stared into each other's eyes, and nodded: the deal was done.

The fiddle band began sawing out a rousing version of "Leather Britches." Solomon took his crumpled top hat off, bowed at the waist, and asked if he might have the pleasure. Then he whirled me into his arm and spun me around until the lights and faces all smeared together. My head kept whirling even after Solomon was ripped out of my arms.

I have recounted what happened next a million times in my head and never once found a way to stop it. To make it all come out different. Only in memory can I force those few seconds to pause. I was standing there, wobbling and laughing, for I thought Solomon was having a bit of fun turning me loose after spinning me like a top, when I saw that a white man had grabbed Solomon. It was Dupree.

Quick as a rattler striking, without a word spoken, Dupree stabbed a bowie knife into Solomon's gut, pulled it down hard with both hands, yanked it out, and disappeared into the crowd.

Chapter 26

L ay that whip on, girl!" I yelled up to Clemmie sitting in the driver's seat of our wagon. I was in the back tending to Solomon, my hand on the spot where the knife had stabbed in, pressing hard to keep the life from flowing out of him.

"Camp's not far," I told Solomon. "You're gon see Sheridan's personal surgeon. Puny as that trashy rascal was, you'll probably only need a stitch or two."

I had nestled Matildy on Solomon's chest so he'd have the comfort of her twining about him while I cooed gentle as a mourning dove for him to rest easy.

"We'll get the General's doc, I promise. You be fine. Trip out West'll be a vacation for you now. Pretty sneaky of you to fix it so's I'll be the one holding the reins, working that jerk line the whole way." I tried to make a joke, but it hung false in the air and only showed off the truth of how scared I was.

Solomon reached up, pulled me close, and in a strangled, raspy voice said, "Cathy, I got money inside my jacket. Take it. Go out West."

"Solomon Yarnell," I said, anger boiling up the way it always did when I wanted to snuff out fear or sadness or weakness. "I told you, I don't want to hear that talk."

"Cathy." He held my eyes. "I'm dying. Let me do it in a bed. Then bury me. Proper."

"No, Solomon. Not gon be that way. We're going out West. You, me, Clemmie, Matildy. Things be different out West."

"Cathy, we never lied to each other, did we?"

"No, Solomon, we didn't."

"Not the time to start now, is it?"

I refused to answer. Refused to let another good man pronounce a verdict I would never be ready to hear.

"Cathy, take the money."

I looked about, frantic for some sign of camp ahead, for help, for a way to stop what was happening. Up ahead, in the darkness, I caught the glimmer of a lantern burning in the window of a cabin at the edge of a burned-out plantation. I hollered for Clemmie to make for it. Double-quick.

"You be in a bed fore you know it," I said, clinging tight to Solomon's hand. "Then we can get you doctored up proper."

Solomon laid his hand on top of mine, stroked it as gentle as he always stroked Matildy, pulled it to his lips, kissed it, and said, "Mighty glad I got to know you, Cathy Williams. You are something else, Queenie. Something else entirely."

Those were the last words of Solomon Yarnell.

Chapter 27

"Stop right there!" a freedwoman ordered, pointing an old muzzle-loader at me as I approached the door of her cabin. She stepped out into the moonlight followed by three children, two young girls and an older boy who held a lantern high.

The woman was a teeny little thing, down to gristle and grit, eyes big and wild as a cornered possum. It was no trick seeing that she'd been beat down hard by slavery and even harder by life after Sheridan burned the plantation house and the crops and the white folks fled, leaving her to fend for herself and her little ones. I could appreciate that she was ready to blow the next person who did her wrong to kingdom come.

"Ma'am," I said, kindly as could be, "I don't want nothin' from you. I got a man here gone just now to where the woodbine twineth. A good man. Needs a peaceful spot to take his eternal rest. That's all I'm asking of you. Just let me bury him here."

She didn't answer.

"I'll pay you."

"How much?"

"Four bits."

"Lemme see."

I counted out a few of the coins I had taken from Solomon's pocket. She snatched them away and tucked them into her bodice without ever lowering the barrel of her muzzleloader. For another two cents, she let me have the use of a half-burned shovel that turned my palms black when I held it. Her boy, Tad, led us around back. The youngest girl, Bethany, followed.

I picked a spot beneath a tall willow with branches long enough that they'd stroke Solomon's grave when a south wind blew. The digging felt good. Stabbing the shovel into the earth hard and regular held off the sadness. Clemmie offered to spell me, but it seemed I couldn't pry my fingers from the handle, so she sat holding Matildy who was chittering with nervousness.

"She'th thcared," said young Bethany, a round-headed child who was missing her two front teeth along with the fear of strangers that kept her mother at the open door, firearm trained on us.

"You wanna hold her?" Clemmie asked.

The girl had a gentle touch that calmed Matildy until Solomon's pet was all but purring in her lap.

With help from the boy, Tad, I worked steady through the night, Bethany chatting away the whole time. "We been livin' on flour dust," she informed us, seeming to speak mostly to Matildy, as though she'd been waiting her whole life for a creature to come along who'd listen to her and her alone. "I's the onliest one small enough to crawl up into the bolting chest after the white folk done locked up the mill and refugeed off down to Richmond. I swept up near three bushel!" she bragged to Matildy. "I picked out the worms and Mammie been baking us up real bread. Leastwise until we run out. We were gon starve so Mammie kilt our mule, Carl, and we ate off him until he went bad cuz we don't have no salt and the Yanks burnt up the smokehouse."

Near dawn I hit rock and asked for a pickax to finish the job, but Tad said the Yankees had not only burned the plantation and the crops, and carried off the livestock, they'd smelted down every plow, harrow, spade, pickax, and anything on the place could be used for bullets. The boy had scavenged the shovel, a plow, and some nails from the ashes of another place been burned out. But no pickax. "Yanks even took our daddy," he finished mournfully.

I didn't mind Sheridan doing the Rebs that way, but he ought to of spared those who were never with them and already been punished more severe than need be.

With no further digging to be done, Clemmie and I said the prayers for the dead that Mama and Iyaiya had taught us. I took what I found in Solomon's pocket: his broken pocket watch, a small button-polishing card, his folding knife, and pipe. Soon as I could, I would get a personal effects box from the graves detail and have them store his things in a pretty little pine container for when Solomon's kin came looking for him. I promised Solomon that I would see him soon in my dreams and in the times when I missed him and in all the moments when I went to ask him something and he wouldn't be there.

When we finished, Clemmie told me, "My unit's moving out at daybreak. They'll take you on. Always need another washerwoman."

I said nothing.

"Cathy, you can't go out West now. Not by yourself. Not without a man to protect you. Come with me. Least we'll be together."

I saw myself scrubbing my life away, my hands chapped and burning from lye soap, no more count to anyone than a draft horse. Or having some ruttish stranger work me over top a barrel for a couple of taters. Or even a sparkly pair of earbobs. Both prospects made me feel like crawling in next to Solomon.

"Cathy, you hear me? We runnin' outta time."

The long night's weariness fell on me heavy as a wet quilt.

"What other choice do you have?" she asked. "These are lawless times. Woman without a man to protect her? No telling. They'll kill you, Cathy. Or worse. Come with me. We'll find you a decent man, get you married off, you'll do all right. Stay alive. Aren't you gon say something?"

When I spoke, my own words startled me for they came out of a place deeper inside of me than I even knew was there. I said, "Mama didn't put me on this earth to be some man's brood sow or work ox."

Then I fell so silent and so still that Clemmie said, "Cathy, you scaring me. You have that Africa look in your eyes. You talking to Iyaiya?"

"I'm talking," I finally said, "but she ain't answering."

"Well, I'm answering and I'm telling you for true, you have no choice. Now let's light a shuck."

My head knew she was right, but I couldn't convince my legs she was right and I remained planted next to Solomon's grave. Bethany was beside me cooing to Matildy and feeding her night crawlers been turned up by the digging. My fingers finally turned loose of the shovel and I sagged onto the ground. I was whipped. As a strip of pink cracked across the far horizon, I accepted the truth: I would be a washerwoman. I would be the lowest of the low, a woman bent over a black cauldron, stirring dirty rags with a stick. I had no other choice.

I was about to follow Clemmie when two lonely figures appeared, sil-houetted against the early dawn sky. It took me a minute to credit what I was seeing: the boy and his mother were plowing, furrowing the earth in a desperate attempt to get a crop in before the weather turned. The plow was too tall for Tad, but he held the forked handles strong and sure as a grown man. Up ahead, wearing the harness and pulling the plow, was his little bitty slip of a mother. Head down, she dragged the iron tool through the earth with will more than strength.

Clemmie was boarding the wagon when I told her to go on ahead with-out me.

"I am not leaving without you, sister," she yelled down at me. "I leave you here and you'll for God sure die then Iyaiya'll haunt me forever and I am not having that. Come on with me now," she ordered. "At least you be alive."

"And spend this one life the ancestors gave me scrubbing the shit stains out some man's dirty drawers? That's not my idea of living."

Clemmie stared hard, fixing to put up a fuss. But I was still the big sister, so instead, she moaned, "Oh, Lord, you got that look again means there's no talking to you anymore."

"My mind is made up."

"Damn, girl, you stubborn as a cross-eyed mule. Always were." Clemmie heaved a deep sigh, turned to bend into the wagon bed where she retrieved my yagger, climbed down off the wagon, and held it out to me. "Here. Take it. You be needing this a damn sight more than me."

I waved away the offer. "Naw, you keep it. Wagon, too. Needs to be re-turned to Sheridan. I can't be sashaying about with no weapon out in the open. We ain't that free yet."

Clemmie plunged her hand between her bosoms, and plucked out a little box-lock pistol. "Here, take my pepper pot then. Woman alone." She *tsk-tsked* and shook her head in despair. "You better have something to protect yourself with."

I fished out some of Solomon's bills and forced Clemmie to take them, saying, "Get you another little gun. Something you can always have ready to hand. Whether you got a man or not, a woman's always alone. Always needs to be ready to stand up for herself." I gently traced the round of her plump cheek. She dropped her head low, throwing her arms around me, so that the top of her head was a bouquet beneath my nose, and I whispered into it, "Be strong, little sister."

Clemmie hugged me ferocious tight, muttering, "Damn you, damn you, damn you. Damn your stubbornness." She turned me loose and pivoted quickly away so I couldn't see her face, but my dress was wet where she'd buried her face.

The light of the new day shone on Clemmie's back as she drove away from me. In spite of how she'd plumped up, given herself more padding against a world she'd learned too young was wicked and mean, her shoulders were stooped again, like she was trying to crawl inside herself and hide, the way she had after Old Mister took her. We were both pretending to be tougher than we really were, but Clemmie had a natural sight more tenderness to cover up than I ever did. She couldn't do what I saw I was called to do. She couldn't be a woman alone amongst men.

After watching until she turned off and disappeared behind a low rise, I called out to the little girl, "Bethany, come here." The little girl approached reluctantly, cradling Matildy in her arms, not wanting to give her new friend back.

"You, too," I hollered to her shy big sister. The sister peered back over her shoulder like I was hailing someone behind her. Finally, she crept out of the shadows of the front door holding a skimpy bag of seed, clearly meant for planting as soon as the sun was full up.

"How you call your name?" I asked her. Though she was but a young girl, I saw that she was someone to be trusted.

"Mercy Jane," she answered.

"All right then, Mercy Jane, I want you to take this." Solemnly, I placed most of what remained of Solomon's money in her hand. "Tuck it away," I added when she didn't pull her hand back. "Now, I want you to give that to your mother and tell her to pack all y'all up and leave this place. Go with the Yankees. Follow them back up North. Ain't nothing here for y'all but hunger and heartache. Never will be. Go on, now," I ordered. "Tell her."

Though so skinny you'd of thought her bones would clatter like a skeleton's when she ran, the girl took off running with a heavy, serious step that made me trust her even more.

Bethany held Matildy up to me and, though I longed for the comfort of the creature's silky body and the feel of Solomon's presence it carried, she could not come with me where I had to go. I asked the little girl, "Do you want to keep her?"

Bethany nodded and answered solemnly, "Yeth."

"Can you take care of her? Keep her safe?" She reminded me of Clemmie when she was young. Clemmie, too, had been the sort of girl who was born yearning for something small and soft to care for. Who, if she had a scrap of cloth and a walnut, would turn it into a baby doll and glue moss to it for hair. Me? I'd blow my nose on the scrap of cloth, crack the walnut open and eat it. So, when I said, "Like a mama with her baby?" Bethany's eyes lit up and I knew no harm would ever come to Solomon's friend.

"Her name's Matildy," I said as I started down the road.

I watched Bethany caper away to join her siblings who were all gathered up around their mama, a tight little tribe who had each other. I thought of how I'd of had that with Solomon and something twisted inside of me so hard I stopped dead and didn't believe I could go on. Not alone.

But the rising sun was as warm on my back as a hand pushing me toward what I intended to do and I set off again. I hastened my step until I was running. My mind was made up: what the world wouldn't give Cathy Williams, Cathy Williams was bound to take.

BOOK TWO

~

Heading Out West

Chapter 28

⁓

"W huh the—" As soon as Dupree's mouth was open, I stuffed his words back into it with a dirty rag. The next sound he heard was the hammer of Clemmie's pepper pot cocking back right next to his ear and me telling him that if he made one more sound, he'd meet his Jesus that very day. I whispered even though the passed-out pack of degenerates littering the ground around the campfire they'd returned to like the morons they were wouldn't have stirred had an artillery round landed in their midst.

Still half jugged and entirely terrified, Dupree offered little resistance when I ordered him at gunpoint farther into the woods.

The forest floor was carpeted with a deep layer of pine needles that deadened our footsteps. I marched Dupree down to where the Appomattox River, churned to mud by the horses and men of two armies, was flanked by a wall of granite that would do to baffle the sound of the little revolver being fired point-blank into a man.

Not wanting to die next to a desolate mud wallow, the bushwhacker whirled around and made to grab the gun from my hand. His buckskin shirt and britches were stiff with filth and Dupree lumbered about with no more grace than a shaggy bear. I easily sidestepped his lunge and he stumbled face-first into the gravelly muck. He flipped over and lay there panting, two white eye holes and one pink, near-toothless mouth in all that slimy brown.

"Rebel," I told him, "you already given me two reasons to blow out your lamp. Don't give me another."

But he did. He scrambled over and made a grab for my ankle. Lord, the man moved slow. I stepped hard on the top of his hand, trapped it beneath my shoe and the sharp gravel and ground down hard. Dupree shrieked as the shards of granite cut into his palm. Though any motion caused his hand to be mashed even deeper against the pointed stones, he wriggled about and yanked on my ankle until I kicked him in the head with my free foot.

Sometime later, when Dupree came to, he noticed immediately that he was sprawled out on his back in the mud, naked as the day he was born. "Whuh? Whuh?" he sputtered, splashing through the shallow water as he tried to crawfish away from the barrel of the revolver pointed straight at his little nubbin.

"Take your boots off," I ordered.

"You can have them," he said, obeying. "I'd of given you the buckskins, too," he added for I was now wearing his filthy garments.

After the boots came off, he struggled to his knees, put his hands together and begged me to let him live. "Listen, I got money. Silver them planters buried. It's all melted down. Buried in a secret place. I'll take you right to it. You can have it. Have it all. Please . . ."

He started blubbering so hard I could barely make out the lies he was confabulating about the fortune in Secesh silver he was hiding so he could go on living off the weevily hardtack he stole from the Union army.

I ordered him to shut up and get to his feet then took my sweet time circling that miserable specimen shivering in the cold, hands cupped over his crotch, runty legs bowed out, arms skinny as hickory branches. If this item'd come wrapped in a black skin, he wouldn't have fetched three dollars on the auction block. He'd of ended his life swinging a grub hoe down in Mississippi.

"Please, please, please—"

"Shut your trap and listen."

His shameless begging fell off to a whimper of the most pitiable sort. When he finally shut up, I advised him, "Next time someone tells you to take your hand off a lady—"

I paused to shoot off the big toe of his left foot and he dropped on his ass, howling and clutching at his four-toed paw as the blood gushed through his fingers and down his skinny shank, before I concluded, "You best listen to her."

Chapter 29

Dupree's sodden pants and buckskin shirt hung on me like a sweated-up horse blanket and smelled a hundred times worse. The drop-front britches did contain one welcome surprise, though. In the pocket was a straight-edge razor. The bushwhacker must of stolen it off a Yankee for it had a fine whalebone handle with a four-master sailing boat scrimshawed into it. I opened it, sliced off my braids, and crammed the stinking coonskin hat onto my head. I didn't know what I looked like. Sure not a woman. Probably something slightly below a man. A muskrat trapper maybe.

Thus disguised, I stood at the edge of the woods and peered out, afraid to take the first step into the new life I had determined would be mine. Though it was barely daylight and there wasn't another soul on the Richmond–Lynchburg stage road into Appomattox Court House, I felt like the noon-day sun and a thousand eyes were waiting to drill into me the instant I revealed myself. Holding my breath the way I used to do back home when I'd jump off Sunset Bluff into the swimming hole, I stepped out of the deep shadows and set to marching back into town.

The road was lined with rail fences that made long, zigzagging curves around land that might have been lush once upon a time before soldiers, blue and gray, had knocked the rails down and trampled the fields into muck. Shivering from the chill and weighted so bad with the heaviness of missing Solomon that I wanted to sit down and never rise again, I put my sorrow away sure as I'd put Old Mister away, whispered, "Hay foot. Straw foot. Hay foot. Straw foot," and ordered myself forward.

So intent was I on hunching over and shrinking away under Dupree's coonskin cap that I was considerably spooked when, first one, then another, and another silent group of men, two and three at a time, emerged from the woods, all heading in my direction. And not just any old men. White men. Enemy white men. Glum Rebels who'd been camping rough with the twigs and leaves in their hair and grimy faces and hands to prove it

In spite of looking more creature than human, for the first time in my life, I felt positively womanly. It suddenly seemed like the nubs of my small breasts had grown into massive udders certain to betray me and snatch my dream away. I ducked my head low as a turtle pulling back into her shell, yanked Dupree's disgusting cap down even further over my eyes, and hunched so far forward that the only thing I could see were my feet.

There wasn't much more to the village of Appomattox than a tavern, the courthouse it was named for, a general store, a squatty little law office, a few houses, a three-story redbrick jail with so few windows the place made me pity those unlucky enough to know its grim justice. But it was mobbed that day. Rebels. Yanks. Ex-slaves, they were all there.

The ex-Rebs all headed for the Clover Hill Tavern where passes that marked them as paroled prisoners of war were being handed out that would allow them safe passage home. Quick as I could, I skinned off away from the Rebs and sidled up to a cluster of men of color. I had to pass unnoticed until I located the recruitment depot.

Space immediately cleared around me due to the excessive ripeness of Dupree's raggedy duds, but I could still hear muttering behind me with one asking the other where he thought the recruitment depot the heroic sergeant had referred to the night before might be.

We were milling about like cattle in a pen, shuffling one way, then the other, none brave enough to ask a white stranger for directions when who should strut up but Justice Vikers, the bespectacled fellow with the piercing voice who'd read out the Surrender Agreement. He led a band of followers that had been made brash by the bold words that swirled around Vikers's head thick as a cloud of gnats.

"What ho?" he called out when he came upon us milling about. "What cause for your delay, good fellows? Have you lost your way in this great metropolis?" I once overheard a bunch of actors putting on a play for the white folk and they had the same high-toned manner of speech as Vikers was putting on.

"Is it the recruitment depot you're seeking?" he asked, switching the words around so what you'd expect to go first come last and vicey versey. "Why don't you simply read the notice clearly posted before you?"

And, sure enough, there was a sheet of paper hung from the square head of a nail sticking out the front of one of the Clover Hill Tavern's porch columns. It was hard to miss for a reading person. For us, however, a piece of paper scribbled up with writing was of as little interest as a gold nugget to a sparrow flying overhead.

Vikers stepped forward, making a show of clearing his throat and cleaning the lenses of his spectacles a time or two before he read the directions written on the paper to himself. Instead of just telling us the way, he led us a couple of miles outside of town, talking the whole way. By the second mile, the peculiar voice and high-toned manner that I had been so taken with when he was reading out the Surrender Agreement was starting to grate. It was plain that, like the actors he reminded me of, Vikers had a need for an audience. The more adoring, the better.

"You were right about that one," I whispered to Solomon. Imagining his know-it-all chuckle comforted me and I shambled on.

Vikers led us to an abandoned farm a mile or two east of town set upon a charred field that sported nothing but a few scorched stalks of what once might have been a fair corn crop along with a rickety old barn that had somehow survived the Burning. With my destination in plain sight, I moved out ahead of Vikers and his followers.

I searched the crowd both hoping and fearing I'd catch a glimpse of Sergeant Allbright. Though I'd of given considerable to look upon that fine face again, I did not want him to see me in my current degraded condition. But neither he, nor any soldier of color, was to be found among the soldiers manning the depot. White soldiers pushed us into lines with shoves so unnecessarily rough that I feared once again we were to be tricked by the whites who were really running the show. I would have turned and left then and there but for the fact that I had no other place on earth to go.

A row of three tables with white soldiers sitting behind them were lined up outside the barn. A few ex-slaves, twisting hats in their big work-hardened hands, stood in front of each one, answering questions while the soldiers filled in their answers on enlistment forms.

Enlistment.

Suddenly, it felt like I was high up atop that shot tower again or someplace a heap higher than I had ever intended to go. I couldn't catch my breath for I'd gone to panting too hard and fast to pull in a proper lungful of air. My hands shook until my fingers near rattled. Sweat that had nothing to do with the gathering heat of the day beaded up beneath the coonskin cap and came creeping down until it was dripping off my temples. Since Mama didn't hold with giving in to emotions, my whole life I'd had to wait for my body to let me know what I was feeling, and at that very moment I came to know that I was terrified.

Chapter 30

⸻

"Form up! Form up!" a bucktoothed lion roared into my face and I barely stifled a shriek that would have announced me as the girliest of girls. On second glance I saw that my nerves had got the better of me, and it was only a round-faced corporal with a bushy blond mustache and beard and front teeth that poked out to where he couldn't close his mouth over them.

I tried to step out of line so I could get my hands to quit shaking and take in the lay of the land before it was my turn at the enlistment table, but the bucktoothed corporal jobbed me a smart one in my hindquarters with the butt of his rifle and ordered, "Step up, boy! Step up! You're on army time now!"

The private behind the table squared up the pile of forms in front of him, dipped his pen into a little ink bottle, flicked the excess off, and asked, "Name?"

Caught off guard, I squeaked out, "What?" sounding, for the one and only time in my life not just female, but feeble-minded to boot.

From behind me came Vikers's high-pitched cackle. His cronies joined in laughing at me. The sweat ran down my face in rivulets.

A drop of ink plopped onto the form from the tip of the private's pen as he stared, blinking into the early morning sun up at me, and ordered, "State your first name."

When I responded by opening and closing my mouth like a gaffed bass, he and his buddy at the next table exchanged little snorts of sad amusement directed, not just at me, but at my people in general. "Step aside!" he ordered. "We got men to process. Ranks to fill. Step aside!"

"Naw, naw," a gentle voice behind me muttered. "Give the man a second." The stranger leaned in and whispered in my ear, "Don't have to be your slave name. Go on. Pick your own name your own self."

The man's kindness steadied me and I said, "Williams."

"Is Williams your first name?" the private barked. "Or is Williams your last name? If Williams is your first name, do they call you Billies for short?"

Oh, how the white soldiers and Vikers and his crew, standing behind me, snickered about that weak little joke.

I tucked my head down, almost crushing my chin into my neck to make certain my voice'd be good and low, and said, "William. First name's William." My voice was so deep I'd of made John Henry sound like he ought to of been serving tea at a quilting bee.

"Last name!" the private barked.

"Cathy, sir!" I barked back even louder.

"Cathay," he said as he wrote down my name the way he heard it. "You are eighteen, aren't you?"

"Every bit of it," I snapped right back, as he'd made it clear that eighteen was what he and the U.S. Army wanted me to be. He filled that in, handed me the paper, and told me to proceed to the barn.

I stepped out of line and got my first look at the kind soul who had come to my aid. He was a bull-built country boy, every solid inch of him, with shoulders like a set of smoked hams. His face was broad and open as whatever cotton patch he'd fetched up out of, and when he smiled, his teeth were big and white with a gap between the two front ones probably made him a champion watermelon-seed-spitter. Soon as he finished with his enlistment form, he stepped over to me, his hand stuck out, and said, "Pleased to make your acquaintance, William." He had the velvety-soft, molasses-slow accent of the Deep South, but his hand was big and hard as a hickory knot.

As he told me about " 'nother William I knows back home though he ain't got your height," we took our place in the next line, this one leading into the barn. The whole time, I kept an eye on Vikers. He was a true leader, a man who could influence those around him. What he appeared to be leading his growing crew toward, though, was being bullies, for they mocked and picked on anyone in their vicinity. Most of them he bullied ended up flocking with his gang as it is considerably more entertaining to bully than to be bullied.

When Vikers stepped up to the enlistment table, he made a big deal of taking the pen from the private and sweeping it around in the air several times before plunging it down to the paper to fill in his name and age. His cronies then begged him to do the same for them. Soon they were all signing their Xs on pieces of paper that I took to be IOUs as Vikers collected one from each man whose forms he filled in and signed.

The barn line was barely moving and Vikers and his boys fell in behind us just as the country boy announced to me, "Why, I believe I'll call you Bill. They calls me Lemuel."

To which Vikers squawked out, "Lummox, did you say? You're saying your mammy named you *Lummox*?" In spite of most of them not having the faintest idea what a lummox was, Vikers's followers knew it to be an insult and and cackled loud.

Lemuel took no offense and merely replied, "No, sir, I goes by Lemuel. Not Lum . . . Lummah . . . Whatever you said."

I winced, for, as I'd learned from Mama, being polite to most men, but bullies in particular, was a terrible mistake. Politeness being the first inch of the mile of misery they'd take from you.

"Oh, excuse me for my error," Vikers said.

"Nuthin' to excuse," Lemuel answered, with a gap-toothed smile. "Folks don't hardly never catch it first time." He offered his hand. "I'm Lemuel Powdrell out of Tallapoosa County, Alabama."

"Oh, I have it now," Vikers replied, turning his back on us so as to address his cronies. "Mule. Mule Powdrell."

Being as I hated nothing more in life than a bully, Vikers's insult made the blood pound at my temples. My fists were balling up and, for one second, I almost forgot that I couldn't be Cathy Williams anymore. I was Bill Cathay and my life depended on passing unnoticed.

And passing unnoticed is just what I'd of done had not Vikers then added, "Well, Mule, maybe you two field apes . . ."

Field ape?

Had that little runt just called *me* a field ape or had I gone deaf from hate? The open guffaws of his gang told me I had heard right.

His next words came in loud and clear. "Perhaps you two hadn't noticed, but you're not standing in some field in Hog Dick, Alabama, picking goober peas, so Mule, if you and your odoriferous friend would step forward . . ." He whisked his fingers at us like he was flinging snot off of them.

Lemuel, who wouldn't take up for himself, now did so when the attack included me and muttered, "They ain't no cause to be so ugly."

"Oh, they *ain't, ain't* they?" Vikers singsonged, mocking Lemuel's country accent. Next he brayed out for the benefit of his buddies, "Lincoln should have given these country boys a brain instead of freedom."

Well, that cut it. I wheeled on him and said, "Listen here, Little Man, Lemuel can learn to speak proper, but you ain't never gon learn to be a full-size man."

Because I caught them off guard, a couple of his new buddies laughed. Laughed hard. The one I'd heard being called Greene was a skinny country boy had a head and eyes the shape of almonds with ears placed so high they were near level with his eyebrows. The whole arrangement made him look like a baby possum. The other one, name of Caldwell, was a strapping fellow nearly as solid built as Lemuel. He had a big head and eyes, no neck, and sloping shoulders, all of which gave him a striking resemblance to a six-foot owl.

Little Possum Greene was laughing so hard he had to hang on to Big Owl Caldwell, as Caldwell hooted out, "Hoo-WEE! Little Man, Little Man, Stinky done hit you a straight lick with a crooked stick!" Hooting and gasping, Caldwell even laughed like an owl.

Lemuel joined in with one of those hard sucking-in laughs sounded like a mule braying.

The only one not amused was Vikers, who'd gone flinty and black in the eyes. He cut his boys with a stony gaze and asked in a voice more low and slithery than his usual high and piercing tone, "Caldwell, Greene, did you two suddenly learn to read?"

That tone even more than the words caused them to snap their yaps shut.

Vikers went on, "If you did, then you won't be needing me to watch out for you, will you? Won't need me to read the papers the army's gonna get you to sign. Won't need me to make sure they don't trick you." Vikers shrugged real casual, like it was their funeral and none of his concern. "Who knows? Maybe you'll sign yourself right back into slavery."

You think that didn't bring them to heel? Then you don't know the least little bit about the unimaginable trickery inflicted by whites upon my people. I fought hard against the urge to lick Vikers's boots myself and get on his good side so he'd read for me, too. Before I had time to turn myself into a toadying ass sucker, however, the door of the rickety barn creaked open and a white corporal came out, blinking into the bright sun, and yelling, "Next six men! Step forward!"

Grinning like there was a taffy pull going on inside that barn, Lemuel said, "Come on, Bill, it's our turn," and practically danced inside. Not wanting any further word or scrutiny from Vikers and grateful to Lemuel for shouting out my new man name at every opportunity, I followed him in.

Coming in from the dazzling sun, it took my eyes a bit to adjust to the gloom inside the old barn. For a few seconds, all I could see were horizontal stripes of daylight shining through the gaps between the weathered boards and the dust motes floating through them. The rusty hinges of the barn doors creaked as the soldier slammed them shut then planted himself in front to guard that no one got out.

As soon as my eyes adjusted, I saw that all the men of color, both those being examined and those waiting, were naked as boiled chickens. I stood there, stunned. I can't say exactly what I expected, but it did not involve airing out my particulars before a barnful of naked men. Surely that pair of lady lovers I had seen slurping on each other back to Cedar Creek hadn't been required to show all that God had given them.

Peacetime be a whole other deal. I heard Solomon's voice clear as if he was standing next to me, complete with his told-you-so laugh.

A private holding a musket with a bayonet attached shouted in my ear, "Strip down and line up!" He jerked back sharp, though, when he caught a whiff of Dupree's rank garments.

I stepped forward to where Lemuel was already bent over taking off his britches. He straightened up and became another sturdy trunk in an orchard of dark-barked trees. I froze, conspicuously dressed amidst that forest of naked bodies. The back of my neck prickled and I glanced around to find Vikers studying me like a hawk focused on a baby squirrel. He glared, letting me know that he had a heavy score to settle on account of my mocking him.

"Bill," Lemuel said, "you best shuck off them leathers, man."

"I need to . . ." I pointed vaguely off toward the back of the barn.

Lemuel gave me a knowing nod. "See a man about a horse?"

When I continued searching for a possible escape route that didn't pass by either Vikers or the guard at the barn doors, Lemuel clarified, "Means you got to go wee-wee. You might could slip in behind one them stalls back there."

I shuffled out of the line, and performed the magic trick that all slaves were good at: I turned invisible. Of course being a walking heap of stinking hides helped.

With folks clearing out of the way of my stink shield, I was looking to sashay on out when Lemuel sang out big as glory, "Bill, hey, Bill! I got your place saved right here. Come on now. You up next!"

Chapter 31

~

There were two stations I could be herded to. At each one a doc examined a naked man. At the first, the doctor carefully thumped on a fellow's chest, looked in his eyes, had him show off his grinners, weighed him, measured him, listened to his heart, had him hop about on one leg, then the other and, worst of all, he took a full tour of the recruit's man business. That first doctor was thorough and competent: the last two things on earth I needed at that moment. At the second station was a sawbones with the swimmy eyes, trembling hands, and swollen, rumbud-blotched nose of a dedicated soak. That was my man. I lurched his way.

Figuring the doc'd have sympathy for a fellow stewpot, I stumbled forward like I was loaded to the gunwales, and pretended to trip so as to near fall into his arms. As I suspected, the doc's tippy, hungover stomach lurched at the stink of Dupree's buckskins. Fighting off the heaves, he shoved me as far from himself as his puny arm strength would allow.

"There," he said, speaking into his shoulder. "Just stay right there." Still keeping his distance, the doctor told me to jump up and down. I flapped about a bit, broadcasting even more of Dupree's fragrance.

"Fine, fine, superb specimen," he said into the hand he held in front of his face. Then, in an accent that marked him as a local, he ran down a list of afflictions that would have tried Job, and asked if I had: Tumor. Teeth unable to rip open a musket load. Rupture. Flat feet. Deafness. A wound of the head that impaired judgment. Convulsions.

I couldn't mutter, "Naw, suh," fast enough to keep up with the ailments he was meant to be looking for himself.

Completely ignoring the double yardstick at his side, the doc asked his assistant, "Corporal, what would you put this man's height at?"

The corporal eyeballed me, said, "He's a tall one, sir. Reckon he'd go five nine minimum."

"I concur," Doc said, and that's what the corporal scribbled down on my enlistment form.

"Weight?" he asked next, paying no mind to the scale the good doctor at the first station was making all his men stand on.

Corporal sized me up like he was buying me by the pound. "He's skinny, but looks to be all muscle, sir. He might be tipping one twenty. One thirty."

Doctor shook his head, muttered to the corporal, "And you Yankees insisted that we mistreated these creatures so abominably you had to go and fight a war to 'free' them. Why, look around at these husky bucks." He waved a hand at all the fine young men. "See what excellent condition they are in. Lies. It was all lies. Why, it was in our interest to maintain our property. And we did. Cared for them like prize bulls. It was *my* people who were starving. *My* people who suffered." His voice trembled and his watery eyes got a bit waterier at the injustice. Shaking his head, he signed my form and waved me off toward yet another line.

Two soldiers stood at the head of this line. Beside them were huge piles of army jackets, shirts, suspenders, and trousers. Each recruit who stepped forward was sized up then handed a bundle of those items. I noted that there were two piles of caps. One pile had the hunting horn affixed to it, which marked out the ground-pounders of the infantry. I'd seen enough during the Rebellion to know that their miserable lives held no glory and little more dignity than a slave's had. The other pile, now, those caps were crowned with the crossed sabers of the U.S. Cavalry, the real soldiers like the General and Sergeant Allbright. The ones that rode tall mounted on a fine horse. No question about it, it was the cavalry for me.

"What's your size?" the soldier handing out the duds asked a man in front of me. He held up a pair of britches in each hand and said, "We got too big and too small," and then without bothering to check if the fellow was a size Too Small or Too Big he thrust a uniform at him.

When my turn came, the private snapped the form out of my hand and went to gathering up my bundle without a word about my preferred service. When he popped one of them horn caps atop the bundle, I piped up, "Gimme a saber cap. Cavalry. I'm going for cavalry." I added politely, "If it's all the same to you, sir, I'd prefer to ride."

The private shot his buddy a look that had that combination of twinkly and scary unique to Paddies that meant someone was about to be taken down a notch or get the shit kicked out of him. Usually a painful combination of both. "Foley," he said to his buddy. "Our man here said he'd *prefer* to ride."

Prefer. That was a mistake.

"You don't say," Foley chimed in. "Well now, meself, I'd *prefer* to be carried about in a gilded coach such as emperors and queens and the like *prefer*. What about you, Byrne? What would be your *preferred* mode of transport?"

"Now that you ask, Private Foley, I'd *prefer* to be conveyed by an elephant painted up like a flowered teapot with a great, bloody plume waving about its head like I was the focking lord of all India."

They interrupted their jackass hee-hawing long enough for Byrne to shove the enlistment form in my face, stab a grimy fingernail at something the rumpot doc had written along the side, and read out, "Says 'Infantry.' Savvy?"

"But they never asked me if—"

"This is the army, Sambo. There ain't no asking. You're too focking tall for the cavalry. Get some sturdy boots, boy. It's infantry for you, you _____."

I was hurried off with the two Paddies cussing me out using unnecessary swears of a racial-type nature that I have no intention of repeating. For, as I'd learned during my time with the army, of all the whites, none could beat the Paddies for low-rating people of color. Excepting, of course, the Missouri pukes, Maryland craw thumpers, South Carolina weasels, Texas beef heads, Mississippi whelps, Georgia crackers, Kentucky corn crackers, and soon as they learned to speak American, the Krauts, dagos, Hunkies, and boxheads could also lay on some heavy slurs. I was sure the Bowery Boys I'd met up with on the Shenandoah Campaign meant us no good with their comments, but as no one could understand their New York City chatter, I couldn't swear to it.

Come to think of it, you could count on near any white getting a dig in unless they were abolitionists, Quakers, or your more advanced type of Kraut. And even then, there'd be a Quaker now and again who had once owned slaves and had yet failed to shake off the habit of regarding us as property.

Outside the barn, I stood blinking in the hazy Virginia sunshine watching the naked men pop hands into shirtsleeves and hop from one foot to the other pulling up their army britches. Complaints rang out as they examined the tattered muslin shirts and stained trousers.

"This ain't the blue suit. I signed up for the blue suit."

"These rags ain't fit to scare crows in."

The bucktoothed corporal appeared and informed us, "What you have there is your recruitment issue. Proper uniforms will be issued at Jefferson Barracks in St. Louie. Infantry will form up here tomorrow at five in the morning to begin the march north. Cavalry will move by rail."

March to St. Louie?

I had already marched down the whole of the Shenandoah Valley with Sheridan, I did not intend to spend the next three years of my life wearing out any more shoe leather for the U.S. Army. I would just toss out my papers and head on with the cavalry bunch.

Then the corporal added, "Each one of you must have the proper enlistment form to be admitted to either group."

That was a nut I did not know how to crack.

As I stood there studying that cap with the stupid horn on it weighing out whether putting on a harness and pulling a plow would be any worse than being in the infantry, I caught sight of Vikers and what looked to be his new bodyguards, Greene and Caldwell. The three of them were making a big show of adjusting their caps so that the crossed sabers of the United States Cavalry on the front caught the sunlight and gleamed like gold. Vikers and Greene were shrimp. But Caldwell. He was one of the few men taller than me. Vikers caught me staring and grinned. I don't know how, but he'd managed to get them all into the cavalry.

Chuckling as they passed me by, the possum-faced Greene yelped out, "Enjoy your tramp to St. Louie, Stanky. Might air you out some."

I watched Vikers and his new cronies strut off. Even in the shabby recruitment uniforms, they seemed to stand taller, walk prouder. It was the cap that did it. That cap with the crossed sabers. It was poison for me to have to ask anyone for anything and I already knew that, besides whatever IOU he would make me sign for his help, Vikers would demand a thorough licking of his hindquarters, but I didn't see as I had any choice in the matter.

Chapter 32

fter the necessary parlay with Vikers, I carried my uniform and the enlistment form he'd "adjusted" to the isolated spot on the river where I'd left my woman clothes and carried them to a secluded water hole.

On the bank, I found a nice mossy spot in a patch of sunshine. I hurled the foul buckskins as far away as possible then carefully placed my recruitment issue and the enlistment form that Vikers had fixed for me atop the mossy cushion. I had to keep the paper safe for Vikers's work in changing my future had cost me dear. I couldn't help but admire his precision as he had dabbed what he called his "magic mixture" onto the word "infantry" along with the company I'd been assigned to. I guessed his secret potion to be nothing more than lemon juice and baking soda, but it did the trick, lifting off near all the ink the private had laid down. What specks were left, Vikers picked away at with a pin, his hand steadier and his eye sharper than any I'd seen since watching Daddy do his fine handwork.

When the space was blank, Vikers set the paper to dry, and placed one of his IOUs in front of me. I asked him what the freight was, and he answered, "First three months' pay and any and all favors and services I may require henceforth."

The money was bad enough, but I near balked thinking of the yards of shit that conniver would have me eat. The whole deal threw a heavy shadow over my dreams of glory aback a horse. Still, I signed my X on Vikers's paper, and in place of my infantry assignment, he wrote in "9th Cavalry Regiment (Colored), Troop J." After I made sure that the swirls matched the ones on his paper exactly, I signed his damn IOU.

It took more than an hour to scrub away every bit of Dupree's filth and stench, but I stepped from the chilly pond clean and fresh as a new-saved soul. I used Dupree's stolen straight-edge to slice long, wide strips from my old skirt. When I'd collected enough to do the job, Iyaiya joined me and I kneeled so as to properly receive the strength she'd come to deliver. I traced my fingertips over the rows of dots that marked me as her Africa grandchild and whispered the words Iyaiya had learned Mama:

I cut strength into you. I cut belonging—me to you, you to me, we to the N'Nonmiton—into you. I cut a warning into you that no unwelcome hand shall ever touch you and go unpunished.

I tried to call the dead soldier back, to feel the touch of his fingers on my woman's body before I hid it away. But he would not come. For a moment, I was sad to know that the bond between us wasn't strong enough for me to call him back even for a moment. Then, like I always did, I put aside any feeling that made me weak and picked up a strip of the skirt's fabric. "Negro cloth" it was called for such was the rough weave that my people wore and I now used it to bind my breasts. I wrapped the coarse, scratchy strips tight, pulling hard so as to make what had once been round flat.

The wool flannel army shirt ballooned out around me while the sleeves stopped near half a foot from my wrists, leading me to believe that the shirt's previous owner must have had the shape of a cannonball. A whiskey barrel would have fit nicely in the sky-blue trousers. The only things keeping them in the vicinity of my body were the canvas suspenders and a belted strap I used to cinch them up until it looked like I was being held captive in a tow sack. The blue sack coat was little better except for this: it had the brass buttons with the eagle clutching his arrows.

I buttoned the jacket and rubbed my palms down the front, pleased that nothing bumped out. I took in a deep breath and was overwhelmed by a feeling I almost couldn't identify as it came from a long time ago. From when my Iyaiya would hold me and sing her Africa songs. I felt as sleepy now as I had back when I was held in the old lady's arms. I gathered up some fallen limbs and a few armfuls of tall grass to make myself a little nest, laid down, and sleep overtook me with a suddenness I hadn't knowed since childhood. Before I blinked out, one word came to me, "Safe."

That's what I felt in the blue suit. I felt safe.

Chapter 33

⁓

"Oooh, Lord. Oh, sweet Lord Jesus."

The faster the train went, the louder Lemuel's terrified moans grew. I had been stunned when he'd boarded the cavalry train and took a seat beside me. There was no way that the hulking country boy, who was my height but had an easy thirty pounds on me, could have made it into the cavalry on the square. I realized then that Lem was a sight slyer than he let on and must have gone to Vikers to get his papers doctored just as I had. I had no chance to bring our shared secret up, though, for the instant the train jerked into motion, my friend took leave of his senses, and as the screeching, speed, and swaying picked up he went completely, moon-baying crazy.

When Lem's eyes commenced rolling in his head, I feared he was about to go full possessed by the spirit and I clapped my hand over his mouth. Our car was packed. Lots more men than seats. Lemuel and me'd been lucky to grab two and I didn't want to lose them anytime soon.

"Lem, don't trouble yourself, man. This the way trains do. Nothing to fret over." But Lem continued making low howls in the back of his throat, his eyes wide and wild. And he wasn't the only one out of his head with fear. Though I let not a trace of fear appear on my face, I was also among those on the verge of making water in their pants. And why not? Fastest I'd ever moved in my life before this was whatever top speed a balky mule chose to attain, and now we were careening along in an iron box at, some said, close to twenty mile an hour.

Add to that the shrieks of the iron wheels against the iron rails, the rocking, the sudden jolts that pitched us all near out of our seats, and the eternal trickery of the white man, and who really knew what was to befall us? No wonder a right smart of the men had already heaved up their guts and the stink had the rest of us wobbling on the edge of doing the same.

And no hope of a breath of fresh air, either, as all the windows had been nailed shut and painted over. The Yankees could order the Rebs to carry us on their Central Virginia R.R., but it was up to the Seceshes how they'd do it. And nailing shut and painting the windows black was how they chose. Both to make the ride a torture for us and so whites couldn't see their worst nightmare come to life: railroad cars filled with black soldiers wearing the blue suit about to be given guns and horses. Just like Solomon had warned, Southerners looked on us, not so much as cattle been rustled away from them, but as the rustlers themselves who'd stolen their God-given property: Ourselves.

Luckily, the painters had done a poor job and if I scooted down in my seat, I had a passable view through a spot they'd missed. What I saw was a country in ruins. The fields where cotton and corn had once grown were nothing but charred stalks. Sheridan had burned every barn and left nothing growing in the fields except stinkweed and bur grass. Soldiers more skeletons than men, their shoes tied to their feet with rags, tramped back to homes that probably weren't there anymore. We chugged past a gaunt woman and her children, thin blond hair whipped about by the train wind that blew hissing steam and hot cinders their way.

Should I have felt pity for these miserable souls? I did not. I wished with all my heart that I could of wiped the windows clean so that every planter, Rebel, pattyroller, slave catcher, and all the poor whites whose fondest hope in life had been to have their very own slave to whip could see us riding high above them. Only two things the South ever had was land and slaves. Now one was burned to ashes and the other was riding away on the railroad.

"Justice Vikers wants that seat," Greene barked, startling me. Being Vikers's buddy had put starch in the spine of that bat-eared fool. Vikers followed and the men packed into the aisle like a cartridge rammed down the throat of a musket made way as best they could.

"Cathay," he said, smooth as a master who didn't need to remind a slave who owned her. One word from him and some army clerk'd start checking the records and find out that Cathay, William, was meant for the infantry.

Reluctantly, I stood.

"You too, Mule," Caldwell, the no-neck one, added.

Lem and I wedged in among those afoot. I put Vikers out of my mind and concentrated on imagining the Southerners out beyond the painted windows watching the source of their wealth and pride and way of life slip from their cruel grasp forever.

In that dark, puke-stinking box rocking us north, I smiled as I delivered the news to Iyaiya, *I have escaped. I am captive no more.*

Chapter 34

We unloaded on the banks of the Mississippi River in East St. Louis and took a ten-mile paddleboat ride downriver. At the dock we were met by a young white corporal name of Withers who was jovial and welcoming even though he had the strangely rosy cheeks of one taken with consumption and a cough that left his handkerchief speckled with blood. We gathered our traps and Withers led us up the bluff to the post, talking and coughing all the way.

As we entered the post, Withers told us that Jefferson Barracks had been a hospital during the war. Eighteen thousand patients, Yankee and Reb, himself included, had come through and left behind a whole quarry's worth of white marble tombstones in a big graveyard.

"Want to have a look-see?" Withers asked, eager as a kid with a new bag of hand-rolled clay marbles to show off.

Graveyards were not one of my people's favorite spots. Especially not when the sun was setting and the lonely cries of hootie owls were greeting the night. But the corporal was already leading us there, carrying on with his own special guided tour. As I'd done during the journey here, I hovered at the edge, away from the other men who were always jostling and bumping into each other, heedless as a litter of kittens. I stayed extra far away from Vikers, who kept his eye on me tight as a planter watching a bad runaway.

No matter how far from my draft group I went, though, Lemuel stayed right next to me, true as a shadow. My back ached from caving my shoulders forward so far my sack coat made a straight line from where I kept it buttoned below my chin down to my crotch. The sweat that collected along the rough bindings strapped around my breasts caused a terrible itching. I yearned to do nothing more than sit off by myself alone somewhere and scratch.

The corporal showed us an immense mound where they had buried the body parts sawed off by surgeons during the war. Then he went on for a bit about the unforgettable smell of gangrene. "Makes you want to cut off your own nose," he promised us. "Just see if it don't!"

After that detour, he led us to Jefferson Barracks. Though the place scared me spitless for reasons I'll go into a bit later, it was a grand post. It set a few miles south of St. Louis, high atop a bluff looking down on the Mississippi River. From up there the river was a surging thing that, though brown as a muddy dog during the day, went golden when the sun set and evening came on.

The buildings were made of white limestone that fair shimmered in the sunlight, and everywhere you looked tall oaks cast a heavy, cooling shade. Long rows of one- and two-story buildings and wide verandas made a rectangle open on one end to the breezes that blew up off the river and set Old Glory to snapping on her high staff.

"And here is where you new recruits will be quartered," Withers announced, stopping outside a plain, wooden structure. "Carlisle Barracks."

We cautiously entered the two-story building, awed by the high ceilings and windows that let in a lavish of light. Though the floors were a good bit tore up and so moldy and rotted in spots that an odor of decay fell heavy about the large room, they were wood. For most who had slept on dirt their whole lives, it was paradise.

"Had the dysentery cases in here," the corporal babbled on. "Tell you what: couldn't pay me to sleep on them beds."

All the Appomattox men kept glancing around. The same question that was on my mind showed on their faces. The old Cathy would of piped right up and asked, "Where's Sergeant Allbright?" but William Cathay had to keep his head down, lay low, and not attract attention.

Finally one of a group of six friends who'd all come off the same plantation in Georgia and been recruited at Appomattox said, "Suh, 'scuse me, suh." His accent was so country Southern the words dripped out of him more than being spoken. Later I would learn that his name was Duchamps but his friends called him Tea Cake. The rest had nicknames like Baby King and Ivory. Four of them were Duchamps's brothers and cousins, but I never figured out which four.

"Yes, Private," the corporal said.

"Where's Sergeant Allbright?"

"Who?" the corporal said.

"Sergeant Allbright. One who recruited us. Said we'd be riding west with him."

"Never heard the name," Withers said. Shoulders sagged all around me. We'd been bamboozled again.

Chapter 35

I will now tell you why this cozy, damn near luxurious, warm, lighted place was hell: no privacy. I'd never expected the army would put us all inside, but Solomon was right again. There weren't any tents where I could get off by myself to unwind the infernal binding and catch me a full breath. I wasn't going to last three years without a full breath.

Worse even than the barracks, though, was when the corporal led us to the colored men's washroom. A long, galvanized tin trough ran the length of one side. The men stepped right up and, with much jolly splashing, sent their torrents rushing down the thing.

In the hubbub, no one noticed me hanging back, the whites of my eyes turning yellow from having held my water for so long. At least on the train, there'd been a bucket off in a little closet. How was I going to do my business here? I'd pictured woods. Privies off by themselves. Just when I was about to give up and shuck off to pull a plow somewhere, the corporal said, "For those that need them, outhouses are around back."

I rushed outside and slipped into one of those rickety, stinking chambers, praising the Lord for delivering me. Those disgusting outhouses would be my salvation.

Next stop was the quartermaster's where we each drew thirteen pounds of hay. Back in the barracks, while we stuffed our mattress ticks with the hay, Corporal Withers informed us that our first duty the next morning would be to report to the bathhouse. "Army requires every man to get him a bath once a week. Keeps the lice down. Some."

Oh, Queenie. Solomon chuckled. *What'd I tell you? You figured you'd be off in your own cozy tent, sneaking on down a lonely creek once a month or so for a wash way soldiers always done, didn't you?* he asked.

That's exactly what I had been thinking, remembering how the only soldiers I'd ever seen naked in water were the two ladies in Cedar Creek. Most of the men never even peeled off their drawers when they bathed. Just wet down a bit, snuck a hand inside, rubbed here and there, and called it a day.

Withers had even worse news. "When the bugler sounds reveille tomorrow, every single one of you will report to Sergeant Baumgartner at the bathhouse."

Baumgartner?

The name had a terrifyingly Kraut sound to it. A bath was one thing, but a bath supervised by a Kraut was a whole other can of worms as Krauts were known for their mania for cleaning every nook and cranny. The prospect of having my own personal nooks and crannies cleaned threw me into a state.

I panicked, imagining being stripped naked in front of Vikers and his men. The corporal had his hand on the doorknob about to leave me to my fate, when he tapped a finger to his head to signal he'd just recollected something, turned and said, "You all have to report tomorrow except for one man. I need a volunteer to carry food to the guardhouse."

Iyaiya had saved me again.

Mine was the only hand that shot up.

Then the corporal added, "Besides the bath, this volunteer will be excused from drill and all duty except . . ."

Every single man put his hand up.

". . . sink duty."

All the hands dropped and even mine quivered a bit for sinks were latrines and I already knew enough about men and latrines that I was gagging at the thought. Still I kept my hand up. Not another one was raised, and I thought my worries were over. Then I spotted one other volunteer. Tea Cake. The other Georgia boy they called Ivory explained brightly, "Tea Cake cain't smell. Not a lick. Not since he got too close when Sherman was running the Rebs out of Atlanta and they done set fire to all them railroad cars loaded with ammunition. The boom knocked the smell right out of Tea Cake's nose."

Tea Cake grinned proudly as Ivory concluded, "Stick a dead possum under his nose, he'll eat that booger and lick his chops while he's doing it."

Tea Cake lowered his eyes modestly at the extent of his gift. Withers picked him for the guardhouse duty.

As soon as the door closed behind the corporal, Vikers, who'd gathered a whole new congregation about himself, brayed out, "All right, men, everyone claim a spot." Which we were all going to do anyway, but him saying it first made it like we were following his orders. Me and Lemuel took bunks as far from Vikers as we could get and settled in for the night.

"Bill," Lem asked. "Ain't you hot, man?"

I was the only person in that stuffy room who still had a jacket on. Most had wadded up their long blue jackets to use for a pillow. Mine was buttoned all the way up to my chin to hide the apple of Adam that I didn't have.

"Naw," I answered. "Catch cold easy. Had a sister carried off by a sniffle."

"Oh. I am sorry to hear that, Bill. Had me a baby sister fell off the back of Massuh's wagon. Curled up and turned blue. Peanut I called her for she was just that small."

"I'm sorry, Lem."

"I appreciate it, Bill, for I loved that baby girl and miss her still."

A bugle sounded. I recognized the call and hollered out before Vikers could, "Lights out. One of you want to douse them lanterns?"

The lanterns hanging off chains from the high ceiling were blown out and the big room went dark except for stripes of moonlight coming in the high windows. I hoped the men, exhausted by five days in a metal box, would go directly to sleep for I had an important mission I needed to carry out. However, excited by all the newness, they jabbered away until it occurred to someone to point out, "They ain't fed us."

A general chorus of grumbling followed, then those who had rations left over from the trip started sharing out their hardtack. The crunching of tooth busters echoed in the big room and someone said, "Sounds like hail hitting on a tin roof."

"That's just your big teef, Cyrus," another voice shot back.

"Least I got all my grinners, Chester. Your smile like a jack-o'-lantern!"

"What I told you 'bout calling me Chester? Ain't no damn Chester no more. Name's Antoine now."

"You ain't no aunt of mine. I'ma just call you 'Big Teef.'"

Next the men debated whether Corporal Withers's nickname should be Rosy for his cheeks or Catfish for the wispy bits of mustache he had straggling down either side of his mouth.

The joking went on, everyone in such high spirits that a warm spurt of pride shot through me as I thought about how a bunch of white men would of acted if they had been done this way. Put to bed with no supper? There'd of been an armed mutiny. And here my people were laughing and sharing out what they had. This caused a lovely vision to appear to me in which, once I'd gained the trust and admiration of all, I could reveal my true nature and be accepted as one of them. Just another soldier in the ranks fighting for a better life and a bit of dignity.

Gradually, the jabbering fell into introductions of a sort, and from every corner of the big room, names and jobs rang out. Not surprisingly, we had us a mess of farmboys, pickers, balers, choppers, strippers, and field hands, with names like Clem, Clyde, and Claude. We also had a Virgil who'd worked in a cigar factory in Virginia as a roller and a Tom who'd been a mechanic in Ohio and even a Thaddeus, a freedman who'd worked the whaling ships out of New Bedford, Massachusetts, and had once sailed all the way to Hawaii before coal oil knocked the blocks out from under the whale oil business.

Hearing the freedmen from up North talk about being bartenders, boot-blacks, chimney sweeps, even owning laundries where they had a dozen women working for them was like the dream I used to have of discovering that our wood-floored shack had endless rooms I'd never known about and were there waiting for me to wander about in.

Vikers waited until the names and jobs had settled down then announced, "Yes, well, I was the editor in chief of a freedmen's newspaper published in Baltimore, *The Colored American Deliverer.*"

Off in my dark corner, I perked up because I was the only one in that vast room who knew that Vikers had just told a whopper. Daddy used to read to me from his beloved *Deliverer* and had always noted with pride that it was published way up in New York City, New York. Not Baltimore.

"Why'd a newspaper editor go for a soldier?" Lem whispered to me in all innocence, as if there must be some detail he'd overlooked.

"I couldn't say," I answered. "But I tell you what, Vikers keeping his eye on me? I got both mine on him."

"Stanky," Vikers called down to me. "I hear you and Mule . . ."

Men that wouldn't have laughed in our faces felt free to hoot in the dark at the nicknames given us by Vikers.

"I hear you talking way off down there. What'd y'all do back home? Then in the war?"

"Well, Little Man," I said, for I couldn't let that "Stanky" nonsense stand, no matter what. "Back home I worked a logging crew." I made my voice as deep and gravelly as any soaker been marinating his vocal cords in alcohol and tobacco smoke for fifty years. "Then, come the war, I bucked logs to build corduroy roads for General Philip Henry Sheridan." That sounded a sight more manly than scrubbing pots and cooking ever would.

But men, being what they are, took my log bucking as some kind of manliness challenge that they were then required to beat. They did this the best way they knew how: smutty talk. I thought I already knew how men carried on. But the nastiest comments I'd ever heard before that night in the barracks were Bible stories compared to the tales they fell to telling.

This one bragged about "all the tail" he'd gotten off "this ole gal back home" who was "hotter'n July jam." Someone else blowed on about a "high yaller gal" who'd beg for it until tears came to her green eyes.

From the way they went on about the women who couldn't get enough of their willies and the women who had never seen such a much of size as what they were packing, you'd of thought every one of them had a magic wand stuck down their britches. It was all I could do to keep my mouth shut and not set the fools straight on the true way of it. How women mostly just put up with the willie part as the price of a gentle touch, a kind word, a bit of attention. Maybe a pretty or two. Or even just a plank of hardtack.

I thought about that girl on the barrelhead back at camp, the way she'd let out all them big moans even while her mind was off studying a redheaded flicker hopping up the tulip tree. And how puffed up Solomon had been when he came strutting back. I also recollected the nights back in our cabin when Maynard's man-fevered mama would have a visitor and how she'd moan like that hardtack girl. Then, after he'd done his business, she'd whimper and beg him to stay, hold her for a bit, whisper more sweet words like before he'd had his way. But her visitors would always ignore her and shuck on out without a glance back, just as convinced as the fools around me that she was as pleased as he was and couldn't wait for more. That his wand had worked his special man magic again.

I was glad that Mama had set me straight early on about not wasting myself on short-weight plowboys.

"Ain't right," Lem muttered. "All this nasty talk. You don't appear to be enjoying it, either."

"Can't say as I do," I rumbled back.

"Bill," Lem went on. "We're different from them others." In a whisper, he added, "Especially you."

Different from the others. Lem knew. I'd let him get too close and he had sussed me out.

Unbreathing, I flushed with heat, feeling like Lem was staring through the dark, through my jacket, shirt, and bindings straight at my naked titties. I was already figuring out whether I should offer him money, friendship, or something nasty to keep his mouth shut when he went on, "You're like me, Bill. You know your Bible. Know that Revelations told us, 'Blessed is he what stays away, keeping his garments on so as not to go about naked where whosoever gonna see what ain't meant to be seen.'"

My new friend was churched. I was safe. "That's it," I said with relief. "You got my number, Lem. Me and the Scriptures is like this." I held up two fingers pressed together tight.

"Uh-huh," Lem murmured. "Thought so. Saw right off that you and me was alike."

As the smutty talk went on, Lem asked, "Ain't none of them been saved?" Then he rolled over, putting the shield of his back between himself and all the wickedness of the world and was snoring half a minute later.

I prayed that the men would leave off and go to sleep, so I could do what I had to do to stay safe. But all the fornication talk had turbulated them so that as soon as they shut up, they set to playing with themselves. Which I wouldn't of given a hill of horse turds about if they'd been quiet. But, Lord, the panting and squeaking and gasping and creaking. I feared they'd pleasure themselves straight into idiocy.

At last, snores replaced the creaking and I slithered off to where Tea Cake slept. I had my hand over his mouth so he wouldn't cry out, leaned in and whispered, "Tea Cake, you got to give me the guardhouse duty."

Tea Cake muttered moist syllables against my palm, which I couldn't make out. I slid my hand into my pocket and took hold of the folding straight-edge razor I always kept there. I was ready to use it to help persuade him when I realized that he was saying, "Only volunteered so's to get me some extra victuals."

I let the razor fall back into my pocket and whispered, "You give me the duty, I'll bring you all the victuals I can steal."

Our deal was struck. I retreated to my spot, snugged my jacket up even tighter around me, tried to blot out the sound of one last man having a go at himself, and thought what a miserable, ruttish bunch of beasts men were. It would never be safe for them to know I was a woman.

I didn't sleep one single wink that long, first night in Carlisle Barracks.

Chapter 36

⁓

The kitchen was a sulfurous place of giant iron vats with mush bur- bling and heaving in them and fires roaring beneath. Pumps groaned as they forced water up from the river through large pipes. When the iron door of a roaring oven creaked open, tongues of hell- fire leaped out. Here and there big lumps of pork sat out on tables. They'd gone greenish in the heat and were buzzing with flies. I wondered what Sol- omon would of made of this sorry operation and wished hard that he was with me.

"You!" a stout fellow in a long, dirty apron, white cap atop his head, yelled at me. "You the recruit Withers sent?"

"Yessir!" I answered, snapping him off a salute.

As his hands were occupied hefting one of the big vats off the fire, he tipped his chin to a tall wheelbarrow, lowered the vat onto it, and said, "There's your cart. Get you some that pork." When I winced, he hurled a colorful variety of race slurs my way. I dropped a slimy chunk onto the cart and set out.

The sun was barely up as I trotted along the big, open parade ground between the two long wings of limestone buildings. A serving girl tossing away a bucket of water out front of one of the officers' quarters spotted me, tilted her head back so she could gaze up at me from beneath her thick eye- lashes, gave a sweet little smile and waved. Why, the hussy was flirting with me! Delighted and relieved that I could fool even another female, I gave her a little salute. She glanced quick up and down the field and, seeing no one about, pulled her bodice down so as to reveal a pair of titties high and tight as two apple halves stuck on her chest. Just another hardtack girl looking for business, she'd have flirted with a badger if she thought the creature had a nickel. I hurried on.

The guardhouse was even more solid than the rest of the post. The cells were limestone boxes with iron bars at the front. Each one had a bed big enough for a man as long as he didn't intend to ever turn over. A chilly dampness hung over the place. I started off passing out breakfast to the white prisoners first.

Food was an occasion here, and at the sound of the cart's squeaky wheels, the prisoners jumped up and thrust their mess tins out through the bars and I dolloped a ladle of mush onto every one. They complained because I didn't bring any molasses and I promised to fetch extra when I returned. Not many took any pork, saying they had to wait until their current case of the driz- zly shits cleared up before partaking again.

One prisoner heaped a world of abuse on me for serving up the green pork as though I was the one had left it sitting out. "Least during the war, they boiled our pork, you miserable _____," he said, somehow connect- ing my race to the rotten meat. "Flies is still alive on this shit."

That unloosed a whole hymnbook of laments on the subject of how much better a soldier's life had been during the war than it was now in peacetime. The stories flew about how easygoing life during the war was, pretty much just a big camping trip between battles. And the town girls! What happened to the patriotic young beauties blowing kisses to the soldiers as they marched through a Union town? Bringing them baskets of apple jelly, ginger cake, and fried ham? Holding ice cream socials for their valiant boys?

"Why, can you credit it?" one outraged fellow demanded. "When I come up with my draft group, dang if we weren't met at the station by a mob of town folk all hollering at us, 'Soldier, soldier, will you work?'" He shook his fist and pulled his face into an idiot frown to show how mad and stupid this mob was, then finished up quoting their answer, "No, indeed, I'd rather shirk!"

Best I could recollect, that particular fellow was actually in for shirking. Not that that slowed him or any the rest down from recounting all the in- stances of ingratitude and outright hostility been showed them by civilians. They gabbled on moaning about "what this country was coming to," and wondering about what had happened to "respect for the U.S. military" as though they couldn't puzzle out how one half of the country destroying the other half and leaving hardly a family on either side hadn't chiseled at least one tombstone might of soured folks a bit on war and those in the business of making it.

There was no such talk among the black prisoners as life had never been a camping trip for a single one of them.

Wheeling my barrow, empty now except for what I'd saved out for Tea Cake, back to the kitchen, I passed the colored men's washhouse and peeked in. The walls and floor of the long room were covered with white tiles. A row of a dozen galvanized tubs ran down the middle of the room. Each one was occupied by a naked trooper being parboiled and scrubbed on by Baumgartner with a long-handled brush. A line of naked men waited their turn.

"Scrub harder!" Baumgartner yelled. "*Das Arschloch und der Hodensack* must be clean or there is coming disease!"

Each man received a minute inspection when he stepped from the tub. The particular attention the sergeant paid to the men's private parts left no doubt as to the meaning of *Arschloch* and *Hodensack* or what my fate would have been had I not eluded what Daddy called ablutions.

As I pushed my cart away, I realized that, like all slaves, I already possessed the most useful skill a recruit could have: the ability to look busy. Just wheeling that cart around gave me the appearance of carrying out an assignment. Away from the parade grounds, I found a porch deep and dark enough to hide beneath and I caught up on the sleep I'd missed the night before.

I emerged from my nap hideout in time to return to the kitchen, refill the vat with mush, and serve that, along with generous lashings of molasses, for lunch. Dinner was slumgullion stew, the recipe for which must of read: to too much water and not enough salt, add every victual needs throwing out or feeding to the hogs. Boil until the green on both cabbage and pork is gone. Serve to convicts and soldiers for the hogs won't touch it.

I finished just in time to join my group at the quartermaster's, where I was issued a real uniform that came close to being my size, complete with a handsome caped overcoat of sky-blue wool, a sack coat with brand-new, shiny brass eagle buttons, a fine pair of boots, a cavalry cap with the crossed sabers, and a long grooming coat made of white duck. But the best was two sets of drawers and shirts that covered a body from ankle to wrist and was made of a wonderful soft cloth.

In the barracks, all the troopers were either strutting about in regulation U.S. Cavalry uniforms or in some stage of undress, hurrying to do the same.

"Bill," Lem asked. "Why you ain't parading that new uniform about?"

"That's right," said Vikers, who'd crept up on us in the chaos of men hopping about, pulling on the first pair of boots'd ever touched some of their feet. "Why don't you go on, strip down, and put on the blue suit?" The man had an unearthly gift for popping up exactly when I most wanted him gone. Also for gathering a crowd with that diamond-cutting voice of his. They were all looking on now, waiting on me to answer back.

"Fixing to wash up first," I answered. "Get my arselock and hodensack just as clean as Baumgartner got yours with his brush all up in your business."

"Hoo-WEE! Hoo-WEE!" A few of the men yelped with joy at my little jibe and danced about. This was an Africa thing. A way to show out when you've been tickled.

Lem whooped, "Little Man! Little Man, Cathay hit you another straight lick with a crooked stick!"

Vikers's eyes and smile got tight as a piano wire, and his tone was viperous mean when he came back at me. "Stanky," he said. "Why are you the only one still wearing those rank recruit clothes? And why was it so important to you to duck out of having a bath that you bribed Tea Cake?"

The whole barracks turned to stare at Tea Cake's face, greasy from the bowl of slumgullion I'd stolen for him. Wouldn't have taken a genius to put that together with me pushing the guardhouse barrow.

"Stanky," he asked. "What else you hiding from us?"

Oh, Vikers had planted an evil seed and I saw it take root on the spot. All the troopers studied me, searching now for what I was hiding.

"Who you think you are, Justice Vikers?" I put some sting on that fake name since we all knew that no master and no mammy had given it to him. "Ordering me around like you're my massuh. Day Abraham Lincoln signed that paper's the last day anyone on this earth be my master." That backed him off enough that I grabbed my new uniform and left.

In the kitchen, quiet now save for the mush and slum making slow, swamp-gas bubbles over low fires, I dipped up a bucket of hot water out of what was left in the vats of water for coffee and retreated to a hidden corner.

I peeled off the bindings flattening my breasts and the skin underneath was so chafed and raw, it came off in flakes big as sycamore leaves. In one raw spot beneath my armpit, new skin was growing right into the scratchy fabric. I had to touch the tips of my fingers to Mama's pearl scars for the strength not to cry out when I ripped the binding from the scabs.

The woman's body I was hiding was like an old friend I missed more than I could say. Gently I sudsed all the parts I had to keep hidden and felt a tiny bit less scared and alone. I whispered to my hidden self and told her that she was my twin, my sister, my secret strength, and that I would always protect her and keep her from the men meant to do her harm. As I washed, I cried without making a sound and that was a relief, too.

Chapter 37

"Sem come lem! Sem come lem!" Lemuel's country accent softened the numbers as he rattled the dice in his hands, stopped to blow on them, rattled a bit more, threw them up against the barracks outside back wall, and crapped out.

"Thank you, Mule, thank you! Always a pecuniary pleasure to play with you." Vikers swept what was left of Lem's first month's pay into his pocket. I'd already signed mine away to him. And by the look of how many others weren't gambling or buying extra food or even the gun-cleaning supplies army regs said we were supposed to purchase out of our own money, Vikers had done a right smart of paper doctoring and hired reading. At least I could stop worrying about him revealing that I was supposed to be a foot soldier since he'd changed so many others' papers.

What Vikers actually collected was half our pay, since none of us recruits'd see our full thirteen dollars until we joined an active unit. And that day couldn't come soon enough. Every one of us hated the barracks food, which, aside from the addition of cold corn bread sopped with "gravy" made of naught but hot water and flour and an occasional treat of three prunes apiece, was the same green salt pork and mush as what I slopped out to the prisoners every day.

While we waited for our group to fill out to the ninety men we needed to make a company, every recruit was worked like a draft mule. And, aside from mucking out stables, never a lick of any of it had to do with guns or horses.

In the evenings, after we were done with our digging, painting, sweeping, mopping, and such, we met up with an old white sergeant who had small, tight, squinty eyes and a small, tight, squinty mouth to get educated about the redskins. He'd come from the Indian Territories and could go on for hours about the depravities that awaited us there if we were ever to be captured. According to him, the best we could hope for from the heathens was a quick arrow through the heart or a sweet crack to the back of the head with a tomahawk.

The old sergeant held us spellbound with stories about how the Indians'd do you if you ever fell into their cruel hands. You'd get scalped, or roasted alive. Or buried in the dirt up to your chin with your eyelids cut off so your eyeballs'd barbecue in the sun while you starved to death. Or staked out naked and spread-eagled over a red ant bed after having your private parts sliced off, stuffed in your mouth, and your lips sewed together. A person tended to remember a torture when the best part of it was getting your lips sewed together.

The point of all his stories was simple enough. "They ain't human," he repeated again and again. "No matter what the nancy boy Quakers and pusillanimous politicians in Washington say, redskins ain't human."

Most of the men, wide-eyed with terror, hands folded protectively over their crotches, nodded in agreement. Sergeant tended to finish up terrifying us by delivering a lecture about how my race needed to "learn the meaning of discipline." I bit my tongue to keep from telling him that "my race" could school every soldier in the U.S. Army on discipline for we'd been learned by the finest whip hands in the South.

It turned out that the entire purpose of Jefferson Barracks was to break a man down and make a soldier out of what pieces might be left. A soldier who would salute, say "yessir," and obey. Questions and "no" were for civilians. Those who weren't snappy enough with their "yessirs" and salutes were taught army discipline by way of being barreled up, marched half to death carrying a pack loaded with bricks, or buck and gagged. This last training technique had a soldier gagged and hog-tied up with an iron bar run through the space between his knees and elbows and left that way. When the man was untied, he couldn't straighten up right for a month.

There were other harshnesses.

One morning, I steered my cart of mush and molasses over to the guardhouse and found a dozen white prisoners creeping out. They were breaking for daylight when two guards, still wobbling from being bashed in the head by the escapees, appeared at the door. Without a single word, not a cry of warning, not an order to return, those guards fired their rifles and laid out four of those boys quick as they could reload. They winged another four and shot two more who'd already surrendered and were coming back with their hands waving high up over their heads. Between that and the bucking and gagging and the redskin scare stories, I saw that the army meant business and I was having my doubts if it was one I wanted any part of.

These doubts took on solid form that evening during another crap game. As usual, we were outside, and Vikers, with his bottomless wad of forgery and reading dollars, was corralling what was left of the men's first pay, leaving them nothing to buy so much as a pasty pie or two with from the sutler to quiet their growling bellies with.

When his pockets were full, Vikers stood and announced that he had to see a man about a horse, and the whole bunch of them rose and adjourned outside where it was dark. As I edged off to the privy, I watched them form a line behind the barracks, and set loose their manly arcs. In the middle of seeing who could hit the Mississippi, Vikers yelled back at me, "Stanky, you too good to piss with your bunkies?"

"Naw, I'm fine. Heading to the—" I pointed to the outhouse.

"Man takes a lot of shits, don't he?" Greene, who never missed an opportunity to suck up to Vikers, announced in a loud voice.

Vikers jumped right in. "He does, doesn't he?" he said, pretending like he'd just now noticed that I never unzipped in front of the others. "Mule, what ails your buddy?"

"Cathay just don't like doing his business front of folks," Lem answered. "Why you care anyhow, Little Man?"

So casually it made shivers run up my spine, Vikers answered, "Next time you call me 'Little Man,' Mule, I will slit your throat while you sleep."

I waited long enough to see Lemuel walk away safe, then rushed to the privy. Soon as I got the door closed, I pulled the bindings off and drew a breath. The past weeks had packed the air hard in my lungs. I couldn't take this army, couldn't take Vikers, couldn't take being what I was not, couldn't take being so completely alone that the only friend I had didn't know the first, not the very first, most essential thing about me.

That night was even more uneasy than most.

As usual, I rose early the next morning so I could get to the washroom before everyone else. The pump screeched as I worked the handle to send a rush of water into the long tin trough. It hit the metal and echoed loud and hollow off the white tiles on the floor and walls of the high-ceilinged room. I'd just splashed water on my face when Vikers and his boys surrounded me.

They were bare-chested, suspenders looping down by their sides. The vicious stares they kept trained on me made my heart gallop. Standing next to me, Vikers plunked his straight-edge razor down on the shelf that ran above the trough, and lathered up for a shave.

Keeping my eyes on that straight-edge, I dried my face and turned to leave, but Vikers, his mouth a black hole opening and closing in the middle of the white foam, said, "Cathay, you're not going to shave? We been here a month, but I've never seen you shave. Have any of you boys seen our man here shave?"

They all muttered how, no, they had not seen me shave.

"So, Cathay," Vikers said. "You never shave with us. You never piss with us. You never bathe with us. Care to tell us why that is?"

The men waited for what I was going to say. If they were dogs, the fur on the back of their necks would of been bristled up, they were that ready to attack.

I rubbed my palm over my jaw, and said slow and casual like, "Thanks for reminding me." I plucked the foamy brush out of Vikers's hand, lathered up, and said, "All that Cherokee blood in me, I almost never have to shave. But when I do . . ."

I snatched Dupree's razor out of my pocket, flicked it open, shaved off a strip of lather, snapped it into the trough, and concluded, "I always cut close."

I finished my "shave" and left. The trembling didn't start until I was halfway to the guardhouse. I had thrown the pack off again, but it didn't matter. Vikers and his curs had my scent. One way or another, they were coming for me. One way or another, if I stayed, they'd kill me.

Chapter 38

⁓

As soon as I finished at the guardhouse, I took my cart, but instead of wheeling on back to the kitchen, I kept right on going. Whatever life I'd have as a civilian surely couldn't be any worse than what Vikers and his men had planned for me.

A mile or so outside the post, a pack of freedmen, women, and children were huddled up next to the road. They swarmed about me, thrusting victuals my way. One woman had a basket of roast sweet taters, two for a penny. An old man, eyes so filmed over they were solid gray, held out a trembling hand with a palm's worth of ground corn. A bold little fellow had a single egg, "stole fresh that morning," that he hounded me to buy off him for a nickel. I told him he ought to be selling brass as he had a mite too much of it.

I was trudging down the road toward St. Louie, when the very distinctly military sound of iron halters and bits jingling, tack creaking, and hooves drumming along smartly up ahead caused me to jump off the road and hide myself behind the cane grass growing there. Five riders approached. One of them carried a swallow-tail guidon that snapped in the wind above their heads.

As they came within sight, my eyes went first to the men's rank insignia. It had become second nature to check that even before looking at a face: a first sergeant flanked by four corporals. Each one was spit-and-polished to such a high gleam that they looked to have been punched out at the Perfect Soldier factory.

Before I could even make out the first sergeant, I knew who he was from the way he sat his horse. I stepped back into the road, my hand frozen in a salute would have done the Kaiser of Prussia proud.

The Sergeant reined up, returned my salute, and asked, "Private, could you direct me to Carlisle Barracks? I need to meet my new unit and begin training as quickly as possible."

I gave First Sergeant Levi Allbright directions, turned my barrow around, and wheeled back to post.

Chapter 39

The real first day of the army for me was the day Sergeant Allbright said to us, "As of this moment, I take command of Ninth Cavalry, Troop J. Today we begin training to become the finest troop in not only any colored regiment, but in any regiment anywhere in the United States Army!" From the first word he spoke, we believed Sergeant Allbright and wanted to follow where he led.

All the bullshit assignments stopped immediately. I was pulled off guardhouse detail. The rest who'd been parceled out laying bricks and weeding the officers' wives' flower gardens stopped that nonsense and we all fell to drilling. I am not bragging just stating a simple fact when I say, as far as marching formations, no one in the troop could touch me. After my time with Sheridan, I'd already been in the damn army for near a year. Plus, the way I came up with Mama? I knew how to hold my head up and tamp down every bit of emotion might ever threaten to play across my face.

The third day, the Sergeant pulled me out of formation and put me at the head of the line so that the fumble-footed could copy me. Out of the whole sorry company, it delighted me to see that Vikers was the sorriest. The man was almost white in how long it took him to get in the habit of following an order. Corporal'd say "Right," and that brain of his, always so busy figuring out the angles, would balk and he'd go left. Ended up there were only five boys out of our troop of nearly ninety privates who had to have straw and hay tied to their feet. And Vikers was one of them. Every night in the barracks he went on about how marching was for "ground-pounders" and that he refused to learn it since "equitation" was his "natural means of conveyance."

He didn't have long to wait, for, very next day, when we formed up on the parade grounds, the Sergeant greeted us from high atop his noble steed, saying, "Today you become cavalry soldiers. Today we begin riding. Most of you have never ridden anything but narrow-headed mules and sway-backed plugs. Many of you have been forbidden by law, perhaps upon pain of death, from even swinging a leg over a fine mount. You have been told that people of color do not make good horsemen. I am here to tell you that that is a lie!

"How do I know? I know because I have seen the Comanche and there are two things I can tell you about those fearsome warriors. They are the finest horse soldiers the world has seen since Genghis Khan and his Mongol hordes. And, like the Mongols, they are men of color. Do you hear me? Men of color!"

"Yessir!" I sang out first and loudest.

"Men, let me tell you this. They are going to give us the worst horses, the worst gear, and the worst duty! And do you know what we are going to give them back?" Silence greeted his question and he asked again, "I said, do you know what we will give them back!"

"What, sir?" I sang out.

"I will answer you with another question: tell me, gentlemen, can I smite my enemy, the enemies of the United States of America, of which we are citizens, with one finger?"

He held his pointer out straight, and tipped off by that Bible word "smite," we called back way you'd call back to a preacher on Sunday, "Uh-uh!" "No, sir!" for we knew a lesson was coming.

"Can I smite him with my thumb?"

"No, sir!"

"Can I smite him with my fist?" He raised a fist mighty as a blacksmith's hammer.

We liked this smiting business just fine. It was what we'd signed up for and we thundered back, "Yessir!"

"Yes!" he said. "We are going to come together like separate fingers clenching tight to make one mighty fist! We are going to drill and practice until no man on earth is our equal on the back of a horse or behind the sight of a Spencer repeating carbine. We are going to abjure pettiness and rise to levels of greatness that the U.S. Army has only dreamed of before!"

His voice hummed through us like a pitch pipe calling out the note that brought every one of us into harmony.

"I repeat, they are going to give us the worst horses, the worst gear, and the worst duty! And, I ask you again, what are we going to give them back?"

He raised his fist high in the air and, without thinking, every one of us did the same. A stillness fell as we waited, fists to the sky, for First Sergeant Allbright to deliver the answer unto us.

"I said, do you know what we are going to give them back!"

"What, sir!" I hollered back.

"Gentlemen, we are going to give them the best damn horse soldiers the world has ever seen! Am I right?"

A roar ferocious as any lion's answered him then. With me roaring loudest of all. Though I had seen my folly in believing Allbright was my dead soldier, damn if his words didn't cause a power to move in me that was not of this mortal earth. It was the same power he'd used back at the recruiting. Same one that had made me feel like he recognized me, saw me, knew me personal. And now, that power was working on every man in the troop. All of us, friend and foe alike, were bound up together. If Allbright had asked us to dump coal oil over our heads and spark a flint to it, not a one of us would of hesitated.

The Sergeant's four corporals began leading saddled horses from the stables and went to matching up mount with rider. I saw right off that most of the nags should have been heading for the glue factory. They were windblown, spavined, swaybacked, trappy, long-toothed, and droopy-lipped. And I couldn't wait to get mine.

A corporal name of Masters came up to Lem and me, took one look and called the Sergeant over.

"Private Cathay?" Sergeant Allbright's lips formed my name, but it was a full ten seconds before I could piece together that a question had been asked of me and that I was standing there with my fly trap open. I cringed at the sorry, tongue-tied impression I was making.

"Sir! Yessir!" I snapped off a salute sharp enough to chop hickory.

"You and Private Powdrell, you are too tall for cavalry."

I tipped my head back to meet his eyes, for Allbright was as tall as Lem.

Allbright sussed out my question and informed me, "I was riding with the cavalry before they instituted the height limits. We demand a great deal of our mounts. The gear we require them to carry along with our weight places a heavy burden on them. Were you two not measured and weighed at the recruitment depot?"

"I sure was," Lem said. "And they were going to put me afoot but for I'm a farrier."

So that was it. Lem was a horseshoer. This was news to me and gives you an idea of how different men were with their friends. Had Lem and I been girls, of the normal sort rather than my tomboy brand, we'd of known everything about each other from favorite color to which of our friends riled our nerves so bad one of us was bound to stick an ice pick in her. I surely would of known that my best friend shoed horses, making him the one person, giant or midget, no cavalry outfit could do without.

"Excellent," Allbright exclaimed. "I was afraid we'd have to train someone. A suitable mount will be found for you, Powdrell. What about you, Cathay? Did some gin-soaked local doctor simply wave you on without so much as a thump on your chest?"

"No, sir," I answered. "I was examined in minute-most detail." It always amazed me how, when I most needed him to, Daddy would place the correct words and the correct manner of speaking them in my mouth. "My minascular abundance of height, so to speak, got shrunk down on account of my conspacious knowledge of horseflesh, having been a groom or, actually, more of a barn foreman."

"You're saying you know horses?"

"I am, sir. That's percisely what I am saying."

The Sergeant narrowed his eyes, showing that he half believed me, half thought I was full of shit, and that fifty percent was about all he could ever expect from me. He told his corporal that since I was a lanky, low-weight sort to bring me whatever they had from the stable.

The corporal paused and asked, "Do you mean . . . ?"

"Indeed, I do, Corporal," Allbright answered, appearing to already know what horse Masters was referring to.

The corporal led two horses from the stable. One was a large chestnut near as tall as the General's heroic black steed. He handed the reins of that prime mount to Lem who lit up from grinning so big.

Masters had a specimen of an entirely different sort for me. He made a show of calling out, "And you, Private Cathay, here is the very special horse you will be riding." Everyone was watching when he handed over the reins of a swaybacked gray with knock knees and the longest set of ears ever seen on a horse. Also the strangest. For they drooped. Hung down like a hound's on a hot day.

By the time Masters announced, "We like to call her Bunny," men all up and down the line were hooting. And though Vikers wasn't a hooter, he fixed me with a smug look that said he had the goods on me. Again.

Chapter 40

From the instant we mounted up, Allbright was calling out comments. "Caldwell," he yelled. "You're not walking a tightrope! Get your hands down!"

"Greene! Your stirrups are too short. Dismount and let them out."

"Vikers! Relax, man, relax! You trying to ride that horse. Not choke him to death! Let up on the reins. Better. Better."

Throughout all this, I had been maintaining a death grip on Bunny's reins for, to my surprise, actually being atop a horse was nothing like I'd dreamed it'd be. In fact, it was flat-out terrifying. I didn't mind heights and wasn't particular about being knocked about, but the idea of another creature being in control had me in a state. Plus Bunny had a terrible gait. She threw me high with every step and I came down so hard I feared my tailbone would break. Luckily, Sergeant Allbright wasn't paying any attention to me flopping about in the saddle.

He was focused on my friend Lem. "Gentlemen," he shouted out, "look at Powdrell! That is how you ride a horse! Watch his posture. He's sitting deep in the saddle but not mashed up against the cantle like too many of you are doing. That might make you feel safer, but your mount hates it. Scoot forward toward the horn, all of you!

"Notice Powdrell's arm position. He's carrying them about lap height and he's got the reins in one hand. That is imperative! You are fighting soldiers. You *will* need a free hand. If we were as good as the redskins, we'd ride bareback, control our mounts with our knees, and have both hands free. But we're not, so keep your shooting hand free! Powdrell, turn to your left!"

Seemed like Lem's horse did just that before the words were even out of the Sergeant's mouth.

"Excellent! These are trained mounts and, clearly, Powdrell is a trained rider. You should only need a slight touch of the rein, a nudge, to get the job done. Think of it as a gentle push, not a pull. I don't want to see any more tugging or sawing on the reins. If you want your horse to turn left, gently, *gently*, touch the right rein to the horse's neck. Many of your horses have been through the Rebellion. They know a hell of a lot more about mounted warfare than any of you ever will. Let them do their job. Thank you, Powdrell. Back in line."

Lem, busting with pride, showed out, grinning at us big.

"Eyes forward, Private!" Allbright ordered.

Lem snapped his head back around, and the Sergeant turned his attention to the rest of us. When he gazed my way, I came completely unscrewed, got my left and right twisted around, and steered poor Bunny straight at him. Bunny's ears flopped up and down with every step and I flopped along with them. Sad to say, neither of our flops was timed up together and I was a big, dumb rag doll atop the goofiest-looking horse in the U.S Cavalry. I didn't need the jackass hee-haws to alert me to the comical sight we presented. Allbright took one step to the side, reached out, grabbed the reins, brought Bunny to a smooth halt, and ordered, "Trooper, dismount!"

My foot got tangled up in the stirrup and the first part of me to touch the ground was my butt end. You think Vikers and his crew didn't have themselves a jubilee of sneering about that?

"Rest of you men, keep circling!" Allbright hollered. "Not a one of you doesn't need the practice!"

When they were all in motion again, Allbright asked me in a low voice, so as to keep the shaming between us, "You haven't been horseback before, have you, Cathay?"

"No, sir," I answered, my eyes straight forward.

"You're not a natural, Cathay."

"No, sir."

"You weren't a barn foreman, were you?"

"No, sir."

He heaved a breath or two as he considered mustering me out then and there. At last, he said, "Show me your riding position." I went to mount up again, but he stopped me with a hand on my shoulder. "No, let's give your mount a rest. Just show me right here."

"Here, sir?"

"Here, Cathay."

I glanced around.

"Don't mind them."

I squatted down.

"Let's see your hand position. Just let your hands drop. Nice and relaxed."

My hands were as relaxed as a couple of cast-iron frying pans dangling at the end of each wrist. Allbright guided them into position. "You're nervous, Cathay. Hands feel like you've been using them for ice tongs."

"Yessir."

Without another word, he put one hand under my butt and the other on the inside of my thigh, far enough from my crotch that there was no danger of him discovering what wasn't there. "Here! Cathay," he said, pressing against those tender spots. "You've got to feel your mount here!" He pressed up on the cleft of my arse. "And here!" He pressed hard against the inside of my thigh, spots no man had ever touched before, and he moved my hips back and forth in a slow rock. "You feel that?"

I tried to answer but couldn't work up the spit to get a word out and nodded my head instead.

"Don't fight it, Cathay." He kept up the motion until my joints unfroze and followed where he was pushing them. "I've been watching you, Cathay. No one better on the marching field than you, but off it you keep your guard up all the time. And the others don't like you."

My lips trembled from stuffing the hot words I had to say on that topic back down my throat.

"I'm not saying they're right," he went on. "Just that it makes you a divisive element. And I can't have divisive elements. Can't have a soldier who's not pulling this unit together. You don't have to like everybody. They don't have to like you. The fact is, you can hate every single man here, but you have to unite with them. Do you understand me?"

I nodded stiffly as he continued guiding my hips.

"All right, better. You're getting the rhythm of it. Thing to remember is that riding a horse is like being with a woman. You know that feeling, Cathay? With the woman next to you, your body and her body making one body? Her smell all up in your head? You know that feeling, Cathay?"

I nodded, for words had slipped even further beyond my power now.

"Smooth, Cathay. Don't fight her. Don't fight us. I'll be watching you.

You might be meant for an infantryman instead of the cavalry. No shame in that. I just can't have a man who's not committed, heart and soul, to making this the best goddamn unit in the army. They're watching us. They want us to fail. We will not fail. You got that?" I gave a feeble nod.

"I'll give you until end of the week, Friday, before I decide. You've got the next four days to make me believe you're fit to ride in the U.S. Cavalry. If you don't . . ." He stood and shrugged. "I guess you can just keep on walking to St. Louie like you were the day I rode in."

I reddened, as I realized that he knew I'd been deserting.

"Caldwell!" the Sergeant yelled, walking away. "You look like a duck. Get your ass down, man!"

That evening at mess, in spite of not eating all day, I couldn't choke down a single spoonful of the slum. Or even the special treat they put out for us: real bread with butter. I was happy to pass mine on to Lem, saying my stomach wasn't right. Which it most definitely had not been since the instant Allbright laid his hands on me.

That night, sleep would not come. I lay awake listening to the sounds a hundred men make at night. Snores, groans, creaks, whimpers, the senseless babbling of someone talking back to his dreams, shrieks when the nightmares came. Crying. Lots of them cried softly at night.

"You awake?" Lem whispered from the next bunk. Though I never made the tiniest sound, Lem always sensed when I was awake.

"Yeah," I answered, my voice extra deep to cover up the girlish spell I had fallen under.

"Pretty exciting day, huh?"

"Yeah."

"Special, huh?"

"First day I ever sat a horse," I said, laying off my giddiness on Bunny.

The snores rose to a crescendo loud as an August noon in a field of cicadas. "Seems we're the only ones in the outfit feels that specialness."

I saw then what kind of special the day had been for Lem, country boy up out of Alabama, nobody'd ever made over him before.

"Sergeant made you an example, Lem. Singled you out."

"Well, you too, Bill."

I snorted for, kind as Lem was, it wasn't any use in pretending why I'd been singled out. "The Sergeant told me I have four days to shape up or I am for the infantry."

"Aw, Bill. I hate to hear that. Can you? Shape up?"

"Like a steer, I can try," I joked, trying to sound game.

Lem chuckled. "I hope you do. Sure would be lonesome without you. Good night, Bill."

"Good night, Lem."

He was snoring by the time I finished pronouncing his name, but I laid there the whole night, so fluttery I thought I'd take flight.

Chapter 41

—

Next few days were even worse. It was a sore disappointment to discover that I wasn't the horseman I'd always dreamed I'd be if only given the chance. Problem was, I was trying too hard. Turned out that riding a horse was one of those things, like sleep or moving your bowels, that gets worse the more try you put on them.

By the end of the day, I could barely stand. Felt like I'd been dropped from a shot tower direct onto the old *Arschloch*. About a hundred times. Walking bowlegged, I led Bunny to the stables for grooming. The stables were my favorite place on post to escape from prying eyes. With Bunny I could relax for a bit, leave off the manly airs that I found so wearying. It was also the only place where my odor wasn't noticeable, for all the riding combined with avoiding the bathhouse had caused me to ripen to such a degree that comments were being passed. Many comments.

The problem wasn't exactly me, though, since I slipped off to wash every other day or so. It was my uniform. Since every cent I made was going to pay off Vikers, I didn't have even the three pennies a washerwoman charged to iron a shirt, much less what it cost to mend, soak, boil, scrub, blue, bleach, rinse, wring, dry, and fold the whole truck. But with Allbright studying on exiling me to the infantry, the least I could do was not stink. I headed for Suds Row hoping to convince one of the gals to IOU the deal.

I was just turning the corner out onto the central promenade when I spotted Sergeant Allbright on the other side, his laundry wrapped up neat inside a jacket and tucked under his arm. My step slackened as I gazed upon him striding beneath the oaks, their leaves starting to make a dark lace against the sky as dusk came on. His walk had the smooth action of a show horse and he didn't seem to spend any more energy covering ground than a hawk did riding a high wind current.

I picked up my pace, cut across the promenade, and intersected him just as he was about to turn off for Soap Suds Row.

"Why, Sergeant," I piped up with a note of surprise that sounded fake even to me. I slipped in beside him with a salute which he only half returned. "Right nice evening, isn't it, Sergeant?"

He nodded stiffly.

"Out for a walk, sir?" I asked.

He pointed to the bundle beneath his arm.

"Soap Suds Row! You don't say. Why, that's just where I'm headed," I said, as if us both headed toward one of the two places anyone off duty'd ever walk to was a coincidence of the highest order. "Be happy to take that for you, sir," I said as I grabbed hold of his bundle of laundry.

Allbright jerked it away, saying, "No need, Private." He started to leave, pivoted, and added, "Cathay, I am still watching you. Still going to have to make my choice based on what's best for the unit."

It was clear that Allbright thought I was brownnosing him, sucking up so he wouldn't send me down to the infantry. Shamed by that realization, I fumbled a salute and hurried away to the far end of the last barracks where I hid at its edge. Far below the bluff the post sat on, the evening light had polished the river up to a shine, but, in my humiliation, I took no notice of its silver ripples and slow, snaking turns. Without thinking, I lowered my face into my hands and caught the barest whiff of his smell of sweat and soap and sun that either lingered there from the touch of his clothes or was put there by my wanting.

As I was sniffing, I felt the spidery sensation of being watched. I dropped my hands, glanced behind me, and there, standing beneath a monstrous oak that had a perfect view of the promenade, was Justice Vikers, grinning for he had seen the whole set-to.

I tried to wait until after lights out to return to the barracks, but a corporal spotted me and ordered me inside. Tea Cake and his bunch were singing field chants to ease their homesickness. In the middle of the room the cots had been cleared away leaving the floor empty and Vikers was running his usual crap game. A stable boy out of Shreveport name of Fernie Teague was clinging to the dice too long. Vikers yawped at him, "You chokin' them dice, Teague! Shake and lemme hear the music! Rattle them bones!"

I made my way around the gamblers to my bunk, surprised that Vikers had passed no comment. Turned out, he had a different game in mind. His first move was declaring, "Uh-huh! Lucy Landreau, that was one fine piece of womanflesh." This Lucy Landreau had made so many appearances in Vikers's accounts of his many conquests that she needed no introduction. He went on as he always did, saying, "Of course, I do have a decided preference for high yellow tail."

I figured I was safe for the night as, once the nasty talk started, it could go on for hours and all any of them were interested in was getting their own story told. During these endless discussions, I liked to pretend the men were talking about horses or food with all their comments about someone being a "fine piece of flesh" or a "tasty morsel." Otherwise, I'd get to feeling like a rabbit hiding from a pack of wolves. I knew most of the men were just blowing big, ruffling up like yard dogs to keep the pack from thinking they were little enough to boss around. But some of them truly believed women had been put on this earth for them to use like animals.

It scared me to think what those men'd do to me if they ever discovered that I fell into the livestock category.

"Me," Greene announced, "give me that dark meat, man." He added the familiar words, "The darker the berry, the sweeter the juice."

Teague said, "Wish I had me a piece right now, any color."

"Me too," Caldwell cut in. "I'm so horny I could—"

I never did find out what horniness might drive Greene to, for Vikers interrupted, and in a voice could tenderize shoe leather, he asked, "What about you, Cathay? What kind of tail you like?" All eyes turned to me and Vikers asked again, "Cathay? You never have said what kind of tail you prefer."

"No, Vikers. I never have." I cut my words off so they flew at him with sharp points.

"Might lead a body to think, maybe, you got something to hide."

"That so?" I came back, holding his eyes hard and fast until he blinked. "We got a saying back home about that," I said, laid it out there, hoping he'd pick it up.

Which he did, saying in a peevish, sneery manner, "Oh, you do, do you?"

He was looking off at his boys, upping his eyebrows, when he asked, "And just what might that pearl of country wisdom be?"

"Old folks say," I began. "'The louder the rooster crow, the less about the hen he know.'"

That was a crowd-pleaser, especially amongst the country boys who outnumbered the freedmen and city slickers like Vikers by a long shot. They whooped it up riotous then settled down, waiting for Vikers to hit me back.

I puffed up, certain he had nothing as he played for time, muttering, "Is that right? Is that right?"

"That's right, Vikers."

"Well, Cathay, we have a saying, too."

Everybody hushed up then.

"Yeah, that's right. Back home we like to say, 'Rooster that don't crow at all. Might turn out to be a capon.'"

The hoots rang out then. "You hear that?" "Got him! Got him! Got him!" "Cut him! Dead!"

Silence fell again for it was my turn and if I didn't cut Vikers back, he would pitch into me even harder. I was trying to cook up some back-home saying the way Vikers had just done when Lem, puzzled, piped up, "We don' have that sayin' back in Alabama. What, exactly, is a kay-pon?"

This time Vikers got the eye lock on me and said, "That's a cock had his balls cut off."

"Oh, yes!" Lem exclaimed. "Makes the meat tender."

Vikers, staring at me dead level, said, "I wouldn't know. I never tried it that way."

"Just keep on a-blowin'," I told him. "Air's not hot enough in here no how." That was lame as a sick kitten and the whole barracks knew I'd lost and lost big. Being called out as a nancy boy was serious business back in those days. Though sodomites weren't generally killed outright anymore, if a man was proved a candy ankle, he'd spend a few years behind bars. And he'd definitely get mustered out of the army faster than even a woman would. First, though, he'd get hard used by anyone cared to have a go at him. Worse even than the way I would be if I was ever uncovered.

When the hee-hawing went on—"Hear that? He got him." "Laid him out on the cooling board!" "Took him to the boneyard!" "Buried him! Clean buried Stanky!"—I turned away and made out like I couldn't be bothered with such childish moonshines.

"Don't mind them ignorant fools, Bill," Lem said.

I slept little that night for, even more than a woman alone, season was always open on nancy boys. I clutched at the collar of my jacket and started at every noise. Most of my barracks mates were fine men, but there were jackals amongst them. Jackals and the easily led. I grew up hearing of what men did to women, but recalling the stories about what they did to boys who'd been singled out as funny made my blood run cold.

On top of everything else keeping me anxioused up, tomorrow was Friday. Last day I had to prove to Allbright that I was fit for the cavalry. Though I wasn't any circus performer and never would be, Bunny and I had smoothed out enough that I could keep up with the rest. What I had to do now was show Allbright that I wouldn't be a divisive element in the unit. Somehow or other, I had to get right with Vikers. Or, at least, appear to the Sergeant's eyes to be.

Chapter 42

⌒

Friday.

As the company fell in and marched to the training field, I felt the Sergeant's eyes on me. I wasn't sure I wanted to be in the army anymore, but I for God sure knew I'd die before I left with him thinking ill of me.

When we reached the field, I saw my salvation: the corporals had set up eight hay bales and were pinning bull's-eye targets on them. We were going to shoot. My heart bumped with joy thinking of how I'd prove myself today.

But the best of it was when wooden crates were pried open and brand-new Spencer repeating carbines were thrust into our hands. I'd already seen the Spencer in action and knew it beat my old yagger and any other single-action rifle all to blazes. I had itched to get my hands on one back when Sheridan's soldiers were being drilled on them. I knew more about this weapon than the instructors walking us through loading, sighting, and such.

After we were split up into eight lines, Allbright explained how we had to be winnowed since ammo was limited and he needed to find the good shots before it ran out. "Our lives will depend upon identifying our finest marksmen," he said. "They will be named 'troop riflemen.' They will ride point and be our first line of defense as we pass through territory held by hostiles."

The winnowing went fast for there weren't but a dozen or so who'd ever held a gun and fewer still who'd fired one. I was last in my line, watching, itching for my chance to show out.

Greene and Caldwell both shot wild and were pulled out of line. Vikers turned out to be a fair shot for a four-eyes. Good enough not to be cut, but not anywhere close to me. The man in front of me was Fernie Teague. He hit an old robin's nest and joked, "Thought I'd shoot y'all down some break-fast." Everyone laughed. Even Sergeant Allbright. Still grinning, Fernie added his magazine to the pile of those handed over by the bad shots and stepped away.

Corporal Masters barked out, "Cathay!" I stepped up to the head of the line. A cloud of smoke from the shooters who'd gone before hung heavy as a black fog and smelled like a battlefield. Blinking, I put that fine Spencer car-bine to my shoulder, flipped up the sight, breathed out, fired, and put one close to the bull's-eye. I sighted in, got my range, and inched closer with the next shot. The third was a dead bull's-eye. I did that five more times then Allbright told me to step back before my carbine locked up from overheating.

I was barely able to suppress my grin for there was no doubt, I was the best shot in the company.

The Sergeant dismissed us and he left without a word.

When the black powder fog cleared I saw that most of the country boys were clumped around Teague, laughing at his joke about breakfast. Vikers had his growing flock all shining up to him like he'd been the one shot best. Other groups here and there complained about how their rifle was out of true or the wind had carried off what should of been a dead shot. Lem would have been making over me, but, as farrier, he'd been excused, so I stood by myself, alone on that big field.

To blazes with them all, I thought. Not a damn one of them had to like me now. Not even Allbright. I'd be riding point. I'd be what was between them and the hostiles. They needed me. And needing was a hell of a lot stronger than liking. I'd proved myself. I was going out West and none of them could stop me.

I was heading for the mess hall when Masters approached and told me to report to the Sergeant's office. I hurried over, eager to hear direct from him that I'd be a troop rifleman.

He was waiting outside his office, standing in the shadows, where he had been watching everything. He gave me an at ease and said, "Congratula-tions, Cathay, you're a fine shot. Best in the company. You'd be a rifleman, if you were coming out West with us."

If?

"But you're not. Though I warned you, it is clear that you have remained a divisive element. I can't have that. Come to my office after reveille tomor-row. I will have your orders issued. You will proceed to HQ for reassign-ment to an infantry unit."

Chapter 43

———

Giving up was such a relief that at lights out I fell direct into the first night of real sleep I'd had since I set foot in the barracks. Soon as I let my guard down, though, the night riders came creeping out of the dark forest where they'd hidden, waiting to pick me off as I rolled away from Old Mister's farm.

Their faces were tombstone white, but the hands they reached out for me were black. I wasn't in the wagon, though. I was running. Trying to run anyway, but I had that damn skirt on again. Though I fought to move, I was frozen in place. They were coming for me. I glanced over my shoulder, but it wasn't the pattyrollers coming for me. The savages were. They would discover I was a woman and use me the way they used enemy women. When they grabbed me, though, their hands weren't red, but black as rotten paw-paws. And I knew I was to be lynched. I tried to scream, but my tongue was frozen and the cry got trapped in my throat. Trapped by a tight strap of cloth.

I woke as a gag was cinched up so deep in my mouth, I near choked on my own tongue. I lashed out in the darkness at my attackers. Kicked one fellow in the head, another in the crotch judging from the loud "Oof!" he blew out.

"Hey?" I heard Lem ask. "Whatcha all—"

The hollow *clunk* of what sounded to be the heavy stock of a Spencer hitting Lem's head was followed by a screech as the iron feet of his bunk raked across the floor when his falling body pushed it aside.

Six pairs of hands cocooned me in a rough army blanket until I couldn't fight anymore. They finished the job by winding rope around the whole package and tying me fast.

They toted me atop their heads like a wild boar they were bringing back to camp to be dressed out. I heard a door open, then close, and we were outside.

They're going to drown me in the river.

I waited for the slope that meant they were carrying me down the steep hill to the Mississippi and tried to work out how to get untied before I drowned.

But the descent I was expecting never came. Instead another door opened and from the way the sound of it closing echoed, I worked out that we were in the washroom with its hard tile walls and floors. This I came to know for a fact when they chunked me on the tile floor, face-first, causing my teeth to bust through my lip so that blood filled my gagged mouth. Then a couple of men hoisted up the draping ends of the blanket and started to swing. When they'd built up a good head of steam, they slammed me against the wall. I wasn't knocked out, only left senseless. I drew myself into a ball as much as I could, trying to protect my head.

"Come on, boys!" It was no surprise to hear Vikers's rasp of a voice. The hatred surged up in me throbbing hot. "Put your backs into it, we've got to give our champion shooter a real ride."

The next few swings were the worst. After that I was beyond feeling anything. Worn out, and figuring they'd killed me, they dumped me on the floor. I played possum. They untied me. Vikers kicked the blanket away from my face with the toe of his boot and I sprung on him like a cougar leaping up to rip out a deer's throat. I would have brought him down had his men not locked a stranglehold on me.

Vikers pulled up straight so that he stood an inch or two over me since my legs had given out and I drooped between Greene and Caldwell. "What did I tell you?" Vikers asked the other troopers'd ganged up with him. "Our *man* here sleeps in his uniform. Never takes it off. Any y'all ever seen our *man* here naked?"

His mob, already scenting even more blood, tried to top each other with insults about me and the nasty doings they claimed they'd seen me and Lem get up to. When they reached the right pitch of blood lust, Vikers pulled out a wicked-looking wire brush last used for scrubbing flaking paint off the stables. "Man never undresses, is a man must not ever bathe," Vikers said. "Wouldn't you agree?"

They keened for me like one of Iyaiya's mobs calling for an enemy prisoner to be thrown down to them.

"I'd say it was past time Stanky had him a bath. Get him on his feet."

Greene and Caldwell jerked me up, and though my mouth was gagged and my throat was nearly ruined with my silent screams, I gargled out a protest.

"Appears Stanky is trying to say something," Vikers observed, playful as a cat toying with a mouse. "What do you have to say, Stanky? Were you going to scream for your sweetheart Mule to come save you? Let's hear what Stanky has to say. Take the gag off."

When they did, I didn't have to work to lower my voice as I promised, "If you touch me, you hard-tailed bastard, I will kill you. Even if I have to come back from the grave to do it, you will die, screaming in agony."

The men's hold slackened a bit. I could of terrified any one of them into letting me go. But Vikers, who feared losing power more than death, said, "I believe this mouth needs cleaning up first."

The pain of a wire brush being ripped across your lips is beyond my ability to describe. But not a drop fell from my eyes, nor did a cry escape from my ravaged mouth after that first cruel stroke. This surprised Vikers, and I took the opportunity to kick him in the face. That broke the spell and they fell on me, Vikers gouging me with the brush, the strokes getting hotter and harder when I refused to scream for mercy.

Panting hard as a roused-up stallion on the prod, his eyes walled, nostrils open wide, quivering in an odd way, Vikers ordered, "Strip him!"

With many idiot remarks about how I stunk and deserved what was coming, his boys tore my pants off, revealing my drawers. I went limp then, defeated by the inevitability of what was to come. Much worse than dying was how those men would use me when they discovered my true nature. There was no evil worse than a man sticking his business in a woman not of a like mind. I wished fervently for death instead of that. They were clawing off my drawers when the sound of a rifle being cocked stopped them.

Sergeant Allbright stepped forward. Lem, blood caked around a gash on his head that showed white to the bone, stood beside him. Allbright, his carbine pointed direct at Vikers, said, "Next man touches that trooper is dead."

Vikers and the rest backed away, and though the pain was terrible when I moved, I managed to pull my uniform on.

Allbright took a long time getting his words out for his mouth was clogged with disgust. "There's one reason and one reason alone that I am not going to hand every man in here a dishonorable discharge. Our orders came in late today. We deploy tomorrow for Fort Arroyo. I won't muster every single one of you out. Not because you don't deserve it, but because we are the first colored cavalry regiment in the history of the United States Army and we get one chance. I will not allow you animals to destroy that chance for those more worthy who will follow you."

He stared, breathing hard against the anger he was reining back. When he spoke, though, it was with a sadness that stung worse than anger ever could. "Damn you all. Don't be the animals they tried to turn us into. You are not slaves anymore. But if you keep on acting like slaves, like something less than men, they will keep on treating us as such. We will only be free men when we act like free men. Now get out of my sight. All of you."

They slunk away beneath his hard stare. Barely able to walk, I shuffled past Allbright and he said, "I'll leave your orders with the regimental clerk." He shook his head, started to walk away, then stopped and added, "Or," he paused before finishing, "you can come with us. If you're fit for service."

I think he made the offer to punish Vikers. Also, I'm certain he didn't believe I would take it.

"I'm fit, sir," I mumbled, blood and pain flowing with every word.

Allbright, disappointed and disgusted, shook his head sorrowfully as he walked away.

Nearly carrying me, Lem helped me outside. We passed Vikers and he hissed, "Something not right about you, Cathay. You know it and I know it. You can hide it here, but no place to hide out there. No place to hide."

BOOK THREE

Out West

Chapter 44

⁓

When we rode out in the black hours before sunrise, I was nothing but an oozing sack of pain slopping around atop Bunny.

"Hang on, Bill. Hang on," Lem, riding next to me, chanted. "All's you got to do is make it down to the river. Ain't but a mile or two. After that, I'ma load you on that boat and you can rest easy. Bill. Bill?"

When I didn't answer, he suggested, "Maybe you should take them transfer papers."

I gave him an animal growl left no doubt how I felt about that. Lem went on talking, but his voice came from farther and farther away and then, along with the clang of the riverboat bells and the rusty croaks of a flock of purple grackles, it stopped altogether.

Next memory I had was of opening my eyes on the terrifying sight of a white plume of steam rising up between two tall crowns of iron that stabbed black points into it as its whistle hooted out the mournful song *Cotton and slaves. Cotton and slaves.* Every splinter of that haunted vessel vibrated its history of evil and cruelty up through me from the planks I laid upon.

"Rest easy, Bill," Lem's voice soothed when, whimpering like a sick dog, I struggled to rise up and escape the terrible fate that waited down the river. He patted me back down, my head resting on his jacket, which he'd folded into a pillow since, even more than I had before, I kept a death grip on my own jacket, buttoned up to my chin. My saddle and other belongings sat next to me in the neat stack where Lem had placed them.

"Hard part's over," he said. "Leastwise for the next few days. All's in the world you got to do now is lay back and heal up." Gently, he patted sweet calendula cream on my ruined mouth, then he brought his canteen to my lips. When he lifted my head so I could drink, he tipped me up enough that I saw how the rest of the company was all sprawled out across the top deck like so much felled timber. This hectic scene doubled and tripled and tilted back and forth for the beating had rattled my brain.

Fearing I would spend the rest of my days trapped in a cartwheeling world, I tried to focus on the paddle wheel turning at the back of the boat. It was a dozen yards wide and tall as a three-story house. Faces, always two of the same one, appeared above me. They were like mirrors reflecting back how bad I looked. The good men in the troop, Fernie Teague, the Georgia boys and them, could barely look upon my battered face. The bad ones had no trouble staring at me with critical eyes. Like I was a piece of poor work-manship. A job that hadn't been done up to standards. A killing that'd gone half finished. I was mostly out of my head for the next couple of days. Every time I opened my eyes ghostly white birds were flying across an overcast sky gray as wash water and Lem was dripping water into my mouth just the way I'd dripped cider into my dead soldier's mouth.

At some point, the boat must of made a stop, for Lem was giving me some bark he'd stripped off a willow tree to chew on to quiet the moans I wasn't aware I'd been making. The long and short of it is, I'd of died except for Private Lemuel Powdrell. He tended to me gentle as a mama to her babe. He'd of given me a sponge bath, but, even when passed smooth out, my wits would collect themselves the instant a hand came anywhere near the uni-form I kept buttoned up around me tight as a second skin, and I would not allow it.

One time Sergeant Allbright's face appeared between me and the white birds. I was mortified to smithereens to have him see me, shape I was in. I was a thorn in his side. At best a nuisance and at worst the reason his troop wasn't coming together the way he'd dreamed black men in uniform ought to. It hurt my heart for him to see me in such pitiful shape and I closed my eyes and slipped off away from that pain, too.

The next time I opened my eyes, the Georgia boys were lined up across the edge of the deck pissing into the Mississippi, wagging their beans about so the streams would crisscross and arguing about who was shooting far-thest.

Lem asked me, "You think you can make water? Want me to help you up?"

"Can't stand," I croaked. "Fetch me that blanket and my mess kit."

Lem unstrapped the bedroll from my saddle and helped me to tent up inside it, and I proceeded to squat like a frog and fill my tin to overflowing. It hurt so bad that if I could of picked one moment to die that'd of been the one. The whistle blew and the black came up again.

Chapter 45

〜

Though we were meant to sail on down to Indianola off the coast of Texas, there was a yellow fever epidemic raging from New Orleans on south. Sergeant didn't want to risk that it had reached Indianola, so we docked north of New Orleans in the town of Vicksburg and unloaded in what remained of the city Grant had bombarded and burned to cinders.

The horses, who'd ridden below in the shade of the upper deck, were led down a wide gangplank. With their hooves clopping big and echoey against that wooden plank, the company gathered its traps and prepared to go ashore. I hauled myself up by clinging to the pilothouse. The instant I put the least bit of weight on my legs, though, I came down in a heap. I wondered what was broken and if I'd be a cripple, seeing double, for the rest of my days.

"Guess I'll haul you off way I got you on," Lem said, and made to scoop me up.

"Naw," I mumbled, for even pushing words out exhausted me. "Got to walk."

And though I leaned on Lem so heavy he might as well have been carrying me for all the good my legs were, I made it ashore on my own two feet. I don't intend to moan any further about my miseries and will simply state that mounting up on Bunny and riding out of Vicksburg was a disagreeable business. But, oh, what a comfort it was to be reunited with my floppy-eared friend. She healed a loneliness in me that Lem, for all his goodness, could not touch. For Lem did not know my secret and Bunny did.

After a few days, my vision leveled out. Then, once I got myself splinted and bound up to where I could sit the saddle again and not fall out from the pain, I found myself embarked upon a right pleasant ride. It was as if the war had never ended and I was once again out camping with the General. The joy of being released from the barracks and away from Vikers's tormenting attention was a first-class tonic. Away in whatever little corner of the forest that Lem and I found to camp in of a night, I was free again. Free to be alone, free to squat and do my business, free to breathe.

We headed south by southwest for over a week through wet grassland and pine forests so thick we rode single file, spread out for miles. In that way, we passed into east Texas where the ringing of axes and the thunder as the giant pines fell told the story that the houses and barns and businesses the war had burned to ash were to be built again. It was odd, though, that the farther west into those piney woods we rode, the heavier grew the spell of the South that fell upon us. Buried within the deep woods, sound and air and even time was stopped so still by those walls of pine trunks that it seemed the war had never been fought. That slavery times not only had never ended in east Texas but would go on for all eternity.

The story passed among us that this state had fought not one, but two wars for the right to own us and build Texas off of free black labor. The first one was against the Mexicans who didn't allow slavery. Then they fought the United States of America to keep my people in chains. I figured this explained why the state seemed double haunted and double damned.

Whenever we passed a work crew, the hands pulling the long saws and swinging the axes were all black. The ones holding the reins, all white. The axmen blinked a time or two as we rode past like they couldn't believe they were seeing black men, armed and mounted, wearing the blue suits of the Union Army. The company, which had come off that paddle wheel boat gay and full of song at being real soldiers riding West, fell silent upon seeing these zombie men.

I summoned up the strength to yell out to the frozen black figures watching us pass, "You're free. Come with us! You're free! Free!" I repeated, but they acted like they either didn't know the meaning of the word or didn't believe it held true in Texas. They were back to their sawing and ax swinging even before we'd finished passing through.

The white masters were another story. Late on a morning, so muggy I feared I might drown from breathing the swampy air, I heard a shot ring out, then a couple dozen terrified troopers came thundering past. One of them was riding double, his passenger clinging to him, eyes wild with fright.

A white boss had shot the man's horse right out from under him and threatened to kill the next black _____ that trespassed on his property.

Later, when I recounted the hardships of my years in the army, the doubters, the ones who called me a liar, would always ask, "If it was as tough and hard as you make out, why didn't you just leave?"

My answer came from the sorrowful, ghostly creatures who inhabited the piney woods of Texas and from the demons who drove them. Nothing could be worse than that.

Lem and I rode on, silent until he said, "Thought things was gon be different out West."

"This isn't the West," a voice pronounced from behind us. Me and Bunny'd been flopping along in our pitiful way, but the instant I heard that voice, I came up straight as a die and my hand cleavered a salute into my forehead.

"At ease, men," Allbright said. "No one out here to see us except that mama turkey down there."

He tipped his head toward a pile of underbrush and it shaped itself into a lanky, lock-kneed gobbler leading a wobbling clutch of six babies through the shadows. I, who thought myself a sharp hunting eye, had not so much as glimpsed that tasty bird and her young. We were alone, we three, for the column, tiptoeing over fallen trees and around marshes, was stretched out far ahead and behind, leaving us with our own space of lonely quiet.

The Sergeant, free from command for a moment, expanded into that open space and said, "No, Powdrell, we're a long ways from where the West begins. What we're riding through here is the worst of the South that will never end."

"Yessir," I piped up, excited that Sergeant Allbright had spoken my thoughts. "It's all this Spanish moss. Stuff gives me the all-overs."

Allbright said, "Like fog and pond scum had a baby."

I noted that Sergeant Allbright had spoken to me without the disgust that usually pickled his face. I think not dying might have graded me up some in his eyes. When we finally rode into a bit of sunshine and glimpsed a patch of sky and a horizon to go along with it, Allbright said, "Let's see exactly where we are."

We dismounted and Allbright dug a beautiful brass instrument he called a sextant from his saddlebag. This he held to his eye and explained as he measured various angles how to pinpoint our precise spot on the face of the earth. Juggling the instrument, he fumbled to write the numbers in his note-book and I offered to do the writing for him.

"You can read?" he asked.

"No, sir, but I can cipher. I do know my numbers. Can write a fair hand when it's not letters."

Suspicious, he turned his notebook over to me, and after shaking the rust out of my fingers, I showed him how well Daddy had taught me. We finished and rode on, the Sergeant clearly lost in his thoughts. After a bit, he asked, as though the three of us had all been part of the conversation he was having in his head, "What was it that slavery required to grow and flourish?"

"Wicked white folk," Lem answered in complete sincerity.

"You can find those anywhere," the Sergeant said. "No, what slavery required was water. No point in slaves unless you had the water to raise cotton, tobacco, sugar. That's what saved the West. Not enough water for slavery to make white men rich in that parched terrain. If they'd had the water, they'd have had the slaves. But they didn't. Which is why true freedom will not begin until we reach the ninety-eighth meridian."

"Is that right?" Lem said, having no more idea what a "meridian" was than I did—just that it was the spot where freedom would begin.

"The ninety-eighth," Allbright went on. "That's where annual rainfall drops off to less than twenty inches a year. That's where we can breathe free. By my measurements, we crossed the ninety-third a while back."

"Five more to go," I said, showing off. I was considerably puffed up to be riding along with Sergeant Allbright, being schooled about meridians and annual rainfall. It was like being back with Solomon. If Solomon had been young and had skin that shone like it had been rubbed with linseed oil and broad shoulders and a lavish plenty of eyelashes that curled up tight as a music box spring and a manner of speaking that was educated but didn't low-rate everyone else.

And then the Sergeant got going on someone I would come to find out was, essentially, the love of his life: Mr. Frederick Douglass. When he started in quoting his idol, a spirit possessed the Sergeant purer and stronger than any preacher I'd ever heard. And so it was that, with Mr. Douglass's thoughts on "color-phobia," which is what that great man called the "disease" of racialism, ringing in my ears, Sergeant Allbright led us like Moses out of that land of bondage and toward the Promised Land of the ninety-eighth meridian.

Chapter 46

Once released from its piney prison, Texas opened out into sugar then cotton plantations, neither of which appeared to have been inconvenienced by the war that had left much of the South east of the Mississippi a smoldering graveyard.

In a pretty stretch of hilly limestone country, we came upon a settlement of Germans who had fought with the Union against slavery and showed themselves to be the most welcoming whites I had ever encountered. Their limestone farmhouses, cedar fences, peach orchards, and cornfields were as neat and tidy as the plump wives and blond children who waved as we passed by. Some even ran up to offer us apples or a kerchief filled with dewberries.

But the true wonders of Texas did not present themselves until we rode into the old Spanish capital of San Antonio de Béxar where grandees with chin beards, thin and sharp as daggers, wandered the city's narrow, twisting streets. A river, cool and green, ran through the city where citizens of all ages swam in the shade of giant cypress and willow trees. If I'd of run off anywhere, it would have been there in San Antone.

Instead, after four days' rest while we resupplied and reshod the horses, we headed west by way of the Emigrant Trail, following in the tracks of a few settlers and a whole herd of prospectors bound for the gold fields of California.

As the Sergeant promised, the farther west we rode, the drier it got. Bit by bit all the greenery that had given me what privacy I could steal, commenced to thin out and dwindle in size. On the forty-fifth day out, we rode for nine hours before encountering any greenery higher than the rough grasses that extended as far as the eye could see. And that was only a patch of prickly pear that barely gave me enough cover to do my squatting business.

By then all the plants had turned on us. Gone were such as the sweet and gentle weeping willow that couldn't of slapped a housefly in a hurricane. Instead of being the kind friends that did naught but feed and clothe and shelter, plants became sworn enemies dedicated to killing us and every other creature that passed by. They had the names to prove it, too: Spanish dagger. Devil's darning needle. Horse crippler. Apache lance. Crucifixion thorn. Coach whip.

As Vikers had warned, there was no place to hide in this barren country and I had to wait until long after dark when the mens' snores grew louder than the yips and howls of coyotes yodeling out their hunting songs to sneak off and relieve myself. One of those endless days seemed worse than all the others with strange cramps deep in my gut caused by my having to hold it for so long. The aching even reached up farther, making my breasts sore and tender beneath the tight bindings. That night, the moon was so full it was near bright as day and I was forced to venture even farther away than usual to find privacy.

In this light, when I pulled down my britches and squatted, the catastrophe that had struck was plain to see: After all these years, my nature had arrived.

I had no choice but to unwind my chest bindings and stuff them into my stained drawers. As I waddled back to my bedroll I wondered why the woman's curse had found me after I'd ducked it for so long. It had to be that, for the first time in my life, out here on the trail, I was eating regular. We had all the game we could shoot, plenty of beans, and even vegetables whenever there were any to be bought. After a lifetime of hoecakes, hardtack, and mush, the long hollows on my body were filling out. My hipbones no longer stuck out like knife blades and I couldn't count every single one of my ribs. Also, hard as army life was, it was a picnic compared to what it had been back at Old Mister's.

I had to conclude that the army had made me soft, soft enough to become a real woman. For a minute or two, the thought that I was normal in this way comforted me. Then the cramping in my nethers almost ripped a moan from my lips and I realized that my woman's body had betrayed me again and just made a hard road even harder.

Chapter 47

⟨athay, you not going to pee?" Vikers yelled back over his shoulder at me the next day. He was lined up with most of the other troopers. They had their backs turned and were pissing onto the hard-baked dirt.

It was three in the afternoon. We'd been riding for ten hours since we broke camp at five and hadn't come across so much as a pile of rocks high enough to squat behind. The prairie rolled on in all directions, endless as an ocean. An ocean set hard on drowning me. The only things throwing shadows across that dry flat land were a long column of horses and men and one girl had to pee so bad she was sweating yellow. No milch cow, hours past milking time, had ever been as full as I was.

Though I'd made sure that neither my unharnessed bumps nor the least stain on my light blue trousers would betray me, Vikers seemed to notice that something was different. He was paying me even more attention than usual, remarking on how I didn't piss with the others and the like. The way he sniffed around made him seem about half wolf, like he'd picked up the scent of blood and tracked it back to me.

A horse nickered and Greene, peeing with the others, jerked to look behind, sending his stream flying over the boots of the soldier next to him who cursed and promised to slit Greene's throat if that ever happened again.

Vikers, mounted now, came up next to me, and asked again, "You're not going to relieve yourself?" His piercing voice had dried out so much it now sounded like a rusty nail being pulled from a cedar post.

I tucked my chin into my neck and came back salty, "What? You keepin' count?"

Vikers's ugly, bow-faced mare nudged in close to Bunny. "Nothing to count. Last two times we stopped, you stayed in the saddle."

"So, you are keepin' count."

"Oh, I'm counting, Cathay. You best believe I am counting."

"You ain't right, Vikers."

He wheeled his mount around so he faced me head-on, plucked his spectacles out, and wrapped the gold curl of one arm then the other around his ears like he was fixing to read one of the papers that decided our fates. And now, in the withering glare of a sun that shone twice as bright as it did back home, he was reading me, and pronounced, "Someone round here *isn't* right, but it *isn't* me. Is it?"

I pulled up tall and stared kerosene waiting for the flame back at him. I'd give the pipsqueak something to read. I'd give him a grandma sharpened her teeth to points so she could rip out the throats of her enemies.

His voice softened until he sounded almost kind and he went on, "I said it before, I'll say it again, something's not right about you, Cathay. Not your fault," he said, sounding like a friend concerned about my welfare, wanting to help me. "You know it. I know it. Every trooper here knows it. It's bound to come out. Bound to."

For one second, I thought about how easy it'd be to confess, clear the air, just be myself the way I always had. I snapped out of that, though, and said, "Step off, Vikers. You crowding me. Man."

He smirked and rode away. I gripped the stock of my carbine, and looked off into the distance, praying for a few scraggly trees, even some piles of rocks. Nothing stopped my gaze, though, until it hit a line of blue mountains could of been a thousand miles away. It took me a bit to notice a few pale squiggles of motion. I figured they were just heat waves rising from the sandy earth, but the squiggles took shape and I saw them to be the pale wolves the Mexicans called *lobos*. They trotted along in the shimmery heat for a long time, watching us with their yellow eyes. Then, in the blink of an eye, that cruel emptiness swallowed them up whole.

Chapter 48

～

Never before or after did I hear coyotes howl the way they did that night. Seemed they were taking the woes of the world and flinging them back at the moon, and the moon didn't care.

When the moon finally sank beneath the horizon, leaving us in darkness, the coyotes left off howling and I was finally safe to creep away from camp. Along the way, I stole half a dozen of the kerchiefs troopers had laid out to dry. When I was far enough off that the embers of the string of burned-down fires the troopers were bedded down next to were pinpricks of orange in the black night, I relieved myself. I tossed away the fouled bindings, replaced them with a pad of kerchiefs then sat down to consider my situation.

I had to conclude that Vikers and his boys were bound to find me out. For a second or two, I wondered whether it wouldn't be better for me to walk on out into the night until I met up with the yellow eyes of a pack of *lobos*. I was wondering if having my guts strung across the prairie by Mexican wolves might not be preferable to getting done in by Vikers, when a rattler, attracted by my warmth, slithered up. I had a rock in my hand and his brains bashed out before he had a chance to raise his tail and shake out even one rattle.

"Thank you, Iyaiya," I said, uplifted mightily by this evidence that my grandmother was still looking out for me. No telegram could of been clearer and I knew sure as creek run to river what I had to do.

Back in camp, I crept over to where Vikers and his boys lay curled around the ashes of their fire, dead asleep. Vikers's special tin coffeepot set on a rock next to the cold fire. I swiped that pot. In exchange, I tucked Grandma's messenger into bed with Vikers then slipped away.

I made for the remuda staked out at the far edge of camp. The mounted guard was Milton Favor, a wheelwright out of Illinois. This was bad luck for me as Favor was a bright-eyed lad when what I needed at that moment was a shirker slumped over in the saddle, dreaming his shift away. Quiet though I was, the horses caught my smell and started snorting and shifting about, eager for their morning grain.

"Hush, hosses, hush," Favor said.

The horses quieted down. I eased forward, took a deep breath, gathered my courage, and chunked Vikers's pot hard as I could into the middle of the herd. It clanged and clattered with a fearsome noise that would of given me away, except that the horses started whinnying and churning about. Favor was so occupied heading off a complete stampede that he didn't notice even when I stood, passed among the milling animals, and retrieved what was left of the stolen pot.

As I'd hoped, it was trampled but good. The gooseneck spout hung on by the thinnest of welds. As soon as I was in the clear, I popped it loose. The spout was exactly the length I needed. Six inches. I worked it down into my drawers and between my legs and secured it so that it wasn't poking me.

I slipped back into my bedroll and slept as easy as a babe in the cradle. I was filled with the kind of peace familiar to those who place their faith in Jesus and turn loose the reins on their lives. My faith was in my Iyaiya. She had made a way for me and I had no doubt that it would lead me out of the sorry place I now found myself in.

Chapter 49

⌒

Shrieks of a pitch to raise both the quick and the dead woke me the next morning. The discovery that he'd spent the night with a rattlesnake had Vikers dancing about in the predawn light, waving his hands in the air, and squealing like a hysterical girl.

"It's dead," his bunkies repeated a dozen times, to no avail, for, as Iyaiya must of known, Vikers had snakephobia bad and he had been driven out of his senses. This was better than I could of ever hoped for in the way of cutting the man down. I gulped down three cups of coffee, eager for the next act of my play.

Vikers quit shrieking around the time my bladder threatened to burst. I strutted off to the edge of camp and faced out toward the line of blue mountains, streaked along the top with orange where the sun was peeking up.

Trying to think of a song that'd get everyone's attention, I recalled a ditty we'd learned off of a stomper who worked in a cotton gin back in Hempstead. Though the man coughed constantly, as, like most of them there, he was dying of cotton lung from breathing in clouds of lint all day, he managed to teach us the words that I bellowed out now.

There's a yellow girl in Texas
That I'm going down to see
No other darkies know her
No darkey, only me
She cried so when I left her
That it like to broke my heart,

And if I only find her,
We never more will part

When I opened up and really sang, I had a voice that could make water tremble in a horse trough. It was a voice you felt in the pit of your gut. Like me, whether you thought my voice was pretty or not didn't count for much, it would get the job done.

And the job then was to get every trooper's attention. Which it did. They shifted their stares from Vikers, who had collapsed into whimpering trembles, to me. I hawked and snorted and spit before commencing the main act. Having gotten bushels more schooling than I ever cared to on how to pee like a man, I took my stance, spreading my legs as though extra bracing was required to counterbalance the magnificent weight being pulled forth, before I dug into the fly of my britches and took hold of what I'd planted there. Then, although there was no one at my side, I performed a maneuver I'd seen the less endowed among the men use and covered up what little of the spout I allowed to protrude with one hand. The other I rested on my hip in the manner of the jauntier troopers. And then, standing straight up, I turned loose of all that used coffee. Though but a dribble, it did squirt out from roughly the right place.

"Hoo-WEE!" Lem said, startling me, as he took his place at my side and unbuttoned. "Thought we already done crossed the Mississippi."

Though Lem was happily occupied in unloosing a majestic arc, I turned away.

"Oh, sorry, Bill," Lem said. "Thought you was over your bashful spell. No disrespect intended."

"None taken, Lem," I answered.

More hawking and spitting covered any telltale clanks of the spout against the pewter buttons of my fly as I tucked my equipment back into its kerchief holder, closed the fly, hitched up my suspenders, and turned to face Vikers. Though he tried to glare back at me, it didn't work as he'd gone the color of cold ashes and his hands were trembling.

I sauntered his way and, when the only sound was the far-off chittering of prairie dogs barking out their good mornings to each other and warning us not to come any closer, I said to Vikers, "Next one'll be alive."

Chapter 50

⁓

Fort Clark, where we stopped for a week of rest, barely merited being called a fort, yet it seemed like Paris, France, to our saddle-sore company as we'd had naught but the stars overhead for a roof and the hard ground beneath our bones for a bed for weeks. The one characteristic that distinguished the ramshackle collection of weather-beat *jacales* and half-burned barracks was, unlike any other fort you'd ever ride into anywhere in the entire country, this one had no flag flapping above it.

The flagpole was nothing but a black stump poking up out of a weedy parade ground for it had been burned down by the Union commander when the Rebs overtook the fort in the first year of the war. Though that Yankee commander surrendered without a fight, he was bound that the Confederate Stars and Bars flag would never fly above Fort Clark. So he set the flagpole on fire. As well as the barracks and whatever else he could torch before clearing off.

Beyond putting the fires out, the Rebs didn't do much with the fort and withdrew entirely a year later to march north as the Secesh intended to capture the Colorado gold mines and California ports for the Confederacy. These conquerors of the American West made it as far as Glorieta Pass, New Mexico, which is where their fancy plan went to smash.

It is not certain whether they were defeated on account of a commander who was a rum soak or because no one out West wanted them there to begin with. Either way, the Rebs vacated that country, headed south, back to the swamps and marshes that are more hospitable to their species, and Fort

Clark sat deserted through the rest of the war. Union forces had barely moved back in by the time we arrived. The barracks were still charred and Old Glory was not yet flying.

The unburned parts of the near-empty barracks were already set aside for whites. The second lieutenant who met us flapped a weary hand in the direction of a moderately scorched building and allowed as how we could bunk there. It had been constructed of cedar stakes set vertically the way the Mexicans did to build their *jacales*. Daylight shone between the upright stakes as the long-ago builders had set them when they were green and they'd dried up and shrunk away from whatever chinking might once have separated what was indoors from what was out.

After batting away years of spiderwebs, we entered and encountered a lavish menagerie of critters. Swallows flew from one end of the large space to the other, escaping out through the large gaps in all four walls. The mice squeaked at us, protesting our intrusion. A loud rattling from a dark corner sent Vikers bolting from the place.

Allbright planted himself in the gloom. As he studied the interior, I was taken by the way the stripes of light peeking through the stakes glinted through the cloud of dust that whirled about him like handfuls of gold dust were being tossed his way. The light outlined his broad shoulders and shot out in rays, making a halo around his wide-brimmed hat. "Any of you men," he said, "who'd rather camp outside are free to do so. Mulberry Springs is a quarter of a mile north, northwest. The water there is clear and abundant. That is all."

As soon as I had Bunny groomed, and turned loose in the fort corral, I made for Mulberry Springs. It was a vision of paradise. The spring water bubbling up was clear as glass and cool as a slab of polished marble. It flowed for miles along a limestone bed. As far as I could see, the stream was overhung by thick stands of oak and pecan trees, making the blessed waterway into a tunnel of green cutting through that dry land.

I wasted no time in seeking out the most isolated, most private spot I could find for I hungered for one thing more than food or air at that moment: a bath. I followed the creek for so long that I couldn't hear even the memory of a trooper hawking up trail dust. That was where I bivouacked. The cool water against my naked skin was almost more bliss than I could stand. The feel of it touching all the soft, round places brought tears to my eyes. I hugged myself the way I would a friend who'd been gone too long. One I missed more than I ever thought I would.

I lathered up with the bar of soap that had been handed out before we left Jefferson Barracks. Having done no shaving and very little bathing with my ration, I had near a full bar left and sudsed up aplenty. My drawers and britches, socks and kerchiefs, were next. Though I'd never have believed such a thing would happen in this hot, dry land, I was shivering by the time I stepped out and dressed quickly.

The sun set and dark came on fast. While I was spreading my wash out to dry, a voice came to me from some distance away, echoing down along that green tunnel. It was Allbright, and, wonder of wonders, the man was singing exactly the tune I had been earlier.

> *Oh, I'm going now to find her*
> *For my heart is full of woe*
> *And we'll sing the songs together*
> *That we sang so long ago*
> *We'll play the banjo gaily*
> *And we'll sing our sorrows o'er*
> *And the yellow Rose of Texas*
> *shall be mine forever more.*

In a moment of silly, girlish dreaming, I lost all sense that his words were being sung or that they had ever been uttered before. That "sweetest girl of color" was me and I would be his forever more.

I made my way to his encampment, and stopped there in the shadows beyond the globe of light cast by his fire. I watched as he arranged his blanket by the fire. I noticed how his movements seemed lightened, now that he was freed from the weight of command, and realized that the Sergeant, too, was burdened by the necessity of putting on an act. He settled himself on the blanket next to a pile of pecans he had collected and started in cracking those plump nuts between a couple of rocks. Even now, all these years later, if I want to calm my spirit, this is the memory I call up. Him cracking and eating those nuts and humming all the while about his yellow rose.

The happiness must of deafened us both, otherwise the intruders never would of snuck up the way they did without either of us hearing the twig that must of snapped, the frogs that had stopped croaking, or the owl that hooted a warning about the invaders. But we didn't and, all of an instant, they were there, five of them, strolling into the safe circle of the Sergeant's campfire light.

One second I thought the intruders were Indians. The next, I was certain they were black men. A moment later, I knew them to be Mexican. Mostly, though, they were invaders who, sneaking up on the Sergeant in the dark, clearly meant him harm. I had not brought my carbine and the Sergeant's was leaning up against a tree, out of reach.

Though I knew those black Mexican Indians would lay me out cold, I burst from the shadows and went for the rifle. The savages reacted to my jumping into their midst, then pulling a cocked rifle on them, with no more notice than they'd of given a tumblebug rolling a tidy dab of shit past their feet.

Their leader looked me up and down, gave a little grunt of dismissal, and said to the Sergeant, "I am John Horse. Are you hungry? We have antelope. Backstrap. The best part. Leave the nuts for the squirrels."

He nodded at me, and added, "Your friend is also invited." Then they all vanished back into the woods.

Chapter 51

The strangers slithered through the woods along the creek quiet as ghosts. Compared to them, Allbright and I sounded like a pair of buffalo. In this way, I was certain that, whatever the exact color of skin, fullness of lip, broadness of nose, or wiriness of hair, they were Indian. This fact became undeniable when we fetched up at their camp and I saw the whole band of around eighty or so men, women, and children of what I learned were Black Seminoles.

Either out of good manners or a strange lack of curiosity, only the children stared and pointed at the Sergeant and me as we stepped into their midst. They motioned for us to sit down, and brand-new, U.S.-issue mess tins were placed in our hands by a couple of flounced and beaded women. On the tins were chunks of boiled antelope and a sort of doughy bread that tasted like it was made from yams and vulcanized rubber.

I ate and gawked at the band.

If God ever put a more handsome group of human beings on this earth, I have yet to see them. These black Mexican Indians had extracted the best from three races and assembled a tribe of people with walnut skin, long black hair either straight or with a bit of crinkle to it, high cheekbones, full lips, and every brand of nose you can conjure. Might even have been a button or two amidst them. The men wore full muslin shirts and moccasins. A few old birds sported turbans made of a plaid wool.

Most impressive of all was their chief, a tall, powerfully built man with straight, black hair that fell to his shoulders, dark skin that had a coppery cast to it, and eyes angled up in Chinaman fashion. He was dressed in a mus-

lin tunic that extended to the middle of his thighs. A vest decorated with
Mexican pesos pounded flat and rows of beads was worn atop the tunic.
Deerskin leggings covered his legs and moccasins his feet. About his neck
was a strand of beads made from iridescent shells interspersed with more flattened pesos.

As striking as he and the rest of the men were, it was their women who
stole my breath away. Let me describe the one I took to be the chief's wife,
though she may only have been a sweetheart for the headman always seemed
to look to one old gal for the final word. In any case, when I gazed upon this
young woman, I felt as though I was staring into the face of my grandmother back when she was one of the Leopard King's Amazon warriors.
Back before the filthy Portugee got hold of her or the cursed Americans
locked an iron collar about her neck. Back when she was free.

This beauty gazed at me directly from beneath a frame of short, straight
black bangs that curved around her face. The rest of her hair was pulled up
into a tall hair hat decorated with a band of red beads woven through it.
Her neck, from just below her chin down to the tops of her shoulders, was
circled with alternating strings of yellow and red beads. The choker gave
her a regal appearance, her head resting high and noble above the garland.
A fantastic cape, trimmed across the top with Mexican peso coins beat down
to broad, flat discs, covered her upper arms.

Of a sudden, the old gal who I figured might be the chief's wife appeared
to notice me for the first time. She was a shrunk-down, wrinkled-up, pot-
bellied copy of the young beauty. A smile played across her queenly features
as she nudged the other women around her, pointed at me, and whispered.
They all commenced then to studying me, scowling and grimacing as though
I were a hard problem they had to cipher. Then they, too, went to smiling,
nodding, and beckoning me to join them. With horror, I realized that they
had all arrived at the same conclusion: I was one of them. I was female. A
female warrior.

I looked away, but my constant fear of exposure had risen into a full-
blown panic. I would of jumped up and bolted right then and there except
that the smiles and waves stopped dead the instant that the headman stood
before the gathering and said in English, "We welcome the sergeant who
leads his men into this land where we will fight side by side."

Though this comment mystified me, there was a muttering and heads
nodding in our direction. Then they all fell silent and the chief went on

speaking to Allbright. "I am John Horse, headman of the Black Seminoles. I led the only successful slave rebellion in the history of this country. Three times I defeated the Army of the United States of America in the swamps of Florida and kept my people free. Have you heard my story?"

For the only time I knew of, the Sergeant stumbled before answering, "No, sir, I have never before heard of people of color defeating the U.S. Army."

John Horse shrugged. "Of course not. We did what our enemies fear most. Why would they share the tale? Three times the army came into the swamps of Florida to claim us. And three times we beat them back. I will tell you of my people's victories, Sergeant, so that you will know who John Horse and the Black Seminoles are. So that you and your Buffalo Soldiers will come to fight beside us. No matter who the enemy is."

The Sergeant gave him a suspicious look.

Horse continued, "I went to Washington two times to speak to the President and tell him that the Black Seminoles would slaughter the whites who try to make us slaves. You must know that, again and again, we were betrayed by generals who promised freedom then imprisoned us when we surrendered. The last time I was tricked this way, they locked me inside the fourteen-foot-thick walls of Castillo de San Marcos. With me was the great chief Osceola and the fiercest warrior to ever fight the white man, Wild Cat, who we call Coacoochee.

"Inside those thick walls, all we saw of the freedom we had been promised was a nine-inch-wide opening fifteen feet above our heads. Though our women wailed, lamenting our lost home, Wild Cat made us strong with his words, saying, 'They may shoot us. They may drive our women and children night and day. They may chain our hands and feet, but the red man's heart will be always free.' We, his allies, some of us his blood kin, were red men. Not the black slaves whose grandparents had escaped bondage.

"We watched the nine inches of sky and we fasted and we waited. We made rope from our bed sacks. And, on a night when the moon did not enter the sky, we escaped. We gathered our bands and took back the swamps. We fought the white man, and again, no general, no army could defeat us. Again, we drove the masters to the bargaining table. And, yet again, promises were made if we surrendered. We were promised our own land in the Indian Territories. Because our children were dying of hunger, we accepted. And, a third time, we were betrayed."

A slave rebellion? Red men and black men fighting together to defeat white men? Escaping out a nine-inch opening fifteen feet overhead?

Could this be true?

Though I had never heard a whisper of such things, when John Horse spoke I could hear my grandmother through him. Her stories of six thousand women warriors defeating armies of men twice that size might also have sounded like a pack of lies to anyone who didn't know that we weren't slaves. We were captives. John Horse had the same iron in his soul that was never going to be bent nor beaten into another shape. I believed he had done everything he recollected and a deal more besides.

"The barren land they moved us to," Horse continued, "was in the territory of our enemy, the Creek. These devils had fought alongside the slavers. They kidnapped us and they enslaved us. The Black Seminole will never be slaves. Not for the white man. Not for the red man. So, again, I led my people to freedom. We escaped to northern Mexico, where the government gave us sanctuary if we would help them fight the Comanche and Apache raiders. This we did. I became el Capitán Juan Caballo and, for many years, we were happy in Coahuila. And then, once more, the betrayals began.

"Because of this, I now come here to Fort Clark. The U.S. Army has invited us to fight the Apache and Comanche with them for, in this, the American soldiers are helpless children. They now offer us good land beside this creek and good rations. Still, my people fear another betrayal and we did not know whether we should accept or go back to Coahuila. And then we saw you. Black men wearing the uniform of the U.S. Army, riding the horses of the U.S. Army, and carrying the guns of the U.S. Army.

"Because of you, we are convinced now to leave Mexico and come to Fort Clark. Then, no matter what betrayals might come, we shall always have allies by our side. But first, my people and I need an answer to a question."

"And what might that question be?" the Sergeant asked, his tone peppery with suspicion.

"We want to know why you are fighting for your enemies, for the ones who enslaved you?"

"You mean the United States Army?" the Sergeant asked, his suspicion turning to annoyance. "Just exactly who do you think you and your men will be fighting for?"

John Horse translated the comment for those who didn't savvy English then answered, calmly, "We will not be fighting for those who enslaved us because the white men never owned us. They never sold one of our children from her mother or used our women as broodmares as they have done to your people. If an enemy had ever done such things to my people, and then, if a great war had been fought to free us, we would never become slaves again."

Peevishness crinkled the Sergeant's fine features and he said, "We are free men, we are fighting for those who freed us, and we are paid well for our service."

At this, a great murmur went through the crowd, the Sergeant was pulled to his feet, and one of John Horse's lieutenants handed him a small bundle wrapped in the plaid wool some of them had tied about their heads as turbans. The Sergeant took the bundle, which caused a wave of happy murmurs of *hink-lah-mas-tchay* and *es bueno*. Though a general jolliness settled over everyone, the Sergeant's uneasiness sharpened. He stood there staring at the bundle like John Horse had placed a bag of boll weevils in his hands.

At that moment, all the ladies, led by the old one I took to be John Horse's wife, rose up as one and headed straight for me. I scrambled to my feet. Though I feared what they had figured out, I didn't think they had any way to blow me as it did not appear that the women spoke English. Then I glimpsed the gift John Horse's wife held in her outstretched hands and I saw that no words would be needed for they were stepping forward with one of the long, flounced skirts that only the women wore.

I pivoted smartly and ran from the gathering. Though a *tsk-tsking* chorus of *hull-wax-tchay* and *no es bueno* followed me into the darkness, I had no other choice. Even then, I feared they'd exposed me. That the Sergeant would put together the two and two of them presenting me with a damn skirt and me bolting and my secret would be revealed.

I was trembling when the Sergeant caught up with me. I was sure he'd have that skirt in his hands and demand to know what it meant. Instead, he said, "Good work, Private. I'd have left myself except that I was too stunned by their proposal."

"Oh," was all I could manage.

"I salute you for your very swift, very correct response to their treasonous suggestion."

"Uh-huh."

"You've a nimble mind, Private. And a loyal heart."

"Sir."

"You saved us by not accepting their bribe. I should have done the same. Instead, they tricked me into allying myself with them in rebellion against the United States."

"You don't say."

"I couldn't believe it either, Cathay. Just by accepting their gift, I betrayed the oath of allegiance I swore when I enlisted."

He heaved the bundle into the woods, said, "Good night, Private," and took off at a fast trot back to his encampment. I started to leave, then went back, peeked twice in all directions, bent down, and plucked up the Sergeant's bundle.

Back at my camp, I unwound the plaid wool. The women had fine weaving skills and the cloth was surprisingly light and soft. It became my new binding. I pulled my muslin shirt on over it. I now had two secrets to hide. The second was: far from being horrified by John Horse's tale, the news that slaves had beaten back the U.S. Army electrified me.

Chapter 52

~

After a week of fixing horseshoes and feeding our mounts up on corn and us on the turkey, antelope, and deer that ran plentiful about, to say nothing of the sunfish, bluegills, bass, and walleyes that fairly leaped from Mulberry Springs, we left Fort Clark.

The second day on the trail, the Sergeant, who believed that I had saved him from turning traitor on the U.S. Army and took my flight from the Black Seminole camp to be the act of a true patriot, graded me up so considerable that he asked me to come on a scouting expedition with him.

First thing the next morning, the two of us rode out ahead of the long column of men. We headed north and reached a plain covered by grass high enough to tickle Bunny's belly. We cut through it leaving the trail of our passing behind. We climbed to the top of a rise and found the vast, flat table land they called a mesa at the top. A cooling breeze swooped up the rise and we halted in the scant shade of a mesquite. The Sergeant pulled out his spyglass and we went to searching for signs of hostile activity.

Glass still at his eye, the Sergeant said, "He was telling the truth."

"Sir?"

"John Horse. I asked one of the white officers. Everything he claims to have done, he did. And a deal more." He took the glass from his eye but did not look at me when he asked, "Cathay, you were a slave, were you not?"

"I was, sir."

"Perhaps I'd feel differently about his treason had I ever been in bondage."

"Yessir, I expect you would, sir." I jumped on the Sergeant's new willingness to talk to me and quickly asked, "So, you were born free, sir?"

He perked up at this question and answered back proudly, "My family was free New Englanders of color." With no other troopers about to overhear him, the Sergeant fell to speaking like a normal man instead of a commander, and went on. "As soon as my grandfather was freed by his Quaker master, he left for the one place where race didn't matter."

"Where would that be, sir?"

"The sea."

After a long silence, I repeated, "The sea," hoping to coax him into saying more.

We watched a flock of killdeer pass overhead and listened to an antelope buck snort in the distance before he went on. "My father signed on as cook with a whaling ship and sailed out of New Bedford, Massachusetts, for months at a time. He hunted the deep waters on expeditions from Greenland to the west coast of Africa. He was a seaman who sailed under the great Captain Pardon Jones, himself a man of color. Pardon's was one of the first ships to hunt sperm whales off the coast of Japan. Like the other New England whalers who made it around the Horn to fish in the Pacific, they wintered in San Francisco. There he met my mother. Daughter of a prominent San Francisco whaling family, I'm told." He worked his jaw a bit before he added, "She perished in childbirth."

"I am sorry to hear that, sir."

"Yes, well." He shrugged, brushing the comment off like he was talking about a misplaced button hook. Since commanders in this peacetime army rarely even revealed their first names, the Sergeant surely couldn't be caught moping about his dead mama. As I knew only too well, it was dangerous, possibly fatal, for one man to show such weakness in front of another man.

But I wasn't a man. I was one of the other ones. The ones men told their secrets to. The ones who knew their sorrows and shame. The ones who would not kill them for being weak. The ones men loved and hated for knowing they weren't made of stone.

I was a woman.

I felt the Sergeant's sadness and longing and the weight of that burden, and because I knew he wanted to tell me, I asked, "What do you know about her?"

"My mother? Oh. Well. Her father came from the Barbados Islands, the son of a Scottish sugar planter. Her mother was a Creole Indian. She was said to be a beauty. But I wouldn't know. I have no memory of my mother's family as my father left San Francisco soon after she died to make his fortune in the gold fields."

"Did he? Make his fortune?"

"Yes. But not from gold. In the way of most who were not broken by that merciless hunt, his fortune was made selling the prospectors overpriced salt pork and potatoes. To the end of his days, which came when I was fourteen, he dreamed of returning to the sea. He gave those dreams to me. He told me I'd be a captain to rival Pardon Jones." The Sergeant gave a hollow chuckle, pretending like he believed the thought was foolish. "Instead," he went on, "I found my home not at sea but in the army."

After a long silence, he raised his spyglass to his eye and asked, "What's that?" He jerked his chin toward a plume of dust rising in the distance.

Miles away, across the grassy valley, the land rose to a ridge gulleyed by runoffs like the backbone of a starved cat with every rib poking out. A few puffs of what might have been dust rose there, though the noon sky was bleached to such a blinding intensity that I couldn't say for sure.

With the Sergeant occupied, I took the opportunity to study him up close. There was no doubt that he had come from a long line of men who'd had their eyes fixed on the far horizon. I saw the seaman in his profile, the man who would of been captain in a better world. And I saw something else that only revealed itself now, with close observation. The skin of his cheeks and forehead was lightly mottled with a faint pattern like the tiniest of stars on a dark night. I figured it to be scars left by smallpox. But it didn't have the look of pox for the scars were too small and they stopped around his eyes and temples in a band.

Just as if a blindfold or a bandage had been tied around his eyes.

I was seized by the image that had long haunted me of my soldier, dead and cruelly thrown into a pit, lye powder being sprinkled down upon his blindfolded face.

"Sir," I asked as he twisted the spyglass about with his extended left hand, adjusting the focus.

"Private."

"Sir, those marks on your face? Did you have smallpox?"

"The pox, no," he answered, bringing his free hand up to touch the light speckles on his cheek. "Surprising you should notice. No one has in so long that I thought the marks had faded completely. It is quite a tale . . ."

His words drifted away. When it seemed none were likely to follow, I asked, "How's that, sir?"

He lowered the glass, stared off as though transfixed by the far horizon, and rolled his lips inward, bottling up the words trying to escape. A time passed before he shook his head and puffed out a little laugh, pretending to make light of what he was about to say. "Every trooper out here must have a sad, lost sweetheart tale. Mine is no different from the rest, though I'm sure it is among the most curious."

I rose out of the saddle and leaned forward as far as I could, straining to catch every word. But none came. He was done. "Sir?" I prompted again.

"Yes, Private?" he asked, pretending not to recall what we were talking about.

"Your story? Why is it curious?" Bunny's flanks quivered beneath me as I'd put a crushing grip on her with my thighs while I tensed, waiting for Allbright's answer. I eased off and reminded myself to breathe.

"Oh, nothing really. The circumstances of our meeting. I was wounded, my eyes were bandaged, and she saved my life. But most curious, ridiculous, really, if examined logically, is the fact that though I never actually saw the woman, I fell in love with her."

Love.

Every sound—the clop of our horses' hooves as they shifted their weight, the soughing of the wind rustling through the tall grass, the jangle of tack as the beasts moved—fell silent.

Wager. Wager Swayne. He was *my soldier.*

Jubilation and an odd shyness collided and kept me from calling out the name I now knew to be his on the spot.

"Stupid, isn't it?" he asked before I could gather my wits. "Yet nothing can erase her memory from my mind. And here's the strangest part." Though he paused for some time, I did not have to urge him to go on. "Though I only 'saw' her face with the tips of my fingers, I know just from that touch and from how she comforted and nursed me that she is the most exceptional of women. I know that she will stand apart from all others because of her many superlative qualities and because of that one day I will find her."

I'd of told him then, "You have found her," but he had long since stopped speaking to me. His promise had been sent to the far horizon, to the place of freedom and equality he dreamed of. To the destination that was forever out of reach in this vast land.

Still, I would have said his true name then, I would have claimed him, except that, with unshakable faith, he concluded, "I will most especially know her because of her womanly beauty."

Beauty.

I sunk back down into the saddle. I had been gut shot.

Womanly beauty.

I knew then clear as glass what would happen if I told him that I was the woman who had saved him, the woman he'd dreamed about, the woman he held above all others. He would not believe me. For, truth be told, I wasn't that woman. I wasn't the woman who'd kept him alive. That woman was beautiful and womanly. I wasn't beautiful. I was barely a woman. I was a woman who could pass for a man.

"What the deuce?" he said, leaning forward toward the patch of movement shimmying through the grass. Abruptly he pivoted in the saddle and thrust the spyglass back at me. "Have a look, Cathay. Tell me what you make of—"

He went silent the instant he caught sight of my face and I knew what he saw written there: love, heartbreak, and a yearning so naked and so deep it all but swallowed me up.

The brass instrument hung in the air between us. I took it from him. The Sergeant spurred his mount and rode on without a word.

The sun was still two fingers above the horizon when the Sergeant halted, but night was coming on and the prairie had already gone violet. He waited until I drew abreast of him. We sat there for a long, silent moment. Without a word or a glance in my direction, the Sergeant stuck his hand out and I placed the spyglass in it. He tucked the spyglass back into its case on his saddle but did not spur his mount forward.

The shadows we threw made long scarecrow shapes behind us. He cleared his throat and, still staring off into the distance, said, "Private, I've seen boys like you before. Never been off the plantation. The first time they see a black man give an order, it . . ." He struggled for a moment to find the right word. When he couldn't, he said, "Well, it has a powerful effect. Sometimes they think it's the man. Do you get my meaning, Private?"

He didn't expect me to answer and I didn't.

"It is not the man, Private," he added sharp and hard. "It's giving the order. Do you hear me?" he asked and repeated, "It's giving the order. It's being the man in the blue suit atop a horse. Do you understand what I'm saying?"

"Yessir."

"Never confuse the two again."

"Yessir."

He rode on ahead, putting enough distance between us so as to remove even the tip of his long shadow from my touch.

Chapter 53

~

The Sergeant believed me to be a degenerate.

From that awful moment through our final days on the trail as we rode to Fort Arroyo, the Sergeant kept his distance from me. It no longer mattered whether he was or was not my soldier, I had lost him forever. I learned what a grievous thing it is when a dream dies. To save myself pain, I erased the name "Wager Swayne" from my mind. From then on I was as insensible to my surroundings as a box turtle. I recorded the passing landscape but stopped feeling as if I was in it. The wondrous sights we rode through might have been paintings hanging on a wall.

I saw an ocean of beeves. Ranch owners who'd gone off to fight for the Confederate cause had turned their herds loose and those horned beasts had whiled the intervening years away mounting and being mounted and pro-liferating beyond anyone's power to imagine. Cowboys, black and Mexi-can, worked gathering up the beasts and putting their bosses' brands on the ones they got to first. We bought up all the beef we could eat.

One day, we found ourselves at the edge of a cliff that dropped a thou-sand feet down to the Pecos River. We had to ride a couple days north to find a crossing. On the other side those bountiful beeves were no more and we were back to beans. Even our salt pork was gone by then.

Near the end of that long ride, we topped a rise and saw a sight so won-drous that, for a moment, it overcame my sadness at losing the Sergeant's regard, for, as far as the eye could see, buffalo covered the rolling plain. We'd seen herds before, but they'd always been far off in the distance. This was different. The entire world below looked to be carpeted with a wooly brown rug.

Lem was the first to break the stunned silence. "I heard they was good eating."

I nodded, having no comment to make one way or another.

"Seems we ought to try and pot a few," he said. "I'm about to perish from the dry wilts eating all them beans."

"You know how to pot a buffalo?" I asked, not entirely sneery for Lem had revealed himself to be a man of a number of hidden skills.

"No, do you?"

"No."

We gazed at the massive horned beasts and Lem asked, "You scared?"

"I wasn't born in the woods to be scared by an owl. Or buffalo, neither," I answered. I was a lot of things, but scared was not on my current list of afflictions. Lem got permission from the Sergeant and a few of us headed down the slope.

As impressive as a carpet of buffalo seen from afar was, coming up to a shifting wall of those spindly legged animals stretching for miles in either direction left us speechless. The sight panicked Caldwell and he took a shot. The herd was beyond the Spencer's range and all he accomplished was to send the beasts fleeing with a pounding of hooves so thunderous it shook the ground beneath us.

Caring not whether I lived or died, it was no great feat of courage for me to spur Bunny on and we charged after the fleeing herd. In spite of her comical appearance, Bunny had the heart of a warhorse and, ears flapping, she tore after the creatures. The great beasts looked like boulders fleeing upon clattering sticks. We entered the cloud of dust they'd raised and were blanketed by a choking red haze that made both seeing and breathing close to impossible.

My heart started up again and kicked into higher and higher gears the closer we came to that stampeding herd whose smallest member could of laid me out simply by veering into my path. Of an instant, a fierce joy filled up all the places inside that had been stomped flat by hurt and humiliation. I plunged in and Bunny took over like she'd been trained to it. An old bull walled its eyes until the whites showed vivid against the black that outlined them. He flung his head side to side and a lasso of buffalo slobbers flew from his mouth and nose. I drew my carbine and fired four times. He dropped.

Hungry as the men were for something besides beans, they made over me lavishly that night as they ate their fill of fresh meat. I noted that Vikers partook, but it was Allbright I studied. Seeking the darkness to relieve myself, I ventured far beyond the light of the dozen or so campfires the troop had built, one for each mess unit. At the head of that string, Allbright sat with Corporal Masters and the rest of his seconds in command. Lem had delivered a hefty cut of the hump to them and it was sizzling on a spit over the fire. The men sawed at it with their sabers. Masters hacked a hunk off onto his mess kit and took it to Allbright.

I watched the Sergeant eat, and imagined that I was sitting beside him. I wondered if he knew that I was the one'd brought his supper down. I crept away wishing I was riding through that red haze again with every thought blasted out of my head. I wandered alone through the desert until near everyone had turned in. Lem, though, was still awake when I returned to our lonely campsite. He grinned when I approached.

"What?" I asked.

"Nothing," he answered. "Just this." He patted a pile of oddments resting atop my bedsack. Among them were a box of matches, a twist of paper containing a quid of tobacco, two stamps, a sliver of soap, two dried apples, and a dozen pecans.

"What's all this?"

"Some of the boys brung it by as a thank-you for the fresh meat."

"Is that so?" I said, examining each of the articles, before cradling the pecans in my hands. "Anyone in particular?"

"Fernie, Milton Favor. The Georgia boys. A few others."

"Oh. What about the pecans? Who they from?"

"Couldn't say. Quite a few contributed this and that."

I held the pecans and believed what I wanted to believe.

Chapter 54

Ten miles outside of Fort Arroyo, we passed through a pitiful collection of weather-beaten buildings attempting to be a town by the name of Matanza. A few of the townspeople pulled back curtains or stood at doors cracked open an inch or two to watch us pass. All the citizens were male, white, and every bit as pitiful as the town they'd made. Their mean stares reminded me of Solomon's warning about Southern men. It was clear that though they might run cattle instead of raise cotton, these were still Southern men. I lifted my head high so as to stare down my nose at the sullen ingrates. I mean, it was their sorry, traitor hides we were coming to protect.

On the edge of Matanza were heaps of pickets, remnants of the abandoned *jacale* dwellings the Mexicans who'd founded the town favored. The information filtered back from the Sergeant that the town's name meant "slaughter" in honor of all the times the Apaches had swept through doing just that.

A mile east of the fort, we pulled up at Agua Dulce Creek to make ourselves presentable for our new commanding officer, Colonel Ednar Drewbott. The men washed and shaved, a good number of them using Dupree's whalebone-handled razor which I borrowed out.

Lem stropped the instrument to a fine edge and spent several minutes marveling over the tiny ship etched into its handle, something he did each time he borrowed it, before reluctantly handing it back, asking, "How'd they do that, Bill?"

When the men were all occupied, I took my canteen behind a pile of boulders and did my best to scrub off a few layers of trail dust and sneak a wet rag down amongst my folding parts.

Boots and tack were shined. Buttons replaced. Tears stitched up. After a quick inspection by the Sergeant and his corporals, we set off to see our new home and meet the white officers who were waiting there.

Fort Arroyo set just off Emigrant Trail on flat ground guarded in the back by a set of sheer cliffs. Out front, we were greeted by a lone soapberry tree that rose up a good thirty feet, the only bit of green above knee-high for miles in any direction. I took that tree as a good sign for it had to of been planted and watered by the first troopers who came here back in '54. Like Fort Lewis, this Union fort had been captured then abandoned by the Rebels after they gave up on their dream of conquering the West for the Confederate cause. Agua Dulce Creek ran nearby and the German Mountains were close enough to hand to supply us with wood. It seemed a decent enough setup.

We passed the soapberry tree and, just before we entered the fort, the Sergeant ordered parade formation and we rode in with our company guidon snapping in the breeze and every man sitting his horse pretty enough for a grand review.

But Fort Arroyo appeared deserted. We halted on the large, flat drill field, surrounded on one side by the remnants of rows of adobe buildings that were melting back into the earth. Yellow sunflowers blossomed here and there atop the scabby stumps of walls. The other two sides of the open rectangle of buildings were formed by the redbrick walls of the post hospital, and the walls of half a dozen officers' houses and one two-story officers' barracks. I say "walls" for that was all that remained of those structures as every bit of wood—the doors, porch railings, window sashes, even the wooden roof shingles—had been stripped off by the Mescalero and Warm Springs Apache Indians during the years the fort was abandoned.

There were signs, though, that the structures were occupied. Ladies' bloomers and drawers flapped on lines out back. Big stones had been stacked up to where the doors had once been. Blankets flapped where those stolen doors had once hung. A couple of toy stick horses lay in the dirt. And, at all the houses, the blankets hanging in doorholes fluttered as the white officers inside got a peek at us.

A feeling as familiar as it was unpleasant came over us: the feeling of being watched by white folks. Horses nickered and pawed as they felt their riders tensing up. Though not a one of us spoke a word or moved a muscle, we all drew closer under the gaze of our new masters. That awareness finished what those long weeks in the saddle had started. We were bonded, to each other and to our mounts. Just like the Sergeant had always wanted, we fused into a unit. Our time out on the open prairie was over. Once again, it was us and them.

So, when Sergeant Allbright ordered us to form up on the drill yard to wait for the Officer of the Day to come out and greet us like army regs specified, we swung into position smooth as any equestrian team you'd ever hope to see. Every boot toe peeking out of every stirrup was polished, every jacket was buttoned to the chin, every cap was centered just so, the swallowtails of our Union blue troop guidon unfurled so prettily above our heads that the feeling of being part of something fine and strong and a whole lot bigger and more important than I was welled up just the way it had when I'd marched with Sheridan.

And there we waited. And waited.

No one emerged to greet us.

The sun rose and beat down. Sweat started to trickle then to pour out from under our caps. Finally, the blanket covering the door of the post hospital swung back. A captain stepped out, held the blanket aside, and a colonel, our new commanding officer, Colonel Drewbott, strode out, hiking his suspenders up onto his shoulders. Though disheveled, he was a pretty man with a head of downy blond hair and a wispy mustache that glinted gold beneath one of those miniature noses that didn't seem capable of drawing enough air to keep a newt alive. At first glance, we took him to be what we all most wanted in a CO: a Northeastern Yankee. Preferably a rock-ribbed abolitionist from up Massachusetts or Maine way whose speech would be so jagged with "ars" and "ahs" that we would have to pretend to understand him.

A sense went through us that we'd lucked out with this colonel, so pale and blond he just had to be from way up North. With the Sergeant leading us, we all snapped into our sharpest salutes. So hopeful was I that I chalked up Drewbott's lack of both jacket and hat as well as the fact that he just barely had his britches on, not to disrespect, but to a looseness that signaled he wasn't a stickler.

As he and the captain sauntered forth, the Sergeant dismounted and called out, "Sergeant Allbright, sir! Troop J reporting for duty, sir!"

Drewbott stopped in front of him, planted his feet wide, and executed a mockery of a salute so sloppy that he might of been flicking a fly away from his face. We dropped our hands and pricked up our ears to catch our new commander's first words. Shading his eyes with his hand, he considered us for a bit, heaved a sigh, and said, "Well, y'all finally made it."

From the instant Colonel Drewbott opened his mouth, we commenced looking back at the long, grueling ride across the Trans-Mississippi as the best part of our service. For, instead of being assailed with the speedy, nasal Yank accent we'd been praying for, Drewbott's words lumbered forth thick with the sludge of a Southern accent. Our hopes were dashed. His accent and insolence added up to only one thing: a butternut Yank. One of those who'd fought to save the Union. A slave-owning Union, that is. We'd heard of officers resigning their commissions in disgust rather than take a black command. Drewbott soon proved that he had decided to hang on to both his commission and his disgust.

"Sir, yessir!" the Sergeant said, staring straight ahead, his eyes fixed on the hulk of the basalt ridge rising up beyond this lonely clump of derelict structures. He pulled a copy of our orders from his pocket, and, still without letting his eyes meet Drewbott's, handed them over. "Troop J, reporting for duty, sir," he said. "Four days *early*, sir!"

Next to me, Lem let loose the tiny gasp of disbelief that all the rest of us were holding in: by raising his voice the slightest bit on "four days early," the Sergeant had come back at Drewbott. Corrected him. Set him straight about us "finally" making it. Pointed out that the only "finally" around here was the time it took for him to come out of hiding. I wanted to cheer.

Southerner that he was, fine-tuned to the slightest hint, real or imagined, of disrespect, Drewbott bristled and thrust the papers at the captain who'd followed him out. "Obviously," he boomed out in a big-dog voice meant to keep a pack of curs, or us, in our place, "we need to establish some ground rules."

He clasped his hands behind his back and strutted back and forth in front of the line, hollering at the ground. "Any incident of drunkenness will be punishable by two weeks in the guardhouse! The highest standards of hygiene will be maintained! Gambling will result in the forfeiture of half a month's salary! Any, and I do mean any, insubordination of any kind will be grounds for a court-martial!" He glared at the Sergeant and asked, "Is that understood?"

"Yessir!" the Sergeant answered, loud enough that Bunny flinched beneath me.

Drewbott made a sour face, turned, and addressed us. "Now, you boys, y'all listen here now. I'ma splain dese here rules so's you kin follows me. You boys get likkered up, you don' wash, you bring in yo' whores, you get uppity, you don't jump when I say jump, you be walking outta here on yo' feets. No horse. No food. No water. Y'all hear me?"

No one spoke a word.

"Do you hear me, Sergeant?" Drewbott thundered.

The Sergeant did not answer.

At his refusal to "yessir" Drewbott's insults, the admiration I held for Sergeant Allbright thundered up in me so furious I felt as if my chest would explode. That admiration was a powerful balm and went a long way toward healing the hurt of losing Wager Swayne and having to bury him a second time.

Drewbott's pink face went red and he repeated, "Sergeant!"

"Yes. Sir."

Drewbott clasped his hands behind his back again and worked his lips from side to side for some time before he said, "My adjutant Major Carter will issue your special assignment," and left.

The Sergeant led us in saluting our new CO's retreating back. I knew Allbright and I knew that we were saluting the U.S. Army and what it was supposed to be. His salute was not, and never would be, for Colonel Ednar Drewbott.

Chapter 55

O ur "special" assignment turned out to be rebuilding the old fort
and adding new barracks.

"Didn't sign up to come out here to swing no pickax," Lem
said, after our second week of construction.

One thing I will say, you put ninety strong, young men who've bonded
themselves over to the U.S. government to working on anything, you will
achieve miracles. We hung the doors and windows that had been freighted
out from San Francisco. Rebuilt porches, railings, roofs. Even dug a garden
for every officer's wife. After that, we patched up the bachelor officers' barracks.

When we started digging the foundation for our own new barracks, Lem
was pulled off stable duty and put on our crew. A few of the older men who
weren't fit for heavy duty ended up as what were known as strikers, house
boys working for the officers and their families. Just like back on the plantations and farms, this was how we found out all the important information
that never made its way up or down any chain of command. One of the first
bits of information the strikers passed along was that Colonel Drewbott was
no more popular with his own men than he was with us.

We learned that most of the officers and their wives were decent enough
fellows, but that some of the wives believed that they wore their husbands'
rank and demanded the special treatment that went along with those stars
and bars. Worst of that group was Drewbott's wife. Mrs. Drewbott was
one of those Southern women bred to be pretty and helpless who, though a

porcelain doll baby on her wedding day, went to fat straight after getting
that ring on her finger.

Drewbott's striker, Milton Favor, the Illinois wheelwright, reported that
the colonel worshipped none other than Sheridan's pet, George Armstrong
Custer. Favor told us that Drewbott never tired of pointing out to Mrs. Drewbott how slim and pretty Custer's wife, Libby, was and how Sheridan was
so taken with her that he'd bought the very table upon which Lee and Grant
had signed the Appomattox surrender agreement just to give to her as a
present. Drewbott also liked to yell at his fat wife that she was the reason
he'd gotten such a "hind-teat assignment commanding a bunch of jacka-
mammies."

Most of the white ladies at Fort Arroyo, though, were all right. Just doing
the best they could to keep a clean house and raise their children in the strange
and hostile world the U.S. Army had tossed them into.

In any case, hadn't been for Drewbott and a couple of other officers, we'd
of been well on our way to creating a paradise there in the desert. Fortu-
nately, Drewbott had no more desire to see us than we did him, and after
that first day's "welcome," he channeled nearly all his communications to
us through the Sergeant.

Mostly what Allbright had to say was: work harder. Summer was ending and we needed to have some walls between us and the sharp bite of the
"blue northers" that the Sergeant warned us were going to be howling down
on us all the way from the North Pole. Every morning, the bugle sounded
at 4:45. After roll call, breakfast, and stable duty, the Sergeant worked side
by side with us, pulling a plumb line, swinging a pick, what have you. After
a day of busting rocks and pounding nails, we dropped hard as felled timber into our bunks. Some too tired to even collect their rations.

The Sergeant, though, he had a whole day's work to do at night for he
kept all the company's records. As the highest-ranking noncommissioned
officer on post, the Sergeant had a tidy little room at the end of the bachelor
officers' quarters. Though he chose to sleep rough out in tents with the rest
of us until the barracks were built, he conducted all troop business in that
little room. It had a window through which I peeked many a night, watching Allbright work by the light of a lantern filling out forms, making reports, requisitioning supplies. He was meticulous in his duties, sitting up so
straight that it was rare to ever see his spine touch the back of the chair.

Many a time, while I peeped at the Sergeant, I saw Drewbott storm into his quarters, just bust in through the door without so much as a knock. The Sergeant would jump to his feet and salute. And Drewbott never once returned his salute. I couldn't hear what the colonel said, but it was obvious that he was giving Allbright hell about one thing or another. I watched the colonel peel strips of hide off the Sergeant and use them to flog him. To make it even worse, when the fussbudget colonel left, it wasn't like Allbright could buy himself a gourd of tonsil varnish from the sutler like so many of the men did, then cuss the colonel out with the boys in the barracks. No, he was our commander and he had to keep himself set apart every bit as much as I did.

Though I had accepted that there never was and could never be anything between me and "my" soldier, still the fact that Allbright considered me either a bad apple spoiling his barrel or a hell-bound sodomite made me so dumpish that I set myself to winning back his good opinion.

I was the first one out in the morning and the last one in at night. No one worked harder or backtalked less than me. Bit by bit, over the next few weeks, I became the prize pig at that hog show. More important, I made sure that if there was measuring to be done that I'd be the one with the tape and the one marking down the feet and inches. The Sergeant needed to be reminded of my ciphering skills. Needed to be reminded of me.

Chapter 56

Near the end of the summer, we finished setting the roof over the first set of barracks. Vikers and those he favored immediately occupied it and left the rest of us to continue sleeping rough. Which didn't trouble me a bit as it was cooler outside than in and I was where I wanted to be: off by myself. I was away from Vikers, had the privacy I needed, and a good friend in Lem. All in all, my life in the army, though not what I wanted it to be, was proceeding in a tolerable fashion. Right up until the moment that everything changed overnight.

As usual, on that day, it was barely light when we all tumbled out for roll call and formed up in front of the Sergeant. Each of us sounded off strong when our names were called then slugged down our daily dose of pulque. It was Sheridan who'd ordered that all his troops out West be given a daily dose of the sulfur-smelling cactus juice. As we didn't yet have vegetables, it was meant to guard us against scurvy. It must of worked for no one was taken by that ailment, though a fair number of the men developed a fondness for the fermented sludge and became pulque pots.

"Men," the Sergeant said that morning, "congratulations on your exemplary work on our second barracks. We're so far ahead of schedule that we've completely outrun the sawmill. So, I am shifting some of you to mill duty. The rest of you will begin chinking the walls of 'B' Barracks. If I call your name, go on to the sawmill and ask Corporal Masters for your assignment. Pool. Day. Childress. Abernathy. Kirk. Coleman, and . . ."

As the Sergeant paused to pick the last man, the chosen ones stepped forward smartly, happy to be spared a day of working with the harsh mixture of clay, ashes, sand, and masonry lime that we used to chink up the gaps between pickets. Never expecting the Sergeant to pick me for anything ever again, I was surprised when I saw him eyeing me.

Now, as I've shown, I was like a crab with my eyes swiveling around on stalks up top my head when it came to observing that man. Not his tiniest wince or squint escaped my notice. And that was how, in the dim light of early morning, I saw him consider me in a manner that made it clear that I was a puzzle to him. One he'd already spent some time trying to solve. So, when he called out the final name, "Cathay," I nearly floated out of the line.

At the mill, Masters put me to switching the mule that turned the sawmill wheel while the rest of them rode off in the wagon to cut timber in the German Mountains. My mindless occupation allowed me ample opportunity, not only to enjoy the view sweeping out all the way to Mexico, eighty miles south, but to recall every glance and word that had ever passed between me and the Sergeant. For, though I might have truly buried Wager Swayne, I could do nothing about my one-sided feelings for the Sergeant.

Absorbed as I was in my memories, the day passed pleasantly. It was late afternoon when the horses in the quartermaster's corral began nickering uneasily. I paid them no mind. Nor did I notice that the prairie dogs had stopped chattering or that the steady, old mule, broke as she was to the harness after twenty years of service, suddenly turned so balky I had to snap the quirt on her several times before she was convinced to continue plodding along on her round path to nowhere. It wasn't until she lifted her head and bared her long, squared-off teeth in a shrieking bray that I turned away from sunny Mayheeko and saw clouds moving in from the north. The desert liked to tease that way, promising rain it never delivered, so I turned back south, harred up the mule and went back to work.

It had been another blazing-hot, wearying day and we were dead asleep that night when in comes a gully washer would of set Noah to hammering. The rain poured down in buckets heavy enough that a wave of waist-high muddy water sluiced down off the hills behind the fort and rolled right through our tents and swept them away.

Determined to spend the rest of the night inside, we stomped through the mud to the finished barracks. The door was barred. Vikers's face appeared in the nearest window. The lantern held beneath his chin cast dark, devil-type shadows upward on his face. "Price of admission into our nice, dry barracks is one month's salary," Vikers announced. "I have the wage garnishment orders waiting for your Xs."

"How can you do us like this?!" demanded Tea Cake.

Ivory backed him up with, "You gon keep us out here in this rain pouring down like Satan hisself pissing all over us? You gon make us pay for a dry spot in some barracks *we* helped build?!"

"That ain't right!" Baby King threw in.

We pounded on that door until it rattled on its hinges.

Vikers must have promised cuts to his boys, for they made a show of stretching out on their nice dry beds and fluttering their fingers at us in mocking waves.

After a few more of our drenched crew yelled threats and insults through the glass, Tea Cake shrugged and announced, "What good's thirteen dollar to me if I be dead of the new moany?"

Pretty soon, they had all agreed to sign Vikers's IOUs.

"No!" I thundered, startling them for they'd gotten used to me with my mouth shut. "What is the matter with y'all? You acting like you're too slow to catch the itch. No! Dammit, no. You ain't paying that man a month's salary to spend the night on the damn floor of a barracks we built."

"Well, what the hell you suggest, Mr. Fancy?" Tea Cake asked, "Mr. Fancy" being one of my nicknames. Along with "Missy Bill" and "Candy Ankle."

They were listening to me now, though, and I said, "I suggest we make us a roof to sleep under. We got all that tar paper we're going to use to roof in our barracks. We take that, go to quartermaster's corral, spread it out across the stone posts, over the top of that chimney, make us the coziest tent you ever seen."

"We'll still be sleeping on mud," Tea Cake objected.

"Like you didn't spend the entire war sleeping on mud," I answered back. "You that particular, get you some hay to put up under you."

They grumbled back and forth, but when Lem said, "Does look mighty cozy in there," I knew that I had lost and Vikers had won.

"No," a familiar voice said. "Cathay's right."

We snapped to attention.

"At ease," the Sergeant said, stepping forward to stand next to me in the small pool of light cast by the lantern. The instant Vikers saw the Sergeant's face, the door was unlocked. I made to follow the others, but the Sergeant said, "Private."

I stopped as the others went in, and he said, "You were looking out for your unit and forestalled a bad decision. Good work."

That hardwood barracks floor felt like a feather bed under me that night.

Chapter 57

After the night of the flash flood things changed fast. The Sergeant put Vikers on the Black List to punish him for creating discord in the ranks, and he caught every nasty assignment that came along. Seeing Vikers cleaning out latrines brought him down a peg or two and he lost some of his hold on the men. And, though I was never destined to be a troop favorite, I was generally accepted as one could be counted on to haul his own weight without bellyaching and to stand pat with his friends. But the real change, the only one that mattered, was with the Sergeant. He started treating me like any of the other men. Then better than any of the other men.

First, he made me his puller. I'd be the one walking the tape out that he held so that he could check measurements. Then he handed me his notebook and had me enter the figures. Then he asked me to do a few sums. Then some takeaways.

After a week of double-checking my figures, he pulled me aside and said, "Private, I could use your assistance in keeping the company records. I have too much to do filing all the reports that the army requires. If you could take over the accounts, it would be most helpful. I can offer you a monthly pay raise of fifty cents."

Though I was doing cartwheels inside and bursting to yodel out with joy, I buried such nancy-boy capers and replied solemnly, "Yessir. That'd be fine, sir."

"Good. Be at my quarters after retreat."

That evening, soon as the flag was lowered and the sun had set as the bugler played the last notes of retreat, I knocked softly on the Sergeant's door.

Instead of hollering for me to come in, he opened the door himself and said, "Private, good, you're here." He wore only his muslin shirt. His suspenders dangled loose from the waist of his pants. His jacket hung from a nail.

He closed the door and, though he always kept the curtains open so the whole company could view us, we were alone together in that small room. I knew every inch of his room from the outside, but now standing inside the four walls of chinked cedar posts made it new. A lantern glowed on the table where he worked. The room smelled of cedar and kerosene and pencil shavings and the Sergeant's scent, which was his own combination of bread baking and sweat and lye soap and clothes dried in the sun. I breathed it in and felt like I'd reached a destination I hadn't known I was heading for. I was where I was always meant to be.

"You can take the stool," he said. Waving his hand at a stack of papers, he added, "These are the company accounts from the day we arrived. Up until this point, they've been kept by Lieutenant Banfield. I suspect there might be . . ." He paused before adding dryly, "Errors in the lieutenant's calculations."

The pages were filled with lines of numbers so smeared and scrawled my daddy would have been disgusted. Even if I was just forming my numbers with a stick in the dust, ready to be patted away should a white appear, he taught me to respect them. To give the four its tidy little roof and the sixes and nines their pretty, curled tails. His rule was, "If the dullest of dullards cannot immediately say what your figure is, you have failed." The lieutenant had failed.

The Sergeant continued, "Since the army demands triplicate of every report, supply order, sick call tally, and disciplinary action, I haven't had time to review these accounts."

He gave me a tall, narrow book, bound with a green cover. The pages inside were blank. With a trembling hand, I picked up a pencil he'd already knife-sharpened to a fine point, and held it above the bright, clean page.

"Just copy these"—he tapped the crumpled sheets, then the page in front of me—"to this. Tally up each page and move on to the next."

My first few entries were a sight and I feared the Sergeant would kick me out. But all he said, after glancing over only once, was, "Easy there, Private. Easy. I've seen you do better than that."

My fingers loosened up then and my numbers were as neat and tidy as any Daddy ever showed me.

From that evening on, I spent the days whistling through any chore set before me, counting the minutes until retreat. Then, after everyone else was settled in for the night, I'd go to the Sergeant and we'd work together in a silence broken only when I finished one long column and needed him to enter in the corrections I had found. And corrections there were aplenty.

Pretty quick it came clear that the lieutenant was either pitiful bad at ciphering or he was a crook robbing the company.

"What are you going to do?" I asked the Sergeant. "You can't charge a white officer."

He patted my green book and said, "That's insurance, Private. You're creating insurance for us. When charges are made, we'll be protected. We'll have the truth."

Him believing the truth would protect a black man was another way he reminded me of Daddy. Much as I knew it wasn't how the world worked, I admired that belief. Like Daddy, the Sergeant needed a woman strong enough to protect him when he found out that the truth was whatever the white man said it was.

Night after night, I sat beside him as silent and companionable as a cat. Over time, he started talking. I quickly sussed out that the one subject he could not resist was his idol, Frederick Douglass. Like that great man, the Sergeant was dedicated to uplifting our race and he figured he'd start with me. Many an evening passed with our reports and accounts ignored as he schooled me in Douglass's teachings.

The Sergeant knew nearly every one of Douglass's speeches by heart and, instead of passing the time talking while we worked, he recited whole chunks of them, a thing he could do without ever slowing down on his reports. The one he favored most, though, came from the same speech he'd quoted us at the recruitment back in Appomattox. He'd stop his work completely and glow like a new-saved sinner when he recited this part.

I know that Congress has been pleased to say in deference to prevailing prejudice that colored men shall not rise higher than company officers. They might as well have passed a law that black men shall not be brave; that they shall not learn to read; that they shall not shoot straight; and that they shall not grow taller than five feet nine inches and a half. The law is even more absurd than mean. Enter the army and deserve promotion, and you will be sure to get it in the end.

"'Enter the army and deserve promotion,'" he repeated, "'and you will be sure to get it in the end.'"

He didn't need to say that part twice for me to understand that it was all ten of his commandments melted down to one word: deserve.

Chapter 58

⁓

The weeks passed, and one day we awoke to the ringing sound of pickaxes and pry bars digging into the stone that underlay much of the desert. Sooner than you'd think, twenty-foot telegraph poles sprouted, running from the far horizon right up to the fort. The black infantry soldiers working that detail shinnied up those poles easy as pie to hang those telegraph lines. The wire, looping from one pole to the next, shone in the setting sun, an endless row of gold necklaces.

Things changed as soon as the contraption was set up. Overnight we went from feeling invisible and invulnerable, lost way out on the prairie where no one and nothing could get at us, to feeling like a big, fat target. Though the only Indians we'd spotted, besides John Horse and his crew, had been lone riders on distant peaks, by the end of the first week of telegrams we felt we were under siege.

Every time a telegram came in, the operator, a white corporal with the wispiest mustache and biggest apple of Adam in the entire single-star state, would tear around the fort yelling the news about every single solitary redskin outrage that occurred anywhere in the entire country. Though it might have been the Sioux up in South Dakota stealing a couple of beeves off a Norwegian settler, or Comanche way off in north Texas burning down a barn, the wire made it seem like the heathens were a vast, united force closing in around us. Drewbott, who'd already shown himself to be a chickenshit of the first order, was powerfully affected by these alarms. He doubled, then tripled the night guard.

Though Drewbott squandered time and worry and scarce supplies on the threat of Indian attack, the fact of the matter was that, in the entire history of the Indian Wars, the heathens only ever attacked a U.S. fort once. They were too smart to hit the places where the men with guns were. Lone farms and stagecoaches were more their cup of tea. If you wanted to mess with Indians, you'd mostly have to go out and track them down. And that was not a chore Colonel Chickenshit much cared for.

Pretty soon, though, reports did start coming in from much closer to home. A band of Mescalero Apache led by a chief name of Chewing Bones had left the reservation they'd been herded onto by Kit Carson over in the Rio Grande Valley. Even though the telegrams kept getting grimmer with news of settlers being burned out, their livestock stolen, women and children kidnapped, and men mutilated in ways so flamboyant my grandmother would have admired them, Drewbott still wasn't inclined to leave the fort and go off in pursuit of the savages.

Then, late one evening, a telegram came in that changed everything.

As usual, I was in the Sergeant's office, stuffing myself to bursting with the pleasure of keeping silent company with him. On that particular evening, I was toting up the number of days all the companies had lost to sick call. "Sergeant," I said, soon as I recorded the totals. "We've only lost thirteen days this entire month. C and F," I said, referring to the two new companies of infantrymen that had joined the regiment, "lost forty-three and twenty-eight."

Sergeant hid his pride at our company and said, "Malingerers."

"Shirkers, idlers, loafers, and deadbeats," I added, parroting back the words I'd learned from the Sergeant. I clung to every word out of his mouth, stored them up, and presented them often as I could for I was ever trying to make a good impression.

"Wastrels, spongers, slouches, and—"

I never learned the next new word he was tossing into my vocabulary for the door burst open and there stood Colonel Drewbott. Sergeant and I sprang to our feet like a couple of jack-in-the-boxes.

The colonel wore a nightshirt stuffed into his britches, one suspender on his shoulder, one off. His hair stood up on the side it'd been slept on. He wobbled at the door, dazed as a goose with a nail in its head until he remembered the telegram in his hand, flapped it at the Sergeant and said, "This just came in from—"

The instant he noticed me, the colonel shut up and handed the wire to the Sergeant. With a sharp eye cast in my direction, Drewbott added, "Mention this to no one until tomorrow. Make a general announcement to all companies tomorrow at assembly. And then set to, boy, set to with a mighty vengeance." He left without returning our salutes.

Though I'd heard Drewbott say it before—that "boy" business—it still shocked me to hear the Sergeant addressed in such a manner. The Sergeant, busy reading the telegram, seemed not to notice. He finished and looked up. I feared someone had died.

"What?" I asked. "Has the president been assassinated?"

That would of been shocking but not necessarily sad. For the current occupant of the White House, Andrew Johnson, the nincompoop vice president who'd slid his tiny feet into Lincoln's giant shoes, was currently trying to turn us all back into slaves.

"No, no," the Sergeant corrected me. "The news is good." He put his hand over his mouth in a girlish way I'd never thought him capable of and pressed against the smile that formed there. "Very good, indeed."

"What?" I asked again, for once not feeling the need to add "sir." The Sergeant suddenly seemed so young and wide-eyed, I was certain I was seeing an expression that had not played across his face since he was a boy.

"I'm not supposed to say," he said.

"Sergeant, you know me. Who would I tell? I hardly talk to anyone but Powdrell."

"Hell, you'll know tomorrow anyway. All right, Cathay." It pleased me when he called me "Cathay" instead of "Private." "What would you say if I told you that the military governor of the entire Fifth Military District was going to pin a Marksman medal on you?"

I could not speak.

He thought my surprise was about the medal and said, "I didn't want to say anything until the award had been approved, but I put you in for it weeks ago."

But that wasn't what had shocked me. "Sheridan?" I croaked, for my old commander was the military governor. "General Sheridan is coming here?"

"Week from today. To conduct a general inspection. Custer will be accompanying him. They'll award all the honors earned until now."

"The General? He's going to see me?" I heard the tremble in my voice, for the instant the General set eyes on me, I'd be mustered out and turned onto the prairie to fend for myself. I wondered what'd kill me first: hostiles, wolves, or a rattler. Of course, a chughole'd do it. Horse trips and breaks a leg and a person afoot in the desert is dead.

"I'm as surprised as you are," the Sergeant went on, beaming. "The first general inspection of the first colored cavalry unit *and* a presentation of honors by the highest-ranking officer in the district?"

Then I realized I didn't have to worry about dying of thirst on the desert: once the General exposed me, I'd never make it out of the fort alive. Vikers and his jackals'd see to that.

"Cathay," the Sergeant went on, more talkative than I'd ever known him to be. "I was having doubts, but this renews my faith in the United States Army. Like all made by man, the army is an imperfect organization filled with members who don't live up to its ideals. But, say what you will, when it comes to the nut-cutting, the army is fair." He nodded and, with stern decisiveness, stated, "No matter what the color of your skin, Private, if you serve, if you *de*serve, you will be recognized."

"Yessir," I answered.

"And, just as surely, if you *fail* to serve, as Drewbott is failing, the army will, I promise you, eventually recognize that, too. No wonder the man's worried. He knows a reckoning is coming." The Sergeant nodded, satisfied, then went on. "According to the telegram, both Sheridan and Custer—did I mention that Custer is coming as well? In any case, they have already sent out advance kitchen staff. And since you served with Sheridan during the Rebellion—"

"Well, 'served with,' sir," I interrupted. "I maybe shouldn't have gone that far—"

"Don't be modest, Cathay. I'm not saying you were a strategy adviser."

"No, sir."

"But you know the man, right?"

"Well, 'know,'" I crawfished.

"Fine. I'm assigning you to meet with his staff. Show them around. Lots to be done, Private," he muttered, already drawing up lists in his head. "Lots to be done. Your old general gives a tough inspection. I've heard he doesn't miss a thing."

"No, sir," I agreed. "General Philip Sheridan never misses a thing."

Chapter 59

⎯

Two generals on post," Pinkney the cook grumbled, slamming a cast-iron Dutch oven down on the counter. "That don't mean work, ain't a hound dog in Georgie."

"Technically," I said, "Custer's only a captain. He was only brevetted to general on account of the war."

"Don't matter," Pinkney grumbled. "That is one white man believes he was *born* a general. Everyone calls him 'general.' Treats him like a general. Don't matter whether he's got the stars to prove it or not. Worse part of it is, they brung their own damn cooks. You ever know a white boy could cook? Tell you what, them white-boy cooks killed off more Yanks than the Rebels ever did. Hughes, hand me that gourd."

Hughes, one of his cook's helpers, passed a gourd of the sort that the Mexican women sold filled with pulque. Like most cooks, Solomon being the exception, Pinkney was a jug-steamed drunk. He tipped the gourd, it glug-glugged down his gullet, and he went back to the tear he was on. "They think they gon come in here, tell Elijah Bountiful Pinkney how to—"

"Ten-HUT!" Hughes bellowed out the instant he caught sight of Major Carter leading two white corporals into the kitchen. Several other soldiers followed behind, but they were blocked from our view.

Carter introduced the two corporals, Adams and Poteet.

Pinkney was whispering to me about the bother it'd be to have them boys underfoot when I saw something that punched the wind out of me. Pushing her way through the clot of men barring the kitchen door, was none other than my beautiful little sister, Clemmie.

The earbobs and face paint were gone, but she was bolder and brassier than ever. And if it was possible, she was even prettier. Her skin had seen the touch of the sun since she'd left indoor work behind and it glowed satiny and near dark as mine. This brought out her eyes to the point that one glance her way left the kitchen helpers struck dumb. She didn't notice those boys as, standing there with her hands on her hips, she appraised the kitchen with a disdainful eye. That disdain vanished when her gaze lit on me. She opened her mouth like she was going to scream. But I shot her a look warning her to shut up and my little sister composed herself on the spot.

Carter pulled a list from his pocket and read, "Here are General Custer's requirements. Colored troops, with proper supervision, may assist Corporals Adams and Poteet in the preparation of the general's food, but they will not serve him at table. General Custer will eat only white meat. See to it that no other is put before the general." He folded the order, returned it to his pocket, and asked the newcomers, "Which ones of you are with General Sheridan's staff?"

Clemmie stepped forward.

"Where are the others?"

"There are no others, sir."

"Oh. What are General Sheridan's requirements?"

"Only has two," Clemmie answered then said no more, forcing Carter to ask, "And what might those be?"

"Hot and on time."

Pinkney and his kitchen boys snickered at Clemmie's sauciness, aimed as it was direct at Custer's fussiness.

"Now," Clemmie concluded and pointed at me, "if this gentleman will show me to my quarters."

Outside, we had to run an obstacle course of men frozen in place, gaping at Clemmie like she had two heads and was shooting Liberty dollars out her mouth. Even if she hadn't been a looker, they'd of stared for, aside from the Seminole women, we hadn't seen a single black woman since leaving San Antonio. Most of the troopers were harmless. They just gaped like they were dying of calico fever and she was the cure. Some of them, though, I knew to be bad men. I'd heard enough barracks talk about "gals putting up a little fuss" even though they'd "asked for it" and "wanted it bad" to know that some of those dogs with their tongues dragging the ground figured Clemmie was asking for it and wanted it bad because she was pretty. Their kind believed the pretty had been put on, just for them, and Clemmie was just waiting for them to come and take it. My sister took no notice of any of them.

I marched us straight to the Sergeant's office. He opened the door and, like the most common soldier in the yard, his eyes bulged out of his head at the sight of Clemmie. This caused jealousy to twine about my heart like the viper it is and squeeze hard.

"Our guest needs quarters," I said, my voice crisp as a dried corn husk.

"Yes, yes," he stammered, buttoning his jacket up to his chin. "I wasn't expecting a . . ." He couldn't so much as say the word "female," he was that struck. "Please, I hope this office will do. There's a small . . ." He stumbled again. This time over the word "bed," and ended up pointing to his neat cot. "The door . . ." He rushed to demonstrate how to slide the iron bar in and out of place to lock it.

He noticed the faces pressed against the window glass and, muttering apologies, rushed over to draw the heavy curtain. The room darkened. This, too, seemed to embarrass him, and muttering "lamp," he hurriedly lighted the lantern, then gathered up his jacket and cap. Even though we were indoors, I snapped to and saluted. As he was backing out of the room, he paused to shift his belongings to his left arm and he saluted me back.

The instant we locked the door behind him, everything disappeared except Clemmie. We grabbed ahold of each other and jumped up and down like a couple of crazy ladies, me saying she'd kill me of apoplexy if she kept popping up out of nowhere and her just laughing. We were out of breath by the time Clemmie stopped and marveled, "You did it. You're wearing the blue suit."

"Said I would," I answered.

She studied me, concluding, "Damn, Cathy Williams, you make a fine-looking man."

"I do?"

"About fine enough make me forget you're my sister."

We got to laughing so hard about that, I had to shush her for the wolves were still out there, circling.

Turning serious, she told me, "You're crazy. You do know that, right? Cathy, there are some hard cases out there. And I've seen a world of hard cases, believe me. But them? Out there?"

She'd only been pretending not to notice. The way girls have to do.

"Those are the most woman-hungry bunch I've ever seen. You know what they'd do to you, they ever found out the truth?"

I thought about the washroom. My head being hammered into a tile wall. I didn't answer.

"Cathy, it scares me to think about it. You are playing a game's a whole hell of a lot more dangerous than you think it is."

"Not if they don't find out."

"I can't believe they haven't already. You're not the *most* girlish thing around, but still . . ."

"Folks generally see what they expect to see."

"But what if you take sick? Get shot?"

"Don't plan on doing either of those things."

She gasped with annoyance just the way she'd always done when she thought I'd gone too far. Then she said, "Well, what about if you fall in love?"

"Don't intend to do that, either."

She gave a sharp bark of a laugh. "Don't intend? Do you think I'm as stupid as you're pretending to be right now?"

"I don't know what you're going on about," I sniffed.

"Can't say as I blame you," she said, playing like I'd admitted everything. "The sergeant is even finer up close than he was back at the recruitment. All oak and iron-bound, no question about it. When'd you completely lose your mind over him?"

"I never!"

She shook her head. "Girl, girl, girl. You got it bad, don't you?"

The softness in her voice drained the sand right out of me and I slumped onto the bed. "He's all I think about."

"I never figured you for the type get her nose wide open, give it all up for a man."

"I ain't given up nothing. It's not like that. *He's* not like that. He's better. Purer. He's like Daddy was."

"Oh, a deluded fool?"

"A man of principles."

She hooted at that. " 'Principles'? Is *that* what he calls it?"

"Let's leave off this foolishness," I said, cutting the conversation short, for the desire to tell her about Wager Swayne was threatening to overwhelm me. And that was one ghost I was determined to keep buried. "I got much bigger problems."

"Like what?"

"I won a medal for sharpshooting and—"

"You don't say. Congratulations. Always could shoot the eye out of a needle."

"Clemmie, Sheridan's going to pin that medal on me."

"So?"

"So, he'll recognize me and I'll be done for."

Clemmie snorted a bitter laugh. "You're seriously worried that General Philip Sheridan, governor of the Fifth Military District, third highest-ranking officer in the United States Army, is going to recognize you?"

"Hell, yes, he'll recognize me. I fed the man every damn meal he ate for almost a year."

"Oh, pea blossom, I know you always believed you were a bend or two above most, but no matter how special you think you were to Sheridan, he's still a white man. Believe me, he'll never recognize you 'cause he never really saw you in the first place. Tell you what, though, them jackals out there." She nodded her head toward the slavering pack. "Day they figure out what you got down there"—she tipped her head toward my crotch—"probably gon be your last."

"Sergeant Allbright'll protect me."

"Sergeant Allbright? Cathy, you put that man on a pedestal all the way back to the recruiting. He's a man. You saw the way he looked at me."

"Did he? I didn't notice."

Clemmie hooted. "Oh, sister, are you jealous?"

"No," I lied.

"Well, you sure are acting like it's my fault for the way men look at me. Like I'm to blame for the way the meat got stacked on my bones."

For some reason, saying this last turned Clemmie gloomy and she sat down on the Sergeant's bunk and stared at her hands. Finally she huffed out a big sigh and said, "Sergeant Allbright saluted you. No one salutes *me,* Cathy. I'm just another pair of black hands. And a woman to boot. Means any white can order me about and any black man believes he can do the same." Then, instead of carrying on about what a fool, dangerous thing I was doing, her tune changed completely and she said, "We have to make sure Little Phil doesn't recognize you."

Chapter 60

⁓

Inspection day dawned hot and bright. Too bright. I'd been praying for rain. At least some clouds. But Clemmie had convinced me that if I just kept my head down and my hat tipped low, the General wouldn't look at me twice since he hadn't ever really seen me in the first place. And now, there he was, inching his way down the long line toward me. Though it hurt, I prayed that Clemmie was right.

Our line gleamed for, like everything else on post, we had all been spit-and-polished to within an inch of our lives. Every button, every buckle, every boot, every saber, every crossed-sword insignia atop our caps shone in the sun. Drewbott had even ordered a couple of men to trim the tall soap-berry tree outside the fort so that a bit of pristine green would greet the General.

No one spoke. The flag on the pole didn't even flutter, as the General made his slow, careful way down the line. He was just as I'd seen him last, standing in front of that farmhouse outside of Appomattox. He might of fattened up a bit now that he didn't spend all day in the saddle chasing Rebs. But he still had that big ferocious head, jaw clenched, eyes black and savage, all set atop his stumpy, bulldog body. He eyed every trooper hard. But, to my relief, I saw that he didn't pay any mind to faces. The only parts he cared about had patches, buttons, or shoeshines on them.

In the stillness, we all heard Drewbott say, "General Sheridan, sir, tell me something."

"What's that, Colonel?" Sheridan asked, not taking his gaze from the trooper in front of him.

"Since this is your first tour of the Lone Star State, what do you think of Texas?"

"What do I think?" Sheridan repeated. "Colonel, I think that if I owned Texas and hell, I would rent out Texas and live in hell."

Custer, standing behind the General, about wet himself laughing. Though the Boy General was now but a lowly captain, Custer had not been demoted in Sheridan's affection. His laughter pleased the General. The instant Drewbott joined in, though, Custer and Sheridan went solemn as judges. They were still the two bad boys together, the outcasts of West Point, sneering at the timid good boys.

Leaving Drewbott chuckling too loudly at a joke that had already been taken away from him, Sheridan snapped, "Colonel, there is rust on the guard of this man's saber."

"Noted, sir," Drewbott said as he added the rust spot to the list he was keeping of every unpolished buckle, missing button, and stray bit of lint that the General observed.

Inspection had already gone on long enough for the sun to rise up noon high. Heat and nerve sweat ran from beneath my cap. I caught sight of Clemmie in the distance, watching from the shade of the kitchen porch. When Sheridan reached the man two down from me, I ducked my head so low all I could see were his boots.

"General," Custer asked in a jokey way. "Did you notice that the band which greeted us was missing a bass drum?"

Playing along, Sheridan answered, "Why yes, General, I did. What do you think happened to it?"

"I couldn't say for sure," Custer replied then lowered his voice and said out of the side of his mouth just for Sheridan to hear, "But from the looks of her, they'd better bring Drewbott's wife in for questioning."

When he reached me the General was too busy snickering about Drewbott's fat wife to pay me any mind. And though he passed by close enough that I could hear his stomach growling, he didn't so much as pause, much less pin that sharpshooter medal on me. I should have been grateful and relieved, but I wasn't. Leastwise, Cathy Williams wasn't. William Cathay was delighted that he wasn't going to be mustered out. But Cathy Williams? She was downhearted that her old commander hadn't seen that she'd done what he said could not be done. And done it well enough that she was getting a medal.

When I spotted another pair of boots raising dust as they moved double-quick toward the General, I lifted my head. It was the Sergeant. As soon as he reached Sheridan, he said, "General, begging your pardon, sir, but one medal has not been presented."

"Is that true, Colonel?" the General asked Drewbott.

"Yes, well—" Drewbott stuttered.

"Why didn't you tell me?"

"Well, that is, I thought, in the interest of time—"

"Damn it, Drewbott, the medals were earned, the medals must be awarded. Where's the blasted medal. Who's the soldier?"

With Drewbott leading the way, Sheridan headed my way. My heart thumped heavy with each step he took. I was near passing out by the time his boots came to rest again in front of me. I peeked up just enough to see Drewbott pass him the medal. A handsome thing it was, too. A brass bull's-eye with four fishtails sticking out like a big, four-petaled daisy. No one else had won one.

"In recognition of superior marksmanship," Sheridan began, "I present Private . . . Private . . ." Drewbott leaned over and told him my name.

"Private William Cath—" He stopped dead for a moment before saying, "Cathy?"

No power on earth could of kept me from raising my head at the call of my name. He was staring at me. I met his gaze. I saluted. He was stupefied. He recognized me. He saw me. He knew who I was. At that second, I didn't care that I'd been blown and would be tossed out to the wolves and red-skins and rapists. Sheridan had recognized me. In front of the Sergeant. In front of Clemmie. They were going to see now that I had mattered. The General remembered me.

I was certain that he would call me out. But Sheridan didn't speak for so long that Custer asked, "General, is something wrong?"

"No, nothing is wrong," Sheridan said, his black button eyes turned to hot coals burning into me. "This, uh, soldier . . ."—he curdled the word so it came out sounding like "piece of pig shit"—"reminded me of someone is all. A contraband by the name of Solomon. Solomon was my cook through-out the Rebellion. He was a fine and honorable man."

The way Sheridan hit those words, "fine," "honorable," and "man," it was clear he didn't feel that any of the three applied to me.

"It is in honor of the years during which Solomon served me so honorably, and for that reason and that reason alone, I present this medal. Is that understood, Private?"

With Custer and Drewbott trading puzzled looks, I answered, "Yessir," though my mouth felt like it was filled with ashes.

Instead of pinning the medal on me the way he'd done the winners of good conducts and the like, Sheridan just handed it to me. Had I not taken it, he'd of dropped it on the ground. Then he turned away, leaving me there with my hand quivering from being hacked into my forehead so hard. The Sergeant, Clemmie, Custer, Drewbott, they all saw that the General didn't return my salute.

"Not quite up to snuff, are they, General?" Custer asked. "Not quite regular army quality," Custer babbled on, plenty loud enough for every fellow up and down the line to hear. "This is exactly what I've been telling you, old man. They're fine in wartime. Burying details, cooking, entrenchments, and the like. But the peacetime army? Actual soldiers? It is folly to believe that Negroes will ever make true fighting men."

"It is not a belief, General. It is a proven fact," Sheridan said. Then, with a hard glance back over his shoulder at me, he added, "That the *men* . . . The colored *men* who enlisted *honorably* have already made fighting men. Their valor was established during the war. During combat." He raised his voice as he stomped off to the mess hall, making sure I wouldn't miss a word. "Combat. The only place where men, real, true, and valiant men, have ever proved themselves."

Custer, at his heels, went on, "Sure, a few of them managed to come up to the mark, but . . ." He fluffed his golden locks up and off the back of his neck, whipping them from side to side. His yellow silk kerchief billowing as he strode along, he added, "No white officer worth his salt will ever accept a colored command. You saw how fast I turned it down when you offered me one. There's your problem, Sheridan. You'll never get a decent white officer to command them. All you'll ever get is a no-hoper like Drewbott."

Sheridan didn't answer, but Custer stayed on his heels and went on, "All the action, all the glory is up North. The Sioux, Sheridan, they're massing. Give me a command fighting those red devils and you'll see an end to your Indian problem once and for all."

Their comments faded out and were lost in the distance. But all of us, including Drewbott, whose fine, pointed nostrils were flaring like a flagged bull's, had heard plenty. Our moment of glory had ended in humiliation. For the single, solitary time such a thing was ever likely to occur, Colonel Ednar Drewbott and I were of one mind: we both blamed our humiliation on the goading of the preening colorphobe, George Armstrong Custer, and we hated him with an equal intensity.

Unlike the chickenshit colonel, though, I was going to do something about it.

Chapter 61

⁓

The tow sack slung over my shoulder was heavier than you'd expect when, the next day, I hauled it into the kitchen.

Pinkney was busy hollering at Adams or Poteet, I couldn't tell one from the other, who were, at that moment, using the edge of Pinkney's oak table to play mumblety-peg. Those pinhead louts were zinging their knives onto the table, *thwokking* the points of their blades hard onto the wood, then snickering when Pinkney jumped as the knives came closer and closer to his hands.

Pinkney was hacking up chickens, and the next time he dropped that cleaver, he was glaring at the pair of dimwits and hit the table hard enough to decapitate one grown man or two undersize dimwits.

Poteet stopped snickering long enough to say, "Uncle, mind how you cut up the general's chicken. Remember, uncle, Custer hates dark meat." Adams laughed at his chum's wit.

That uncle business, that was the final straw. Pinkney yanked Poteet's knife out of his worktable, held it up high with that pig-sticker blade pointed right at its owner, who, seeing the murder in the cook's eye, shut his maw. Pinkney stood with the blade trembling for a moment, then flipped it up high, caught the beechwood handle without ever tearing his eyes from Poteet, cocked it back, and sent that piece of carbon steel flying with a masterful flick of the wrist that cartwheeled it through the air.

Thwok! It landed at the toe of Poteet's boot. No, on second glance, I saw, it had landed *in* the toe of Poteet's boot, stuck into the bit of sole protruding along the front, pinning that little toad where he stood.

"Oh, excuse me, suh," Pinkney drawled. "It slipped."

As the two corporals rained curses and threats down upon Pinkney, who was now smiling and whistling, I hurried past them to where Clemmie was pulling the pin feathers off some chicken carcasses. I hefted the sack off my shoulder and dropped it on the worktable next to her cleaver.

Clemmie stifled a shriek and jumped back, hissing, "Get that away from me! I told you I didn't want any part of this. Told you not to do it. But when have you ever listened to—"

My back to the white boys, I leaned in close, whispered, "Don't worry. They're dead," and opened the sack a crack.

Clemmie yelped when she saw my fine, fat, dead rattlesnakes. "I told you, I didn't want any part of this. I like my job. Like being—"

"Do you like Custer?"

"General Goldilocks? That prissy bastard can burn in hell. All that mess about only eat white meat, only be served by white troopers, would never take a black command, that just about fries my gizzards."

"Well then, we need to hit him back only way we have." I dumped a carcass onto the cutting board. Clemmie threw a dishrag over it, and hissed, "Why do you want to take a risk like that after you lucky enough to make it through inspection? Huh? Why do you always got to push things?"

I lifted the towel and chopped the creature's head off with one whack of the cleaver. "Because if you don't push, you never move ahead. Come on, Clemmie, you're not Old Miss's house girl anymore. Old Mister is dead. We're free, Clemmie. Maybe we can't speak up, but we can do this. We can get back a little of our own."

Clemmie heaved a big sigh, took several glances back at Adams and Poteet bullyragging Pinkney, and gave a nod of agreement. I had those venomous creatures skinned, dressed, and chopped into dainty portions before Poteet and Adams had finished cussing Pinkney out.

When we passed the word later to Pinkney about what the secret ingredient in Custer's dinner was going to be, he had only one objection: that he hadn't thought of it first. We worked together on creating a special dish for Custer. Pinkney made a white sauce that finally had me believing his claim that, before the bottle took him, he'd been a cook at the Astor House in New York City.

"Man," I told him, stealing another taste of his sauce, "you could put that on a roof shingle and have you some fine eating." He slapped my hand away

as he did something he told me was "napping" and blanketed a choice selection of deboned chunks of rattler with his sauce.

Word spread fast. By suppertime, the serving area off to the side of the
officers' mess hall was crowded with troopers foregoing their own evening
meal for a peek at Custer eating his.

The mess hall was done up with candles and bunches of wildflowers
that the wives, under the supervision of Mrs. Drewbott, had arranged.
Sheridan, Custer by his side, presided over the long table lined on either
side by every white officer on post and his wife if he had one, arranged in
order of rank, with the bachelor lieutenants sitting at the end.

Adams and Poteet, in their dress blues, wearing white gloves on their
hands, hair gleaming with pomade, swept plates covered with silver domes
down in front of Sheridan and Custer. They were followed by a small army
of white noncoms, recruited so as to save Custer from having to glimpse
a black face while he ate.

"What's he doing?" Caldwell asked in a whisper, craning to get a glimpse
at Custer.

"He's using his hand like a fan to waft the aroma up his nose," I told
him.

"Oh, now," said Clemmie, "he's spearing him a big chunk of prime rattlesnake."

The crowd closed in tighter around me. "He's chewing," I related to those
in back who couldn't see. "He's chewing and . . . yes! He swallowed."

A couple of the men tapped their hands together in applause that was as
gleeful as it was silent.

Next we all heard the rattler-eating Custer tapping on his glass with his
knife. The big room fell silent and he spoke. "My compliments to your cook,
Drewbott. I have been told that he created this dish, Poulet Fricassee à la
Custer, especially for me." He held up a morsel for all to admire. "White
meat, eh, gentlemen? No one can deny its inherent superiority. It is all I shall
ever eat." He popped that chunk of rattler into his bewhiskered grub hole,
chewed, and through a mouthful of viper, said, "It is all I shall ever command."

We all about exploded then, blown up as we were by stuffing the laughter that bubbled up at the sight of Custer smacking his lips over Pinkney's
rattler fricassee. The only officer not digging in was the General. I saw that
he was in a black mood and didn't appear hungry enough to eat much of

anything, let alone that hind leg off the Lamb of God he used to talk about.

Custer and Drewbott fell to gassing on about how President Johnson was packing the army with coloreds to clear us out of the South where we were "malingering" and "stirring up unrest."

Drewbott said it was just so the army could get our cheap labor and have us doing the jobs "decent" whites wouldn't touch.

"Cheap labor is all well and good," Custer answered back, "but tell me this: what's to prevent our coloreds from joining up with the coloreds they're supposed to be out here fighting? The black man and the red man? Like joins to like, correct? The coloreds' natural allegiance is to other coloreds. Bear that in mind, Drewbott," Custer warned. "Next time you're out in the field alone with nothing but a company of coloreds and surrounded by more of their kind, what's to keep the coloreds from joining up with the redskins and slaughtering all of you and then having their way with your wives?"

An uneasy silence fell over the party as the wives exchanged glances. Even tubby Mrs. Drewbott fancied our men were lusting for her. Just like I'd seen him do back at Cedar Creek, Sheridan had gone quiet. Dangerous quiet.

Showing that he couldn't read his commander any better than Colonel Terrill had at that other officers' dinner party, Drewbott, his face red from being wallpapered on the fine whiskey he'd had freighted in, stood, raised his glass, and brayed out in his jackass voice, "May I propose a toast to our most esteemed visitor for honoring our humble post with his presence. To General Philip Sheridan, who led us to victory in the recent unpleasantness and will do the same in eradicating the redskins. To the Generals Sheridan and Custer!"

Chairs were scraped back, all the officers except for Custer and Sheridan popped up, and a hearty cheer was raised. I watched the General's face turn to stone and felt like a play that I had seen before was about to commence.

When the cheer was done, the officers stayed on their feet with their glasses raised high, waiting for Sheridan to stand.

The General didn't move a muscle other than his tongue. "Sit down! All of you fools," he ordered. They did. "I might as well speak plainly and to your face, Drewbott. As all present are fully aware, you were given this command because no competent officer would take it. I expected little of you, Drewbott. You have delivered less."

Drewbott's face went from red to pink to white and settled at green.

"Drewbott, the United States Army has not expended considerable resources, scarce resources I might add in this new day with both the people and the Congress against having a standing army at all, for you to waste in establishing this fort. That money, Drewbott, was not appropriated so that your wives could grow _____ petunias!"

The old, familiar curses came back as Sheridan grew hot.

Mrs. Drewbott gasped and pressed her hankie to her mouth. Ladies back then, white ladies at any rate, were never supposed to hear such salty language.

The General didn't slow down a whit. "The _____ mission is to, as you yourself put it, 'eradicate redskins.' You seem to believe, Drewbott, that this is a mission that I will accomplish on my own. Might I remind you that I am but the head. My _____ commanders in the field are my hands. And, you, Drewbott, have done nothing but sit on yours. Thus far, you have failed to so much as even map the _____ savages' water holes. That is a crucial piece of reconnaissance in helping us to shut down the _____ redskins' pantry by eliminating the buffalo."

No food, no fight. Solomon's words came back to me and I realized then that the General was going to do the redskins the way he'd done Old Mister and all the other Rebels in his path: starve them out.

"The _____ war may be over, Colonel, but we are still _____ soldiers. And soldiers soldier, Drewbott. Soldiers soldier. Soldiering is something you have done precious little of during your tenure. Instead, you have turned this fort into your own personal hidey-hole where you have sat on your fat _____ backside waiting for the redskins to come calling. As you have been told many times, Drewbott, they will not _____ come to you! You must get up off your _____ plump posteriors and hunt the _____ savages down."

Gasping and trembling, Drewbott looked as though his heart was failing him. And still the General did not let up.

"We are daily inundated with reports of the depredations committed, in particular by the renegade chief Chewing Bones and his pack of hyenas. Not fifty miles from this very _____ post a farm was raided. Crops and buildings burned. Livestock stolen. The man's wife was cruelly used by the savages to the point of death. His two maiden daughters were carried off. The settler and his sons were slaughtered in an unspeakable manner. Are you in receipt of that report, Colonel?"

"Yessir, I am, sir."

"Ah, good. And tell me, Colonel, would you care to be knowing how I learned of this atrocity?"

Drewbott, who barely squeaked out "Sir," appeared to know how dangerous it was when Sheridan fell back on the "me boyo" talk.

"From my superior officer, General Sherman. General _____ William _____ Tecumseh Sherman. He was not happy, Colonel. Perhaps you've not seen General Sherman when he is not happy. This report and your failure to do one _____ thing about it did *not* make the Commander of the United States Army happy."

Sheridan stood so suddenly that his chair tipped backward and crashed to the floor. He flung his napkin onto the table and thundered, "By Christ, Drewbott, you shall either begin immediately hunting down and exterminating Chewing Bones and his murderous band and driving the _____ savages from this territory or a soldier in possession of a functioning pair of testicles will be found who can!"

Chapter 62

When I reached her the next morning, Clemmie was already packing her traps onto the kitchen wagon. Sheridan, Custer, and their staffs had cleared out right after supper rather than spend another night in Fort Arroyo.

"There you are," she said. She sounded mad. "I need to tell you something."

I peeked around. As usual whenever Clemmie appeared, most of the company flocked around, all of them bobbing their necks about like geese going after June bugs trying to catch a peek of my sister.

I moved in close so she wouldn't be talking so loud in case she called me "sister" or talked about our mama. We'd spent every second we were free together in the Sergeant's quarters and some of the men had already started teasing me about my "sweetheart."

"What's wrong?" I asked.

"I will kill you, strangle you with my own two hands, if you get yourself laid out. You hear me?" Though she spoke hard, tears trembled in her eyes.

"I am not gonna get killed."

"You might have to go after the renegades. Only the idiot whites believe those bloodthirsty savages see a dime's worth of difference between white and black. They'll come after you, Cathy. If they ever get hold of you . . ." Her anger cooled and she whispered, "A woman? Lord." She'd heard the stories, too. "Killing'd be the best thing they could do to you."

"Me?" I said. "Don't you know I am killproof? Already had one army, one gang of bushwhackers, and one Old Mister try to get the big job done. And they all failed, didn't they?"

She smiled and hugged me. This last I didn't resist for every single man gawking at us would of given up his crossed-saber cap for so much as a kind glance from my sister and there she was lavishing me with affection. For them to behold an actual hug and water running from the eye of the prettiest woman in the state on my account? Well, that was sure to do my standing as a man a power of good. With everyone except Vikers, of course. For, there he was, sneaking around as usual, watching our farewell hug with his head tipped to the side, trying to work out what was really going on.

Dust hadn't settled behind our visitors before the Sergeant passed along Sheridan's order that we were to "map, blow up, or poison every location where a redskin might get a sip of water." He read off a list of those he'd chosen for the expedition. To our surprise, me and Lem were on it. It seemed that my "romance" with Clemmie had taken the degenerate stink off me.

I gathered up my gray wool blanket, ground cloth, Spencer carbine, and one-quart canteen. Since it was a warm April with the barrel cactus already dotted with yellow flowers and the prickly pears blossoming pink, all of us on the detachment left our heavy overcoats with their handsome shoulder capes behind.

We were each issued sixty rounds of ammunition and five days' rations. A pound of hardtack and three-quarters of a pound of salt pork. Knowing how tedious this fare could become, I traded Pinkney two gourds of pulque for a couple of onions and three potatoes. Once we got our personal gear stored, we used every minute of the remaining time overhauling our horses and their gear.

I had Bunny's saddle and bridle gleaming bright as the day they were issued. And Bunny, herself, I groomed until she was pretty enough for the state fair.

We were ready to take to the field.

Chapter 63

When we rode out in the dark, chilly hours before dawn, the country smelled like spring, like the earth getting ready for warmth and growing. We knew that the heavy hammer of summer heat was about to fall on us again, so we enjoyed shivering a bit in the saddle before the sun came burning up.

The Sergeant divvied us up into three details of ten men each and sent us out to scout water holes, springs, seeps, any place the savages could get a drink. He kept me, Caldwell, Greene, another fellow whose entire job was to lead a mule carrying two crates of black powder, and five others in his unit of ten. The Sergeant handed me a little notebook and the stub of a pencil, told me I'd be marking down his sightings from the sextant, and we hit the trail.

Bunny loped along next to the Sergeant's mount with a right jaunty snap to her step. Caldwell and Greene and the rest kept well back, which was fine with me for I had hard feelings about that pair that time had not, and never would, soften.

Just like when I was keeping accounts for him in his office, the Sergeant was silent for a good while as he studied the plains, here and there bouqueted with wildflowers, a few glistening with the last drops of morning dew, before starting in the way he did, as though I'd been privy to the conversation he was carrying on in his head. "It couldn't have come soon enough, right?"

"That's right," I agreed, knowing he was talking about finally getting out of the fort and putting some miles between us and Drewbott.

"I love this country," he observed. "Open and wild and free. Endless possibilities."

"Yessir, being able to see a hundred miles in any direction does have a freeing effect on the mind. That and being west of the cursed ninety-eighth meridian."

"You remembered," he said.

"Sir," I answered. "I remember every word you have ever spoken to me."

I'd never of said something so personal if we'd been indoors. But he was right, this country was freeing. And it had the same effect on him. He responded, "You have a fine mind, Private. You're not like any other freed slave I've ever met. You go your own way."

"Thank you, sir."

"It's not a compliment, Cathay. Not for a soldier."

"Yessir."

"On the other hand," he continued, the way he did when he was chewing something over. "Our people will never be free if we always obey."

"No, sir. I figure on obeying much as I can right up to the point where I get me that pension. That'll be the last day I ever 'sir' anyone."

"What will you do after?"

I hadn't actually given much thought to the matter of after. But the Sergeant had a way of causing dreams you hardly knew were there to crowd in and I piped up as though I'd had it all planned out for months. "I propose to have my own little business."

"Yes! A business," he exclaimed, like I'd come up with the right answer to a tough problem. "It's just like Brother Douglass says, 'We must acquire property and educate the hands and hearts and heads of our children. Races that fail to do these things die politically and socially, and are only fit to die.'"

It puffed me up considerably that me and Brother Douglass were of a mind.

The Sergeant asked if I'd stay out West when my hitch was up and I said I would. "Nothing for me back East. Even less down South."

"Nothing for any of us, Private," he agreed. "And every day it gets worse as President Johnson shows how deeply he is in the pocket of the planters. With a few strokes of his pen, he continues to give back with ink what was won with four years of blood. There is no hope for a decent life in the South. Not with a bunch of defeated Rebs who are determined to use the law to enslave us again."

For a minute or two the only sound was the clopping of hooves as we made our way across a high mesa. Finally he spoke, asking, "You know where you should head?"

"Can't say as I do."

"San Francisco," he answered. "My father told me stories of how all the races mingle freely there. That'd be the place to open a business." His eyes gleamed at the prospect. "You could bring Clemmie if you two have an understanding," he added. "As for me, I have a feeling that I will find my own heart's darling waiting for me there by the sea."

It hurt me to think about this heart's darling he'd be finding.

"What sort of business do you have in mind?" he asked.

"I was thinking about a laundry."

"Oh, no." He cut me off. "Not a laundry. Where's the dignity in that?"

"It wouldn't be me doing the scrubbing," I corrected him. "I'd hire some gals."

"No, no, why, you'd be barely better than a slave owner then. No, what you want to do is open a small dry-goods store."

I agreed that that was a fine idea, but it had one hitch. "I'll never have enough money to rent a place with high shelves, much less stock those shelves. I figure I could swing a couple of washtubs and some lye soap. But ever have enough to open a dry-goods store? Uh-uh. I'd as soon catch a weasel asleep."

"Not if you had a partner."

"A partner," I repeated, thinking I'd misheard or heard what I'd never even dared to dream about.

"Why not? If we throw in together, our pensions along with what we've saved up, we could swing it. Our hitches are up at about the same time. I trust you. I think you trust me."

More than anyone I've ever known, I wanted to say, but didn't for fear of sounding candy ankle.

"Think about it, Cathay," he said, riding back to gather up the stragglers for we had come to the edge of the mesa.

Farther on, the ten of us picked our way down a series of ravines that led to a canyon the like of which I'd never seen. It was a trough with walls that rose far overhead and had a floor of sandstone that bathed the cliffs in a reddish glow. Hooves clattered on the hard rock bed. The orange cliffs on either side were wavy as buttercream icing slumping off a cake on a hot day. Lost in gaping, I fell behind the rest. I was having my doubts about finding water for every inch of stone was sunbaked with not a patch of earth nor tuft of grass.

"Cathay!" The Sergeant's call echoed back. I rode forward and damn if he wasn't standing beside a little pool, pretty as a round looking glass reflecting the blue sky high overhead. A series of such seeps, none much deeper or bigger than a red clay washbasin, stair-stepped down the canyon, trapping whatever little rain or dew ran into them. The dust around each one had been disturbed by the unshod hooves of Indian ponies.

The Sergeant pulled his sextant from a saddlebag and proceeded to calculate latitude and longitude. I wrote down the numbers he reeled off in my notebook so that they could be mapped later.

"Are we going to blast them?" I asked, for that was why we'd brought along the black powder.

His right eye clamped to the sighting mechanism, the Sergeant answered, "I hope that's not a serious question, Private. We'd have to drill into sandstone to plant the cartridges. Then where would we run once the fuses were lit? Not to mention the danger of creating a rock slide. And for what?" he asked, sliding his sextant back into the saddlebag. "To blow up a few shallow basins?"

We clopped along the canyon until it opened out into a gully with a thin trickle of water running in it. Pitiful as it was, the Sergeant shot the coordinates anyway and I wrote them down.

For the next few days, we ambled about a newborn world waking up from winter, mapping anything wet we came across. On the fifth day, the Sergeant told the others that at dawn the next morning him and me and a couple of packhorses'd be heading out alone. "There is supposed to be a spring fifteen or twenty miles due west. Cathay and I will make better time and use less water if we go alone."

That evening, I filled a bucket with water from one of the kegs and took it along with a flake of hay to where I'd staked Bunny for the night. She dipped her head into the bucket, soaking her floppy ears, as she guzzled her nightcap. I broke up the flake and, whiskery muzzle twitching, she gathered the dry stalks into her mouth and ate, her jaw slewing from side to side. As she mulched up the hay, I groomed her, and whispered the good news about how the Sergeant had picked me.

We were up the next morning before any of the others except Lem, who had named himself camp cook. He had coffee ready and brought cups to me and the Sergeant. It was to be a short foray and we were traveling light. All-bright had his canteen looped over his saddle horn and a spyglass in its leather case on a strap over his shoulder.

The day dawned bright and hot, the sun already flexing for the summer to come. Like the rest of the men, the Sergeant wasn't wearing his jacket. Of course, I was. But no one passed comments anymore as I was known as either modest or crazy and "Bill's ways" had come to be accepted.

"Y'all take care, Bill," Lem hollered after me. It was unusual for one man to call another by his first name and I didn't like him yelling it out like that. It sounded nancy boy, and I didn't want to put that thought back in All-bright's head after Clemmie had taken it away. So, though I could picture Lem behind me, waving good-bye, waiting for me to wave back, I never did turn around.

After a few hours on the trail, the land began, ever so gradually, to slope down. We continued poking our way through the typical assortment of vegetation bent on stabbing or crippling us. The day turned so warm that the Sergeant took the liberty of unbuttoning his shirt. We went to a gallop for a bit to feel a breeze on our sweaty skin and his shirt flew open, baring his chest and shoulders.

Lord.

I had to look away.

We settled into an easy walk so that the Sergeant could tip over to the side in his saddle, and study the ground. He was cutting for signs of red-skins. This wasn't like tracking back home, though, where a deer'd leave a tidy set of hoofprints clear as a map in the soft earth. No, here he studied what looked to me like bare rock, searching for "disturbances" and for "what's not there."

He halted at the top of an arroyo so deep it was almost a little canyon and tilted his ear down toward the ravine, listening for the bird chatter that wasn't there and the prairie-dog alert barks far ahead that were. Then he looked to see what was disturbed. Leaves crushed. Twigs broken. Thorns sprouting hair from a horse's tail. When Bunny nickered, Allbright held up his gauntleted hand, ordering silence. I leaned down and rested on Bunny's neck, stroking her black mane to keep her from getting snorty. Clouds moved in and provided a bit of shade to cool us off.

We rode on, following the arroyo below us. Within its shaded recesses, I spotted several jacks and a couple of white-tailed deer stirring amidst the desert willow and shaggy salt cedar that sprouted along the creek bed at the base of the ravine. We came to an old cottonwood that had been swept away when some long-ago flash flood rose up, then dropped the fallen tree here. A covey of quail skittered out from beneath the whitened branches of the dead tree and fishtailed after their mama to safety farther on down the ravine.

The Sergeant said that we were close and we couldn't risk the horses giving us away, so we left them tied to the fallen cottonwood and continued on foot. Now that I was closer to the ground, I could see what the Sergeant had been following. What had looked like nothing from horseback, showed itself to be a trail that had been brushed over with a leafy branch. Here and there, part of a hoofprint appeared.

The wind started kicking up then and long strings of gray clouds flapped across the sky. The clouds erased our shadows and the wind whipped away any sound we might make. Bits of blown grit and sand stung my face. I snugged the hold bead of my hat up tight under my chin to keep it from blowing off and peered up at the sky. The entire northern horizon behind me was blanketed in towers of clouds that rose up into dark gray anvils.

"Sergeant," I said. "Begging your pardon, sir, but I think we got some weather moving in."

He barely glanced up from the trail to peek at the clouds and say, "We're getting close."

At the leading edge of the massive anvil cloud was a thin line of bright blue. I'd heard of such a thing before. "I believe, sir," I said, "that this is what's called a 'blue norther.'"

He mumbled, "*Hmmm,*" and carried on. The Sergeant had what you might call a one-track mind and his was roaring down the rails toward mapping the water hole the prints were leading us to. "Not much farther now," he said again, hiking the straps of the spyglass and sextant cases up farther on his shoulder, and setting off at a ferocious pace.

But it was farther. Far enough that I wished we hadn't left the horses behind. Far enough that the temperature started dropping like a rock. The wind turned chilly and I knew we'd be cold the instant we stopped. Especially the Sergeant without a jacket and hardly enough fat on him to keep a sparrow warm.

After an hour or so, he stopped suddenly and dropped to his belly. I lay down beside him close enough that a seam of warmth opened up along my side where it touched him. He pulled the spyglass from its case, rested on his elbows, and made a tripod of his arms. He put the glass to his eye and peered down the ravine that ran straight before us. A wind funneled up and blew the brim of his hat back so that it was mashed up flat against the crown. His body next to mine tensed at what he saw and I knew we'd come upon a party of Apache.

Chapter 64

⌐

As I lay there, waiting for the Sergeant to speak, every story the old sergeant back at Jefferson Barracks had told us and every one of the telegrams I'd heard read out came back to me with the words "mutilated," "raped," "unmanned," and "burned alive" jumping out. My blood galloped through my veins harder than it had in my moment of cowardice back at Cedar Creek. Redskins were even more terrifying than Rebels, for at least Rebs weren't murdering savages like the redskins, who were more animal than human, who gloried in killing the way a wild animal would.

"Have a look," the Sergeant whispered.

With a trembling hand, I put the glass to my eye, and braced myself to see a treacherous brave, his mouth still red from eating the heart of one of his victims. Instead, the glass filled with the sight of a young mother gazing down at the infant sucking at her breast with a tenderness to break the hardest heart. Her long, black hair, parted in the middle, framed a face gentle and wary as a doe's.

I glanced about at the rest of the band, camped out amidst a heavy growth of brush with a wallow dug in its center that had filled with muddy seep water. I counted half a dozen women and old men and twice that many youngsters, skinny specimens slinging rocks at each other with leather pouches. A small remuda of Indian ponies was picketed a ways down from the band. The women and old men sat with stiff blankets tented around their shoulders for the wind had picked up even further and was howling now so strong that we could of started shouting and they'd of never heard us.

This band wasn't at all the fearsome gang of bloodthirsty murderers described by the old sergeant. First off, they were all half starved. The old ones were down to gristle. A couple only raised their heads to cough. Still, I reminded myself, sad and pitiful as they might seem, they'd slice my throat soon as look at me.

My heart was hardening toward them again when Iyaiya whispered to me, *They were here first. They are warriors. They fight the enemy. They will not be captives.*

As I took one last look, a big wind gusted up and lifted the mama's long black hair so it rose off her blanketed shoulders like a raven taking wing.

The Sergeant had the sextant to his eye. I wanted to ask if we couldn't just skip this one water hole. What would it matter if we let some women and babies and old folk live? But he whispered, "Coordinates," and I fumbled in my pocket for the notebook. When I had it and the stub of pencil in my hand, he dictated to me the numbers that would reveal this secret spot to the army and they would come after us and blow it up or poison it.

I wrote the numbers down.

Progress back to our horses was slow as the wind was against us. The temperature kept dropping. When we reached the horses, the Sergeant had trouble untying the reins as his fingers had stiffened and he was shivering hard. I worried about him not having a jacket and wished I could give him mine. We mounted up and, for a minute, he peered about, looking almost dazed, like he was trying to recollect where he was and which way to go. I spurred Bunny ahead, he followed, and I led us out.

The Sergeant, though he was trembling so much he shimmied in the saddle, was able to pick up our trail when we left the arroyo and he took the lead. Though the wind cut straight through my jacket and set me to shivering, I figured we'd be okay. All we had to do was follow our trail back to camp.

The northern wind blew Bunny's mane so hard it flew straight out from her neck like a black flag. My bare hands on the reins were numb as stones. Wind-whipped water streamed from my eyes, blurring my sight and chilling my cheeks. And then it started to rain. The icy rain blew in at us sideways by the bucketful, soaking us to the bone. Thunder boomed. Lightning cracked and the sky showed a poisonous violet in the flash. The signs we'd left coming out, the hoof marks chalked onto rocky ground, horse plops, trampled brush, they were all washed away. It was dark, we had no signs to follow back to camp, no light to see by even if we had, and nothing to shelter us from the cold and rain.

We went on by dead reckoning. I rode next to the Sergeant and saw that he'd stopped shivering. He looked calm and unworried. That eased my mind, until, stiff fingers fumbling at the buttons, he started to take off his shirt. I'd heard stories of men lost in the winter, stripping off and rolling in the snow. The stories always ended with them being found naked and dead. Like those poor souls, the cold had taken his mind.

"No!" I screamed, and he stopped. His face was blank. The reins dropped from his hands and he wobbled in the saddle. I tied his reins to my saddle horn and mounted up behind him on his horse. He slumped forward and didn't resist. I opened my jacket and leaned forward, covering his back and giving him what warmth I had. I harred Bunny up, loosened up on the reins, and let her pick the trail. She was a good night horse and could see a sight better than me in the dark.

We trudged along, the Sergeant mashed up against my chest. He listed to the side. Even though the rain had stopped, we were both stiff and cold as boulders. I hugged him and whispered into the back of his neck, asking him not to die.

Of a sudden, Bunny picked her pace up to a jerky canter. I figured that her brain had frozen, too, and we'd die when she tripped on a hole. A minute later, I heard a tinny sound that turned to a clanging as we drew closer. A speck of light, so small it vanished when I blinked, appeared in the distance, growing steadier the closer we came.

"We made it, Sergeant," I whispered. He slumped and it took all my strength to keep him from tumbling off.

The speck became a bonfire. Lem was silhouetted in front of it, banging on a big tin kettle with a ladle. My friend was there to catch me and the Sergeant when I dismounted and my legs folded up under me. The Sergeant's arm over my neck was stiff as old putty as Lem helped me carry him to the tent. We laid him on his cot. Lem lit the stub of a candle. His eyes were open, but he wasn't seeing anything in this world. His wet clothes had frozen to his skin in spots and we had to melt them off before wrapping him in his blanket.

Lem left to hunt up more blankets. I knelt beside the cot. The Sergeant lay still as death, his eyes closed. In the light from the candle, he looked like he'd been carved out of marble. A statue or some other thing too perfect for this world. I pressed my ear against his chest, but I heard nothing.

I felt like I was falling from a great height and heard myself whimpering, "No, please, no. Sergeant. Please."

I listened again. Only when I stopped breathing could I catch the sound of a slow thump. Something else came to me along with the faint beat of his heart: his smell. It was the first time I'd been close enough to smell of the Sergeant since those long days and endless nights when I had brought him back from death and, with just that one whiff, hard as I had tried to deaden him, Wager Swayne came alive again in my heart.

Just as I had saved my soldier then in that wagon rolling away from my girlhood, I would save him now. I opened my jacket, lifted the blanket, and pressed my warm chest against his. I laid my head against his neck and blew my warm breath against it.

For nearly the first time since that terrible moment when I accepted that I would never be the phantom woman he loved, I allowed his name, the name of my soldier, back into my thoughts. And then for the first time ever, I spoke it out loud. "Wager," I whispered. "Wager Swayne." When I said his name, it was in my own voice. The voice of the woman who'd kept him in this world once before and was bound to do it a second time.

"Wager Swayne. Wager Swayne. Wager Swayne," I crooned. I let his name swell with all the love I had tamped down until it became a chant as strong as the one Mama had blessed me and Clemmie with. His heart thumped a tiny bit louder as I let my love pour forth. "Wager," I pleaded, speaking directly to his spirit and calling it back. His chest rose and fell. But the breath that came forth was icy as death. I put my mouth on his and breathed up heat from the pit of my belly, but his lips against mine did not warm.

"Wager," I whispered and became every woman he had ever loved. Every woman he'd ever wanted. Every woman who had made his life sweet enough to go on living. I became the woman he dreamed had saved him. I put my lips against his and pressed my need into them. His breath came back up then, stronger, warmer, heavier with life, and I kissed him even more deeply. He was alive. My love had brought him back from death and no one would ever tell me different. Not even after what happened next.

He yanked his head to the side, jerking his lips from mine, reared back and stared at me, his eyes snapped wide open in horror. With what strength he had, he shoved me away.

"It's not what you think it—"

"Shut up, Private. Just shut up." Anger unfroze his throat.

"I saved your life. I—"

"Shut your damn mouth, man. Stop talking in that strange voice. Stop. I warned you once before. And now, if you say one more word to me, ever, I will have you court-martialed for moral turpitude."

"Sergeant, listen—"

"Get. Out. Of. My. Sight."

Every word was a punch to the gut. I couldn't of spoken if I'd wanted. I spun around. Lem stood at the tent opening. I pushed past him.

I went to Bunny and would of ridden off that night, but she was played out. I fed and watered her, staked her out for what was left of the night, and went to the tent I shared with Lem. Without making a sound, I wept. Lem lit his candle, came and sat next to me and wrapped his blanket around both of us, but nothing could stop my shivering.

"Bill," he said, his words soft and consoling, "I'm sorry your heart is broke. I know there ain't no pain to compare with lovin' someone don't love you back."

Even if he was talking about a man loving a man, what he said was true and little shuddery gasps I could not hold back slipped from me.

"There now, Bill," he said, pulling me closer. "It's gon be all right. Just gon take time's all. Trust Lem, okay?"

His kind words and friendship after being alone for so long caused all the sand to drain out of me. I leaned my head against his shoulder and wept, slumping more and more into him as the fight went out of me.

Lem wrapped both his arms around me and I snuggled against his chest. "I can't stand to see you hurtin' like this, Bill," he said. A moment later, his mouth was on mine.

I tried to pull away, but it was like being trapped beneath a bank vault.

"I love you, Bill," he murmured. "Loved you from the start. I'll take care of you. Treat you good. You won't never have no man treat you better."

"Get off me!" I screamed. "I'm not like you!" This last I accompanied by pulling the razor from my pocket and holding the blade to his neck.

He stood, and asked, more hurt than mad, "You put a blade to my throat? After everything . . . ? After . . . ?" He did not have words for how wrong I'd done him.

"We're quits, Bill. That's the last time I ever speak your name and I'll thank you not to ever say mine again."

Chapter 65

⁓

Lem was as good as his word and, from that night on, I stopped existing both for the Sergeant and for him. Back at the fort, he paid Tea Cake three dollars to switch bunks with him. Neither he nor the Sergeant would so much as glance my way. The misery and loneliness of the year that followed, I do not care to return to even in memory and will say only that the days were long and the nights were longer.

I came to many a cold dawn during those long months with my mind set on deserting. A couple of times, in the dark of night, my saddlebags stuffed with stolen potatoes and salt pork, I actually skinned out. Once Bunny and me made it all the way into the nearest town, Matanza, but then, coming upon that grimy settlement, I thought of the faces I would see there. And that put me in mind of all the faces I'd see for whatever remained of my miserable life.

Realizing that there would never again be even the slightest chance that the Sergeant's would be among them caused me to turn around and head back. Though, once again, the Sergeant might regard me as the worst sort of sissy degenerate, a twist who'd taken advantage of a man when he was out of his head, I'd rather of died straight-out than live without ever seeing his face again. Though there wasn't the speck of a hope of a chance for a future, I could not stop how I felt. Wager Swayne or Levi Allbright, I was devoted, heart and soul, to the man and would be until the day I died.

Only thing that kept me from killing myself during that awful year was knowing that Iyaiya was waiting for me on the other side and I couldn't endure an eternity of the wrath she would rain upon me if I took my own life.

After months of no one speaking a word to me that wasn't an order, I got so lonely I rode into Matanza just to have a bit of company. Matanza had livened up considerably since I'd last passed through. Five saloons, four with whorehouses upstairs, had sprouted along the single street, an avenue of either choking dust or hoof-churned muck. Chubby thighs collared with lace garters, dainty toes pointing, poked out of second-story windows luring white cowboys into one of the whites-only establishments.

All this growth among fancy houses and watering holes, to say nothing of a dry-goods store, a bank, and a hotel was because of the ranch owners who'd turned their herds loose when they went off to kill Yankees for the Confederacy and had come back to find that those beeves had gone forth and been most astonishing fruitful. Quick as the army and the slave owners could set their men free, the ranchers hired them to gather up the herds and drive them to San Francisco along the old Emigrant and Butterfield stage trails. Covering about twelve miles a day, the first big herds out of San Antonio arrived in Matanza during my second spring, my second at Fort Arroyo, when I was a friendless outcast.

The black cowboys, who made up about a fourth of this army of saddle tramps, had to straggle on past the saloons to a rickety, two-story structure, set off a ways out of town. I'd of been shot or lynched if I'd set foot in any of the white establishments. So, on that lilac-skyed evening at the end of a particularly lonely day, near the end of a particularly lonely year, I headed for the one place in town that catered to my people, The Last Chance Saloon.

The Last Chance was a mean, bare-walled place barely better than a barn in construction but considerably worse in aroma. Everyone inside was black except for a few of the girls and the white owner and bartender, Barney, a two-time Confederate deserter who left the Army of the South for good after being branded with a *D* on his hip. Most of the customers were cowboys with a sprinkling of soldiers. All of them were talking loud and acting like jackasses.

The Last Chance smelled like old beer, sawdust, sweat, wet leather, and every form of chewed, spit, and smoked tobacco you can imagine. It was packed that night as a large herd up from the Valley was bedded down outside of town. A couple of men waited in a line on the stairs leading to the four rooms on the second floor where the daughters of Eve plied their trade. All six of the card tables were filled.

I was sorry to see that Vikers, who'd risen over the past year and was more powerful than ever, sat at one of those tables with Greene and Caldwell guarding his back. But, since Vikers was a card cheat and had a table full of cowboys eager to get swindled, I didn't think he'd notice me much, so I went on ahead and took a place at the crowded bar.

I'd just ordered a beer and settled in when I spotted a face reflected in the mirror that ran along behind the bottles. The mirror was so cloudy and spotted and cracked that the face came to me like a faded memory. It was Lem and he was staring back with none of the hostility he usually directed my way when I encountered him at the fort. Hoping he'd finally forgiven me, I smiled and raised my hand. Lem picked up his drink and turned his back to the bar. I finished my beer in one long swallow and ordered another.

From the loud remarks the men were passing back and forth, I figured out that Vikers had lured in a couple of wranglers and one big, fat pigeon. This last was a cook they called Frenchie as he was a Creole-type fellow out of New Orleans. Next to the trail boss, the cook was the most important man on the drive and he pulled down sixty dollar a month. Though Frenchie's words were sweetened with the honeyed accent of his region, he was as surly as any other cook I ever knew right back to Solomon.

"Soldier boy!" Frenchie yelled at Vikers, who was studying his cards in a way meant to show he was worried. "Feels better in, man. Ante up! Ante up!"

Vikers fidgeted, acted uncertain, and played the greenhorn.

"Got a hunch, bet a bunch!" Frenchie urged, his nose wide open, smelling the pot he thought was his.

At the top of the stairs, Beulah, a heavy white woman corseted up like a battleship with her bosoms heaved high, bawled out, "Who's next?" She kept her doughy face angled off, presenting a profile that featured a high forehead, thin lips, and a minimum of two double chins, as well as the aforementioned bosoms. Though there were three men waiting on the stairs, no one stepped forward.

"What's wrong with you smoked Yankees?" she roared. "Ain't you out here, standin' in line for pussy?"

"Not off no half-nose woman," a corporal with a haystack bush of dusty hair yelled back.

She howled insults of a racial nature, turned to advance on the man, and exposed the other side of her face, revealing a nose had been et up by the pox.

In the silence that followed, the sound of moist, snuffling breaths being sucked into and blown out of that black hole left every pecker in the place soft. This being bad for business, Barney flew out from behind the bar, holding a quirt, which he used to threaten Beulah back into her room. Lust brought folks to a low state. It was a sad business all around.

The only other one of the soiled doves I'd heard of was Mary the Murderer. Stories had passed around the barracks that Mary had opened a drifter up from his tail to his scuppers with a straight-edge razor after he beat her up then passed out. Scariest part of the deal was that Mary had no remorse for filleting the lout. Mary was a laudanum addict, and it was said that she'd dosed her victim the night of the murder. I'd never set eyes on the girl and had no desire to do so.

Back at Vikers's table, one of the wranglers, a long-headed dimwit from somewhere back in hookworm country, prodded Vikers. "Push in or push off."

Finally, Vikers, who was still acting hesitant in spite of the aces and kings he was known to keep up his sleeve, matched the pot, and cards were dealt. The long-headed wrangler picked his up and yelped, "Ooo-wee! Hell broke loose in Georgie!" The boy was as country as red flannel gravy and twice as thick.

"What you say?" the dealer asked the other wrangler.

"Hit me," he answered.

The dealer flipped him a no-account up card. The Creole cook cackled and told the boy, "Eat acorns, son."

The long-headed boy said, "Pull off again," and drew a down card that made him say, "Shee-yit."

Upstairs, doors opened and closed as the ladies did their business and boots clopped in and out as the men did theirs. Vikers kept fumbling and acting like he wasn't sure how to bet. The pot built. Pretending to be fidgeting over his poke, counting the bills, Vikers slid one of the cards waiting up his sleeve into his hand then pushed his whole roll into the pot.

The two wranglers folded, throwing their cards down in disgust. Frenchie didn't bother to hide a self-satisfied smirk as he believed he'd suckered Vikers. The cook matched the bet and raised. Vikers pulled out the wad he kept tucked into his boot for just such occasions and slapped that down.

The cook all but licked his chops for he was holding three aces. Vikers laid down a jacks high straight.

"Well, just goes to show, don't it," Vikers said, pretending amazement as he scooped up the pile. "Even a blind hog'll get him an acorn now and again."

Frenchie, seeing the way of it and that he'd been cheated, was going for the derringer tucked into his boot when he heard two revolvers being cocked. One at each side of his head where Greene and Caldwell had him boxed in.

Since Vikers wasn't occupied anymore, it was time I left before he noticed me. Staring at the back of Lem's head, I downed my beer and headed for the door. I wasn't quick enough.

"Hey, Stanky," Vikers hollered. "What're you leaving for? Fun's just starting."

I was shoving the door open, could see Bunny hitched up outside waiting for me, was all but gone when hands fell on my shoulders and stopped me.

Caldwell and Greene shoved me back to Vikers, who looked me up and down, and said, "Well, well, if it isn't our old friend Stanky. You've been laying pretty low. Hiding out. Don't recall seeing you about much. You boys," he asked Greene and Caldwell, "you recall seeing Stanky much? Like, oh say, the washroom?"

Oh, Lord Jesus, not again.

"Sure don't," Caldwell chimed in.

"Nope," Greene agreed. "Never knowed anyone as soap shy as this here nancy boy."

"Maybe it's time we give him that bath was interrupted before. Allbright's not here to save his pet," Vikers said. "Strip him down, boys."

I struggled, but there wasn't any point. Vikers's game had caught on with the drunk cowboys and they'd all joined in. I thought about how they nearly quirted a white woman in this place just because she showed the disease that had been shoved into her by these very men, and I did not want to think on what they'd do to me once they got my britches off.

I fought like a cougar, but my jacket was half off when Lem drew his sidearm, pointed it at Vikers, and said he'd burn him down unless I was turned loose.

"Look who we have here, boys," Vikers said, happy as a cat with a new mouse to torture. "It's Mr. Fancy's wife, Mrs. Fancy. I thought the happy couple'd broken up. But here he is ready to defend his sweetheart's honor. Is that what you're doing, Mule? Defending your sweetheart's honor?"

"Leave him be," Lem said.

The drunk cowboys crowded in, waiting for Vikers to give the word. Knowing Lem didn't have it in him to pull the trigger, Vikers said, "Have at him, boys," and they lunged for my pants. I was grabbing around for a gun or knife to kill myself with when Lem fired off a round, and the mirror behind the bar shattered.

Everyone halted. The jackals dragging at my pants and the fellow with his fist cocked back ready to chug Lem in the face, they all froze.

"You want to know why Cathay don't wash with us?" Lem demanded. "Because I know. I know something none of y'all know."

Of course Lem knew my secret. He probably figured it out while he was trying to have his way with me. If he was ever going to throw me to the wolves and tell my secret, now'd be the time. The mob was about two seconds from finding it out for themselves anyway. I hoped that telling on me now would help Lem a mite. That'd make what was to come worth the dying.

Vikers, seeing a way to stretch the torture out a bit, said, "Tell us."

"It's because . . ." Lem looked over at me with so much hurt and betrayal in his eyes that I near accepted what was coming as my due. "It's because . . ."

He's a woman. Say it. Get it over with. Least I won't have to face Iyaiya as a suicide.

"It's because," Lem started again then paused until the men holding him turned him loose. "It's because he's been cat-hauled."

The hands dropped off me like I was on fire. Every slave had heard the whispered tales of cat-hauling, the most wicked of all the wicked tortures visited upon our captive bodies.

This worst of penalties was reserved exclusively for the slave who could not be broken. When whips and chains failed, the blackhearted master would tie the rebel to a tree, bare his back, and drag a furious tomcat across his naked skin. And that is only where the pain started. The true agony began when every cut made by that filthy, shit-burying animal inevitably went bad and festered. The smell, that's what they said was the worst. The smell of a man rotting to death.

Lem had every ear when he spoke again. "Cathay never wanted anyone to see those terrible scars."

The men turned us loose and, eyes averted, they backed away. Though shame bowed the others a bit, Vikers continued staring straight at me, eyes narrowed, trying to figure out what angle I was playing. Finally, he said,

"That being the case, Cathay, I would like to apologize, for you have suffered enough. In addition, I would like to do something to make it up to you. I would like to give you a reward for surviving the cruelest of tortures."

I did not like the way his lips twitched in the start of a smile. I tucked in my shirt, grabbed my hat, said, "No need," and was heading for the door when Caldwell and Greene grabbed me again.

"No, I insist," Vikers said. "It would be my honor. I, Justice Vikers, insist upon treating you to a poke."

This idea caught on fast and the soldiers crowded back in around me.

Lem was the first to grab me. He slipped his gun into the deep pocket of my sack coat before I was swept upstairs. Vikers led the mob that halted outside the last door at the end of the hall. Vikers hailed the occupant inside the room. "We've got a customer for you, Mary."

"Not Mary!" I screamed as the mob shoved me into the room of Mary the Murderer.

Chapter 66

⁓

I was in a fix, no two ways about it, and was about to jump straight out of Mary's window when the little whore emerged from her swamp of dirty bedclothes, propped herself up on a pile of ratty red velvet pillows fringed in gold and ordered Vikers and his boys, "Get out!" Mary the Murderer looked a lot more like a puny brown girl dying of consumption than she did a bloodthirsty harlot. She seemed harmless right up until you noticed all the straight-edge razors she had tucked here and there about the room.

With surprising energy, she leaped up, plucked an especially wicked-looking blade from beneath a pillow, flipped it open, and swished it to and fro at the men crowded at the door. "I told you donkey-balled, dirt-eating, fart-lickers before. One at a time. No shows 'less everyone pays."

All the boys except Vikers backed up.

"Especially you, you card-sharpin', bottom-dealin' sneak," Mary added, making to slice up Vikers's nasty face. Preferring my odds with Mary, I hopped in and snarled at Vikers, "You heard the lady! Get the hell out fore she slits your throat!"

Soon as the door was shut, Mary slumped back down, hiked up her skirt, and exposed a pair of legs so bowed and coppery brown that I knew she'd grown up ahorseback, making her, most likely, an Indian. She wore no underclothes of any sort and when she threw her legs wide, she exposed her parts to me and all the world. They were of a purplish-brown color not too dissimilar from my own.

Hearing muffled scratchings and whispers, I flung open Mary's door and

Greene and Caldwell stumbled in, pushed forward by the crowd behind. I pulled out Lem's sidearm, a .58 Remington, the finest percussion pistol ever made. The sight of that piece caused the hall to fall silent for they knew it could blow a dandy hole through a two-by-four.

"I am going to shut this door, count to three, and start blasting. You still the other side, you *will* meet your Jesus tonight." The pack was gone and down the stairs before I could slam the door shut, lock it, and stuff my yellow kerchief in the keyhole.

"You shoot up my door," Mary snapped. "You gon buy me another one. Don't want no shot-up door."

I slid the .58's cylinder out and told her, "That won't be a problem. Gun's not loaded."

Mary pulled her filthy skirt up even higher, and said, "Well? What you waiting for? I ain't got all night. Get your damn pecker hard and do your business."

I turned away for she'd started thrusting her hips in a fashion she fancied would put me on the prod but which gave me the creeping willies. "Yeah. Okay," I said, thinking hard for Vikers would be sure to demand a full report of my performance from Mary. "Give me a minute. I need to get in the mood."

"'The mood'?" Mary repeated as though hearing the word for the first time. "You got thirty seconds, then I scream for your friends to come and drag you outta here!" This last Mary hollered at the top of her lungs to the audience I could hear scraping around again outside her door. The pack had returned. Mary added, "Perverts like them outside pay for such details. The more humiliating, the better."

Oh, Mary was a vicious little guttersnipe. The prospect of humiliating me perked her up to an alarming extent and Vikers's trap closed in around me even tighter. I had to shut Vikers up now, tonight, or I might just as well take one of Mary's razors and open up a few veins. I looked around her room, desperate for a way out.

"You're costin' me money, nigger," Mary grumbled. "And you or Vikers is sure God gon make it up to me. My medicine's expensive."

Mention of her medicine inspired Mary to refresh herself with a healthy swig of laudanum. A moment later, she drifted into a light doze and started snoring like a little kitten.

Hoping to find something of use, I quickly studied the few bits of girlishness atop Mary's dresser: a locket with one half of the heart broken off; a tin of lilac talcum powder; a small glass vial with the gooey amber mess of what had once been perfume clogged inside; and the lacy remnants of a dainty hankie.

I picked up the hankie and found my salvation hidden underneath: a set of the strange beads exactly like the ones the General used to say his prayers on. Recalling their power to make even that hardened warrior blubber, I grabbed the pearly string by the tiny bleeding Jesus drooping on a cross at its end.

A cough and the shuffling of feet came from outside the door. The pack was closing in, hungry to rip me apart if I failed to prove myself a real man.

I went to Mary's bedside and dropped to my knees. Her eyes flickered open. I whirled the tiny Jesus in front of my head and shoulders the way I'd seen Sheridan do, kissed the tips of my fingers, bowed my head, and started working those beads through my fingers. With the heat of a true believer, I repeated, word for word, what I remembered of the Mary prayer Sheridan had said so many times.

"Hell Mary! Full of grapes. Blessed Arthur. And blessed is the fruit that I won. Oh, Jesus! Oh, Jesus! Oh, Jesus!"

Staring at me dreamily, Mary asked, "Are you Catholic?"

I was glad for all the times I'd put on Sheridan's Paddy accent to try and get a smile out of Solomon, for it came right back to me and I answered, "And what else would ye be thinkin' I am, lass?" I used Mary's moment of stupefaction to pull her skirt down and cover what ought be covered.

"I didn't know there was no nigger Catholics," she said.

"Oh, hell yes, they's a mess of us," I shot back, quick. Too quick, for I'd left off the accent. I hurried to replace it, asking, "Shall we be praying together to Hell Mary, me dear child?"

Something about the accent or the beads or the laudanum, or maybe it was just being spoken to kindly, but Mary puddled up. Big tears pooled in her dark eyes, making her look even more like a child, one haunted by things she never should of seen. Her lips trembled and, in a small voice, she said, "You sound like the Black Robes back on the reservation."

"Will ye not kneel beside me, my child, and ask Hell Mary for forgiveness?"

She dropped her head and tears splashed down onto her bosom. "Forgiveness? For me? After all I done?"

The way Mary bowed her head down in shame for what she'd been forced to do reminded me of Clemmie. After Old Mister A spasm of anger gripped me, and I said, "You only did what you had to do to survive. Nothin' wrong in that. Come on now. Jesus and Hell Mary love all their children."

Mary was too lost in sorrow and memory and laudanum to notice that I'd let the accent slide. She lay there, propped up on those red pillows, crumpled into herself, sniffling away. Finally, in a little mouse voice she squeaked out, "Even me?"

"You more than anybody." Mary looked so pitiful and lost that I added, "Let me tell you something I don't tell just anyone."

She lifted her eyes a bit and asked, "What?" in a voice sharpened by all the times she'd been lied to in her young life.

"I am a bona fide minister of Hell Mary."

"You are?" She sniffled.

"I am. You want Hell Mary to forgive you, come on down here and pray with me."

After a moment of debate, she slipped out of bed, kneeled beside me, and commenced to pray. Mary mumbled the way a poor reservation child, kneeling in one of those big, stone Catholic churches with a sad-eyed, bleeding Jesus looking down on her, would have been taught to do. But mumbling was not what I required at that moment and I demonstrated what was needed by calling out, "Oh, Hell Mary! Mary! My God! Mary!" I punctuated my cries by jiggling the bedsprings loud as I could.

Mary joined in, yelling out to Hell Mary. I suggested that maybe she should try appealing directly to Jesus and she switched, calling out, "Oh, Jesus! Oh, dear Lord! Lord, God Almighty!"

I led her in some selected prayers, my voice rising to a shout then dropping to a whisper as I said, "OH, GOD! Please hear our prayers. I AM COMING, OH, HELL MARY, to ask forgiveness for your sweet daughter who has been lost and now is found. I AM COMING! I AM COMING! I AM COMING to ask you to welcome her back into your love." To Mary, I whispered, "You might want to second the request."

"Yes, dear Lord," she added.

"Got to show Him you mean it," I suggested.

I led her on a rising crescendo of "yesses," that climaxed with my telling her that her sins had been forgiven. Upon which Mary slumped, crying, onto the bed.

In the silence that followed, I heard Caldwell say in his deep, bass voice from out in the hall, "Well, shoot a bug. Whenever I topped Mary, she ain't never said shit. Cathay be a sissy, make me a dog damn mule!"

Muttered agreement was followed by the clomping of boots as the men abandoned their posts. I kneeled beside Mary, patting her back, and telling her that her sins had been washed away. We continued on in this way for such a long time that several customers came and pounded on the door saying it was their turn. Mary yelled for them to go eat owl shit and carried on praying and calling on the Lord. After she was worn out on confessing her sins and me washing them away, she curled up on her bed, took a nip of her medicine, and dropped off to sleep.

It was near dawn when Bunny and I made it back to the fort. Only then did I realize that I had left my yellow kerchief stuffed into Mary's keyhole. It was too late to go back for. I slipped into the barracks, crept over to Lem's bunk, and placed both his sidearm and my scrimshaw razor on his pillow.

An hour later, at first call, I awoke to find two sugar plums on my pillow and Lem back in the bunk next to mine.

Chapter 67

"hy'd God invent tumbleweeds?" I asked the Sergeant, trying to make a joke to jolly him out of his sour mood. This was a month after Lem had saved my life and gone back to being my friend. I had to yell my question for the Sergeant and I were sitting up top of a stagecoach tearing down the Butterfield Stage route.

The Sergeant didn't answer. Just kept on glaring ahead at the team of six stout, barrel-chested sorrels. The sound of hooves pounding, wheels creaking, and wind roaring past filled the silence between us.

He was not happy to be on this run, guarding the stagecoach. And he was really not happy to be squashed in next to me, up top with the driver, Rube Burrow. He'd heard about me and Mary and, apparently, had just added that to my disgusting list of degeneracies.

Me? I was singing with my tail up to be out with the Sergeant for guarding the coaches was a prize assignment. Troopers fought for it. The Sergeant could of easily, and rightfully, claimed the duty for himself whenever he chose. Instead, he passed it among his men as a break from the eternal wood runs and mucking out stables. He'd never picked me to make a run. But yesterday, that changed when Drewbott made a rare appearance at assembly and barked out an order. "Allbright, you will make the stage run tomorrow."

"Sir, I already have two men detailed for that run," the Sergeant had answered.

"Allbright, did I not make myself clear?" the colonel demanded. "I said I wanted you to make the run, not a couple of your nappy-haired plantation monkeys." The colonel had been freer of late with his insults, passing along some of the humiliation that Sheridan continued to deal him, for Drewbott still refused to leave the fort and chase Chewing Bones.

You'd of had to know the Sergeant to notice the tiny quiver in his left nostril that meant he was furious. Drewbott's insults had worn him so smooth that every one went straight to nerve now. But his lips remained sealed tight.

"I cannot emphasize enough," Drewbott went on, "how important the run tomorrow is. You will be escorting Miss Regina Armstrong into town." He paused for a second like he expected the name to cause the Sergeant's eyes to light up. When they didn't, he added, "The mayor's fiancée. Precious cargo, Allbright. Precious cargo, indeed." He pointed my way and added, "Take the sharpshooter with you."

"Begging your pardon, sir," the Sergeant answered. "But I don't think Cathay is the man for this detail."

It stung that the Sergeant didn't even want to be alone with me atop a bucking stagecoach driven by some old whipcracker with tobacco juice leaking out of his mouth.

"Are you questioning my order, Sergeant?" Drewbott had demanded.

"No, sir."

"Good, because this isn't your usual run, Allbright. We need the best you've got. You shall have the honor of safeguarding the passage of the first decent white woman into these parts."

"Yessir," the Sergeant had answered then, his mouth puckered as if he was sucking on a green persimmon. "Quite an honor."

But the day was so spring beautiful and the joy of escaping the fort to sit next to the Sergeant jouncing across the prairie high up on the back of a fine coach was so keen that my stupid riddle about why God had invented tumbleweeds had just bubbled out. Instead of answering, though, the Sergeant looked at me like I was the most miserable speck of nothing on earth.

Rube the driver, though, he piped up, "Finish your damn joke." Rube was a scrawny fellow had the look of a jockey been put out to pasture. Or a monkey, for though he had nothing much of a body, the long, ropy arms attached to it became part of his whip when he cracked it.

Though the Sergeant had dampened my joke-telling mood, I finished, "So cowboys'd know which way the wind was blowing."

Rube whooped with delight for drivers looked down on cowboys same way cowboys looked down on soldiers and white soldiers looked down on black soldiers. Truth of it was, pretty much everyone looked down on black soldiers. Especially the stupidly ungrateful settlers whose towns, ranches, and farms only existed because we were out here guarding them and herding the savages onto reservations.

The joke tickled Rube so much he hee-hawed himself into a coughing fit and had to calm himself with a chaw on his quid of tobacco. Like all coach drivers, Rube loved his plug and had two half-moon curves of brown juice on either side of his mouth, staining his white mustache to prove it.

The Sergeant held his silence, glaring out at the rocky terrain and the billows of white clouds puffing up against a sky as blue as a cornflower like he held a grudge against nice scenery.

"Right pretty day," I finally ventured.

"Oh, it's perfect."

He spit that out with so much vinegar, I had to say, "Sergeant, sometimes you remind me of a man I knew back during the Rebellion. Never satisfied. It'd be raining silver dollars, he'd complain about not having his umbrella."

At that, he turned to study me straight on. What he saw did not please him. He checked to make sure Rube was occupied in wrangling the team for we were passing over ground so rough that the coach was pitching like a little boat riding out a bad blow. Though there was no chance Rube could hear him, the Sergeant still leaned in and whispered, "I thought you were smart."

I didn't know how to answer that and so I did not.

This seemed to make him even sourer than he already was about being forced into my degenerate company and he hissed, "Do you know what we're carrying back there?" He nodded down at the passengers.

"A drummer, a captain and his wife bound for Fort Bliss, and Miss Regina Armstrong," I answered, saving for last the name of our "precious cargo," a beribboned and furbelowed woman well into her spinster years. Though she might have been a bit shopworn, and lightly mustached into the bargain, she carried herself in a fancy, high-nosed way. "And a dozen or so sacks of mail," I concluded, wondering what the Sergeant's true purpose was in having me recite an inventory that he knew well.

"We're carrying," he said in a low, harsh voice, "the end of the West for black folks."

"What are you talking—" I started, but he interrupted.

"It is over for us, Cathay. Once their 'decent white women' arrive, it is over for the black man."

"What about the officers' wives already here? They're decent enough."

"They're army. That's different. They're not permanent. They're not living in town. It's the towns where the trouble starts."

"What kind of trouble? We're Union soldiers, Sergeant. We got the blue suits, the horses, the guns, the whole damn Union Army behind us. We're safe."

"That's what those three black troopers in Fort Hays thought," the Sergeant said. "Pulled out of a jail cell by a vigilante mob and lynched."

"But Sergeant," I said, for I had heard about the Fort Hays incident. "Those troopers shot a civilian to death. Black barber testified he heard them swear they were gon shoot the first white men they came across."

"Did I say those men were angels?" he asked, hotter than need be. "Am I saying any of us are angels? Not much doubt they did it. Lot of murdering in Hays City. But when it's whites doing the killing, they don't get hauled out of the jail and strung up on a railroad trestle way those three black troopers were."

"Well, that's Kansas," I said, feeling that the state was a world away.

The Sergeant snorted out a bitter laugh before he set me straight. "Cathay, open your eyes." He stabbed a finger at the rocky ground rolling beneath the coach's high wheels. "This? Where we are right now? This Lone Star State? It's the most colorphobic of them all. Not enough of the war took place here to beat the fear of federal troopers into these un-Reconstructed Rebs. Didn't you hear about that civilian over near Fort McKavett who murdered a black private name of Boston Henry? Also shot Corporal Albert Marshall and Private Charles Murray dead when they went to bring him in?"

I shook my head. I hadn't heard a word even though Fort McKavett was less than three hundred miles away.

"And you know what kind of sentence the jury, the all-white jury, in Austin gave that civilian who laid out three of our men?"

I knew I wasn't gonna like the answer.

"None. They set that murderer free. Blue suit don't mean shit when it's on a black body. Soon as they can, they'll get rid of all of us."

"Beg pardon, Sergeant, but that's crazy. Matanza, none of these little towns could even exist without us. They need us."

"For what?" he asked. His anger was too hot for him to keep on freezing me out. "Why do they need the black man? To kill the red man so they can steal his land for other white men."

It knocked me sideways to hear the Sergeant talk this way. "You sound like John Horse. I thought you said he was a traitor."

"A traitor to who?" the Sergeant asked. "I've come to see that the man who is true to his own people is no traitor." The sourness had peeled away to show a misery beneath that had nothing to do with me. As always, his real friends and enemies were the big ideas battling it out in his head. "Once we do their dirty work, then what?"

"Then we get us some land. We have us our own towns."

"Do you really think they're going to let that happen?"

"Sure. Look around." I waved my hand at the open prairie rolling on forever in all directions. "All this land. Has to be a corner we can tuck ourselves into and have a decent life. Has to be."

He shook his head, pitying me for my stupidity.

"Sergeant?" I asked, thrown hard by his change of heart. I waited for him to explain, but he just shook his head like the job of setting me straight was too big for him to take on.

Though Matanza was only ten miles from post as the crow flew, the ride took hours for the trail was gullied and, in a couple of spots, we had to climb down and shove away boulders that blocked our way entirely. Through it all, the Sergeant was so lost in whatever big argument was raging in his head that we didn't exchange another word.

Instead of heading into the stage depot in the center of town, Rube halted at the edge of Matanza where a welcoming committee, led by the mayor, waited. Behind them was a new church. Though it was hardly bigger than an outhouse, it was a church, and I figured that the mayor thought a house of the Lord'd make a better first impression on Miss Regina Armstrong than the saloons and bawdy houses we had to pass to reach the depot.

The handbrake screeched as Burrow set it. The seat bounced beneath us when he hoisted himself down. The mayor, himself no more of a prize than his bewhiskered fiancée, having a pair of hunched vulture shoulders and but a few strands of hair, which required coatings of axle grease to remain plastered across the bald dome of his head, was a perfect match for Miss Regina Armstrong in the fancy airs department. He actually bowed as he held his hand up and helped his fiancée to step out of the coach. Hats swept off the pale, untanned tops of the men's heads, and they shook the tips of Miss Regina Armstrong's fingers, welcoming her to their "it's not much, but we call it home."

Through it all, the Sergeant, glum as a toad, sat up top with me. Far out on the other side of town, a plume of dust rose high into the still noontime air. I nudged the Sergeant. "Look, the inbound's coming in from the West."

The Sergeant and I climbed down off the stage and set out to catch the inbound back to the fort as was the practice on special short runs like this. Soon as our feet touched the ground, though, the dozen or so men in front of the church clustered around Miss Regina Armstrong like she was a sparkling jewel and us a couple of thieves. The mayor, his eyes held tight on us, scurried off to chew Rube's ear. The Sergeant and I had hardly gone more than a few steps when the driver called after us, "Uh, boys, uh, hold on there. I need to talk to you."

The Sergeant stopped dead, but he didn't turn around. He made Rube hustle over to us on his stumpy jockey legs.

"What is it, Rube?" I asked. "We got to get to the depot before the inbound leaves without us." Though the icy looks being directed our way by the mayor and his cronies chilled the mirth right out of me, I gave a fake chuckle and added, "Long walk back to the fort."

"Well, now, that's the thing," Rube, who stood half a foot beneath me, started off. "The thing is . . ." He put a hand on the back of his neck where it had to have been prickling, nervous as he suddenly was. "That is . . . Well, dammit, the mayor thinks it's time for a change."

"Change?"

The Sergeant grinned in a mirthless way and looked up at the clear sky like he was reading every word that was to come up there.

"Shitfire, boys," Rube went on. "Were up to me, wouldn't be no changes. But that damn mayor . . . What with ladies coming in and all . . . Well, the long and the short of it is, he don't want all y'all on the stage anymore."

"All us what?" I demanded, commencing to heat up. "All us soldiers of the United States Cavalry?"

"No," Rube answered, his face pickling up like the words he had to spit out were sour. "Dammit, you know. You Aunt Hagar's children."

"Us what?" I asked for I had never heard that one.

"The Affrish," he muttered. To his credit, Rube was embarrassed, and hurried to explain, "This ain't my idea, I had no part in it. But, well, fact is, mayor and the sheriff and them"—he pointed a thumb back at the men glaring at us—"they'd prefer it if all y'all'd keep out of town entirely."

The anger jumped into me so sudden that I yelled at those brave townsmen who'd sent a jockey to do their talking for them, "You want us United States Army soldiers who are out here keeping the Indians from scalping every damn person in this damn town to keep out? Is *that* what you're saying!"

The men all started bunching together, putting themselves between us and Miss Regina Armstrong, as if the Sergeant and me were lusting to get at that withered-up hank of mustachioed gristle.

"You got something to tell me," I hollered. "Step on over here and say it to my face!" They packed in tighter but made no movement in my direction. "Or are you too chickenshit? Makes sense. Bunch of Rebel deserters, appears you're still too scared to face the United States Army."

Even as I was stomping it into the dust, I knew that I'd crossed the line. Instant I did, that bunch of fine, upstanding gentlemen protecting their first upstanding white woman turned directly into a lynch mob.

Rube hurried away from us as fast as his stubby legs would allow, clambered back up onto his seat, tossed down his canteen and bedroll, tipped his chin toward the men, and said, "You two best head for the high line, right quick." He cracked his whip like a clap of thunder and rolled on, leaving nothing except wheel tracks between us and the welcoming committee.

The Sergeant stared straight at the citizens, daring them to come on ahead.

They moved forward.

The instant the danger pointed at the Sergeant, I grabbed hold of his jacket and tried to pull him away, but he didn't shift.

"Sir," I pleaded, trusting that he'd do for one of his men what he wouldn't for himself. "I don't want to die today."

He kept staring hate and vengeance at the mayor until I begged him again, my voice cracking for the word "lynch" had bored into my brain. Only then did we start putting distance between ourselves and the cracker assholes of Matanza.

Chapter 68

⁓

"I told you it was over," the Sergeant said once we were out of sight of Matanza. After that, we tramped on without him opening his mouth again except to spit out the bile rising from his liver.

The trail rose then fell in a long, gradual slope toward the fort. It dropped away on the south side down into the valley that Agua Dulce Creek ran along. I was watching a hawk dive through the sun-bleached sky when the Sergeant startled me by saying, "To hell with this." He stopped dead in the middle of the trail and, seeming to notice me for the first time, asked, "Why should we kill ourselves getting back to the fort?"

"So we won't get hunted down and shot for deserting?"

He spit, then reached back under his waistband, brought forth a small, flat brown bottle, uncorked it, tipped it my way and said, "Here's to you, Private. You're a man-humping degenerate and more trouble than you're worth, but the way you called out that egg-sucking pisspot of a mayor? That took more guts than you can hang on a fence."

He gulped down a long tug, then passed the bottle to me. "Come on, Cathay," he said, "we're going AWOL." He left the trail and disappeared down the hill we'd been climbing.

I was like a cat watching two pieces of yarn get pulled apart. I didn't know what to be more stupefied by: the Sergeant revealing himself to be a spitting, cussing, drinking man or one who seemed to be deserting. The dust settled around me and I was as alone as Adam before he lost a rib. I thought for a moment, maybe two, about a firing squad all aiming at my deserter chest and then I followed him off the trail.

Though I galloped down the steep incline, following the twisting path that the Sergeant was scraping in the sandy dirt, I couldn't catch sight of him. His trail wound through high boulders that abruptly gave way to a stand of desert willows and cottonwoods just tall enough to throw some shade. The willows were heavy with pink and lilac blossoms that looked like orchids and smelled like sweet talcum powder. The creek running through them was clear and, I discovered, cool.

The desert willows, greedy for that rare moisture, grew thick along its banks, blocking my view and swamping me with the womanly powder smell of their blossoms. I pushed through a dense fringe of long, skinny leaves and found the Sergeant standing naked in a water hole that reached up to his waist. Cottonwoods shaded the large pool and their heart-shaped leaves floated atop it amidst the squiggly patterns traced by water striders.

He held the brown bottle up high like he was saluting me with it and called out, "Thought I'd lost you. Come on in." Even more astonishing, he was grinning.

I didn't move.

"Don't worry," he said, running the palm of his hand across the still pool, scattering leaves and water striders. "I already scared off the cottonmouths." He tipped his head up and drank. I watched the long column of his neck work and did not move.

"Can't you swim?" he asked, taking my stupefaction for fear. "It's not deep. Look." Holding the bottle up high, he dunked his head under, and came back up, flinging crystal droplets from his hair. The water came up to his waist when he stood. Water sluiced down over his shoulders, chest, and belly.

"Suit yourself," he said. Taking another long pull from the bottle, he lowered himself into the water and leaned against the boulder at his back. Arms to either side, eyes closed, he was the picture of a man taking his ease.

I ducked behind a thick stand of willows, stripped off everything except my shirt and drawers, double-checked to make sure the bindings were on tight, and waded in. The water was cold and I shrieked. Catching myself, I turned the girlish cry into a grunt and stifled the impulse to fold my arms across my chest.

"Nice, huh?" he asked.

I turned shy and dove underwater.

It was like going home, all the way back to the times when I'd hide out in the creek that ran through the woods around Old Mister's farm with a reed in my mouth and the world above my head turning into smeary blues and greens. The water around me now was all the greens of the willows and cottonwoods and the velvety moss growing on the round rocks. A small cloud of perch swam through my fingers. The Sergeant's legs wobbled, sliced into gleaming walnut sections by wavy shafts of sunlight. I quickly looked away from the dark patch where they joined.

The water made my drawers and undershirt so soppy that they sagged and clung. Afraid that too much would show if I stood up all the way, I only popped my head and shoulders out of the water.

The Sergeant took no notice of me as the peaceful pond had sent him into a dreamy mood. He said nothing, just handed the bottle my way.

I squat-walked over to him and took it.

"Nice, huh?" Allbright asked again after a few more passes of the bottle.

"Yessir."

"Come on, now, Cathay, don't 'sir' me out here." Even his voice was different. It had a low gentleness to it that hummed through my belly.

"Yess—" I stopped myself before the "sir" jumped in there.

The Sergeant stared off at a buzzard making long, slow pirouettes through the cloudless sky. He watched it for a long time before he shook his head and chuckled like he'd just told himself a joke that wasn't particularly funny, and said, "Army can make a white man salute the uniform, but it can't make him give a man the respect that goes with it."

"They're civilians, sir. And fools. Forget about those corn-cracking, piss-drinking skunks. Not a one of them's fit to tote guts to a bear."

This got the first real laugh of the day. "For a degenerate sissy, you're a good man, Cathay."

"Thank you."

He leaned against the boulder, his long arms stretched out, head lolling back. Drops of water sparkled in the tight whorls of his dark brown hair and in the coiled spring of his lashes. He studied the depthless sky. In the shaded sunlight, his eyes showed flashes of amber. I swallowed.

Girl, quit eye-eating the man.

I looked away, but not before he caught me staring at him like the lovesick sodomite he took me to be. He snorted a weak laugh, amused and unbothered by what he seemed to have accepted as my peculiarity, and went back to his lounging and drinking.

Eyes closed, he said, "It's too late for us, Cathay. Doesn't matter where we go in this country, they'll be waiting for us. The corn-cracking, piss-drinking skunks. You know what our only hope is?"

"What's that, Sergeant?"

"Our children. It's like Brother Douglass says, it's easier to raise strong children than it is to fix broken men. And that's what we are, Cathay. We're broken men. We have to create a new generation built from the ground up of strong, capable men, true and brave."

"And women," I added, quietly.

He chewed on that for a moment or two then sat up abruptly and slapped the water with his free hand. "Damn it to hell, Cathay, you're right. It takes someone like yourself who doesn't have the normal man feelings about women to see that they're the key."

"Well, men can't do it alone," I pointed out. "This creating a new generation."

The gleam came to his eye that meant he had been seized by an idea. "The problem is finding a woman whose spirit hasn't already been broken. Who hasn't been warped beyond repair. Made into something that she's not. Like you and Lem. In your own way, not that I approve, but you two haven't let anything change who you really are, have you? Not slavery. Not a civil war. Not even the U.S. Army."

I thought of all the ways I was not who I really was and said nothing.

Too fired up to notice my silence, the Sergeant went on. "You and Lem. He's your all in all and you don't give a hang what the rest of the world thinks."

Lem and me?

"You have that steel inside you to know who you are. That's the kind of wife I need. One with that unbendable steel. I've only ever met one woman made of such strong stuff."

I didn't know if my heart could stand hearing him speak again of the dream woman I never was and never could be.

Nothing moved except for a light breeze shimmying through the dainty leaves of the mesquite tree. The buzzing whine of the cicadas filled the silence before he finally asked, "Have you ever had a memory so perfect you were afraid that putting it into words would spoil it?"

I nodded. I did. Yes, I did.

"Cathay, remember when I spoke before of the woman who saved my life? Whom I loved though I'd never even seen her?"

"I do," I answered, the jealousy I felt for the woman I both was and could never be twisting like a knife through my guts.

"I don't know what it is about you, but, in spite of, or maybe because of, your 'peculiarities,' you are the only one I've ever breathed a word about her to."

I nodded. Too sad to comment, I watched a water strider carve a V into the still water that grew wider and wider until the ripples reached almost to either edge of the water hole.

"Cathay, I need to apologize to you."

I bit back the "Sir?" that sprang to my lips and said nothing as he went on. "I was wrong. For condemning you. Who am I to condemn anyone for who they love when my heart belongs to a woman whose name I don't even know?"

He flicked up a geyser of water with his thumb like he was shooting a marble, the drops pattered down around us, and I muttered, "It's fine."

"It's not though. Not when I think of how besotted I am. How often I've tried and failed to chase her from my mind. My heart. Yet still I cling to the conviction that I will find her and will know her when I do. And here's the oddest part of my odd story. I will know her because she bears six rows of scars, marks of Mother Africa, raised upon her skin like the most perfect of pearls."

I came close then to yanking down the neck of my wet shirt, showing him those very scars, and . . . and what? The sight would destroy the only bond I truly had with Wager Swayne: the memory of our days and nights together. And all I would have then would be Wager's embarrassment and disappointment at seeing the marks which belonged on the womanly beauty of his dreams on a body that was neither womanly nor beautiful.

The drone of the cicadas became a mean buzz in my head so loud and painful it took me a second to hear that the Sergeant was asking in a pleading way, "Damnation, Cathay, why do they always think we want their women?

Why is that? The last thing on God's green earth I want is a finicky, stringy-necked, prissy, dried-up white woman. What I want is . . ." Longing even deeper than what burdened me silenced him.

He sucked in several breaths before he stated a truth wrenched from his deepest soul. "I want a black woman."

The words stacked up one atop the other like he was erecting a statue. Once it was up, the rest came tumbling out. "You know how it is, Cathay? Well, maybe you don't."

It didn't matter if I answered or not. Or even if I was there or not, his voice ragged with desperation, he was saying what he had to say.

"No other woman smells like a black woman. Feels like a black woman. Feels like . . ." He stopped again, bound not to break down in front of one of his soldiers, one of his men. He took another drink then stood up and walked out until no part of him was covered. Water streamed down his naked backside.

At the edge of the pond, he stopped and, determined to say what he had to say, no matter what the cost, he turned and faced me. Standing tall and lean and strong, he was as I had imagined he would be. He was as God had imagined a man should be. His broad shoulders caught then turned loose of the sun as they heaved up and down a fraction before he composed himself and concluded, "No other woman feels like home." He nodded and repeated to himself, "Like home." I could barely hear when he concluded, "A black woman. I want to hold. A. Black. Woman."

I'd never heard such loneliness in my life. Angry at all that had been taken from him, all he'd never had, he bent over, snatched up his uniform, and walked away.

I dove beneath the water, and sunk like a stone to the bottom where I sat and hugged myself, my right hand pressed against the rows of scars as my body remembered who I was.

I ran my hands over my breasts. Being a man, eating mens' rations, living in a man's guarded body, had made me a woman. My breasts had filled out into pretty, budded things. There was a flare to my hips now that hadn't been present before.

"Private! Cathay! Where are you?"

Underwater, the Sergeant's voice sounded distant and wobbly, like he was calling to me from a long time ago. From back in the free time when I would have run wherever my feet and heart carried me and I would have loved and protected a king.

I pulled off the undershirt and the drawers. Then I unwound the long strips of muslin from around my breasts. They twirled, floating and dancing about me like white smoke rising from damp wood.

I was naked. I rose to the surface.

Chapter 69

⁓

Without so much as a ripple, I walked onto the flat rocks at the edge of the pond.

The Sergeant, dressed in shirt and trousers, suspenders looping down either side of his waist, was sitting with his back to me, tugging a boot on. He didn't know I stood behind him, dripping water, feeling the thirsty wind sucking the wet off me, and he yelled out over his shoulder, "Private! Move it, man! You're burning daylight." He was a commander again, one who was plastering over the weakness he'd let slip out, making sure nothing but a hard wall showed.

Chalky minerals were drying on my skin, leaving it ashy and rough. Out of the water, my womanliness was already parching. I stood there, a creature too tall, too strong, too ornery, and too plain to be female. To be beloved.

The Sergeant glanced back, saw only my naked legs and ordered wearily, "Cathay, get your uniform back on, man. What the hell's wrong with you?"

My back hurts and my shoulders ache from crouching.

That's what the hell was wrong with me. And I wasn't having it anymore. In the end, it was as simple as that: I was tired of the pinch in my shoulders and the ache in my back from stooping and crouching. I straightened up and threw back my shoulders. I stood taller than most men and any woman I'd ever known.

When I didn't answer the Sergeant turned, got a good look at me, and jumped to his feet. For a long moment he stood there, bumfuzzled, not able to credit what he was seeing, probably thinking he'd either lost his mind or was seeing some brand of sissyness he'd never encountered before. "Get your uniform on, man."

I stepped closer, hardly feeling the sharp rocks poking into my bare feet. My walk was a woman's walk. I let my hips sway as they wanted. His eyes walled as he watched me advance. I stood before him and, in my soft woman's voice, said, "I am not a man. I am a woman. A black woman."

He put his hand out to stop me or touch me, I didn't know which. It trembled. Spooked, he snatched it back, still not convinced that I wasn't some unnatural thing or a vision he'd conjured up out of loneliness and longing.

I took his hand and placed the flat of his palm against my cheek where I'd dreamed so many times it might once again rest. I no longer cared what might follow. Even if the Sergeant turned from me now, from the plainness of my features and the manly ways I'd had to claim as my own, this touch was worth whatever it cost. For one, terrible moment his hand froze and then he pulled it away. I dropped my gaze, shame already beginning to burn through me. Shame at my naked body. Shame at loving someone so far above me. Shame at being a woman who could pass for a man.

I walked away, gathering up my uniform as I went, clutching it against my chest, slouching again to hide who I was.

"Wait."

His hand fell upon my shoulder and turned me to face him. He gaped, not at me, but at my scars. Unable to speak, he tapped his fingers beneath his own collarbone.

I nodded but would not speak the words.

Yes, these are the scars. Yes, I am the woman.

He ran the tips of his fingers across my scars, all the while whispering, "You. It's you. But you're not . . ."

"Pretty?"

"No, you're not."

"But I'm here and I saved your life twice and I love you and you loved me until now. You know what's inside me. Outside's the only part that's different."

The battle going on in his head played out across his features. His dream of the fine, beautiful woman who'd saved him was crashing into the strapping length of muscle and bone that stood before him now. His face prickled with the effort of making the two fit together. He shook his head for the pieces weren't coming together, and he started to back away.

"I know I don't please you in the usual man-woman sort of way," I said. "But I am good and true and will give you strong children who will build a new world for our people."

"I don't—"

I stopped him before he said what couldn't be taken back. "If you touch me," I promised, taking his hand, "you will make me beautiful."

I put the palm of his hand against my cheek and curled into it like a bird into the nest she's flown her whole life to reach. I tilted my head into his palm and kissed the lines that foretold his life, pressing myself into them with my lips, making his future our future.

His palm, roughened by reins, brushed over my cheek, my neck, my shoulder. I was as good as my word for every place he touched turned velvety soft and beautiful. He traced his fingers across the scars and down to the swell of my breast. When he whispered, "You are a woman. You are her," there wasn't a molecule of either doubt or command in his voice.

I reached for his face and, like I was pulling the sun down, brought his lips to mine. I had kissed the Sergeant twice before. This time he kissed me. The scent of dogwood and sage rose from my body and the chalky mineral dust floated off of me in a cloud.

He put his lips on my neck, inhaled, and said, "You smell like home."

We were both home. I was his home and he was mine.

He rolled out the coach driver's bedroll and we lay upon it, facing each other. He put his lips on my lips and on the scars and on my breasts. I learned everything I needed to learn about him. I learned that his skin was the color of a baby fawn that was prettier than the sunset next to my smoky quartz tone. I learned that he had been with many women and was disciplined and tender and kind. I learned that too much joy and too much pleasure make me weep.

Later, a violet and orange sunset shone through the green lace the cottonwoods tatted against the evening sky. We did not speak until the light was gone and a fire built. There was a slight chill in the air and he held me against his chest, both of us facing the fire.

"Why," he asked, running his hand along my arm, "didn't you tell me who you were?"

"As soon as I was sure you were you," I answered, "I did. Or tried. Remember? When we were out on patrol that time?"

"I do. I thought—"

"You made it clear what you thought. The next time I tried, when you were sick and I called you back from the dead using your given name and blowing warm breath into you, you threatened to have me court-martialed for moral turpitude.

"After that," I went on, my voice small, "I stopped trying. I didn't want to wreck the vision you carried in your head of the woman who saved you. I wanted to stay beautiful to you. Beautiful and womanly."

His hands stroked me. My breasts, my belly, between my legs. He kissed my shoulder, my neck. "You are womanly."

He manned again. I took him into my body. This time he held himself away so as to look at my face in the firelight and he held back until a frenzied jubilation overtook us that was as keen and thrilling as riding the high line ahead of an electrical storm and I knew I pleased him.

When we finished, the night was chill. The Sergeant pulled the blanket about us, and we moved closer to the fire, sitting there with me cradled between his legs, his back resting against a warm rock. He had hardtack in his pocket and we ate that, washing it down with spring water. With his arms cradled around me, I rested my head on his chest.

"When you saw me?" he asked. "At the recruitment? Did you know?"

"I thought I did, but the man in the wagon's name was Wager Swayne. Not Levi Allbright. Which one is really your name?"

"My name was Wager Swayne until the burying detail pulled me out of the grave. I was lost amongst the contrabands for some time. Barely able to walk. I didn't know where my unit was or how to find it. When I recovered enough, I enlisted under the name of Allbright as the depot was across the street from the All Bright Lantern Company."

"Why didn't you use your real name?"

"Because Wager Swayne had been infantry. Too tall for cavalry. But by the time I went in again, I knew who I needed to pay to get the assignment I wanted."

"What should I call you?"

"Wager was my mother's family name. My father was Emmanuel Swayne, seaman."

"Wager," I repeated. "Wager Swayne." I liked saying the name his mama and daddy had given him. A name that only I knew for a person that only I knew.

"And you?" he asked. "What do they call you back home?"

"Cathy."

"Your name really is Cathay?"

"Well, Cathy. Yes, it really is Cathy. Cathy Williams."

"Your name really is Cathy," Wager repeated, then burst out laughing so hard that the muscles of his belly bunched up and bounced hard against my back. The chuckles rose to a hard cackle.

I pivoted around and there were tears running from his eyes, he was hee-hawing so hard. "What exactly is so damn hilarious about my name?" I asked.

"I . . . I . . ." Wager tried to explain before collapsing again. He finally pulled himself together and said, "Cathy Williams, you sure did go the long way round to do it, but you have got to be the first soldier ever made the United States Army call him by his first name."

"Her," I said. "Her name."

"Her," he repeated. "Oh, yes, very much her." And then Wager Swayne kissed me. Me, Cathy Williams.

Chapter 70

T he pond has grown to an enormous size. The gauzy strips of binding flutter after me like long wings as I swim through water that is
alive with dust motes sparkling bright as gold dust. I soar forward,
my hands pointed out in front cut through the water like the prow of a
boat. Then I remember that this is how to fly. I leave the water and take
wing, I rise into the blue sky and swim through it. I am doing something
no other person ever has. I am flying. Wager stares up at me, overcome with
admiration.

As I fly, I become aware of the new place inside me, between my legs. It
is soft and tender as a baby's foot the first time it is ever walked on. The first
time it discovers what a foot is for. Now, in my dream, Wager is with me,
clinging to my back. His weight presses down and I flap harder. I am strong
enough to lift us both and he admires that, too. We rise higher and higher
with each flap of the tatters of my binding wings.

Below us, on the drill field, everyone in the company cranes his head back
to watch in wonder. I am as beautiful as an angel and I can do something
no one else can. That is when I recall that, as Mama warned, it is dangerous
to capture the gazes of men. I see now that the hand that grips me is black
with rot.

I glance back over my shoulder. It is not Wager clutching my shoulder,
eager again for the soft place within, it is Old Mister. And then it is Vikers
riding my back. And then it is all of them. Caldwell. Greene. The mayor.
The stage driver. Drewbott. Dupree. Even Lem and Solomon. They all know
my secret and they are all coming for me. I flap harder and harder, but I sink

now, falling from the sky until murky water covers me. It is dark and Old
Mister waits there to use me as he used Clemmie because I am Clemmie now
that I have shown myself.

"Cathy. Cathy, you're trembling."

Wager held me, my breasts soft against his chest, the stubble of his chin
beard a nice rasp against the crook of my neck as he cooed and gentled me.
"Shh-shh-shh. You had a nightmare. It's over. I'm here. It wasn't real."

I sat up, the nightmare and sleep still heavy on me. The moon, which
had been near full when I fell asleep, has set. Wager patted away the tears
with his yellow silk kerchief then tied it around my neck, replacing the one
I'd left in Mary's keyhole and leaving his own neck bare, and I said his name,
"Wager."

He answered, "Cathy," whispering my name as tender as if he was saying "darling." Wager had laid my clothes out on the flat rocks to dry in the
desert air. He'd rolled up the long strips of gauze, and now he unspooled
them around my breasts, binding down again what only he had seen. I pulled
my shirt on. He kissed me. The kiss deepened. He tried to stop me from
buttoning my shirt, but it was late. We had to leave.

A cool breeze lifted up the yellow tails of the kerchief Wager had tied
about my neck and they floated behind me as we hurried through the night.
In the distance, a pack of coyotes celebrated a kill with yodeling howls. A
pair of owls called back and forth, their songs a funny woofing sound that
bounced higher with every note. A screech owl hooted its mournful call
from the branches of a mesquite. Deer and armadillo rustled through the
scrub brush. A peccary snorted and grunted nearby. Each noise caused Wager to smile at me as though the animals were clowning just for us. He took
my hand and held it for most of the way back to the fort.

As soon as we came in sight of the flag snapping smartly in the breeze,
for it was brand-new, having just added a thirty-seventh star after the Territory of Nebraska became a state, I dropped Wager's hand and took off his
kerchief. When I tried to give it back, he refused. I straightened my uniform, and whisked away a few blades of grass from my trousers.

The fort still slept and we crept in silent as two Indians. Though it was
dark, I felt exposed, as if a bright light shone on me and eyes I could not see
were trained my way, tracking me like hunters in a blind. I shrunk back
down into my uniform, slouching and slumping so that the familiar pinch
in my shoulders and ache in my back returned. I feared for myself, but I feared

even more for Wager since, in that big-brained way of his, when an idea seized him, it seized his whole being. And he had been seized by the idea that I was really a woman. A woman strong enough to be his. I was terrified that he was too honest to hide what had happened between us. To hide what I was. But he had to or we would lose everything.

So, when we stopped in the darkened corner beside the barracks door, and he leaned in to kiss me, I jerked away as if a rattler were perched on his shoulder. Glancing about nervously, I tried to duck into the barracks before the first rays of sun exposed us. He grabbed my shoulder and whispered, "Cathy—"

"No," I silenced him, fear making my command sharper than I'd meant it to be. "You can't," was all I could say, adding before I slipped into the barracks, "We'll talk. Later. When it's safe."

I lay in my bunk trembling, more scared than I'd been since that first, long night back in Jefferson Barracks. Wager claiming me as a woman had turned me into more of one than I had ever been. I had to reverse that. Fast. Before the near hundred men sleeping about me woke. But every tender, yearning, astonished thought I had about Wager stripped me back down to a frail girl. I made myself think about what Vikers'd do to me if I didn't snuff out that girl. That thought was the knife at my throat that forced me to harden back up enough to meet the new day. By the time we formed up for assembly I was Private William Cathay again. At least until Wager strode onto the yard.

Wager.

I thought his name one last time, wobbling and unbreathing as I did, then I banished it. Here, in the fort, he had to be Sergeant Allbright. And I had to be Private Cathay. If I wasn't, if he wasn't, the future I'd kissed into the palm of his hand, ours, together, would be destroyed. I did not meet his glance and, without another peek in his direction, I marched off with my detail.

Lem and I worked together on the colonel's latest project, a bakery. After a few hours of digging post holes, Lem said, "You steady her and I'll tamp her in," as he raised a double jack with both hands to drive a cedar post deeper into the hole we'd dug. Everyone in our crew, Caldwell, Greene, the Georgia boys, had their shirts off. As usual, Vikers kept to the shade, pretending to be busy, but mostly he watched. Me. I always hated the feel of his spectacled gaze, but that day, his peeping brought a hot, prickly sweat to my brow and the back of my neck, making me aware of the Sergeant's kerchief tied there. I was certain he'd see the Sergeant's bare neck and guess every-thing.

"Bill?" Lem asked. I'd let the shaggy cedar post in my hand list to the side while craning around to keep an eye on Vikers keeping an eye on me. I straightened it up and the hard wood thrummed in my hand with every pound of Lem's hammer.

"You're mighty quiet today, Bill," Lem said, as we moved on to the next spot.

I *humphed* in answer and we got busy with our long iron digging bars, jabbing them into the dry, sandy earth. Out of the corner of my eye, I watched Wager, no, I watched Sergeant Allbright off to the side with Drew-bott and Carter. They were studying the plans for the bakery Drewbott had ordered us to build. The colonel held his hand out to indicate where a wall was meant to go and the Sergeant left his side, pulling a string line off that way.

"Can't wait for them to get that bakery built. Can you, Bill?"

"Yeah, a bakery'd be good," I managed, watching the Sergeant drive a stake into the ground and tie the string line to it to use for a guide in building the south wall. When he finished, he glanced up and caught me staring at him. Though I whipped my gaze away, praying no one had no-ticed, I'd seen a tender expression on his face that made my hands go cold in the heat.

"I'm tired of cracking my teeth on hardtack was stale back when the Rebs fired on Fort Sumter," Lem said.

"Uh-huh," I muttered, my throat suddenly dry.

"Fresh bread," he sang out. "Can smell it now. Slather some butter on it warm out of the oven. Nothin' finer on this earth. Ain't that right, Bill?"

I *uh-hummed* and we continued in this way, me unable to pull my eyes from the Sergeant, ready to burst out singing one minute then wet my pants from terror the next.

Which is why Lem caught me off guard when he said, "Heard you creep in near dawn. What in blazes was you and Sarge doing out there all night? Then you tossed and turned in your bunk like you were breaking a fever. Something happen on that run, Bill?"

A sharpness in his tone put me on alert that he didn't want any more lies from me and I mumbled about being put off the stage by the damn town folk and having to walk back to the fort.

"Yeah, but that's not no all-night walk, is it, Bill? Could of made it back by nightfall easy."

"We were tired. Camped out."

"Why'd you do that? Didn't bring no gear with you."

"We made do, all right?" I snapped back.

"Yeah, I 'spect you did," Lem said. "Way you're acting. Eyes glued on the sergeant. 'Spect you made do just fine." He winked at me and, because he was my only friend and had saved my life, I winked back.

"Knew it," he gloated. "Knew Sarge was one of us."

For the next hour the only sound was our digging rods clanking into rocks and the pound of the sledge as we drove the posts in. I refused to so much as cut my eyes in the Sergeant's direction. Pretending like nothing had changed, I said, "Never signed up for no post-hole diggin'. When we gon go out hunt them renegades like we're supposed to be doing? Can't believe Drewbott's held Sheridan off for a whole year. This here's infantry work we're doing?"

"Ain't right," Lem amened.

It calmed me to settle into our normal to and fro. "I mean," I said, "it's been so long since we rode out proper ain't even any horses need shoeing. Here you are, the best farrier this side of the Mississippi, and they got you pounding fence posts. Ain't right. Just ain't right."

"Strikers say Drewbott sends Sheridan fake reports just to keep him off his back. Man is terrified of redskins." Lem leaned in close, his face lit up the way it did when he had some juicy gossip to share, and whispered, "Way I heard it, Drewbott makes his wife sleep on the side of the bed closest to the door. Figures on making the redskins go through her carcass fore they can get at him."

"Well, at least Chewing Bones isn't on the warpath."

There had been no attacks in our area since Chewing Bones and his band had been herded onto a reservation.

A few swings of the heavy sledge later, Lem yelped in pain, dropped the hammer and held his hand out to show me where a blister had burst. The skin was pale where it sagged away from the red flesh left exposed on his palm. "I got to go wrap this," he said, hurrying off in search of something to bandage the oozing sore with.

I picked up the heavy sledge he'd dropped, choked up on the hammer, and steadying the post with my free hand, tried to tap it in myself. I was so intent on the job that I started when a hand reached out and grabbed the post. "Here. Let me hold that for you. Private Cathay."

The Sergeant said my name too loud, calling it out for others around us to hear like it was a joke between him and me that none of the others would get. He took the hammer from my hand and pounded the post in for me.

I whipped my head around, praying no one, especially not Vikers, was watching, and hissed, "What in billy hell are you doing?"

"Just helping out one of my *men*." He near hollered the last word.

"Shut up," I whispered, looking away so's it'd appear I wasn't speaking directly to my CO. "For God's sake, Sergeant, please shut your mouth."

"I was only—"

"You are *only* going to get me mustered out or killed."

"Cathy, calm down. You sound crazy. You're safe. I'll kill the first man lays a finger on you."

"What?" I hissed. "You gon be by my side every minute of the next year until my hitch is up?' Cause that's what it'll take to keep a woman alone safe amongst these jackals."

"What am I supposed to do?" he asked.

It threw me to hear him asking me what to do until I realized that he was the one standing naked and scared as I'd been yesterday when I'd revealed my true nature to him.

"Forget what happened?" he asked in a whisper, leaning in closer than any commander ever would have. "Forget who, what, you really are? Forget how I feel?"

How I wished we were still alone on the prairie, but we weren't, and even at that moment, Vikers was huddling up with Greene and Caldwell, staring hard at us.

"Yes," I answered, refusing to look his way. "That's exactly what I want you to do."

"That's not possible. Cathy, last night changed everything for me. Didn't it for you?"

"What did it change?" I hissed "I've still got a year left on my hitch. It didn't change that. You know that the army is all I've got in this world. Don't take it away. Please."

"We could get married."

"Then what?" I whispered. "I trail around after you from post to post? They're never gonna give a black soldier a little house where I can put flower boxes on the windows. That's for officers. And the only officers this army will ever have are white. What about our babies? Who pays for a decent place for children to grow up in? For food? Shoes? Only job I can get is laundress or whore and I'll die first."

"Cathy, I make nearly twenty a month. Be a solid twenty-one soon as my promotion to sergeant major comes through."

I snorted a dry laugh, astonished that such a smart man could say such a stupid thing. "Why are we even talking about this? The instant they find out what I really am, we're both done. We'll both be mustered out so fast your head will spin. That is, if we're lucky. If we're not, they'll bring you up on charges and lock you up in Fort Leavenworth. Me? Think about what'll happen when the barracks jackals find out they got a woman, all by herself, no one to protect her, who's been tricking them for two years. Think about it. Think about what they'll do to me. Vikers already hates me."

The memory of the widow harnessed like a mule to a plow came back to me and I begged him, "Let me finish my hitch. Get that pension. You finish yours and then, maybe—"

"Not 'maybe,' Cathy. Then we'll be together."

"If you let me finish out my tour," I said.

He didn't answer.

"Sergeant, you got to understand the way Vikers and his boys watch me. Nothing slips by them. You can't touch me, can't say my name, you can't so much as glance my way from now until the day I muster out."

"I don't think I can do that."

"No think about it," I said. "It has to be that way or we might just as well ride on out of here tonight."

"Desert?"

I nodded.

He said, "They'll come after us. Find us. Shoot us."

"They will. I've only got eight more months on my hitch then, maybe—"

"I already told you, no 'maybe' about it. We'll be together. If it means that until the day you muster out, you're nothing but Private William Cathay to me, then that's what you'll be. But you have to give me your promise."

I nodded.

"Say it," he said.

"We'll be together."

"Say my name."

I dared a glance into his face and said, "We'll be together, Wager Swayne."

Right then, I'd of taken it all back and we'd have run for the high line, but since the Sergeant was the Sergeant, he kept his word, he did the right thing. He stepped back and walked away. What had to be, had to be. We had a plan. We'd be together.

Chapter 71

—

Wager. *Wager. Wager. Wager.*

Only in the dark of the barracks when all around me were calling out in their sleep for their beloveds could I allow his name back into my head. And then only to heft it for the weight of the hope and the worry it brought and to calculate if I could bear either for another day. Another day that would bring me one step closer to finishing out my hitch, getting that pension, having a life with my all in all.

In July news came that helped knock my worries aside: Chewing Bones and his band had left the reservation and were raiding and massacring again. The news and rumors flew so thick and heavy that it was impossible to tell what was true. If I was to believe every tale of atrocity told in the barracks after lights out, I'd of had to give Chewing Bones credit for more devastation than what was wreaked upon the entire Shenandoah Valley by Sheridan and the Union Army.

Every night the rumors got more gruesome. Like the settler who was clubbed in the back of the head as he tried to run away then had his scalp lifted. And would of lived except that screw worms burrowed into his bald skull and ate his brain.

"Mutilation" was everything the savages did beyond the regular scalping and porcupining someone with arrows. The strikers brought the best stories back. With a fiendish glee that came straight from the officers' dinner tables, we heard of the renegades chopping off fingers, hands, ears, eyelids, entire human hides. Chewing Bones himself was said to have hacked one fellow's heart right out of his chest, leaving him alive long enough to see it give its final beat. Stories of such butchery, however, were always just a warm-up for the accounts of the ultimate outrage: when a man got his parts chopped off. In the mathematics of the barracks parts getting chopped off equaled up to a couple dozen killings by any other means.

And then there were the endless kidnappings and violations of "innocent white women and girls." The nastiest stories always came by way of the colonel and his wife. They told of brave pioneer wives being hauled out of their cabins by the hair for all the braves to have a go at. Then they'd stake the white woman out in the sun with her eyelids cut off. The braves'd kidnap whatever girls were of age, or close to, to take back to their squalid teepees and use at their leisure. Or to let their women henpeck to death. Or, ransom back to the whites. Usually via a gang of comancheros who'd also use her in highly imaginative ways.

I'd heard variations on this tale so many times, I stopped paying attention until, one night, Vikers said, "The worst depravity has to be what happened to a young girl by the name of Matilda Lockhart who was carried off by the Comanche to the Guadalupe Mountain. She wasn't but thirteen years old, though already well developed with a fine, high bust."

Fine, high bust. Vikers played the barracks boys like a fiddle.

"The savages held her captive for two years. Every one of those lustful heathens used that little girl in the most despicable of ways."

In the dark, I made a sour face thinking of how, night after endless night, they did nothing but brag on the despicable ways that they themselves used women.

"But the squaws," Vikers droned on. "Those redskin squaws were even worse. They beat little Matilda constantly. Even when she tried to sleep they'd torture her. Many a time they woke her by pressing a hot coal against her tender flesh. Especially her nose.

"When her family got her back after two years, her nose was burned down to the stump. She was so utterly degraded by those beasts that she couldn't hold her head up again in civilized society and died two years later."

I could of let this story go, *should* of let this story go for my own good, but Vikers had whipped even the Georgia boys up.

"Animals," Tea Cake said, genuinely outraged.

"Rabid animals," Ivory added. "Need to put them down like mad dogs."

"First redskin I get my hands on," Baby King swore, "I'ma burn *his* nose off, you just see if I don't."

The frenzy kept building until I had to point out, "You all know that this happened back in eighteen and forty, don't you? This Matilda Lockhart y'all so het up about's been dead now lot longer than she was ever alive, and yet she's still got the U.S. Army and every settler ever headed west slaughtering Indians for her. And one other thing. It was the Comanche took her. Chewing Bones's pack is Apache."

"So what?" Greene said. "They're all bad."

"Eighteen and forty?" Tea Cake asked. "That true, Vikers?"

Vikers gathered himself up and came back, "I doubt that one true thing's ever come out of Stanky's lying mouth."

"Yeah," Caldwell said, "he got too many other things stuffed all up in there."

Oh, they howled and slapped their thighs at that reminder of the unnatural acts I was supposed to be getting up to. When the cackling subsided, Lem spoke up and said, "Cathay's right, I been hearing 'bout this burnt-nose white girl since I signed on. Seems a world of heathens been shot up, burned out, and starved on account of her. Now here we are gettin' riled up all over again over little Matilda been dead longer than I been alive. It sets me to wondering. Makes me to ask y'all a question. Didn't none of y'all never see a master do near as bad or worse to one of our girls? Back where I come from, they got used any way Master saw fit. And weren't never no army riding out to venge those sweet baby girls."

I remembered then. It was an afternoon in late fall when gray clouds hung low and a chilly wind sliced across the yard, blowing bits of dried tobacco leaves and twine left over from tying up the bundles. I was working beside Mama that day. We were all out, rechinking the oldest curing barn on the place, and our hands and arms were white and whiskered up to the elbow from the ash and hog bristles mixed into the mortar we'd been daubing onto the chinks.

Across the yard, Clemmie was on the porch, sweeping the stairs. As she stepped down onto the bottom one, the sun cut through a slit in the clouds and shone directly on her. She was waving at us, smiling, when Old Mister came out of the house and put his hand on her shoulder. Instant he touched her, the smile dropped from my little sister's face. He turned her around, led her back into the house, and shut the door behind them.

I saw it again, Old Mister's hand on my little sister's shoulder, guiding her up the steps, into the house, into his bedroom, and the rage roaring through me melted and ran out my eyes.

Tea Cake noticed and nudged Ivory. I lowered my head and waited for the bullyragging to commence. But it didn't. Instead, I heard them whisper, "Cat-hauled," to one another like that explained everything.

Late that night, when I couldn't sleep, I went to the window and stared out across the drill field to Wager's quarters where his lantern shone behind the drawn curtains. I was feeling so low and mournful that I didn't even care who might see me mooning there. Let them take me for a sodomite, I thought. It'd be worth it for just a glimpse of his shadow passing behind the curtains.

I held my post until day broke.

Chapter 72

⁓

The next day, we were all jumpy, waiting for the order sending us out after Chewing Bones to come down. Tired of listening to the rumors and guesses, I went to the stable to hide out with Bunny. I plucked a few carrots from Mrs. Drewbott's garden and fed chunks to Bunny while I munched on one myself. Her whiskery lips were brushing across my flat palm, herding a nice orange chunk into her mouth, when I caught sight of Major Carter and his pal Captain Grundy coming in. I ducked down in the stall with Bunny as I had little regard for either one.

"Hello!" Carter called out. I watched them from between a gap in the stall boards.

"Anybody here?" Grundy asked. When they were sure no one was about, they set to doing what they'd sought out this secluded spot to do and that was gossiping like a pair of old ladies rocking on a porch.

"So it's true?" Grundy asked. "We're finally moving out?"

"Drewbott told me to pass the order tomorrow at assembly. Sheridan himself telegrammed. And Grundy, I'm telling you, that wire . . ." Carter whistled long and low. "It scorched my eyes to read it. I can't believe Drewbott left it out on his desk."

"Man's a mental defective," Grundy said. "Doesn't have the sense God gave a turnip. What did Little Phil say?"

"He said, and I quote, 'I will come down there myself and rip the eagles off your shoulders and replace them with chicken feathers if you do not get up off your hindquarters and bring the renegades in.'"

Grundy chuckled. "That's old Smash 'em Up for you. I guess we'll see now if Colonel Yellow Belly is more scared of Chewing Bones or Sheridan."

"You know who he's most scared of?" Carter asked.

"His own shadow," Grundy answered.

Carter snorted a laugh, then turned serious and said, "The darkies."

Grundy sounded surprised when he asked, "The darkies? Why?"

"Guilty conscience is my guess. Drewbott being from the South and all. He knows what was done to them down there. Knows he'd kill the man who'd ever treated him as the slaves were treated."

"Doesn't make sense," Grundy said. "Aside from the usual rowdies and drunks, the darkies are the most docile, biddable group of soldiers I've ever come across. The white outfits are the ones to be scared of. They're full of killers and thieves, dipsomaniacs and deserters. You read the report, didn't you?"

"I had a look at it."

"The colored regiments have the lowest rate of desertion and highest rate of compliance of any west of the Mississippi. And Company J leads them all."

I swelled up with pride and could hardly wait to slip out and give the Sergeant this news.

Of course, leave it to Carter to take the shine off of anything sparkly. He came right back with, "Biddable, indeed. Like children, aren't they? The darkies. Happy all the time. You ever pass by the barracks at night, they'll be singing and laughing and capering about. Too dumb to even realize that this is the ass end of all assignments."

"Well, really," Grundy said, "what else have they got? It's not as if they could go back where they came from. Johnson acts like we fought the war just to clear out the slaveholders and let this new bunch he's in cahoots with take over. The Clue Clucks something or other. The ones terrorizing the ex-slaves. Riding around in bedsheets and dunce caps."

"Yes, they're a dim bunch," Carter agreed. "But the darkies, they're children, I tell you. Someone's got to keep them in line."

Grundy sighed. "I suppose so."

Carter leaned in close. "I'll tell you this much, if Drewbott really does get off his hind end and go after Chewing Bones, you better believe he'll have at least two officers between himself and the darkies. He'll have someone guarding his back at all times. Someone white."

"You know who *should* keep a guard at his back?"

Carter gave that nasty little laugh of his and answered, "Allbright. Lord, Drewbott does hate that uppity coon, doesn't he? He put in to have him transferred a month ago. Mark my words, if that request is denied, Drewbott will find some other way to have him removed."

As they left the stables, Carter's words drifted back to me. "No, it wouldn't surprise me one little bit if *Sergeant* Allbright meets an untimely end on this mission."

Chapter 73

~

"Cathy," the Sergeant said when he opened the door of his quarters late that night. It was long after lights out. I couldn't see his face, but his voice was thick with sleep. He caught himself and demanded, "Private?" loud enough that anyone passing in the night could hear.

I told him straight out, "They mean to kill you."

He pulled me into the dark room and shut the door. He wore only his muslin drawers. His shoulders and chest were bare. Still honoring his promise, he quickly stepped away from me.

"What are you talking about?"

"I heard Carter and Grundy in the stables. Sheridan has ordered Drewbott to go after the renegades. Drewbott, he's going to kill you while we're in the field."

"Drewbott?" he scoffed. "That pansy? I'd half respect him if he had the sand for such a thing."

"Listen to me. I'm serious. Drewbott already requested you be transferred."

"Transfer, huh?" the Sergeant asked with a casualness that worried me.

"The man hates you. He's eaten up with it." My words seemed to make no impression on him and my voice went shrill as I warned him again, "He will kill you if he gets the chance."

This caused a little smile to play across his lips and I had to ask what on earth was wrong with him.

"Nothing," he answered. "I just like hearing your real voice. Especially like this. Full of emotion and . . ." He paused before adding, "And worry. You're worried about me." He sounded like he barely believed it possible.

"I am. Of course, I am. Every second of every day."

The smile he gave me had a sweetness to it I hadn't seen before. "Don't worry, Cathy, Ednar Drewbott is not what's going to put me in my grave."

We stood in silence. I'd said my piece. The moment came for me to leave, to hold to the promise that I'd forced him to make, but it passed and I did not turn from him.

"You should leave," he said. But I couldn't move. Couldn't leave. Couldn't not touch him. *Wager.* The forbidden name hummed through me. My head grew heavier until, of its own accord, it leaned over and came to rest on Wager's warm, bare shoulder. I pressed my lips against his neck and breathed in his scent like I hadn't had air for all these past weeks.

"Cathy?" he said, making my name into a question.

"Wager," I said, giving him my answer.

Dim light from the new-risen waxing crescent moon streamed in through the window. He took off my jacket and shirt, angled me so that the light fell across my face, untucked the end of the binding that held it in place and unwound the strips of fabric. Gently, he peeled the long loops away, gathering them up in his free hand like a wilted bouquet then let the loops uncoil and fall to the floor. Moonlight dappled my throat, my shoulders. As soon as my scars were bared, Wager licked each pearl like it was a gumdrop. He lapped at my bare shoulders, throat, breasts as though he could lick the silver glow from my skin.

He laid me upon his bed. We faced each other, the eagerness of his body touching mine. His hands rounded over my cheeks, shoulders, hips. I was grateful to the ones who'd taught him to love so tenderly. Beneath his touch, I felt small and dainty and feminine.

"Did you think of me?" he asked, his need to talk winning over the other need. He wasn't the one Mama had warned me about, the man, any man, all men, who'd do me wrong. She'd never met his like. Neither had Clemmie. Nor, maybe, had any other woman ever except me.

"Wager, I never stop thinking of you."

"Can I tell you a secret?" he asked, his finger tracing the curl of my ear.

"I hope so," I answered. "I told you the biggest one I will ever have."

"I was drawn to you, from the start. I didn't know why. I sure didn't want to be. Some part of me, though, knew. Knew you were a woman. Knew you were the woman who'd saved me."

"Didn't stop you from trying to run me off, telling me I was a 'divisive element'?" Small laughs puffed between us.

"You were. You are. But I still favored you over the others, didn't I? Found reasons to be alone with you. It worried me. Wanting to be alone with a man. But it was there. Right from the start."

"Wager, I loved you from the moment I saw your bandaged face in the back of that wagon. It wasn't peeling away those bindings made me a woman, it was you."

He didn't say the words back, didn't say he loved me. But I hadn't expected he would.

Chapter 74

⟶

Colonel Drewbott refused to go out after the renegades until he had "trustworthy" scouts. By this he meant "white scouts." The great John Horse and his men, veritable bloodhounds every one, would not do. "Too unfamiliar with the area," Drewbott had harrumphed to Wager when he explained the delay. "Too colored" was more like it.

Drewbott's chickenshit dithering gave Wager and me three more nights together. By then, we were both past caring whether or not the entire regiment took us, as Lem did, for a pair of sodomites. One night, hell, one minute with Wager was worth all the gossip and snickering the company could slander us with. Many, maybe most, couples can spend a lifetime together and not know each other the way Wager and I came to know each other in those few, stolen nights together.

We made plans. Come hell or high water, we'd each finish out our hitches so we'd have those pensions to build us a new life together in California. We'd light out for that far land which had not been poisoned by slavery. Maybe I'd cook for one of the fine hotels in San Francisco. Or even open a place of my own. Nothing fancy. Simple food for simple folks.

Wager thought he might take to the sea like his father and come home to me and our fine, unbroken children with stories of adventure in the South Seas, his pockets fat with wages. These were the conversations we had for three nights as we lolled in each other's arms and built our future together, one kiss at a time.

At general assembly on the morning after our third night alone together, a very flustered Drewbott issued orders for a detachment of sixty men to make ready to ride out at first light the next day. Wager, Lem, and I were on the list along with Vikers, Greene, and Caldwell. Like any decent cavalryman, I spent most of the day in the stable, tending to Bunny.

There are those who don't believe that a horse can understand human feelings, but Bunny knew I was happy for those floppy ears of hers nearly stood up when I gave her the news that we'd been ordered into the field. I tested, repaired, oiled, and polished every bit of her tack and curried her until she gleamed. Though most everyone else still adhered to the "3 Bs," bleeding, blistering, and burning, to treat their mounts, I would have laid out the first quack veterinary ever dared to come at my Bunny with a bleeding cup. No, I bought calendula cream at the sutler's out of my pay to dab on every scratch and sweet feed to make her coat glossy.

Late that night, I went to Wager. We were sitting on his bed when the door burst open and there stood John Horse and two of his men. They stepped in without waiting for so much as a how-dee-do. Instead of beads and deerskin leggings and vests decorated with Mexican pesos, they were all wearing army uniforms. John Horse held the rank of corporal, but still wore his plaid wool tunic.

"They said you would be here," John Horse said.

"I thought Drewbott wanted white scouts," Wager said.

"He did," John Horse answered. "Sheridan didn't agree." The chief nodded at me then at Wager and asked, "You two?" He jabbed his pointer finger in and out of a circle he made with the pointer and thumb of his other hand in a gesture as crude as it was universal.

"He knows?" Wager asked me.

"He knew from the first," I answered.

"But how?"

John Horse translated for his men and they laughed. "How not?" John Horse asked. "I knew by seeing she is a woman."

"But how?" Wager asked again.

"How did you not?" John Horse asked, laughing with his men. John Horse clapped Wager on the back and concluded, "You have been with white men too long. You only see what you think should be there. Not what is right in front of you."

He looked around at Wager's quarters, nodded and said, "We'll sleep in here with you. In the barracks there is too much farting and . . ." He mimed masturbation and concluded, "What do you have to eat?"

Chapter 75

———

At the stable before dawn, I breathed in the good smell of fresh bedding hay as I all but skipped to Bunny's stall to get her tacked up for the big day ahead. The stall was empty. I ran outside yelling for Fernie Teague, who was second to Lem and now in charge since Lem was coming with us.

"What you hollerin' about?" Fernie demanded as he hustled up to me, pulling his long white grooming coat on over his uniform.

"Bunny? Where's my horse?"

"Oh, right, I was going to tell you first thing—"

"Tell me what?" My heart had stopped dead.

"About Bunny. She took sick. Glanders's what it looks like."

Glanders.

I thought my legs would drop out from under me, glanders was that fatal bad.

"Whoa, whoa," Fernie said. "She ain't dead yet. Quarantined her over to the back pasture."

I started to go to her, but Fernie grabbed my arm and stopped me. "Sorry, doc said no one's allowed to get close to her. People can catch glanders and that ain't a pretty way to go. Horse or man."

"I have to take care of—"

"Order's an order, Cathay. Don't fret. I'll leave water and feed for her. She'll be comfortable."

"Will you . . ." I couldn't finish. "If she's suffering."

"Count on it," he answered. "Comes to it, I'll put her down gentle and fast. Doc says to give her till tomorrow morning."

Fernie loaned me a sturdy brown gelding and I made myself forget that I'd never known of an animal to recover from glanders. Like always, I put my sorrow to the side, did what had to be done, and was mounted and ready time we moved out.

Carter's prediction turned out to be right. When we rode out, heading south toward Mexico where Chewing Bones liked to hole up across the Rio Grande, Drewbott had four white officers riding between him and us. But the man didn't stop there. He'd also assigned Carter and Grundy to ride directly behind Wager. As soon as I saw that Drewbott had put two gunmen at Wager's back, I unholstered my carbine and kept it out, resting on the saddle. I held the reins in my left hand, rifle in the right, with my finger on the trigger.

We rode through a land that, while still vast and magnificent, no longer seemed as untroubled as it had when Wager and I scouted it a year ago. The spring rains hadn't come and where miles of grass should have carpeted the prairie, only stubbly clumps lay here and there. Even the cactus and scrub oak looked exhausted by the drought.

At night, Wager, Lem, and I bedded down with the scouts, far away from the others. Wager had warmed considerably to John Horse. Instead of thinking him a traitor, he asked Horse to tell him again about defeating the United States Army in the swamps of Florida and escaping from capture in that thick-walled prison. He listened to Horse now like the chief was Frederick Douglass sitting amongst us with a plaid wool turban atop his head.

Wager and I both noticed that Horse and his men always spoke of their white commander at Fort Lewis, Lieutenant Bullis, with the same kind of fondness and loyalty that the Buffalo Soldiers who served under Colonels Hatch and Grierson spoke of those officers. Not only did those white COs treat their troops with respect, but they had them doing more soldiering than pick-swinging.

"I guess not all white officers are chickenshit colorphobes," I said. "Appears we just got stuck with a bad apple."

"'Apple'?" Horse whooped. "Drewbott's a whole barrel of stinking turds is what he is. You need to put in for a transfer to our unit."

"To scout?" Wager asked.

"Sure. Why not? I'll get Bullis to request you. Don't appear Colonel Turd'll object."

"And the private?" Wager asked, nodding toward me.

"Oh, sure, the 'private,'" Horse echoed, winking at the other scouts. "The 'private,' sure, I'll put in for 'him,' too."

"We'd like that," Wager said.

"And Lem, too?" I asked.

John Horse agreed. The other scouts laughed, apparently delighted that the three of us were, in our various ways, pulling one over on the army. Taking this jolliness as a sign that the Seminole accepted his brand of love, Lem grinned.

This plan, this answer to our prayer, made me half-witted with happiness. As for Wager, the corners of his mouth turned up, which was like him doing handsprings and jumping for joy. I saw us together, settled in beside Blackberry Creek, finishing out our hitches with friends on either side. I wanted badly to take his hand and squeeze it. But though at this campfire we were among friends, I never forgot that enemies were always watching.

At the center of camp, in front of a fire bigger than it needed to be, was Drewbott. Hearing our laughter and being thin-skinned as a dewberry, he believed we were having sport at his expense. His eyes narrowed and his nostrils flared in agitation as he studied us. Off in the distance a coyote howled and, startled by the sound, Drewbott jerked up so fast the cup of coffee he held splashed down the leg of his pants. He shook his head and glared our way as though, on top of all the other miseries of his life, this, too, was our fault. Was Wager's fault. His sour expression reminded me so much of Old Mister that a cold bolt of fear lodged beneath my breastbone. I pledged that that shoulder-strapped carbuncle would die before he ever raised a hand to Wager. And that I would do the deadening.

Chapter 76

⁓

Nothing of much account happened during our first few days in the field except that we drank the water wagon dry. Drewbott sent word down that water would not be a concern as he possessed a map of the savages' water sources. He meant the map that had been drawn up from the locations Wager and I had scouted a year ago. We camped that night beside the first water we'd found, and mapped on that last trip. It had been a creek back then but was now barely a trickle.

On the morning of the fifth day, John Horse and his men left out before dawn, headed to the Klatt Ranch on Sulfur Draw, seventy miles away, where the last reported renegade attack had taken place. The scouts would cut for sign and pick up the trail from there. Drewbott and Carter studied the water map and sent down word that we were making for Playa del Oro, thirty miles south. We splashed the slurry of coffee and grounds left at the bottom of our cups into the embers of our breakfast fires and Wager passed among his men reminding them, "Fill up your canteens. All of you. No man leaves without a full canteen."

Before they could obey, Drewbott, with Carter and Grundy flanking him and Vikers and his boys bringing up the rear, marched over. The bolt of fear lodged in my chest twisted tighter. Drewbott stopped a ways from our campsite and bellowed, "Allbright!"

With a quick glance at me, Wager strode over, snapped off a salute, and waited at attention.

"First Sergeant Allbright!" Drewbott rumbled out, loud enough for everyone to hear. The men halted what they were doing. Saddles were held out frozen in front of them, one man's carbine hung open, waiting to be loaded, a mule danced about at the end of a rein waiting to be harnessed, and the men going to fill canteens halted.

When everyone's attention was on him, Drewbott announced, "First Sergeant Allbright, you are hereby relieved of your command and demoted to corporal. I am brevetting Corporal Vikers to the rank of first sergeant. He will assume your duties, effective immediately."

"What are the charges?" Wager asked, not a speck of the shock that had gripped me and the rest of the detachment showing on his face or in his voice.

Vikers stepped forward with Wager's sextant and spyglass and Drewbott announced, "These were found in your saddlebag."

"Of course they were," Wager answered calmly. "They're always in my saddlebag. How else am I supposed to map and navigate?"

"That's about enough of your smart lip, boy," Drewbott snapped. "You're not on this expedition to do either one. We have a white officer, Grundy, to do that. So, since you clearly knew that there would be no mapping, why would you bring these instruments along?"

Wager said nothing.

"Admit it," Drewbott thundered with such force and suddenness that the officers beside him widened their eyes. That was when I saw that Drewbott had the red-eyed gauntness of a man who wasn't sleeping right. "You are searching for your confederates out there!" He held a trembling finger out toward the vast emptiness.

For the first time, I saw worry wrinkle Wager's face.

"First Sergeant Vikers," Drewbott ordered. "The command is yours."

Vikers, chest puffed out, stepped up and ordered, "Boots and saddles, men! Boots and saddles! Get a move on! Colonel expects us to make forty miles today! He wants to be splashing about in Playa del Oro by nightfall! Are we going to do it for the colonel?" he yelled out.

We all recognized Vikers's toadying up to the master for the sign of the bad overseer that it was, and Greene and Caldwell were the only ones to hurrah him back. So Vikers, staring threats, asked again. This time everyone except me, Wager, and Lem yelled agreement.

As we rode off, Wager betrayed no more emotion than a statue carved from marble. Only I saw how his jaw bunched from the rage he was swallowing down. He separated himself from us and I knew to let him be.

The sun rose and, as the dry miles got dryer and hotter, it came out that many of the men, rushed by Vikers to saddle up, had not filled their canteens at the creek we'd camped next to. Worse, Vikers was not enforcing water discipline. He hadn't made the men nurse along what water they did have, the way Wager would of. By noon, a fair number of the men, mostly the new recruits, had already drained what little water they had. They didn't worry overly much, though, for we were making for a marked water hole, the large shallow lake called Playa del Oro that we had mapped spring before last.

I told Lem about how Wager and I had seen more different kinds of animals gathered at Playa del Oro than Noah had on his Ark. Skittish pronghorn, snorty wild horses, braying burros, a flock of spindly-legged cranes, skunk, lizards, javelina. I told him how flocks of white wing dove rose and settled upon the broad, shallow lake thick as leaves whirled by an autumn wind. We'd even seen the prints of puma, wolves, and the long-nailed track of a bear pressed into the mud around the banks of the shallow lake.

In anticipation of this vast watering hole, Lem made free with his water, gulping down what he had.

"Wait," I told him. "Best if you ration what you got. Save some for tomorrow."

"Why?" he asked. "Tomorrow we be splashing with the cranes."

"Maybe. Maybe not. Look." I pointed to the sky.

"What? Nothing up there. Not even a cloud to give us a bit of shade."

"That's what I'm talkin' about. Last time we were here, sky was full of white wing dove flocking this way. And, have you seen a single pronghorn? They've left, Lem. That's a bad sign. I'm telling you, slow down."

Lem stoppered his canteen and we rode on.

Playa del Oro sat atop a high mesa. The climb was steep and the footing unsteady. The sound of men panting and the clatter of horse hooves unloosing torrents of loose rock filled the hot, dry air. Full dark was coming on by the time we approached the mesa. The parched men pushed hard to reach the top where the broad water hole waited.

The first ones to reach the peak stopped dead. We gathered up next to them and gazed out on a vast dry depression scaled with curls of crisp gray dirt.

Drewbott made a great show of unfurling Wager's map and calling out, "Either Allbright got these coordinates wrong or this 'playa' he reported never existed in the first place."

I watched the muscles of Wager's jaw work, grinding so hard I could hear the sound, but he did not utter a word. Not at that and not when Drewbott sent out a couple of his officers to scout the area, ordering them, "Find the water that Corporal Allbright says is supposed to be here." I wanted to scream at Drewbott that only an idiot would expect water to always be where it had been in a desert.

Without a word, Wager pulled an entrenching spade off of one of the supply mules and walked out across the Playa. I followed. The disks of sun-baked dirt crunched beneath our boots. Near the center of the shallow basin, we commenced to dig. Wager with the spade. Me with my saber. When we got down far enough, water seeped slowly into the hole. Sad that I had to dirty it, I flattened the kerchief Wager had given me down into the puddle to filter out the mud, sank my cup into it, then held it up and called out, "Who's thirsty?"

Soon all of the recruits and most of the men were digging. Drewbott and his officers, along with Vikers and his bunch, stood away and pretended to be amused at us "wallowing like pigs in the muck." When all the men were done, we led the horses out to drink at the seeps.

That night, Lem, Wager, and I made camp as far from the others as we could go without officially deserting. Stars spangled the sky from one edge of the mesa to the other. Even when the three of us were alone, Wager didn't speak, just studied the sky like he'd find an answer to this ultimate betrayal of all he had once believed in up there. When I heard Lem snoring, I moved my bedroll next to Wager. He took no notice of me. He was too occupied in parsing out how his grand ideas and noble thoughts had let him down. He was finding his way to knowing what I knew: the time for noble thoughts had passed. We were captives and we had to escape.

The moon went down and the stars settled around us, so close and radiant it seemed like I could flap my arms, swim up through them, and lead Wager and Lem to freedom.

Chapter 77

The next morning, we noticed dried mud on the knees of the trousers of Vikers and all the white officers except for Drewbott. No doubt, in the dark of the night, the colonel had ordered someone else to scoop up his water from a hole dug by one of us. I hoped there was horse shit in it.

Though the seep water slaked our thirst, it griped our bellies. When the recruits complained about their guts cramping up, Wager told them, "That's only the gypsum in the water. Just be thankful it wasn't alkali water. Gyppy water'll run you a little ragged at first, but you'll get used to it. Alkali, though, alkali will kill a man long before he ever gets used to it."

Wager reminded his men to fill their canteens from the seeps and then we mounted up and rode on to Sulfur Draw where we were to meet up with John Horse.

We smelled what was left of the Klatt Ranch before we saw it. That odor of smoke and ash and burned flesh reminded me of the Shenandoah Valley after Sheridan had finished with it. Difference was that back then the burned flesh had all been animal. We found Mr. Klatt's blackened remains spread-eagled on a wagon wheel resting atop the ashes of the fire he'd died upon. His wife, naked, rested a ways off. Her back was spiked with a dozen arrows from the renegades she'd died running from. We buried the wife. Klatt, though, had fused onto the charred spokes and we had to chop the cinders of what was left of him off the wheel before we could bury his remains.

While we were filling in the grave, an officer approached quaking with rage and holding up a corn husk doll. "Look what I found over there!" he yelled, pointing south. "They took her! Those red-skinned animals took a white girl child!"

The other officers and then most of the company, black and white, fell to wrathful proclamations, cursing the heathen and vowing revenge for this defilement. Like the times back in the barracks when the men would whip themselves into the most heated frenzies as they told old tales of white girls being kidnapped and white women violated, my reaction was so cold that I worried I might have a heart as evil and unfeeling as those savages.

Just like back in the barracks, all I could think was, *What about Clemmie? What about Iyaiya?* And I sure didn't see any answers in the faces twisted with rage for a corn husk doll.

The last wisps of smoke swirling over a burned sorghum field caught my eye. On second glance the wisps formed up into John Horse and his men riding forward out of the woods.

John Horse led us to a trail so broad and obvious that Drewbott brayed out, loud enough for every man in the unit to hear, "I don't know what the army is paying those black savages for. A blind man could follow this trail. Even without the . . ." Here he paused, then continued, his voice throbbing with outrage. "Without the fallen plaything of an innocent girl child to guide us."

The trail was, indeed, impossible to miss. White hoof strikes marked gray rocks, brush was trampled by what had to be close to fifty riders, long mane hairs fluttered from the thorns they'd snagged on. Drewbott was right. It was easy following the renegades' trail as they rode south, making for refuge in Mexico. Following Wager's map, Drewbott had us veer off the trail toward a spring we'd marked. It wasn't running and, once again, Drewbott blamed Wager. We retook the trail and pushed hard to make the next marked source before dark.

Lips cracked in the heat. Shirts and kerchiefs hung limp. Near midafternoon, a recruit who'd finished all his water the day before wobbled, then toppled off his saddle. Within an hour, three more greenhorns had fallen out. Drewbott ordered the strongest to stay behind and help the weakest. That was a mistake. Our column soon stretched out near two miles.

We entered the canyon Wager and I had mapped. Again, I rode between orange cliffs that had reminded me of buttercream icing slumping off a cake on a hot day. All the seeps we'd found the first time were dry and the sound of Drewbott cursing Wager and promising to have him court-martialed echoed off the red sandstone walls until we emerged and rode south on into the desert. Wager caught my eye and shot me a look that asked why Drewbott wasn't heading for the arroyo we had mapped. I shrugged, pretending not to know the answer.

Around four that afternoon, the column halted. A clump of men, mostly officers, along with Vikers and his cronies, were clustered around John Horse, who squatted in the dust holding an ocotillo blade long as a coach whip. To keep from disturbing the trail, Horse pointed the long branch to what appeared to be just more rocky, sandy earth punctuated here and there with clumps of prickly pear or scrub oak.

Wager glanced at me for John Horse was pointing toward the spring we had mapped, saying it was thirty miles or so to the west, hidden away in a deep arroyo.

Drewbott, hands on hips, demanded, "Why are you trying to tell me that the renegades rode west when it is as clear as if a herd of elephant passed by that they're heading south? All the spoor and all the reports say that they've got their hideout across the river in Mexico. Why would they detour off?"

John Horse stood. He towered over Drewbott and let that fact speak for a few moments before he answered, "Water." He left off the "Sir." And the salute.

"Just how stupid do you think I am?" Drewbott hissed. "Who left this?" He went about pointing at broken twigs, snagged horse hair, and asking at each sign, "And this? And this? And all of this?" The last, piles of manure so fresh it was still formed up into nice, round apples without a bit of crumbling, was his prize exhibit. "Why, their trail is so obvious a child could follow it."

John Horse slid his eyes to the side, away from the colonel and said nothing.

"Corporal, answer my question or I will bring you up on insubordination charges so fast, it will make your head spin and your turban unfurl."

The officers chuckled quietly at Drewbott's little joke, but Vikers nearly herniated himself laughing.

Finally, John Horse intoned, "Yes, I see. A trail has been left that even a child could follow. A stubborn, blind, stupid, spoiled child."

Drewbott went red as a stewed tomato at this disrespect. Then, trembling with rage, he unfurled the water hole map that had been drawn up based on Wager's readings and the figures I'd written down for him. Drew-bott held it up in the chief's face and, stabbing at it, hollered, "There are no water sources within three days' ride west of here!"

Wager looked at me, questioning, and I nodded: yes. It was true. I had written down the numbers he'd told me that would reveal the location of the spring where the band of starving women and children had gathered. But I had written them down backward.

Wager spoke. "Sir."

"Yes, what do you have to add, *Corporal*?" Drewbott said to Wager in a sneery tone. "Do you agree with this black Indian scout that there is a water source to the west?"

"Yes," Wager answered. "John Horse is correct. There is a water hole west of here."

"There is?" Drewbott asked in his snide way. "And yet you did not see fit to mark its location?"

"Sir," I said, "I was the one didn't mark down the coordinates of the spring that Sergeant Allbright read out to me."

" 'Coordinates,' " he repeated, in a mocking voice that said I didn't know what that was and couldn't of written them down if I had. "So this 'spring' even has coordinates. Care to tell us what they might be?"

"I don't recollect the exact figures," I answered.

"That's awfully handy, isn't it?" Drewbott asked.

"The private's failure is my responsibility," Wager said.

"I know that," Drewbott snapped. "So, *Corporal,* you're saying that, though you did not see fit to mark it, there is water west of here, and we should now follow these black Indians to it?"

"Yessir, I am," Wager answered, never once glancing Drewbott's way. "It's our only chance for survival. There are no marked water sources south from here to the Rio Grande."

Drewbott lowered his head, held his hands behind his back, and paced back and forth, muttering, "Uh-huh. Uh-huh," like he was considering what Wager and John Horse had said. Of a sudden, he halted, raised his head, pointed at Wager and ordered, "Lieutenant Meinzer, Captain Grundy, seize this enemy agent prisoner. Vikers, Caldwell, Greene, seize the Indians."

Hands were laid upon Wager and the Seminoles.

"This treasonous conspiracy," Drewbott sputtered, "must be stopped. We won't be led by these traitors into an ambush. The prisoners are to be kept under watch at all times. During the day, their hands are to be tied in such a way that they can still ride. At night, they will be bound, hand and foot.

"As for the rest of you," he screamed at us. "Colonel Ednar Drewbott promises that justice will be swift for traitors and deserters. There will be no questions asked and no mercy shown. Wherever you run, I will send the strongest men with the most powerful weapons to hunt you down and shoot you like the treasonous dogs you are. Take the prisoners away."

Wager, John Horse, and the others were bound and rudely led off. Drewbott hollered after them, "Put three men on Allbright. White men. He's the ringleader of this mutiny. He's the dangerous one."

Chapter 78

———

Sleep was fitful that night. Men coughed and panted hard as dogs trying to cool themselves. The moon was so diamond bright that the ocotillos threw shadows like spiders crawling across the sand. I woke Lem and whispered to him, "We have to go for water."

"How's that?"

"There is water to the west. A spring. I saw it, just didn't mark it down right. But it's there."

"You talking desertion?" Lem asked. "They'll hang us."

"Rather go that way than dying of thirst. What you say?"

"Tonight?"

"Have to. Drewbott's bound on killing the Sergeant. Lem, no two ways about it, you stay, you will die."

Lem nodded.

"Good. Soon as I can set the Sergeant free, be ready to jump up and dust. I'll watch for the officers guarding him to drop off."

And, while Lem slept, that is what I did. But the three officers must have had orders from Drewbott to keep up a constant guard. Each one took duty, switching off every couple of hours. Halfway through the night, Lem woke and said he'd take a turn. I closed my eyes and dropped off.

I woke a few hours later and found Lem snoring with his mouth open, John Horse and his men gone, and Wager staring at me from between the officers lying fast asleep beside him. Though a dozen sleeping men, one smoking fire, and several clumps of prickly pear separated us, I raised my hands, my wrists held together, then separated them and pointed at him. He nodded, understanding that I meant to free him and held up three fingers, then laid his head to the side upon his hands and shut his eyes. I nodded that I understood: the guards slept at three.

At breakfast, the greenhorns who'd been without good water the longest tried to eat hardtack, but they were too dry to swallow. They opened their mouths and the crumbs fell out, parched as cornmeal.

Convinced that he was following the savages to water, Drewbott led us farther south. Soon, the rocky ground gave way to sandy soil that was exhausting to move through. The horses were close to giving out. Hoping to spare our mounts, we continued afoot. Our progress slowed even more, as we shuffled along, heads drooping, feet dragging. All that long day, I kept my eyes on Wager, riding up ahead in front of his guards, my spirits lifted by knowing that tonight we were leaving.

We walked on. Few spoke for our tongues had swollen in our mouths. No one had made water for the past day. Several of the new recruits were staggering like they were drunk. Two men fell out and had to be slung across their saddles.

We followed the clear, deep tracks of the Indian ponies leading us ever farther south. I snapped to every now and again and found that I'd slept while I marched along. At the edge of a dry arroyo, Baby King's mare staggered and slid down into the ravine. Without making the slightest nicker, she came to rest on her side and made no effort to stand. Just lay there in a heap, panting hard.

Baby King scrambled down the slope after her. He hung on to either side of her throatlatch and tried to tug the downed horse to her feet, pleading, "Get up, hoss. Come on, please," and repeated what we all knew, "Man afoot's a dead man out here, you know that. Come on, baby, please."

The mare wouldn't budge. When Baby King turned loose of her, the mare's big head dropped down and she lay there, dust puffing up with every big exhalation. She closed her eyes and her breathing slowed and grew shallow. She was laying on Baby King's carbine, so I gave him the loan of mine. I walked away as fast as I could, but that shot was still the loudest one I had ever heard. I thought of Bunny and hoped that Fernie had made good on his word to let her go gentle. I was glad now that she hadn't come. Man or beast, thirst is a terrible way to die.

Late that afternoon, we made another dry camp. I told Lem that we'd move out at three next morning when Wager had said the guards would be asleep. We all lay huddled up in whatever shade we could find or make and waited out the long hours until our enemy, the sun, left the sky. Lem and I slept a bit. The stars, when they finally appeared, seemed frozen instead of wheeling across the sky as they usually did, while I counted down the minutes until Wager and I would be free.

I watched the first two officers guarding Wager do their tours. The third guard barely had enough strength to sit up when they shook him awake. After only a few minutes, he went to listing to one side, then the other, and I knew it wouldn't be long. My blood, thick and sludgy as it was, jumped in my veins as I took a grip on my knife. The instant he tumped over, I'd have those ropes sawed off Wager, and the three of us would be gone. At last, he tipped over to one side and did not sit back up. I moved into a crouch and made my way through the sleeping camp. Wager saw me coming and heaved himself up into a sitting position. I was poleaxed by the sight of his face flooded with moonlight and stumbled, kicking a rock that pinged off of Vikers's coffeepot. I held my breath, but no one moved and the snoring went on uninterrupted.

Wager raised his hands, beckoning me to cut him loose. I knelt beside him. My blade was on the rope when a shrill blast cut the air. Behind me, the bugler had found the spit to sound "Boots and Saddles," the order for us to mount up.

"Get away," Wager hissed.

"I'll try again tonight," I promised, backing away.

Vikers, Drewbott standing behind him, croaked out, "Colonel says to mount up if your horse is fit. We're going to backtrack. Head back to the mud seeps at Playa del Oro."

In the darkness, with no one's face exposed, the men grumbled loudly, the threat of death causing them, for the first time, to question an order.

Go back to that mudhole? That's crazy.

We'll never make it.

Ought to stay right here and send out a rescue party.

Need to get the best horses, best riders, have them tear ass down to the Rio, bring water back.

"The next man who opens his mouth," Drewbott tried to yell, but his voice was weak and thready. "Will be hung for insubordination."

He stared at us, panting, his eyes wild, his words raspy. "I am fed up trying to command you gorillas in uniform. It's not possible. No one can do it.

Do you think I want to be here? Do you think I wanted to throw away my career and risk my life for a bunch of niggers?" A sob rose up and choked him off. Drewbott turned away, pretending to be having a coughing fit.

Everyone's eyes popped open at the sound of the commander, the man responsible for getting us back alive, breaking down. For a lot of the plantation boys, whose every breath until then had been dictated by a white boss, it was a new and terrifying experience to see the one that their lives depended on even more lost than they were.

Carter, Grundy, and the other white officers traded glances as the "coughing" fit went on. And on. When Carter saw that Drewbott wasn't getting hold of himself, he stepped forward and quietly ordered us to prepare to move out. We would march in the cool of the night.

Trying to cover for his weakness, Drewbott drove us hard through the dark night as we backtracked along the trail. Men fell and no one was dispatched to stay and care for them or even to make a note of their positions. They were abandoned. Panic gripped the troopers as they realized it was every man for himself. For the first time, they started talking the mutiny that Drewbott had lived in fear of since his first peek at us. The men abandoned Vikers and clustered behind Wager, following him like he was Moses who'd lead them out of the wilderness.

At first light, I saw that our detachment had shrunk in every way you can imagine. Over half of those we'd started with had fallen out. The rest of us were shriveled up like we'd all aged thirty years. Our pants hung on bodies drying out into stalks of jerky. We all panted through open mouths ringed in white from dried sweat and puke. Swollen lips showed red where they'd cracked down to the meat.

We continued to shuffle into hell with the fires out.

It had become a rare occurrence for a horse to pee, but when the mount of one recruit so young his voice still cracked slowed to do just that the boy grabbed the empty canteen from around his neck and unstoppered it. The horse spread his back legs, stretched forward, tilting one hoof in like he was pigeon-toed, and loosed a stream of dark piss. The young recruit stuck his canteen under the horse, caught as much of the flow as he could, and drank. Though he had to stop and retch, he went back and finished what he'd caught. Soon, every time a horse stretched out his back legs, men were fighting each other to get their canteen under it.

I did what Wager would of done for his men and passed among them, warning, "Lot of salt in horse piss. It'll dry you out and you'll be worse off than before." But thirst drove the men too hard for them to listen to reason and so many men went on drinking horse piss that Vikers had his boys hand out sugar to put in it. A couple of men tried to eat the sugar, but they didn't even have the spit to dissolve that and it fell from their mouths as dry as it had gone in.

As soon as it was full light, a horrible realization struck us: whatever tracks we'd been following, they weren't ours. We were lost. Still Drewbott ordered us on. After that, the sun got suddenly brighter and everything around me went shimmery. I trudged along believing one moment that I was chopping weeds in Old Mister's tobacco fields. The next I saw Solomon's wagon ahead of me, so real I could touch it. He turned in the driver's seat, looked back, and waved for me to come up and sit with him. I'd be happy for a second or two then realize that my brain was shutting down and these visions were just a sign that I'd be dead soon.

I was jolted out of my stupor when the brown jerked on the reins I was leading him by and tried to break away. All along the line, the silent horses came to life nickering and lunging against the reins as they tried to break free.

"Water!" Lem shouted. "They smell water."

"Mount up!" Vikers passed along Drewbott's order. "Mount up and give the horses their heads!"

The thirst-maddened horses jerked free and charged toward the water they smelled. The unmounted men staggered after them. It took everything I had to keep the brown under control as we approached a shallow lake. The brown reared and snorted at the sight. The lake looked to have been made of pewter. A crusted rim of dried white powder ten feet wide ringed the water hole.

Alkali.

I yelled at the men on foot limping past, "Stop! The water's bad! It'll make y'all sick as dogs! Lem," I screamed at my friend. "Lem! Stop!" But he was already splashing into the tainted water with the rest of the men and the horses, all guzzling as much as they could hold.

By nightfall everyone except me and Wager were doubled over heaving their guts up or writhing on the ground with their bellies cramped into hard knots. Lem lay beside me panting and moaning.

"We have to leave tonight," I told him.

"I can't," he groaned. "I can't move."

"Have to," I answered. "Stay here and you'll die."

"You got any guarantee we'll find that spring? Or even that it'll be running when we get there?"

"None," I answered. "None at all."

I stood and walked amidst the men whimpering and clutching at their bellies. The officers guarding Wager were stricken bad. Though they could barely lift their revolvers when I stepped in amongst them and cut away Wager's bounds, I heard Meinzer cock his.

"We're going for water," I told him. "Who has the Sergeant's sextant and spyglass?" Meinzer pointed to his saddlebags and I retrieved the instruments.

Wager helped Lem into the saddle then went about quietly gathering up a few empty canteens and promising his men he'd return with them full. At the edge of camp, we came upon Drewbott, squatted down, emptying his liquefied innards onto the desert. He went for his revolver, but was too weak to stay squatting and tipped over into his own mess.

"I remember the coordinates exactly," I told him as we passed. "When the sun comes up, Sergeant Allbright will shoot them and we'll ride straight for the spring."

"Why," Drewbott croaked out, "didn't you tell me?"

"Because you're the enemy," I answered. "And we are captives."

The moon wasn't up yet and we rode west into black emptiness.

Chapter 79

—

Wager, happy that we would not have to navigate by dead reckoning as he'd thought we would, shot the coordinates I gave him as soon as the sun rose and we rode and walked all the next day. Though Lem passed in and out of consciousness, he stayed in the saddle. We reached the spring as the moon was rising that night. Though considerably slowed, it still trickled clear and fresh from its granite bed inside the ravine.

Wager and I took turns drinking our fill and tending to Lem. Gradually, he came around enough to drink from the canteen we'd filled for him. But he didn't come completely to his senses, just talked about "play pretties" with imaginary friends then passed out again.

Which is the condition he was in when Wager asked, "Has he made water?"

I shook my head.

"Keep an eye on him. Might mean his kidneys have failed. If that's the case, we're going to need to ride on. Take water back to the men without him."

"Wager," I asked. "You're not serious about going back, are you?"

"Of course. Did you think that I'd abandon my men?"

"I'm not going back there."

"We have to. Men will die if we don't."

"*We'll* die if we do."

"No. We might be court-martialed, but the truth will out."

"Wager, we escaped," I pleaded. "We're free. We don't have to go back."

"Cathy, I can't do that. You know I can't."

I didn't answer, for all the noble ideas crowding his head would of blocked out my words.

"Cathy, they're my men. A fair number of them signed on because of me."

"I don't care about them. I care about us. About the life we're supposed to have together."

"Would you want the man who could turn his back on the ones depend on him most?"

"Yes," I answered. "I want that man alive any way I can have him."

He stood with his hands on his hips and bit back the harsh words I knew he wanted to speak. Finally, walking away, he said in a flat voice, "I recall seeing a prickly pear patch down that way."

The darkness swallowed him up, but I watched anyway. After a time, a rusty voice I barely recognized said, "That's a good man."

I helped Lem sit up. He gulped down several big swallows and I asked if he needed to pee.

He nodded and I helped him up onto his haunches, opened his fly, and fished out his pecker. His pee was thick and near as dark as coal oil. But he was sweating again and making sense.

Lem put his hand on mine and said, "I heard what you and the sergeant was saying. I see now that he is your all in all and you his. Bill, you been a good friend. Best friend a man could of ever had. I'm sorry I ever wished for more and let jealousy twist me up the way it did. Stupid of me to think a fine man like you would of ever choiced an old plow-pusher from Georgia."

"Lem, no," I said. "Don't downrate yourself like that. Anyone would be proud to have you. I'd of been proud myself, but—"

"Don't matter," he said, his voice thick with hurt. "I hope you two's happy together."

"Lem, it's not like that. I'd of been proud to have you, but I never could of. Not that way. Lem, I'm not a man."

"You're all the man I ever wanted," Lem answered.

"Lem." I unbuttoned my jacket and stretched the bindings apart until a raisin-dark nipple popped out into the moonlight.

"Oh," Lem muttered and fell silent.

I closed my jacket.

"Have you always been . . . ?" he asked.

"Female? Yep. Born female, enlisted female, served female."

He considered my revelation for a much shorter time than I would of expected before smiling his beautiful, easy smile and saying, "So, Bill, you're a girl. That makes sense. All my best friends always been girls." He puzzled through all this a moment longer before asking, "And so, the sergeant? He's not?" He wobbled his hand back and forth.

"No."

Learning that Wager wasn't a sodomite pleased Lem. "So he'd of never choiced me, either. All right, then." He nodded, satisfied, until a final question furled his brow and he asked, "If you were born a baby girl, why'd they name you Bill?"

"There's lots to explain, Lem, and we've got a long ride back to camp tomorrow to get it all done." I had accepted that Wager was going back with water for his men because that is who he was and I was going with him because I couldn't not go with him.

A short while later, Wager returned with his pockets full of prickly pear fruits.

"Look at those beauties," I said, taking the fruits he handed me.

Wager glanced at me sharply, startled to hear me using my woman voice in front of Lem.

"I know," Lem trilled.

Wager's face clouded with anger.

"Don't worry," Lem hurried to assure him. "I ain't never gonna blow." He wagged his finger from me to Wager. "You two's sort of made for each other. Ain't a drop of backdown in either one of you."

Even Wager twitched his lips in what passed for his smile. We filled our mouths with the sweet prickly pear meat, crunching down on the soft black seeds and letting the red juice run down off our chins. The happiness of being with the two men I loved best and, for the first time, not having to hide who I was made me so giddy that I did something I hadn't since I was a young girl playing with Clemmie. I giggled. Lem, seeming to have done a right smart of giggling with girls in his time, joined in. Wager snorted something like a laugh and shook his head.

After we drank our fill of water, I helped Lem to his feet. With me steadying him, he was even able to climb out of the arroyo—"Don't want to foul our drinking water"—and do his business.

Before we went back down into the ravine, he said, "I expect you and the Sergeant have plans for, you know, after your hitch."

"Plan to make for California," I answered. "Might set up a laundry. The Sergeant might ship out on a whaler."

"Oh," Lem said. "Y'all'll be all right out there. Heard California's pretty. Weather's good. Never had no slavery. Yeah, you two will be happy. You'll both have someone." He stared out onto the prairie.

"Lem?" I asked. "You want to come with us?"

"Wouldn't care to intrude."

"You wouldn't. You're my best friend."

"A livery," he suggested, shyly. "I thought a time or two about maybe I could open a livery."

"Hell, yes. A livery! What you don't know about caring for horses ain't worth knowing. Come to think of it, a livery'd suit me better than being a damn scrubwoman. I could do the books, help you however you need."

Lem glowed and muttered, "I like that plan. Like it just fine."

I started to help him back down into the arroyo, but he waved me away, saying, "Y'all probably want to be alone."

I tried to persuade him, but he declined, nodding toward our horses that we'd picketed up top to graze. "Naw, think I'd rather just be up here with the hosses and the stars." I took his bedroll to him, and Lem spread it there where he could see the stars and hear the horses.

After Wager filled all the extra canteens we'd brought, he hauled them up to the top of the arroyo, so that we would be ready to leave long before the sun rose.

Imagining the livery the three of us would open, I fell asleep with Wager's arms wrapped around me. Late that night the sound of an animal strangling out its dying cry jolted me awake. I sat bolt upright, my body knowing before my mind could catch up that it wasn't an animal cry. I grabbed my carbine and scrambled up the slope of the arroyo. At the top, by the light of a pale moon, I saw Lem being driven to his knees by an Indian who had my friend's hair gathered in one hand and was about to slice his scalp off his head with the other.

I dropped the brave with one shot then fired on the other shadowed forms. Wager reached my side in time to see three braves leading our horses away. It was too dark to hit them, but we came close enough that two of them dropped the reins of the horses they were stealing and rode off into what was left of the night.

I tore off across the prairie after the two loose mounts. Only when sharp rocks and cactus thorns stabbed my bare feet did I realize that I was as naked as the day I was born and my feet were bare. It didn't matter. If I couldn't gather up the two horses the renegades had turned loose, Wager and I would die.

Luckily, the horses were old army plugs not given to wandering far from their nosebags. I grabbed their reins and tried to lead them back, but the pain in my feet stopped me dead and Wager had to carry me back.

Lem's body had slid halfway down the side of the arroyo. He had five arrows in him. One had gone through the yellow kerchief around his neck.

"Put me down," I asked Wager. "Next to him."

I touched my friend's face gently, curling my palm against his cheek, loving him the way he'd wanted to be loved. I took his broad hand in mine. It was gloved in calluses from his years of pounding out horseshoes. I lifted it to my lips, pressed it against my face and the tears ran over his knuckles.

I don't know how much time passed with me kneeling beside my friend, clutching his hand, before Wager said, "We have to go now. They'll be back."

Wager buried Lem as best he could, marking the grave well so that we could return and give him a proper burial when it was safe. When Wager saw my feet, he winced and took the bindings that had flattened my breasts, soaked them, and tender as a Massachussetts nurse, wrapped my wounds. He set me atop the brown, then went to fetch the extra canteens.

He returned a few moments later having found only one canteen. "We can't waste any more time. We'll need to ride hard for a day or so. Keep the renegades off our trail. Can you do it?"

I nodded but said nothing as only sobs would of come from my mouth had I opened it. Wager spurred his mount and I followed. As we rode toward the light of dawn I saw what was left of the canteens, trampled and crushed by horse hooves in the attack, their spilled water already dried away.

Chapter 80

After a long ride, we reached a meadowland bursting with wildflowers. A creek cut crooked through it. I turned and asked Lem, who was riding beside me, "Have you ever seen such pretty country?"

Lem answered that he never had and started singing the song we'd learned back in Hempstead. I joined in, and we sang it the way that made sense for Lem.

Oh his eyes are bright as diamonds,
And sparkle like the dew.
You may talk about your Dearest Joe,
And sing of Johnny Lee,
But my brave man of Texas
Beats the beaux of Tennessee.

We were laughing at singing out his secret when I heard someone shushing me and remembered that I was in church and the white folks' preacher was yelling Bible verses at us. "Slaves are to be submissive to their own masters in everything; they are to be well pleasing, not argumentative, not pilfering, but showing all good faith, so that in everything they may adorn the doctrine of God our Savior."

Old Miss and Old Mister sat on either side of the preacher nodding. My heart thundered for I was a captive again. Heat poured over me as I was in hell and had never escaped.

"Cathy, wake up. Cathy."

I came to my senses and remembered. First about Lem, then about my feet, the pain in my body mixing with the pain in my heart to bring me so low that I couldn't tell which hurt the most. We were riding back to camp, back to Wager's men, with only one canteen, and I didn't have the energy or wit to fight that bad decision. It took all I had to stay mounted, for hot pain was creeping up from my feet, through my legs, and into every bone in my body. And then the pain stopped until I came to with Wager holding me.

"You're sick, Cathy," he whispered. "You have to rest."

We stopped atop a high mesa where we could see for three hundred and sixty degrees in all directions. Wager scanned behind us with his spyglass for Indian pursuers, but didn't see so much as a puff of dust. We rested in the dappled shade thrown by a couple of mesquites. He unwrapped my feet and cursed the festering mess he found. Both feet had swollen until the skin was tight and pus spilled from the cactus cuts and mesquite thorn punctures. They were useless for standing or walking.

He felt of my head. "You've got fever. Do your bones ache?"

I nodded.

"Infection." He used too much of what water we had for wetting down the wrappings. I tried to stop him, told him to save every drop. But he shushed me and put all the salt we had left on the wet wrappings to help draw out the poison.

When I had been tended to, he staked our horses out to graze. We still had my brown and Wager's horse, a mare he called Belle.

Wager sat with me atop the ridge where we caught the breezes that swept up from the valley below. He pointed out how the land was starting to slope down toward the Rio Grande. I leaned against him and he put his arm around my shoulders. I closed my eyes and the visions started right up again. Solomon, Mama, Iyaiya, Old Mister with his black hand, all the wounded boys lying beneath their Dying Tree, noble King Ghezo and crazy King Andandozan with his hyenas, they all returned.

I don't know how much time had passed when Wager tensed beside me and I jerked awake. He sprang to his feet and squinted at the horizon. I tried to see what had riled him, but nothing appeared. He grabbed the spyglass from his saddlebag, fit it to his eye, and announced, "A rescue squad. Cathy, they're coming for us." He handed me the glass.

I twisted the focus ring on the glass and a fresh troop of soldiers jumped into my vision. Leading them was John Horse, who must of seen the way of things and gone for help when him and his men'd skinned out the night Drewbott took them into custody. And now he was leading the soldiers first to water, then to us. Tender green shoots of hope sprouted in me. With John Horse there to tell the true story, we'd be safe.

Excited, Wager said, "If we leave now, we can intercept them before dark. We'll get fresh mounts and you and I can ride back to the men with what water we have, while this detachment goes to the spring to fetch more, and," he added, "to retrieve Lem's body."

I couldn't take the glass from my eye and was staring at our deliverance when, before I even knew what I was seeing, something deep in my belly clenched. I kept staring, trying to make what I had seen disappear. But it would not and joy dropped off me like green leaves gone dead and brown fall away in the chill of winter.

"Cathy?" Wager asked.

"No, Wager," I finally said. "We're not going back. We are never going back."

"Yes we are," he answered as though that ended the discussion.

When I didn't move, he knelt beside me, and, recalling that fever was playing with my mind, he added patiently, "Cathy, we've been over this. I don't agree with everything the army does or how they do it, but I will not be a deserter. I took an oath. I will honor that oath. For myself. For those who come after me. I stopped believing for a while, but this rescue squad proves that Douglass was right. We shall have our day in court and justice will prevail."

I knew then that the reason I truly loved Wager was that he had been blessed. He'd been born free and raised strong. He had the luxury of believing and I was about to take that away from him. "Wager," I told him. "Maybe, someday, justice will prevail. But not today. Not for us." I handed him the glass and said, "Look careful. At the man riding point. Tell me what he's carrying."

He held the glass to his eye and studied the trooper I'd pointed out.

Wager didn't answer, but his jubilation fell away as he kept studying what he was seeing but could not yet believe.

I told him what he already knew. "Man's toting a Sharps rifle. Nearly four foot in length, no mistaking it. Sticks out near a foot more from his scabbard than the carbines the others are carrying. Shoot today, kill tomorrow," I muttered and said no more. Wager already knew that that was what they called the Sharps as nothing came close to it for long-range accuracy. Buffalo hunters were just starting to use them. Set up on a tripod, they could drop a full-grown bison six hundred yards out. But that man down there, he wasn't a buffalo hunter. He was a soldier toting a long arm with a telescopic sight and Wager knew what that meant.

"Sniper." Wager pronounced the word that was his death sentence. All the big ideas in his head fought to boot this one terrible new fact out and he argued, "But we went for water. And we're riding back to tell them where that water is. To save the men. No jury would convict us for that."

"It's not a question of a jury, Wager. That sniper is here to make sure that you never stand in front of a jury and tell the true story of how Colonel Ednar Drewbott was an incompetent jackass who nearly killed every man in his command. If you truly believe that they sent out a sniper for any other reason, and you want to bet your life and mine on it, then let's ride out right now to meet them."

Wager kept staring at the Sharps through his glass, trying to make the evidence of his own eyes square with all the noble beliefs that he'd built a noble life around.

Gently, I said, "Wager, you'll never have a day in court. That man has orders to kill you on sight. And probably, anyone with you."

Only when I mentioned myself did Wager take the glass from his eye, mash it shut between his palms, take a deep breath, and ask, "How much water do we have?"

"Maybe half a canteen between us."

"Half a canteen of water, two played-out nags, and you crippled," Wager said. "What chance do we have?"

"About what a pig in a dog race'd have."

"I doubt we can make it to the border."

"Impossible."

"Of course, I'd never have thought a woman could survive two years in the Buffalo Soldiers."

"Do we ride?" I asked.

"We ride," Wager answered.

Chapter 81

Wager dragged a leafy mesquite branch behind us to blind what trail we might leave on the rocky ground as we rode down off the mesa, descending to the valley below. My feet smelled like something a surgeon in the war would of cut off. Long red streaks crept up my ankles, pus leaked from the cuts and if a feather'd lit upon them, I'd of screamed in agony. But I had to ride. Since I'd been the one to see the way of things and talk Wager into deserting, it was my obligation now to save him. That gave me the strength to keep my mind right.

We rode all that night, pushing hard for the border.

When daylight came, I couldn't stop peering over my shoulder, fearing the sight of a plume of dust on the horizon closing in on us. But there were no signs of life other than the lizards that scurried past, their tails cutting curlicues in the dust, and the vultures that always seemed to be spiraling around overhead, the feathers at the tips of their wings reaching down to us like fingers.

We came down off the high plains into the heavy heat that hung over the lowland. The few breezes we'd caught up on the mesa were gone now, the air turned too thick to breathe. Heat from my ruined feet rushed up through my legs until every bit of me throbbed. Fever sweat poured off me though I'd had but a few swallows to drink. And then, of a sudden, the pain stopped. The sun grew brighter and brighter until the vultures overhead were wisps of pale gray winging through a white sky. The air was light and I breathed easy.

Creatures I'd never before seen on the prairie appeared. A leopard prowled about me on spotted legs that ended in feet made of the skulls of enemies. A pack of hyenas tore apart the bodies of both Mary the whore and the mother who'd pulled the plow. A lion crushed the golden curls of Custer between his bloody teeth. General Sheridan ordered the lion to turn the Boy General loose. An elephant, roaring and snorting, stampeded toward him. Iyaiya chased behind, holding her shield low and her spear high. My grandmother threw her head back and shouted joy to the heavens. I was in the band of warrior girls singing back to her. The elephant wheeled about and charged my grandmother. I lifted my spear to save her then remembered that my feet had been amputated and only the pain was left.

"Cathy, swallow. Come on, darling, take a drink."

Mama held a cup to my mouth. Iyaiya hovered behind her. Another voice called me. I ignored it and Mama and Iyaiya and I were floating in the cool, green water and nothing hurt anymore. They'd been waiting for me. Helping me all they could. It was time to be with them again.

"Cathy, open your eyes, heartstring. Please. We're almost there. Don't leave me now. We'll rest on the other side. Cathy, don't die. Please open your eyes."

Mama and Iyaiya were so close. Just a minute more and we'd be together again. And Lem! And Solomon! I swam toward them, my mother, my grandmother, my baby brothers and sister, all the ones I'd lost. They looked back at me, smiling. Even Solomon and Mama smiled. They held their hands out, urging me to hurry.

"Private! This is a direct order! Open your eyes!"

I snapped my eyes open. They all vanished.

It was too bright to see anything, then a face came into focus.

Wager.

He gathered me into his arms, brought his canteen to my lips, and I took the last swallow.

"See that, Cathy?" He pointed down to the valley, stretching out at the base of the bluff we sat atop. "That low ridge off in the distance that's turning pink now in the sunset?"

The sun was setting, but through the haze of dust and distance, I saw the pink ridge a few miles away and nodded.

"Cathy, that's Mexico. See the silver thread running along in front of it?"

I nodded.

"That's the Rio Grande River. That's the border. We cross that and we're safe. Once we're on the other side, they can't come after us. The sovereignty of the United States stops there. We'll be safe. We're almost there. We'll rest here a few hours then push on."

"Why did you stop?" The words felt like razors cutting out of my throat and the world tipped and spun whenever I raised my head.

"You were raving, Cathy. Out of your head. I had to get some water into you or you wouldn't have made it. You're still in danger."

I put my hand on his. He brought it to his ravaged lips, kissed it, and said, "We'll rest here a bit. As soon as Belle is ready, we have to push on."

I glanced over and saw Belle slewing her head back and forth as she cropped off wads of grass. My mount was nowhere in sight. "Where's the brown?"

He shook his head.

"We only have one horse?"

"I'll walk and you can ride. It's not that far. Even walking, we'll be in Mexico before dawn. Will you be ready?"

"I'll be ready," I answered. I wanted to say more, but needles of pain were poking me. I struggled to hold my eyes open and my throbbing head upright.

"Don't leave me now, okay?" Wager said. "I don't want . . . I can't do this without you. We'll get your feet doctored in Mexico."

I nodded, wondering idly if they'd have to amputate them. I hoped not, but if it stopped the pain, I'd make that trade.

"Cathy."

I looked at him. The fever and weakness made the feelings I had for him rise up and pour from my eyes.

For a long time he said nothing, just stared back at me. Finally, he spoke. "You make a hell of a man, woman."

"Wager," I said, naming my world.

We embraced, him looking south, off to the country where we'd build new lives together, me staring back behind at the country we were running from. The one that had no place for us. He fortified my spirit by whispering of his plans to find us a plot of land away from anyone and anything where he would build us a house with his own hands from bricks made of adobe. "We can grow a few crops. Raise some chickens?"

"And goats," I whispered, for those beasts could survive anywhere.

"And children," he added. "We'll raise fine children as strong as their mama."

"And as pretty as their daddy."

After that, I slumped against his shoulder, too exhausted to speak, to hold my head up. Even taking air in caused my heart to hammer. I was closing my eyes against the needles stabbing them when I noticed, far off behind us, a giant flame rising up, a torch of wildfire, hazy and orange in the distance.

"A brush fire," I whispered.

Wager looked back over his shoulder, staring to the north, and said, "Goddam them to hell."

It wasn't a wildfire. It was the trail of dust, burning orange in the last rays, led by a sniper with a buffalo gun riding hard toward us.

"We'll ride double on Belle," he said.

One look at the worn-down beast, though, told me what was there for both of us to see. "She can't do it, Wager. Maybe with one, but two'll kill her before we make a hundred yards."

"I'll strap you on and I'll walk." He bent down to scoop me up. I held him off.

"Too slow. They'll catch us."

"Okay, then you take Belle. Ride for the river and I'll make my way down."

He meant it. One more second and he'd of ordered me to ride.

"No, Wager. I stay. You go."

"No—"

Anger gave me the strength to say, "Listen! Instant Drewbott finds out what I am, he'll send me packing before word gets out he had a female in his command for two years and never knew it. You, Wager, it's you he's gunning for. You he got the sniper for."

The words were costing me. I gathered what little strength I had left so that he'd understand how it had to be. "Wager, here's what's gonna happen. You gon take Belle. Get across the border. Get safe. Wait for me. I will come and find you."

"I can't, Cathy. I can't leave you."

The men were closing in. There was no time for argument. "Wager, you only have one choice to make here now. Ride free and live. Or stay here and draw their fire to both of us. If you leave, if they don't capture you, that'll give them one more reason to keep me alive. To make me tell them where you are." He hesitated and, in a voice that came directly from my grandmother who was a warrior-wife of the Leopard King, I ordered him, "Go. Now."

Wager Swayne forked his leg over the saddle, reined Belle around, lifted his heels to spur her, then stopped, reached his arms down to me and said, "Cathy, come with me. We can—"

I'll never know what his next words were to be for I gathered up a handful of gravel and hurled it at Belle's backside. She reared and took off with enough speed going down the slope that gravel avalanched down the hill. I watched until they rode into the shadows beneath the bluff and were swallowed up.

The thump of the soldiers' hooves riding hard from the north grew louder. By the time they arrived, Wager's dust had settled and it was almost too dark to see. Tack creaked. Hooves clattered against rock. The smell of men and horses, leather, boot black, and gun oil engulfed me. Gravel pelted my face as the major in command reined up and bellowed down, "Where is he?"

The sniper, a white sergeant, pulled up beside him. Two more white officers flanked him and ten troopers crowded in behind. John Horse was not with them. I chose to believe that, after leading them to the spring, he refused to help track me and Wager. The officers at the front had the look of Civil War vets who'd made the army a career because they liked a hard life with hard rules. One of the troopers led a horse that carried the familiar form of a corpse rolled in a blanket. Lem. I was relieved. He would be buried properly.

"Where is the traitor?" the major yelled down at me.

Traitor. So that was the story Drewbott had told. Thank the Lord I'd made Wager leave. The major continued screaming, ordering me to tell him what direction Wager was heading in.

My eyes closed of their own accord and the voices drifted farther and farther away until a voice called out, "Major, look at this!"

"What is it, Belton?" the major demanded.

"I got him in the glass, sir! See that streak of light cutting across over there. He's making for the river, sir!"

My brain, then eyes, snapped into focus.

The major pulled out his own glass and zeroed in on something that made him sit up. "You," the major shouted at the sniper. "How long to set up your tripod?"

"He's too far out of range, sir," the man answered.

"Well, then, saddle up, we're moving in, I've got a bead on the traitor!"

"Belton," the major ordered the black trooper with the spyglass. "Stay here and guard the prisoner! The rest of you, move out!"

I heard the clop and drag of hooves as horses were wheeled around. Then the *snap* of quirts being whipped against hide. Again I was pelted with gravel as they rode off. I struggled to sit up. My arms wouldn't hold me.

"Belton," I called up to my guard, a slump-shouldered fellow with a bit of a gut who was still mounted. He didn't hear my feeble whisper as his attention was on his troop mates charging down the hill.

"Belton!" It was agony to raise my voice, but I caught his attention. He glared down. Seeing how close I hovered to death, though, he softened. I beckoned him to come closer, and, after glancing around to make sure that everyone was, indeed, gone, he dismounted, squatted beside me and demanded, "What?"

"Let me look," I asked.

"I ain't giving you my glass," he snarled.

"Please, I want to see. Belton, I'm dying. Please don't deny a man his dying wish."

Reluctantly, he handed over the glass and I fit it to my eye in time to see Wager emerge from the shadows. Belle had slowed but she was upright and trotted onto the sandy ribbon of land that ran along the river.

Four hundred yards or less behind him, I spotted the sniper setting up his tripod. A few moments later, the first trooper emerged from the shadows. Wager would be out of range in a few seconds. But if Belle tripped or stumbled or broke stride, or if Wager didn't make it across the border before the sniper sighted in, they'd have him. The first trooper pulled his carbine from its scabbard, aimed, and shot wild. The report startled Belle and she put on a burst of speed, breaking into a gallop.

The rest of the troopers emerged and swarmed after Wager. I stopped breathing. He was so close. Two other troopers fired. Belle surged forward. Her front hooves hit the water. Carbine fire pocked the river. One shot exploded half a foot behind Wager in a spray so big it had to of come from the Sharps. The sniper had his range. Next one'd get him.

Belle's back hooves kicked up a rooster tail of drops that fanned out behind, shining in the low evening light like handfuls of gold coins sprayed up by the river. When he was halfway across the broad divide, the major held up his hand and his men reined to a halt.

Wager had crossed the border. He was on the other side, beyond the reach of the United States Army. The shots stopped. He was safe. Wager was safe. I sagged back against the bedroll and darkness took me.

Chapter 82

———

The sound of a faraway conversation gradually formed into words.

"Did you get any water in him?"

"A mite, sir. A trickle or two."

"That's not going to be sufficient, Private LeBlanc. He's been out for two days. You better get some water into this boy or he is going to die. He'll probably die anyway, bad off as he is."

"His feet ain't pussing the way they were."

"Hmmm. Yes, well, the carbolic acid stopped the putrefaction some. Yours is a hearty race, LeBlanc. You don't feel pain the same way a white man does. Your people can endure unimaginable hardships. Nonetheless, this boy is on the brink." The doctor heaved an exasperated sigh and added, "Well, if he is going to die, you might as well get him undressed before rigor mortis sets in. Remove his uniform."

"Sir, listen, sir. He's moaning."

"Ah, yes, poor wretch. Death rales. Carry on."

Though I ordered every bit of my being to fight, my eyes refused to open nor my arms lift, and my jacket—my armor, my shield for the past two years—was unbuttoned and stripped off me.

"Uh, sir, you might want to have a look at this."

The smell of quinine and whiskey engulfed me as the surgeon moved close to gape at what had been uncovered. "What the blazes? This man has been wounded. His entire chest is wrapped. I don't recall any injury being mentioned? Oh, well, cut those bandages off him. Let's have a look at what killed him."

Snick.

The cool blade of the scissors rested against my breastbone and took their first slice.

Wager.

Wager was waiting for me on the other side. I had to stop them. I forced life into my hand and pushed the blade away.

"Well, look at that, LeBlanc, a sign of life."

The blade continued slicing downward through the bindings that had protected my secret. I ordered myself to wake up. The cool steel of the scissors' bottom blade slid downward until it rested between my breasts.

"No." My protest was a gargled groan, lost in the final *snick* of the scissors. Brushed by the rare touch of air, I felt my nipples pebble.

"What the deuce?" the surgeon asked.

With hard effort, I pried my eyes open and beheld the whiskery face of the sawbones, his nose and cheeks spotted with crimson rum blossoms, his pendulous lower lip drooping down, mouth open in amazement. His orderly, LeBlanc, a dapper, light-skinned fellow who oiled his hair until the tight curls were plastered down like they'd been scrolled into his skull, was gaping for all *he* was worth. The fools acted like the circus had come to town.

"What?" I croaked, anger lubricating my throat enough for me to speak. "They're titties. Ain't neither of you never seen titties before?"

The way those two were blinking and gasping, it seemed that the answer was "no."

The rumpot surgeon was the first to collect himself and announce, "Colonel Drewbott must be informed. Immediately," and bustled off, so discombobulated that he left his medical bag sitting on the bed beside me. The orderly, unable to peel his eyes from my chest, stayed behind. His trousers were tented out so far in front that I could read his intentions a mile off. When he moved on me, I grabbed up the longest, wickedest scalpel from the medical bag, pointed it right where he was bulging, and said, "One more step forward and you'll back off a gelding."

He jumped away, saying, "Wait until Vikers hears about this. Just wait."

No, I didn't think I'd wait for that seven-sided son of a bitch, and whatever mob he'd whip up, to pay me a call. Though I was weak as a washed kitten, I stuffed the scalpel into my pocket and tried to stand, but tumped over screaming when my feet touched the floor. I made it onto all fours, crawled to the window, hauled myself up until I could see the yard and found

what I feared. LeBlanc stood at the center of a thunderstruck crowd, shouting, "A woman, I'm telling you! Cathay's a woman! I saw her titties with
my own eyes!"

So they knew. Now they would come for me. I threw the bolt lock on
the door to the ward and wrapped my fingers around the scalpel.

Boot heels struck loud and hard on the wooden stairs of the infirmary
porch. Heavy steps pounded down the hall. Shoulders slammed against the
door. Fear was bigger than pain, and I managed to stand on my massacred
feet.

Brawny shoulders thudded against the door. It opened a crack. A slice of
Vikers's face appeared on the other side. "One! Two Three!" he ordered. The
men grunted as they bore down and crashed the thick door open. Vikers
pushed through first. The rest of the mob, a dozen men, maybe more, forced
their way in behind then stopped, staring at me google-eyed.

Someone in the back whispered, "Lordy God, it's true."

Another man added, "Tits."

"I told you," Vikers shouted. "Told you from the get something wasn't
right. Greene, what'd I say from day one?"

"Said something wasn't right with Cathay. Said it from the git. You called
it, Sergeant."

"A woman," Vikers crowed. "Only two reasons a woman'd go for soldier. One, to be with her man. Two, to get her some tail. Cathay doesn't
have a man. So . . ."

"So," Greene yelled, "let's give her the tail she come for!"

They made to move, but Tea Cake elbowed his way in, threw my cut-
up jacket around my shoulders, and said, "Now, hold on a minute, y'all.
What's Cathay ever done to y'all? He served. Weren't no shirker. Never beat
on a duty. He done his hitch good as any of the rest of you. Where's the fault
there?"

"How slow are you?" Caldwell asked. "'He' ain't done nothin'. 'He's' a
'she.'"

"So?" Tea Cake asked. "Seen plenty of women in my time could out-
work, outfight, outbrave any two men."

"She lied to us," Vikers squawked. "Lied to every man here. Lied with
every breath she took passing among us as a man. As one of us. You think
she hasn't been laughing her ass off at us this whole time? Playing us for
chumps. Holding out on us."

"Yeah," Caldwell added, a new ugliness curdling his tone. "She's here putting on she's a real man. Woman needs to be schooled in what it takes to be a real man!"

Caldwell stepped close enough that I could smell he had a bad tooth. But I stood my ground. I wasn't going to run. If they were going to take me, they'd take me standing. Like dogs puzzled when the rabbit doesn't move, they froze.

"Are all y'all hiding pussies, too?" Vikers clamped a hand on my wrist. I didn't fight him. "I'm going to get some tail off this bitch."

With his free hand, Vikers fumbled with his fly. I pulled the scalpel from my pocket and tried to stab it into Vikers's eye. I hit the bone of the socket instead, but that was good enough. He shrieked and blood sheeted his face.

I held the scalpel like a spear and asked, "Who's next? Let's get this over with. The Sergeant is down south waiting for me on the free side of the border and I need to get to him."

I figured that Drewbott must of told them that he'd killed Wager, since the news caused a stir among the men. They looked at each other and exchanged whispered comments. Though I couldn't make out what they were saying, they shrank back an inch or two.

"'Less you kill me," I went on, "I'm riding to him tonight. First thing out of my mouth when me and the Sergeant are together again's gonna be your names and how you done me here today. So, come on, let's get this over with."

Not a one of them moved or would meet my eye. Shame rose off those curs strong as the stink of rotten meat. None more so than Greene and Caldwell who, for all their licking of Vikers's ass, thought as high of Wager as any of them.

Blood running between his fingers from where he held his hand to his eye, Vikers squawked, "Caldwell, you a bitch, too? I told you, take her. Give her what she came to the army to get. Put the bitch in her place," he ordered.

Caldwell's eyes narrowed, and he didn't move.

"Caldwell, are you deaf along with being dumb as a stump? I just gave you a direct order."

Blinking as he reeled from the insult, Caldwell glanced from side to side, but he still didn't move. Still didn't obey Vikers's order.

"That's it, Caldwell, you're finished. You're ruined. Greene, you're my first in command now. Take the bitch!"

Greene wheeled on Vikers and barked out, "Why don't you put your own damn pecker in that"—he waved at me—"that half-man hank of jerky?"

"Yeah?" Caldwell demanded. "Why you always giving us orders? Who you think you are? My massuh? Just cuz you read off a few pieces of paper, gave me scraps of all you stole off every one of us here, don't make you my massuh."

Vikers had skinned near every man in the mob. Of a sudden, the ones still paying him off saw a way to make their debts disappear. The instant that doing the right thing became a financial advantage, that mob of curs turned righteous about raping me and Caldwell commenced to leading them out of the infirmary.

"Goddammit, Greene, Caldwell!" Vikers screeched. "Get your black asses back here!"

The man did not know when he was holding a losing hand and, in the face of a mutiny about to turn ugly, he went on screaming out orders. "Goddammit, Caldwell, I'm cutting you off unless you grab this bitch cuckolded all of us. Now get to it! Tumble out! Tumble out!"

That was the fatal mistake: Vikers had barked at them like an overseer.

Without a word, Caldwell came back and smashed his anvil of a fist into Vikers's face. Vikers dropped on his ass. Blood poured from his nose. Shards of the shattered lenses of his mangled spectacles glistened in the blood.

Greene stepped up and pronounced sentence. "That's the last order you ever give, and you raise up to me now, they will also be the last words you ever speak on this earth." As the mob left, Greene added with enough contempt to blacken a barn, "Little Man."

Chapter 83

—

Bunny was alive.

"Wasn't glanders after all," Tea Cake, who'd helped me dress before we left the infirmary, said as he carried me to the barn.

After all that time out to pasture, Bunny smelled like earth, fresh turned in the sunshine, when I hugged her neck. Having Bunny gave me heart. Her living and being healthy enough to carry me to Mexico was a sign that things were going to work out.

Tea Cake got her tacked up, lifted me into the saddle, and led Bunny out of the stable.

Fernie Teague ran after us, demanding, "What you think you're doing? You aiming to steal this horse?"

"Yes. I am," I answered. "And the saddle, tack, and all the feed I got packed up back there, and the canteen I filled."

"I don't believe you can do that," Fernie said, confused.

"I'm doing it."

"I'm a report you."

"I hope you do. Tell Drewbott to send a detachment. And tell them to be ready to shoot the woman he commanded for two years in the back because the only way I'm coming back here is dead."

Outside, I found a couple dozen troopers waiting in the yard. They were a mournful crew, heads lowered, none of them even able to look my way. I took it as shame and a sort of apology for not stopping the mob and allowed as how they might not all be mangy curs.

Pinkney the cook stepped forward, dumped some potatoes and onions into my saddlebag, looped a couple of full canteens around my saddle horn, and said, "Cathay, before you go out there, I need to tell you something," he started off, his old watery, stewpot eyes filling up.

"No need, Pinkney," I cut him off. I didn't have time to listen to him blubbering in the way drunks were wont to do while he told me how sorry he was he hadn't stood up for me. They were all ashamed, thinking of what I was going to tell the Sergeant about them.

Unable to use my heels to spur Bunny on, I clicked my tongue and my sweet, loyal, good, and true mount ambled forward at the speed she preferred, a tortoise-slow walk. We rode on through the silent crowd of men. A couple of them glanced up, almost started to speak, then stopped. I guessed that shame was crushing the words right out of them.

Night was falling and the barracks Wager and me and the rest of the company had built were lost in shadow. My hitch had been hard and had ended bad, but I'd done it. Done every blessed thing any other trooper had done. And I'd met Wager. And that was worth it all. Worth another fifty years if it came to that.

Wager. Wager is waiting for me.

I sat up straight in the saddle. The barracks blocked my view of the open prairie beyond. Stars shone in the navy blue sky above them. It was stupid to set off this late, but I didn't care. I'd keep the North Star shining on my back and ride south without stopping. To Wager who'd lift me gently from the saddle and take care of me.

The lone soapberry which had greeted me when we first arrived was a black silhouette now against a sky nearly as dark. As it had welcomed me to the fort, the tall tree would send me on my way as I passed beneath it heading south. As I drew closer, however, a broken limb dangling oddly from the soapberry caught my eye. The limb was thick and the branch it hung from bowed with its weight. Bunny shied back and I reined her to a halt.

Before I really knew what I was looking at, I had started praying to Iyaiya, all the ancestors, the Twin Goddesses, and Lord Jesus Christ to make the shadowed form I saw hanging from the soapberry tree a trick of the darkness. It couldn't be a man, his face hidden by a hood. It couldn't.

I was clucking Bunny forward, when from behind came the loud clicks of many rifles being cocked.

"Halt!" Drewbott ordered.

The white officers surrounded me. There were seven of them. They didn't move or speak. Into the silence came the mournful hoots of a couple of billy owls. The snuffling and grubbing of a skunk pawing at a cholla root. The lonely sob of a Mexican wolf rose in the distance.

Drewbott faced me.

I knew what hung from the soapberry tree. "He crossed the border," I charged Drewbott. "He was in Mexico. You're not allowed to go after a man in Mexico. He was free."

"We're the goddamn United States Army," Drewbott barked, his voice still shrill from being dried out in the desert. "No one's free until we say they're free. Carter, seize this . . . this deserter."

"Colonel," Carter said, his voice low. "Are you sure you want to do that?"

"Why? Do you have another bright idea? Your brilliant plan to let Vikers and his men go to the infirmary and 'deal with the problem' didn't quite pan out, did it, Carter? What else do you suggest?"

"Let her leave."

"Wouldn't that be a fine example to set? If we let desertion go unpunished, the darkies will turn on us. We'll have a full-scale mutiny on our hands. They'll come for us. All of us. Our wives. Our childen. Is that what you want, Carter? The deserter must hang."

"Sir, are you sure you want such a, uh, public proceeding?"

"What would you have me do? It's too late now for the sniper. Sheridan himself has taken an interest. He telegraphed. This person is known to him. A report must be submitted. Protocol must be observed."

"Yes, yes, of course," Carter said. "But isn't this just the sort of story that might whet the appetite of a newspaper reporter? Woman goes undetected in a peacetime army command? That's news, sir. In any event, a trial means there will have to be an official admission that—"

Drewbott finished Carter's thought. "That I had a . . . a . . . female under my command for two years."

"Under all of our commands," Carter added. "After the recent events . . . ? The deaths in the desert? The unsuccessful hunt for Chewing Bones? There is certain to be an investigation. Maybe even—"

"A court-martial?" Drewbott said, his voice wavering.

The men's conversation meant less to me than the wolves howling in the distance. It was too dark now to see even the outline of Wager's body hanging from the soapstone tree. My thoughts were muddled. All I'd been certain of from the instant I knew that Wager was dead was that I no longer had any reason to go on living. Since I had no weapon to turn on myself, I decided to charge the men. They would be my firing squad.

My mind was made up, I was bracing for the final pain of thumping my heels against Bunny when Drewbott said, "Yes, yes, Carter, I see your point. We simply let her ride away. We'll muster her out later. Discharge her for medical reasons. Have the quack in town sign the papers. You're right. Who cares if she tells her story? No one will ever believe that a woman served for two years in the Buffalo Soldiers. Most citizens can't believe niggers of any sex can be real soldiers. Yes, let her go."

I don't know if Wager or Iyaiya put this knowing into my head or if it came to me on its own, but I saw clear as day what was going to happen: these white men would erase us. Not just me, but all of us. The noble and the wicked. Wager and Vikers. Lemuel and Caldwell. No history book would show us putting up the telegraph lines and guarding the stagecoaches, tracking Indians and making the West safe. Hell, they might not even show the armies of black cowboys that rode the Texas ranges. Or any of our boys who fought in the Rebellion. Solomon? Would they erase Solomon, too?

I'd been as good as dead the instant the soapberry tree came into view and I cared naught for my life. But Wager? And Solomon? Lem? And all my people who'd died serving the United States of America? I'd be damned if I would let them bury us all twice.

I came to the sad conclusion that I had to live.

I made to ride off and Drewbott spurred his mount forward. "Give me that jacket," he demanded. "You're not leaving here with any evidence of your . . . your treachery!" he exploded.

"Drewbott," I answered, forever done with "sirring," "if you want this jacket, you're going to have to give me all the sweat I put into it first."

"Go," Drewbott hissed. "Get out of my sight."

"Happy to, you half-witted, yellow-bellied horse's ass."

A burst of chain lightning stitched across the black of the north sky. From way off in the night the Mexican wolf called out his sobbing wail. His mate up North answered with her own heartbroken cry. Bunny and I headed in her direction.

BOOK FOUR

Up High

Chapter 84

⁓

I rode into darkness and that is where I remained for many a year, not caring if I lived or died. Though I'd of preferred to die, the fear of being bullyragged through all eternity by Iyaiya for taking my life stilled the knife in my hand and kept me from seeking the high cliff. To give you an idea of how low I slipped, I became a laundress. It was as such that I made my way to Trinidad, Colorado.

Coal had been discovered there and I was sudsing for the black miners who brought up that soft bit coal. Worst job I ever had. Worse even than chopping tobacco. Every man with fourteen cents to pay for getting a dozen items washed—two bits if I supplied the soap—believed he was my boss. Believed he was better than me.

I tried a time or two, two hundred maybe, to set those coal-grubbing nitwits straight. I let them know that though I might appear to be nothing but a bedraggled scrubwoman, I had served for two years in the Buffalo Soldiers. All that got me, however, was a reputation as a flannel-mouthed liar. The mockery of those gum-booted gophers got so bad that back in January of 1876, ten years after I rode away from Fort Arroyo, I agreed to let a reporter from the *St. Louis Daily Times* who had heard a rumor about a female soldier interview me. I expected my life would change when the facts came out printed up in a newspaper. And my life did change. Just not in the direction I reckoned it would.

Where I thought my reputation would climb out of the muck that had been thrown on it and shine the way it ought, it went south in a hurry after the story appeared under the title "She Fought Nobly." That soft-palmed dandy of a reporter got that much right, the "fought nobly" part. He even got a few of the bones of my life, but there wasn't a bit of the real meat left on them.

As I said way back at the start, what stank the whole deal up was that he wrote that I had "an assumed formality that had a touch of the ridiculous." "Assumed"? With just a few words, he made me out to be a fraud and every word out of my mouth a lie.

From that day on, the snickering behind my back stopped. Instead it came right round to the front door and the sorriest souse in Trinidad, Colorado, felt free to throw off on me and call me a liar direct to my face.

I showed them, though. When the mining company built a few rows of cheap houses for the black miners who had families, they also opened up a boardinghouse for bachelors. And guess who the single, solitary black female in town able to manage it was?

Since I was tired of my name getting dragged around in the mud, I called the house Miss Kate's. As Miss Kate's was the only place in town'd take single black men, the louses and souses figured out double-quick they could either show me some respect or sleep out with the prairie dogs. The slow learners, I helped along with some tutoring from my right hook and a swift eviction. Once I was set up proper, I sent for Clemmie.

She arrived on my doorstep having acquired the helpful ability to read and a shiftless husband that I sent packing. Me and my baby sister, together again. Running a respectable business. I had Clemmie with me. Our bellies were full. We were sleeping indoors on beds. No one told us what to do or when to do it. In this way, we passed a dozen happy years. Without hunger driving me, though, I began to dwell on what I did not have. Which was, first, the pension I was rightfully owed by the United States Army for my years of service. And second, Wager's personal effects.

All I had of him was the yellow kerchief he'd given me after I became his woman and it wasn't enough. I wanted that pretty little personal effects pine box that regulations required the army to put aside for the time when loved ones came to claim it. Well, the time had come for the army to do right by me. By Wager. I was his loved one.

Of course, it was possible that the army never put Wager's belongings aside on account of him being hanged as a traitor. One way or the other, though, I needed to know for certain sure, and there wasn't but one man who could give me my answers.

Clemmie helped me with the letter to the General. I had her put in that there'd be sweet tater pie waiting for him at Miss Kate's if he'd care to noon with us. Three months later, when she read the letter that arrived from Washington, D.C., her face went pale. She looked up from the fine parchment paper trembling in her hand and squeaked out, "He's coming. The General is coming to Trinidad."

Chapter 85

～

May 12, 1888

I didn't need the rooster to wake up that morning as I'd been in the kitchen most of the night, filling it with the cinnamon and vanilla smell of pies baking. In the letter I'd received from the General's current aide-de-camp he'd said that Trinidad was Sheridan's last stop on a tour of the Territories and that "the item" I had requested would be delivered on Sunday, the fifth of August, "as the General's schedule allowed."

Clemmie read from the *Trinidad Chronicle* that the mayor, a brass band, a troop of old veterans, and most of the town would be meeting General Sheridan's train at nine oh five. A choral concert in the park, a "Review of the Troops," and an "Official Proclamation of Gratitude to General Philip H. Sheridan" would follow.

And though it wasn't printed up in the *Chronicle*, Clemmie and I knew that the General would then proceed to Miss Kate's Boardinghouse for Sunday dinner. Though my feet were never the same after running across cactus, and had gotten so bad since then that the doc wanted to take both of them, I ignored the pain and hobbled about best I could, determined to pass inspection again.

"Just how many pies you intend on making?" Clemmie's question startled me.

"Enough to get it right," I snapped back at her.

"What?" she demanded, tying an apron on over her skirt. "Those six you got cooling on every windowsill in this kitchen ain't right enough?" The kitchen was hot as I'd had the oven roaring most of the night and sweat beaded her face. Her beautiful face. Clemmie's beauty seemed made of hard maple, for the years had done nothing but polish it up even more.

Not wanting to let my willful, prideful sister see my admiration, I ordered her, "Get that table set and best not let me hear so much as a saucer land wrong."

"I cannot believe that—"

"Not now," I cut her off. What she could not believe was that I'd bribed the head steward at the Claremont Hotel Restaurant for the loan of some fine china and glasses. I'd of perished before I served the General off the house's collection of battered tin plates and chipped mugs.

For the next few hours, Clemmie and I cooked and cleaned together smooth as a span of mules been working in harness for years. The house filled with the smell of fried chicken, corn bread, fried okra, greens seasoned with ham hock and vinegar, and, of course, sweet potato pie. By noon, we had the finest meal ever served at Kate's Boardinghouse laid out on the long dining table set for that one day only with real-glass glasses and china plates didn't have a single crack on them.

At one o'clock I went to ferrying the chicken and greens in and out of the oven so that the General would have his food the way he liked it: hot and on time. A bit after two, Clemmie burst into the kitchen and announced, "Your boarders is getting narrow at the equator. They already been waiting on their dinner for two hours."

Since Clemmie had been giving me this alert every ten minutes since noon, I ignored her.

"You hear me?"

I didn't answer her foolish question.

"Cathy, you might ought to consider that he's not coming."

" 'Not coming'? What's that supposed to mean? The General says he's coming, the man is coming. Just got held up by the mayor giving his speech and a pack of old shipping-clerk soldiers won the war from behind a desk in Washington, D.C."

"Cathy, you invited him, but he never said he was coming."

"The hell he didn't! What else are the words 'be delivered' supposed to mean?"

"Sister, this ain't exactly what you'd call his side of town."

"When you're General Philip Henry Sheridan any side of town you want is your side of town!" I stabbed a serving spoon into the bowl of collard greens I'd just reheated for the third time.

"Calm down. I just don't want you getting riled up the way you do when folks don't believe you did all you did."

"I don't give a red piss about what folks believe," I lied. "They'll see the truth of it soon enough. Letter said the General's going to 'honor my request,'" I reminded her. "Clemmie, the General's bringing me Wager's things."

Though I jerked away before Clemmie could see the water come to my eyes, she heard the soppiness in my voice and patted my back, saying, "I know, I know. It's just that the newspaper said he'd be done with all his events by noon and that was nearly two hours ago and that means . . ."

I knew what it meant: Sheridan wasn't coming. Probably never intended on coming. I had a choice then: bust out boohooing or carry on. I grabbed up that bowl of greens and, though my feet ached, I stomped heavy into the dining room where my beautiful table waited. Also waiting, right around the corner in the parlor, were my boarders, all nineteen of them. House rule was no one was allowed in my kitchen and no one ate before I said so.

Charles, a head miner who could bring up three thousand pounds of coal a day, clean of rock, demanded, "When we gonna eat?"

I gave him my back and put the bowl on the table.

"You hear me?" Charles shouted. "Already two hours past dinnertime. We tired of waiting!"

I heard them shuffling about, standing up, getting ready to move on me, and I whirled around, faced all them broad-shouldered miners, shirts Sunday-clean for the day, nails grimy-black forever, making the few chairs in the parlor look like dollhouse furniture, and, since I was still always willing to let anger burn away pain, I said with plenty of pepper, "Any y'all not happy with the way Miss Kate's is run, you're free to go on live wherever you please."

That shut them up quick for, tough as they were, weren't a one of them tough enough to make it through a Colorado winter living in a tent. I went back to straightening my perfect table. All that came from the parlor behind me were the sounds of stomachs grumbling and some low muttering. Gradually, though, the muttering built in volume.

Of course, Charles was ringleading. "She actually believes that the Commanding General of the U.S. Army's gon come here to her sorry ole boardinghouse," he said.

L.J., a slit-lip boy who was an expert with black powder, grumbled, "Hell, woman actually believe she was a Buffalo Soldier."

"I hear y'all over there!" I hollered, continuing to line gleaming forks and spoons up next to gleaming plates. "Folks can believe any fool thing they want. I know what's true. I know I got a letter saying General Sheridan is coming to my boardinghouse. And I know that when the General says he is coming, he comes. I should know. I rode with the man."

Charles snickered. "Rode *with* the man? She maybe rode *under* him one night somewhere."

L.J. added, "One *real* dark night somewheres."

Curtis, a small man, only good for load cleaning, piped up, "Oh, yeah, she was a Buffalo Soldier. Buffalo Soldier *laundry gal.*"

"That's right. That's right," Charles said. "Washed out them Buffalo Soldier drawers!"

"When she wasn't trying to get into them," a fourth man whose voice I couldn't pick out said.

They were all snorting and chuckling when I stepped into the parlor. I had near half a foot of height on one or two of them and I used every inch of it when I boomed out, "You all got something to say, say it to my face."

That shut them up. Until Charles stood. Charles towered over me and answered back, "Yeah, matter of fact, I do got something to say." He glanced at the other men who nodded him on. "We *all* got something to say. You all the time going on about how you was a Buffalo Soldier. How you tracked the Indians. Got the Marksman medal. Now you telling us the Commanding General of the United States Army is coming? Here? To a colored boardinghouse? To pay a call?"

Whispered words like peas out of a shooter snapped into me. *Liar. Crazy.*

Charles went on, getting hotter with every word. "Our Sunday dinner's been sitting out there on that damn table getting cold going on two hours now. How much longer we got to play pretend?"

"No pretend to it," I shot back. "Now, sit back down fore I shove you down."

But Charles didn't sit down. Instead, one by one, the miners stood. Maybe in the past, when I was stronger, I could of faced down a full-scale mutiny, but seeing now that the General wasn't coming, that he wasn't going to get me my pension, and that I'd never have even the least little bit of Wager to hold, to smell, again, unstrung me. Before the men caught the scent of my weakness, I stomped off to my room.

Their voices, puffed out now, crowed, "She a Buffalo Soldier, where the proof? Where the pension check?"

"She got some old uniform 'bout et up by moths, could of belonged to anybody. That ain't proof."

"Don't know about y'all, but I ain't waiting another second for no pretend general 'fore I eat my supper."

Chairs were scraped out, cutlery rattled against plates, serving spoons clinked against bowls.

"Take and rake!" Charles bellowed his version of grace.

I slammed the door of my room to cut out the sound of my perfect meal being treated like slop in a trough. I went to my trunk, opened it, and took out my old uniform. I'd stuffed a few bits of the bindings that the orderly back at Fort Arroyo had cut off me into the pocket and they hung from it like old, dead weeds. I had to touch my chest to remember the feel of them chafing, to believe again that it had all really happened the way I'd said it had.

I put the jacket on. It actually fit better now than it had when it had been issued to the half-starved girl I'd been over twenty years ago. I pushed aside the scraps of Bunny's last saddle blanket I'd saved and the muslin shirt that had belonged to the husband I'd had for three months, a no-account drunk who'd stolen my pocket watch and twenty dollars and run off. At the bottom of the trunk was a cedar box I'd had made special to keep what was inside as safe from insects and time as possible.

I opened it and lifted out the yellow kerchief Wager Swayne had tied around my neck as we lay beneath the cottonwoods and that scarf had made me his more surely than any wedding ring ever could. Though the years and that long-ago soaking in a mud seep had stolen the silk's bright daisy color, I still pressed it to my nose and hunted for his smell amid the fragrance of cedar. It was gone. I had nothing and I never would. Carefully, I returned the kerchief to its cedar box and shut the trunk.

I thought I'd barricaded myself from grief, but imagining what might have been in Wager's box of personal effects—his leather gauntlets, his folding knife, maybe the notebook he'd carried—swamped me with longing for what I'd never have. I'd never stroke my own cheek with the glove that had cradled his hand. I'd never trace my fingers across the words he'd written. I cursed myself for making the same tragic mistake as Wager had and believing in a white man's army.

"Cathy!" Clemmie burst through the door.

"What!" I snapped, hiding sadness with anger as I whirled around. "Don't you ever knock?"

Clemmie stood there, her mouth working but no words came from it.

"Sister, what is it?" I grabbed her plump shoulders, fearing for a second that she, too, would slip away from me. "What's taken you?"

Finally, she stammered, "The General. His carriage. It's pulling up out front."

In the dining room, the miners, all staring through the screen door out at the street, had been turned to stone. Their hands, reaching for the pitcher of sweet tea or wiping a napkin across a mouth, were frozen in the air. I froze for a moment, too, when I saw that a four-wheel brougham, lacquered a shiny black and pulled by a handsome pair of mahogany bays, was parked on the dirt road.

The screen door blurred the scene outside, making it appear as though it was happening far away. Or in a dream. For a moment, I feared I was imagining that fine coach just because I wanted it to be there so bad. But if I was cooking the vision up in my head, so were all the miners and their families peeking out the front doors of their small company houses and gawking in wonder.

The driver clambered down, set a stool beneath the carriage door, opened it, and helped the first of the two passengers out.

Was my General always so short?

That was what I wondered when a stooped old man emerged. The trim cavalry officer who had ridden out of Winchester, Virginia, like Lucifer was on his tail to save the Union Army from rout and help Lincoln win re-election had gone to fat. An apron of blubber hung beneath his chin. My General's hair, once patent-leather black and smooth, was wispy and gray as ash. Most befuddling of all, though, was that he wore civilian clothes. How could Smash 'em Up be Smash 'em Up without a saber and gauntlets? A high-collared jacket buttoned to his chin and riding boots up to his knees?

A young colonel stepped out and buzzed about the General in the wifely way of an aide-de-camp and I wondered if Terrill had retired or died. The colonel glanced around uncertainly at all the black faces and whispered in the General's ear. Annoyed, Sheridan waved him off and then snapped his fingers. The aide-de-camp fetched a small pine box and my heart lurched.

He approached. Though he'd slowed down, Philip Henry Sheridan was still the bulldog who put his head down and charged forward no matter who the enemy or what the odds. When he came close enough, Iyaiya put a vision in my head and I saw a cloud of black crows circling his head. Death winged about my General. Death was the enemy he was charging now and the only one he would never whip.

"He's coming," Charles said. "Here."

I stepped out into the deep shade of the front porch.

The boarders, napkins still tucked into collars, followed. The front yard had filled with neighbors who stared from me to the Commander of the United States Army, trying to conjure up a world wherein the two of us belonged together.

The General stopped short of the porch steps, visored his eyes, peered into the shadows, and asked, "Cathy, is that you?"

Not a soul made a sound except for Charles who gave out a grunt of astonishment.

Every salute, every drill formation, every inspection, they all reclaimed me. I gathered myself up straight as a flagpole, stepped into the light, descended the steps, formed up in front of my old commander and knew sure as gun is iron that he hadn't come to give me something. He was there for what only I could give him.

"You look well," my General said. The smell of smoke no bath would ever scrub away poured off of him. Black powder smoke from all the terrible battles. Campfire smoke from every pot of water I'd ever boiled for his cups of "tay." Wood and crop and corpse smoke from the Burning. Tobacco smoke from when he burned Old Mister's farm and took me from Mama.

Seeing no reason for anything but the truth at this point, I answered, "You appear about ready for the undertaker, General."

A few in the crowd, fearing the retribution that was sure to be visited upon us all for such insolence, slipped away for they did not know that I had just given Philip Sheridan the gift that only all that smoke, all those fires could allow me to give him.

They were surprised when the General laughed, but I wasn't. It was a fine, rich sound that pulled pain and stuffiness, even age, out of him with each gust until he was, again, the cocky cavalry commander who could sleep on the ground, spring into the saddle the next day, and charge after Rebels like an avenging angel. Wanting nothing more than to be that young soldier again, even if for only a moment, even if only with the lowliest, most fraudulent trooper he had ever commanded, my General asked, "Remember the first thing you ever said to me?"

"Yessir. I told you I'd be singing at your funeral."

I knew that the General had asked the question to hear again the rough exchange of his younger years that no one but me could give him now that he was powerful and old and sick. He smiled. That's what he had come for: to be young again for a moment. Not to be dying.

"Ah, you were a cheeky one," the General said, the accent of his boyhood creeping in. "We always had that in common."

"Outcast of West Point," I said.

A murmur passed through the crowd. Charles said, "She ain't lyin'. She really knows him."

"What?" Sheridan demanded. "'Know her'? Why, this woman held our line at Cedar Creek. Took an old muzzle-loader off a Johnny Reb and opened up! Woman could shoot, too."

"You pinned the Marksman medal on me yourself," I put in, and waited for the General to give me what it was that I wanted. I waited for him to recognize me.

But Sheridan said nothing.

"Back at Fort Arroyo," I prodded.

His eyes narrowed, but still he made no answer. A second time, he denied me, denied my service. He was angry I'd mentioned it. He wanted me to be a sassy cook's helper.

When the silence went on too long, Clemmie stepped up and said brightly, "Well, come on in here into the mess, General. Cooked you a meal, make you feel like taking Cedar Creek all over again!"

"Solomon's sweet potato pie?" he asked.

"Enough for a regiment," Clemmie answered.

"Just thinking about it," Sheridan said, looking straight at me, "makes me so hungry I could eat—"

Though he had denied me my young years as a soldier, I couldn't do a dying man the same way and finished up, "The hind legs off the Lamb of God."

"Ah." Sheridan sighed. "We had some grand times, didn't we?"

"We did, General. That we did. We showed them all." I stepped aside. "Come on inside, sir. I even have you a cup of your Paddy tay."

Sheridan took one eager step forward before his aide-de-camp stopped him to mutter something in his ear that caused the General's brow to lower.

"Blast it all, Colonel!" Sheridan exploded. "Why did you allow that _____ of a mayor to keep us so long? Surely there's time for a piece of pie with my old campaigner."

"I'm sorry, General," the colonel said. "But if we don't leave immediately, we shall miss our connection and you shall be late for your nine A.M. meeting with the President on Tuesday."

"'Meeting.'" The General spit the word back at the colonel. "Cleveland's going to set a gaggle of _____ Quakers and other _____ Indian sympathizers on me for 'eradicating' the redskins. As if that were not the direct order of the American people twenty years ago. Now that it has been carried out and the savages herded onto reservations, I am to be the scapegoat."

He went on a bit longer, cursing the Southern newspapers for blackening his name. Suddenly, he turned to me and finished up as though I was the jury and him the condemned man pleading his case. "Sherman, who left most of a state in cinders, Grant, who issued the _____ orders, they've been welcomed back to the South. Honored. I alone have been barred, reviled."

The black crows beat their wings louder. They made the sound of the judgment my General had begged Mary to pray away now and at the hour of the death that was coming to him.

It was gone. The moment of being young that I had given him was snatched away.

"The box," Sheridan ordered testily, gesturing for the colonel to deliver it to me. With a sweep of his hand in my direction, he turned and began to hobble back to the carriage. The colonel rushed ahead to open the carriage door.

"General," I called out. "Sir."

But the old man couldn't hear me, wouldn't hear me.

"Little Phil!" I shouted. "Smash 'em Up!"

Again, I called back the young soldier, and pivoting his whole body, he looked at me.

I was bound to have what was mine. I stood at attention. My hand quivered at my forehead like a shot arrow and I became every soldier he had ever ordered into battle. At Opequon Creek. At Tom's Brook. At Fisher's Hill. At Cedar Creek. Every soldier who was loyal and true to him and to the country that they both served.

General Philip Henry Sheridan returned my salute.

The silent crowd expelled the breath it had been holding in a gasp of astonishment: the Commanding General of the U.S. Army was saluting a woman. A black woman.

The weight of years of denial and disrespect lifted off me until I was nearly light enough to float up the stairs as I hurried into the kitchen to fetch the prettiest pie.

When I returned, Sheridan was shaking away his aide's helping arm as he heaved himself into the coach. Once he was settled in, I passed the pie through the window. His eyelids closed of their own accord as the smell called him back to his green and eager years.

Then he regarded me for a long moment before asking, "We showed them, Cathy, didn't we?"

I nodded and answered, "We did, indeed, General. We showed them all."

General Philip Henry Sheridan slapped his hand against the roof of the coach and it jerked to life. As it carried him away, my boarders and neighbors crowded around, eager now to hear my story, but I would not speak. I watched in silence until the black coach was but a speck lost in the distance.

Chapter 86

Late that night, while the big house slept and the only sound was the coughing of the men whose lungs had gone black, I sat on the edge of my narrow bed with the pine box perched upon my knees. Shadows cast by the lantern's jittery flame jumped across it.

The box was light. I shook it. There was a muffled rattle. That meant there wouldn't be uniform, I wouldn't have Wager's living scent to inhale. But something. I would have something of his.

My fingers trembled to where I could barely open the box. When I lifted the lid the trembling stopped and my hands fell still as death onto my lap when I saw what was inside: a straight-edge razor with a fine four-masted sailing ship scrimshawed upon its whalebone handle nestled upon a faded yellow kerchief with a tear through it stained by blood that had turned the color of rust.

I picked up the razor to make sure I wasn't seeing things then dropped it for I had to cover my mouth and stuff down the bark of bewilderment that leaped out of me. I fetched my own box, the small one made of cedar that I had returned Wager's kerchief to only a few hours before. Inside, folded neatly again, was the only kerchief Wager Swayne had owned. The one he had given me, leaving his own neck bare.

I ran my fingers over the engraving of the sailing ship. It was exactly as it had been when I gave it to Lem to tell him I was sorry. Next I studied the kerchief. I scratched at the splotches of blood that surrounded one of the holes in the cloth and saw my friend again, an arrow shot through his throat.

The body hanging from the soapberry tree had been Lem's.

My heart slammed against my chest once, twice, three times.

The patrol had found Lem's grave at the springs and taken him back to the fort. But instead of a proper burial, Drewbott had hooded my friend's face and hung him in Wager's place as a warning to those who would mutiny. Who would not be captives.

Wager had escaped.

For a long time I sat there still as a stone while the north of my life for the past twenty years became south and all the meridians I'd pegged that life to shifted and reset themselves to a whole new compass.

Wager had escaped.

I rose to my feet. I would leave tonight. Now. I would ride to Mexico and find Wager. But after punishing my ruined feet all that long day, no amount of want to would make them hold me up. I tottered a moment or two before coming down in a heap onto the bed.

The questions battered me. Did Wager wait at the border for me? Did he sneak back over and try to come after me? Did he return to the crossing again and again over the years? Did he question every gringo, white or black, asking, as I'd once asked if anyone had seen rows of black pearl scars like jewelry no one could ever steal?

Did Wager believe that I had broken my promise to find him?

Near dawn I was overtaken by a vision so real I knew it to be the truth of what had really happened to Wager.

In that vision, I galloped hard following Wager. The lowering sun cut into our eyes and set the Rio Grande ablaze as we crossed it. Bullets from the long-range Sharps pocked the dirt, but we paid them no mind. Wager laughed as the tiny dust devils fell farther and farther behind, never touching us. Never even coming close.

Ahead of me, Belle splashed through the river. Her back hooves crunched against the gravel bed then flung up rooster tails of drops that fanned out and shone in the low evening light. I was so close to Wager that the drops Belle kicked up hung before me bright as handfuls of gold Liberty dollars tossed into the air before they pattered down, cooling my face.

Wager reached the other bank and rode onto the free side to wait for me there.

Overhead the clouds ripened with the most marvelous blooms of color.

Strawberry red and kumquat orange against a background of sky so blue it went all the way to heaven. Ahead was an ocean of rabbit brush bursting with yellow blossoms. The prairie under hoof was lavender in the dimming light.

As the sky dimmed from marigold to turquoise to darkest indigo, I drew up next to Wager and we rode, side by side, into Mexico, captives no more.

Historical Note

On August 5, 1888, General Philip Henry Sheridan died of congestive heart failure at the age of fifty-seven. He is buried beneath the Sheridan Gate at Arlington National Cemetery.

In 1892 Cathy/Cathay/Cathey Williams disappeared from the census rolls. Neither her death certificate nor final resting place has ever been found.

In 2016, one hundred and fifty years after Cathy Williams served, the U.S. military officially allowed women to enlist for combat service.